T0354552

Given A Second Chance

The Novel

Pat Gillespie

iUniverse, Inc.
Bloomington

GIVEN A SECOND CHANCE
THE NOVEL

iUniverse books may be ordered through booksellers or by contacting:

iUniverse
1663 Liberty Drive
Bloomington, IN 47403
www.iuniverse.com
1-800-Authors (1-800-288-4677)

ISBN: 978-1-4759-7460-7 (sc)
ISBN: 978-1-4759-7462-1 (hc)
ISBN: 978-1-4759-7461-4 (e)

Library of Congress Control Number: 2013902976

Printed in the United States of America

iUniverse rev. date: 2/28/2013

I would like to dedicate all my works in Loving Memory of my mom and dad, Roy and Virginia Gillespie, for their continued support of what I love to do. Words could never express how much you'll be missed.

Chapter One

Tossing and turning in her sleep, Jessi's disturbing dream continued, one that she could not bring herself out of just yet. For as she got closer to the old farmhouse, that's when it happened. Coming from within the old house, was a cry she would never forget, as it echoed over and over in her head, *"No___! No___! No___!"* came the sound of a man's voice crying out, while filling the night air with such an eerie feeling about it. Then, without any warning, came the sound of a gun going off, silencing him forever.

"Oh, my God, no ___!" she cried out, horrified, when finally able to wake herself out of the bad dream, to the familiar surroundings of her old room, back at her parents' home, while there visiting, with her two teenage daughters.

Sitting up, she found herself shaking tremendously, when her mother, Ginny Sellers, a matronly woman, in her mid sixties, came rushing in. "Jessi...?" she called out, coming over to her daughter's bedside. "What is it? Are you all right?"

"Oh, Mom...!" she cried, throwing her arms around her mother's neck.

"For goodness sakes, what's wrong, dear...?" she asked, soothing her daughter's frightened state of mind, by taking her into her arms to hold, until she could calm her down some.

Finding her voice, Jessi cried out, pulling away to look into her mother's, gentle brown eyes, "They killed him, Mom...! They killed him...!"

"Killed who?"

"The man in the farmhouse."

Thinking for a moment, she never heard anything about someone getting killed. "Where was this at?" she finally had to ask.

Shaking her head, Jessi couldn't honestly say, but just looked away.

"Jess, was this a dream you had?"

She didn't have to answer that, it was simply in the way she looked.

"Oh, no, honey…! You were just having a bad dream," she tried explaining, while brushing the long, brown hair out of her daughter's tear-dampened face. "That's all it was. Just a bad dream."

"Oh, but it felt more like a nightmare…!" she cried, while letting out a shaky breath. But then looking around her old room, her eyes fell upon the old Victorian clock that sat on an old dresser, off in one corner. Seeing it, she smiled, thinking of her dear, departed grandmother, who had given it to her. Then it hit her. With a cry of how late it was getting, she jumped up out of bed, and hurried over to her vanity. "Is it that time already?" she asked, while taking a moment to fix her face, as her mother got up to walk over to the door.

"Yes, dear, it is," she replied, warmly. "Now, why don't you get yourself washed up, and then get the girls up, and come downstairs. Breakfast is on."

"All right," she replied, as her mother was about to leave the room.

At the age of thirty-five, and divorced, Jessi Rae couldn't believe how shaken she was from the dream she just had. "Where is all this coming from?" she asked herself, while staring off into her mirror, before gathering up her things to go in and get a hot shower.

Once in the confines of the bathroom, getting her shower ready, she slipped out of her pajamas and stepped in under the hot, running water, to allow its magic to do its work on her tired body. While there, the thoughts of her dream returned. She mostly saw the man's face, as he got out of the red, 1984 Chevy pickup. *'Why,'* she wondered, *'did it have a look of fear on it, and yet, anger?'* As the thought continued on, the tall, handsome man, looking to be in his early forties, with thick, dark brown hair, ran up into the old two-story farmhouse, as if trying to get away from someone. *'But who?'* she asked herself, while rinsing the remaining soap off, before getting out to towel off.

Turning off the water, to dry off, she shook off the thought, before putting on her clothes, to go in and check on her two girls.

Upon her arrival, to what used to be her younger sister's room, across the hall from her own, opening the door, she saw the covers pulled over their heads. *'Sweet,'* she thought fondly to herself, while unable to help but smile. *After all they have had a very busy year, since buying Inn, and deserve the rest. However, it's getting late, and we need to be getting back to the others,'* she laughed quietly, thinking about her two closest friends, who has their boutique on the main floor, across from her office. "Girls..." she called out, going on in, "it's time to get up...! We have to be getting back on the road soon...!"

"Oh, Mom..." Cassi cried out first from beneath her blanket. "Do we have to...?"

"Yes."

"But we were supposed to go out back with Matt, to the pond, to try and catch some fish before we go."

"You guys still do that? I thought you quit years ago."

"No..." came a grumble from beneath Lora's blanket, "we still do that whenever we come down. That's why we were gone so long yesterday."

"Oh? But I thought the two of you were over watching TV with your uncle and them, before I came over!" she was asking, in regards to her big brother, David, who lived nearby with his family.

"Nope," Lora continued from beneath her warm blanket.

"Well, just the same, I have an Inn to run. Or have you forgotten that?"

"No... I haven't forgotten," Cassi grumbled, once again, before rolling out of bed. "I just wish we could leave a little later, is all."

"Sorry."

Like their mother, both girls had long brown hair, and hazel green eyes, but Cassi, the fifteen year old, who was taller, with blue eyes. Her sister, Lora, seventeen, and somewhat shorter, was the tomboy of the family.

After taking a moment to explain why they must go, while standing there folding an extra blanket, Jessi's mind drifted back to the dream she had earlier, of a man getting killed in what seemed to have been an old, abandoned farmhouse. But where, she had no idea, or why she would be having such a dream.

In the dream, she recalled how the sky looked dark and threatening, as if a thunderstorm could hit at any time. But just as the scene in front of her began to unfold, the man in the pick-up looked to be frightened, and yet at the same time angry.

Jumping out of his truck, he ran up into the old, faded, two-story house, just as the dark blue sedan pulled in, driven by a man in his late forties, with thinning black hair and a nasty scar above his left eye, making him look rather sinister looking. As for the other man riding with him, looking to be in his early forties, and an average built stubbly kind of fellow, he looked as if he wished he were somewhere else.

Getting out of their car, the two followed the first one inside.

'Just what are they going to do?' she asked, thinking to herself, while holding onto the blanket she had just been folding, as her dream kept playing back in her mind. Meanwhile, standing by her car, watching helplessly, she discovered she wasn't able to move away from her car. And then it was too late. Coming from within the old house was the same sound she would never forget, his cries, followed by the sound of a gun going off. Hearing it, it played over and over in her mind, as she shivered inwardly, while the scene went on with the two men running out of the house, and back to their car to leave, before anyone could spot them.

'Oh, my God…!' she nearly cried out, when Lora spoke up, interrupting her thoughts.

"What time is it?" she asked, in a sleepy-like voice.

"W…what?" Jessi asked, realizing where her mind had drifted off to, when she turned to look back at her daughter.

"What time is it?" she repeated, not having seen the look on her mother's face, as Jessi turned back to hide the horror of what the dream was doing to her.

Knowing that she was going to have to get a hold of herself, before letting such a dream take over her conscious mind, she forced back a sudden shiver, before turning back to answer her. "It's eight thirty,' she replied, but then turned back to act as if she were straightening up the room. "*This is crazy!*" she continued, while struggling to keep control of her wits yet again. *'I don't understand any of this. Where is all this coming from?'* she asked herself, while attempting to hide her, now shaky hands. *'I've got to get control of myself. This was only a bad dream, like mom said it was. Just a bad dream, that's all!'* she repeated, while feeling somewhat calmer. *'Okay, now, let's try this again.'* Turning back, as she headed for the door to leave, she asked, "Who's hungry? Grandma's fixing eggs and bacon."

"Food…?" Cassi squealed out, while jumping out of bed to race passed her mother in the doorway. Stopping first, she gave her a hug before going off into the bathroom to get ready.

"Okay…! I guess this means you're hungry?" she asked, while unable to help but laugh.

"Yes…! How did you guess?" she laughed along with her.

"Just lucky, I suppose," she returned, as Cassi went on in to get washed up for breakfast.

At that time, Lora sat up in bed, rubbing her eyes, and scratching her head. And with that twisted grin of hers, she got up and walked over to her mother, who was still standing in the doorway, to hug her. "Good morning," she mumbled.

"Good morning, yourself, sleepy head. Are you hungry?"

"Yeah…" she replied tiredly, when the two turned to walk out together.

"Good. Get washed up, and then come on down to breakfast. Grandma says it's on now."

"All right."

Turning, Jessi headed down the stairs of her parents' Cape Cod home, after leaving her two daughters to get ready. Upon reaching the main floor, she found her father, Roy, a seventy-five year old, retired accountant, with graying hair, and hazel eyes, in the living room, listening to the news. "Good morning, Dad," she greeted on her way into the kitchen.

"Huh? Yeah, good morning," he returned, looking up to see who it was, as she went on into the kitchen, to find her mother standing near the stove with a spatula in hand.

Although at the age of sixty-three, her mother's hair, though graying, still had a lot of brown in it. "Good morning!" she greeted, when looking up from the stove to see her daughter walking in. "Are the girls up yet?"

Before having time to answer, her father commented from the living room, "They are probably too tired to get up."

At the thought of his comment, she stood back against the doorway, thinking back when she was her girls' age. Growing up, she and her father had their usual conflicts. However, over the last several years, their relationship had grown closer, since she had to raise her girls alone. Now, with a warm smile on her face, she went over to pour herself a cup of coffee, before thinking back to the night before.

"Jess…?" her mother interrupted.

"They're in now getting washed up for breakfast."

"Oh?" she asked, having seen her daughter's expression. "What is it? The dream still?"

"No, though it was rather intense!" she sighed, while turning to go over and plop herself down on a nearby chair.

"Any idea what brought it on? It wasn't a movie you watched over at your brother's last night, was it?"

"No. In fact we were out on his patio most of the time, while the girls were in watching TV with Matt."

"Well, it had to been something, that's for sure!"

"I don't know. It just seemed so… r…real!" she cringed.

"Well, try and forget it, for now, breakfast is about ready."

"I would like nothing more than to forget it. It's just that, I'm not looking forward to the drive back home. Although, we do have to be getting back soon."

"Well, at least you and the girls can go on a full stomach," she returned, while dishing up a few plates of food, before carrying them over to the table.

"Yes, and speaking of which," she laughed, "I'm sure going to miss your cooking, but I have to say, Annie does come in a close second to you," she teased, referring to her cook back at the Inn.

Annie, though, being your average, motherly type person, who always had a kind word for everyone, felt that all problems could be solved, or soothed, by something good from the kitchen. And with her light brown hair, and eyes that lit up whenever Jessi would pay her a compliment, this fifty-three year old, was a joy to have around.

Breaking into her daughter's thoughts, once again, she heard her mother give a chuckle, while turning to carry a couple more plates over to the table, before setting them down. "That's always nice to hear," she was saying, while continuing to laugh.

"Well…!"

"You know, your father and I are glad that you have someone like her in your corner. So now, before the food gets cold, why don't you go and call the girls down. It's time to eat," she added, before calling her father into the kitchen.

"All right," she agreed, heading up to get them.

"Pop…!" Ginny called out, while setting a container of milk and orange juice out on the table, before taking a seat, while waiting on the others to join them.

Chapter Two

After breakfast, Jessi helped her mother with the dishes, while talking about the Inn. Shaking her head, she commented, "I can't believe how things have been going for us. The Inn is really bringing in the guests, and we are already nearly booked up through June."

"I know. Which brings me to asking, who watches over the place, when you're not there?"

"Annie and Hank."

"This Hank, isn't he the head stable hand you've been going on about?"

"Yes, the one with a rugged, down home disposition, who came highly recommended for the job," she laughed, thinking about the man in his upper fifties, with salt and pepper colored hair. "Not to mention, who pretty much watches over everything. In fact, he's been like a second father to me, at times. It feels really nice, too, when I get to missing you guys, that is."

"I can imagine. He sounds like a good man. In fact, speaking of your father, we are both very proud of you for how you have been doing with the place."

"Thanks, Mom that really means a lot hearing you say that. It's just that I have wanted to do so much for my girls, since the divorce," she let out a brief chuckle, then added, "Though, I don't see much of a chance for a marriage in my future."

"Give it time, Jess," her mom was saying, when they finished with the dishes, "the right one is out there, somewhere."

"Perhaps so, but where?" she was asking, when her father spoke up from the other room, sounding worried.

"Hey, you might want to come in and listen to this!" he called out, after having just heard some distressful news, about bad weather, coming their way.

"What is it, Dad?" Jessi asked immediately, when she and her mother walked in, just in time, to hear a bit of what was going on.

"They are saying that there's a severe storm heading our way, and it's coming from up north, across the state line."

"Great. That means it will be cutting across my path in getting home," she complained, having hated storms, while growing up.

Listening more intently now to the weatherman, she and her father got up, to get a closer look at the sky, as some dark clouds were rolling in. Going out onto the front porch, where they could get a better look at the growing, dark clouds across the road, she shivered at the thought of driving through it.

"This doesn't look good," he commented, shaking his head.

"You're right, Dad, this doesn't look good," she agreed, turning back to her father. "But who knows, perhaps it will just blow over," she replied wishfully. *'Or not,'* she had to admit, seeing how bad things looked, when she turned back to see just how dark and ugly the clouds were getting.

"Yes, that would be nice." She heard him say. "But still, I don't like the way they are coming in."

"Huh?" She broke away from what she was thinking to pay closer attention to him.

"I was just saying, how it looks like it could get pretty bad for you and the girls, on your way home."

"I know, but we really should try to get back, before it does."

"What...?" He looked at her in shock. "But you might be driving right into it. Why not just wait it out? At least until it all blows over!"

"I wish we could. But we have so much to do yet, before the Memorial Day weekend comes. And that's just right around the corner from here."

Shaking his head, sadly now, "I can't believe it. Well..., if you're going to try, you had better be getting your things loaded up then. They say it's going to last through tonight, and into the early morning hours."

"Okay, I guess we should be doing that, then," she returned, feeling bad for having to make him worry so, while turning to go back into the house.

Once inside, she tried to ease her father's mind of its worries.

Hearing this, her mother asked, from the kitchen doorway, "Does this mean what I think it means? You're going to chance driving back home in this weather?"

"I have to!" she exclaimed, while turning to the stairway, to call her girls, to bring their things down.

"I still wish you would change your mind, and wait it out," her parents were both saying, while walking her back out to her car.

"I know. I wish we could," she replied, turning back to see the worried look on their faces.

Just then, her mother went back inside to get something, while leaving the two to talk.

"Then what's stopping you?" her father went on. "You have people taking care of the place, don't you, while you're out? And this storm, it looks to be pretty bad from what they're saying about it!"

"We just have to!" she cried, knowing they could have waited. Then, feeling the pain of what she had put her father through once before, when having first moved out to be on her own. She hated having to do it all over again. "Dad…" she fought hard not to break down in front of him, "it's my responsibility to run the Inn, not theirs. You of all people taught me that."

Looking more worried than usual, her father shook his head again. "I taught you about safety, too."

"Yes," she smiled fondly, "you certainly did. And now it's up to me to get my girls back home, safely."

"Not without first saying goodbye to me, you're not!" her brother said, walking up, after getting a call from their mother, about Jessi wanting to head back with a bad storm on its way.

"David…" she laughed, turning back to see him coming up, when she went up to give him a hug, "I wouldn't do that to you…!"

"So, is it true?" he asked, shaking his head, too. "You're really going to try driving home in this?" He pointed at the sky.

"Oh, not you, too…!"

"Well…?"

"Yes. We have to," she groaned, feeling even worse than before for causing her family so much worry, when just then they heard the first sounds of thunder rumbling overhead.

Looking up, she shivered, knowing how only one other person, besides her girls, feared storms as she did. That was her cousin, Jodi, who had always been more like a sister to her than her own two sisters, at times. Though, as close as she and her sisters were, they were nowhere near as close as she and Jodi, having gone through similar experiences, with having both lost their first love in tragic accidents, and both divorced, leaving each of them to raise their own two daughters alone.

"Jessi…" David broke into his sister's thoughts, knowing how she felt about storms.

"David…" she snapped back, regretfully.

"Jessi, no, you don't have to do anything of the kind," he stated firmly, when taking her arm to study her expression more thoroughly.

"David…" she began, when at that moment, their mother returned with a paper sack, containing a variety of sandwiches, and a few other items to tie them over, until they could get back home.

"Here you go," she spoke up, handing Jessi the bag. "I went ahead and fixed you and the girls up with something, on the off chance you had decided to go. At least you won't have to be stopping off anywhere along the way. Just try and make it home safely."

"Thanks, Mom," she replied, while leaning over to give her a hug.

"Well, at least be careful driving," her father added, before she and her girls got into her car to leave, once their things were loaded up.

"I will," she said, when turning back to her brother, who was still shaking his head in disgust. "David, we'll be fine."

"Yeah, sure. Take care, sis."

"And call if you have any trouble," her mom added in.

"I will. Oh, and tell Matt, sorry about the fishing," she added. "We just had to get going, before the storm hits."

"I will," David was about to say, when Matt showed up, during another clap of thunder.

"Tell me what?" the tall, lanky, blond haired teenager asked, when coming to a stop next to his father.

"We have to be getting back, on the account of the storm," Jessi returned, regretfully.

"Yeah, but wouldn't it be safer to wait it out?" he asked.

"Matt…" David warned.

"I know," he smiled, nodding his head. "You have to be going. Sure."

"Matt, you're not making this any easier for me. The others have already succeeded in making me feel bad. Can't you just try to understand? I have to do this. God, it would be so much easier to simply stay, but…"

"Jessi," her father spoke up. "We understand. We're just worried that you and the girls might get into some trouble along the way."

"I hope not. But if we don't go now, it's only going to get worse on the way."

"Before you go, do you have enough gas?" her father asked.

"Yes, just filled it up on the way down here."

"And how about those wipers, are they working all right?" he added, more worriedly, as another clap of thunder rumbled overhead.

Turning them on for everyone to see, she smiled, before starting up her red mid-sized sports car. "I just had them replaced last week. They're fine."

"Good."

Seeing how they were starting to relax some, she waved her goodbyes, and pulled out to head home in what was sure to be a storm she would never forget.

"Do you think she'll make it all right?" her mother asked, while the four of them continued to watch, as she drove on out of the driveway, and onto the country road, heading for the highway home.

"She will call, if she runs into any trouble," David offered, knowing how this was really eating away at their parents. *You had better, sis, if you know what's good for you.'*

Chapter Three

After what seemed like hours on the road, Cassi spoke up, sounding hungry, "Mom, can we stop off and get something to eat, before getting home?"

That was another thing about her daughter, Cassi. She was always hungry, and yet, she never seemed to gain any weight.

Running the slender fingers of her left hand through her hair, Jessi looked worried, while responding to her daughter's question, "There's a sack, sitting next to you, in the back seat," she pointed. "You will find some sandwiches in there that grandma had made so we wouldn't have to stop, along the way. That will have to do for now."

Meanwhile, looking around, she noted a very dark cloud moving their way. When all of a sudden, there came a large streak of lightning across the sky, bringing everyone up on the edge their seats.

"Mom… did you see that…?" Lora cried out, in horror, over a loud clap of thunder that followed.

"Yes, and that was too close to suit me," she cried nervously, while wondering just where the next one might hit.

"What are we going to do?" she went on crying, with fear in her eyes. "It's too dangerous to keep going, don't you think? Maybe we should go back."

Before Jessi could say anything to comfort her, the answer came to them, but not quite what they had expected. When out of nowhere, came something even more dangerous. A bolt of lightning emerged out of the clouds, hitting a large oak tree at the side of the highway, causing it to come crashing down toward them.

"Oh… my… God____!" she screamed, while reaching over with one arm to shield her oldest daughter, while going for the brakes. "Hold on____!" she cried.

At that very moment, everyone in the car started screaming, when the car began swerving off to the left side of the road, just as a large tree branch came crashing through the passenger side window, while scattering glass in its wake.

When the car came to a stop, Jessi turned in her seat immediately, "Lora, Cassi, are you all right?" she asked, while giving them a quick going over.

"Y…yes_____!" Cassi answered first, while sitting back up in her seat, though, slightly shaken.

Not getting an answer from Lora, she leaned over to check her out, asking, as she saw a trickle of blood, coming from a small cut, at the right side of her forehead. "Lora? What about you? Are you all right?"

"Yeah," she replied, flinching, when she touched a finger to the cut.

Examining her further, Jessi noticed then she had a nasty bump on her head, along with some minor cuts from the branch having broken through the front passenger window. However, for the time being, she seemed all right.

Reaching over to pull out some napkins from the glove box, Jessi then reached around into the back seat and grabbed one of her bottled waters to moisten the napkins, before applying them to her daughter's cuts. "Hold that there for now, we have to find some kind of shelter to get out of this storm. It doesn't seem to be letting up any," she was saying, while looking around to see if she could get passed the tree. Unfortunately, that was out of the question, as the tree was blocking most of the road. "So much for that way." she commented, while sitting back in her seat, shaking her head in disgust. "It looks as if we're just going to have to turn around and find another way home."

"Darn it, Mom," Lora spoke up, sounding like her old self again. "You said we were going to have a lot of fun, but this isn't fun anymore."

"Yes, well," she half laughed, feeling relieved at hearing her daughter's sarcasm, "I'm certainly glad to see you're back to your old self again. How is your head?"

"It'll be all right. It just hurts a little."

"Good," she returned, while going on to strain to look out the front window for any sign of another way home.

Seeing how it wasn't going to be an easy task, the rain was coming down even harder, making it difficult to see anything farther than a foot in front of their car. At that point they had no choice but to turn around and go back to find another road home.

After having driven a few miles back the way they came, Jessi spoke up, still unable to see where she was going, "Can anyone see anything?"

"No, how can we?" Lora continued to sound sarcastic, while at the same time, sounding frightened.

"Lora…"

"Mom, I can't help it. What if a tornado was to come?" she asked, while fidgeting with the electric door lock.

"Let's hope not. But just in case, let's see if the radio has anything to tell us," she suggested, while reaching over to turn it on, only to find static.

"Great," Lora complained.

"We have no radio?" Cassi spoke up, fearfully.

Before Jessi could answer, Lora cried out quite suddenly over the sound of rain beating down on the roof, "Slow down…! Slow down…! I think I may have seen something…!"

"Yeah!" Cassi, too, shot up in her seat, calling out. "There_____!" she pointed off in the same direction her sister was looking.

"What is it?" Jessi asked, looking out through the pouring rain.

"Up there! Go! Go up a little further," Cassi shouted, while pointing to a road on the left.

"You're right! I see it, too!" she replied excitedly, while turning off the highway, onto a dark and wooded country road.

With the storm and all, there wasn't much light to see by. Finding, now, she was going to have to use her headlights, she switched them on, and drove ever so cautiously.

"What now?" Cassi asked, while resting her arms on the back of the front seat.

"I don't know. Perhaps look for a place where we can get out of this storm for awhile."

"Great!" Lora muttered, looking out her window.

"Lora, I'm sorry…" she began, only to be cut off by her own daughter, who, though, was acting purely out of fear.

"Mom, why couldn't we have just stayed at Grandma and Grandpa's for awhile longer? We wouldn't have been out in this at all then."

"I know, but I had hoped that it would have passed by like any other normal storm would have done by now."

"Well, Mom," Lora went on, "in case you haven't noticed, there is nothing normal about this storm."

She laughed. "Oh… I've noticed, all right," she agreed, shaking her head. "For now, how about we just keep our eyes open for anything at all."

"Like that house up there?" she asked, pointing out her window to an old two-story farmhouse, standing all alone in the storm, surrounded by trees and a half broken down picket fence, lining the front yard, making it look even more scarier than it really was.

Seeing what she was looking at, Jessi pulled off to the side of the road so she could get a better look at the old graying structure, standing back off the road.

"Mom…" Cassi cried. "This place looks scary. We aren't going to stay here, are we?" she asked, pulling away from the window.

"We just might have to," she returned, while studying the old house through the continuous down pour of rain. "We can't stay out here in the car, it isn't safe out here."

Feeling bad, she could tell her girls were frightened, but what other choice was there?

Then looking around for a driveway, the only sign of one had a tree across it. *'Great! What now?'* she wondered, while looking elsewhere.

"What now?" Cassi asked.

"Why don't you stop whining, and start looking?" Lora scolded her sister frustratedly.

"Lora," Jessi snapped back. "Stop jumping down your sister's throat. She is just scared. We all are."

"Yes, but there was a house back there a ways," she pointed.

"Why didn't you say something before?"

"Sorry. I didn't catch it, until we passed it already."

"And Cassi, to answer your question, since we are already here, I'm just going to have to get out and look for another way in on foot."

"What_____? No_____!" they both cried. "Why couldn't we just back up and check that other place?"

"Because, it's getting too dark on account of this storm! Not to mention, the road looks a bit too narrow to try backing up. What if we wind up in a ditch or something?" she asked, while grabbing for her jacket and a flashlight.

They couldn't argue with her, she was right.

Meanwhile, getting out of the car, she hurried to put on her jacket, and cover her head, before turning back to look at her girls. Doing so, it was plain to see they were frightened about being left alone. "I'll be right back," she said assuredly. "Until then, I want the two of you to stay here, in the car, where you'll be a lot safer."

"But, Mom_____!" Lora cried, as she started across the front seat toward her.

"What?"

"I don't want to stay in the car. I want to go with you."

"Are you sure?"

"Yes," she cried firmly.

"Well... all right," she agreed, hesitantly. "Come on. Cassi, we all might as well go and see if there isn't another way in."

With Lora and Cassi at her side, they headed out on foot to find that other way up to the house, which stood alone, looking deserted.

Finally after a few drenching moments of walking around in the rain, lightning, and an

Occasional clap of thunder, the three found a pathway, in front of the house, big enough to take the car up.

Shining the flashlight over it, she discovered that it too, was once a driveway, unlike the other one she saw before getting out of the car that lead off into the darkness, somewhere along the right side of the house. This one, coming in off the road, as well, took it around to the left of the house, where it would end up at the back of the house.

At that moment, she turned to Lora, "Do you feel brave enough to go back and get the car?"

"Y...yeah, sure," she replied, looking over at where they had left it, "I...I think so...!"

"Good. We'll wait here with the flashlight, until you get back."

"Okay," she agreed, looking to her sister first.

Seeing how she didn't want to go alone, Jessi conceded by nodding her head understandably, "Okay, go with her, Cassi, but be careful, and hurry back."

Taking each other's arm, the two ran as fast as their feet would allow them.

"Okay now, let's see what we are getting ourselves into here," she thought out above a whisper, as she took that moment to have a look around.

"I can't believe we are doing this," Lora commented back at the car.

"Yeah, well it is better than being out here in the car."

"We wouldn't have to be if mom would have just waited it out!"

"Yes, but you know how she feels about being away too long."

Looking back at her mom, she nodded her head and got on into the car.

Meanwhile, back at the house, while waiting on her girls' return, Jessi noted how some of the windows were broken out, and the yard was overgrown with weeds. "Well, this place sure looks abandoned," she commented outwardly. But then, unable to resist, she went on to laugh nervously, when looking up at an upstairs window. "Uh... huh, the makings of a real haunted house," she continued, before turning away, when feeling as though she weren't alone anymore. But where was the feeling coming from, she wondered, while turning circles in the bone chilling dark and eerie front yard.

Just then, Lora drove up into the driveway, at the left side of the house, where her mother was waiting to give her further instructions.

"Lora..." she called out, "stay in the car until I find out if there's anyone living here."

"All right. But from the looks of it, I can't imagine anyone wanting to live here."

"So, sure, it needs a little work, but it will do for now."

"Uh huh."

She laughed, and turned back to head for the door.

"Mom?" Lora called out.

"Yes?" She turned back, while still having a smile on her face.

"Don't be gone too long."

"I won't."

With that, she gathered up her courage to go and see if anyone was living there.

After knocking at the front door, and getting no answer, she went around looking in the front windows, before going around to the side of the house, where she saw another broken window. Only this one was up too high for her to climb in once she discovered the place must have been abandoned.

"Great," she grumbled, having decided to have one of her girls do it for her.

Meanwhile, the girls were starting to get worried, when then they saw their mother coming back around to the front porch to motion for them to join her.

"What did you find?" Lora asked, getting out of the car first to run up to the front porch with her sister right behind.

"Well, for one thing, it doesn't look like anyone lives here anymore. Secondly, there is a window at the side of the house…"

"Yes? And…?" Lora groaned, knowing there was going to be a number three by the way, she hesitated.

"Yes, well it looks like I'm going to need one of you to climb in and open the front door. So who is it going to be?"

"Oh, great," Lora moaned.

"Lora," Cassi complained, "it doesn't always mean that you have to do it yourself."

"No, but I'll do it anyways," she said, bravely, just to get her mind off the storm, if only for a few minutes.

"Are you sure?" her mother asked.

"Yes…!"

"All right, but be careful," she warned, and then took her daughters around to the side of the house that the broken window was on.

Once there, after clearing away just enough of the broken glass, Jessi gave her daughter a hand up, before taking Cassi back around front to wait on Lora's to open the front door. Meanwhile, Cassi, taking that moment to make fun of her mother's drowned out attire, she laughed.

"What is so funny?"

"You. You ought to see yourself in a mirror."

"Why?"

"You look like a drowned rat!" she laughed.

"Gee, thanks, Cassi!" she laughed back, while swatting at her daughter's arm.

Just then, Cassi took on a more serious look. "Mom?"

"Yeah?"

"What if someone does live here?"

"It's not likely. It looks too empty. Besides that, who would live in a house with all these broken windows?" she asked, looking around one last time, just as Lora opened the door.

Going inside, she suddenly felt a presence all around her, one that didn't come across as evil, but that of deep sadness, as she closed the door behind her. "Mmmm," she shuttered a moment, before rounding the corner of what must have been the foyer, to be faced with the living room, she assumed. "Girls…" she spoke up to advise them. "Be careful where you walk. The house is pretty old, and probably in bad shape."

"All right!" they returned, sounding a little excited then, while exploring their new surroundings.

"Hey, Mom, look what I found!" Lora called out from across the room.

"What is it?" she asked, while shining her light over to where Lora was standing.

"It looks like a sleeper sofa."

"Good! We can use it, along with that fireplace there," she gestured with a point of her flashlight. "That's if it works, and we can find some wood."

Going over to have a closer look at it, she shined her light around the mantle, where she found some candles. Lighting a few of them, the girls went back out to unload the car.

"Well…" she thought out loud, while going into the kitchen to look for some water. Unable to find any, she felt slightly discouraged. "Now what?" she asked, while continuing to look around the room. "Could there be another source of water somewhere else?" Going over to the back door to open it, she found for some strange reason it wouldn't budge. Then, at that moment, she felt a strange tingling sensation going up through her hand. "What the heck?" she asked, half under her breath, while attempting to pull away from the now, suddenly cold doorknob. "Oh, God, no_____" she cried in a hushed-like tone, so as not to be overheard by her girls, when they walked back in. But then, just as she began to let loose, the door opened for her and with it a sigh of relief, as she thought for a moment, before going out into the backyard to look around. "Well, do I dare?" she asked, seeing a woodshed off in the distance, and next to it, an old fashioned well with a hand pump still attached. Seeing it, she thanked, God, and headed out to it, while breathing in a sigh of relief, as she pulled her jacket up more around her neck, as the rain kept coming down.

In no time, she was able to get some clear water coming out of it.

"Girls…" she called out, "I could sure use your help filling a few of these containers, I found here in the kitchen, with water. And then, too, carrying in some firewood to keep us warm until it's safe to leave."

"Okay!" they hollered, while running out to assist her.

Once back inside, after dropping off the water in the kitchen, the girls did the same with the wood in the living room, before going back over to the sofa to get settled in.

"Thanks, you two. And while I'm getting changed out of my wet things in the bathroom, why don't you do the same here?"

"All right," Lora replied, as their mother took a candle and a change of clothes, and headed across the foyer, passing a staircase to the upstairs, to go into the bathroom.

After going in, and closing the door, unaware she wasn't alone, she went over to set the candle on the sink, before removing her wet things. But then when it came time to take off her scanty laced bra, she cooed, once she had gotten it off, "Mmmm… now that has to feel better," she thought quietly, while pulling her wet hair out of the way, before going on to take off the rest of her things. When she did, she turned just enough for the candlelight to catch the fullness of her breasts in the mirror, when a sudden chill caused her blossoms to rise. Without warning, the candle went out, leaving her in total darkness. "Lord, what now…?" she cried, feeling more nervous now than she did before.

Fumbling around in the dark to get the rest of her things changed, she didn't waste any time putting on an oversized T-shirt, before exiting the room, while taking the candle with her.

Though just outside the door, she leaned back against the wall to collect herself, before going on in to rejoin her girls. "Lord, I was only kidding about this being the makings of a haunted house. Gees, can't you take a joke?" she groaned quietly, as if to answer to some unknown source to what has been causing her to feel as she does.

Once back in the living room, Jessi was relieved to see the girls were already snuggled in for the night. "Good. And seeing how we aren't going anywhere with the storm doing its thing outside, just maybe, I can get some sleep, too. As long as I can shake off what had just happened to me in the bathroom," she thought, while going over to make up a bedroll next to the fireplace, in order to keep an eye on it.

However, unbeknownst to her, sleep was not going to come quite so easily.

Chapter Four

It wasn't long before having her bedroll made up, she turned to go over to the front door for a moment to step out and say a prayer. Opening it, she groaned quietly, as there it was again, the same chilling feeling she felt before, surrounding her, as though someone had a hold of her. *"But who?"* she asked herself, while closing her eyes to let out a soft cry, "Mmmm… no…! This can't be real…! It is only the night air…! Do you hear me? This is not real…! It is only. I repeat. Only the night air…!"

Then, as if things couldn't get any stranger, she felt as though her head was being tilted back, as a chilling feeling began to travel up the back of her neck, causing her womanly buds to perk up even more at the sensation this presence was doing to her. Not to mention, her emotions, while continuing to be taunted by whatever had her frozen to that spot, as it grew more intense by the moment.

"Mmmm…!" she breathed. "P…please, whoever you are, don't do this to me…!"

Suddenly, no sooner had she said what she did, the feeling began to subside. Now she was finally able to move again. And move, she did. Having decided to cut her prayers short, she closed the door and went straight to bed.

"Yes, sleep," she whispered softly, while watching the light of the fire dance off the walls in the living room, and part of the foyer. "Go to sleep."

When sleep did come, so did the dream. Although, at first, it was just a simple outdoor scene, on a beautiful afternoon. And there he was again, the same man, looking to have been in his early to mid forties, with dark brown wavy hair, and deep blue eyes, driving up in a red Chevy pick-up. With his ruggedly handsome face still having a look of confusion on it, he kept looking behind him.

Just then, there came two other men in the dark blue sedan, as if they were following him.

"But where?" she asked, unable to tell. When, *"Oh, no! It's the same men! And they are after the guy in the truck. But why?"*

Getting out of his truck, the man ran up into the two-story house, wearing a blue denim, snap down shirt, with the sleeves rolled up just beneath his elbows, along with a pair of blue Levis, as the other two got out of their car to follow.

Wanting to know what was going on inside, she found this time she was able to move, and quickly went up onto the front porch to have a look in the window, just to the right of the door.

Seeing the first man's face looking as though he were in shock, he yelled quite suddenly, "What do you want with me...?" he shouted, while looking somewhat terrified.

When there was no answer, to Jessi's horror, the man with the ragged scar over his left eye took out his gun, and as if in slow motion, pointed it at the first man.

"Oh, God_____!" she nearly cried out in her sleep, while watching on in horror, as the second man slowly pulled the trigger, sending a bullet out, hitting the first man directly in the center of the chest.

"No_____!" he cried out in pain. "No_____! No_____! No_____!" the sound went out, echoing over and over again, in her head, as it had in her earlier dream.

Feeling the sudden impact of the bullet, as it hit, causing him to be thrown back slowly onto the floor, near the staircase, where his arms went flailing out to the side, as he landed.

"No_____! Oh, God, no_____!" she screamed, backing away from the window, while covering her mouth to muffle, yet another scream. *"Oh, God_____ this can't be happening_____! They just shot him!"* she cried. But then after seeing the first man fall to the floor, she came back to look in the window again. There, she saw the blood begin to seep out from within its wound. *"No_____!"* she went on crying, while tossing and turning in her sleep.

As the dream went on, the stubbly guy went over to pick up the other man's wallet. Taking out his driver's license, he glanced down at it in surprise. "Tony..." he spouted off, though knowing all along it wasn't the right man, "this ain't who you was after! It says here his name is Craig Matthews, not McMasters! You shot the wrong one!"

"Damn you, McMasters...!" the man growled heatedly. "Well, then, I guess we will just have to wait for the right time to go after him, won't we?" he sneered.

Angered, Tony turned, knocking Craig's wallet out of the other man's hand, and onto the floor, next to his body. "Let's go," he snarled, while leaving Craig there to die.

"What? No_____" Jessi continued crying, while feeling the heat of her own tears, as she stood helplessly by, watching the men flee the scene, before going over to the front door to try the knob.

Once inside, she went right over to kneel down by the man on the floor. Looking in his eyes, she saw the tears of pain, as he went to raise his right hand to gently touch her face. Taking it into her own, she listened carefully, as he cried out to her.

"P...please_____" he began sadly, "help me_____! I don't want to die_____!"

"B...but how_____?" she returned, feeling his hand start to give way in hers. Then his eyes, as they slowly closed. *"No_____! Please don't do this to me! I don't understand! What am I supposed to do! Please_____ come back! Tell me what I am to do! Oh, God_____ how am I to help him?"* she continued, while sitting there, crying over him.

Sometime later, she woke to find her T-shirt drenched in perspiration, as she sat up. "Oh, Lord..." she cried out quietly, feeling shaken over what had just taken place, "what does all this mean?" she asked, sitting there, huddled in her blanket, before getting up to go into the kitchen.

Getting there, she saw the two containers she had just filled, before turning in, empty.

"What...? No_____!" she cried quietly, while going over to pick them up. "I just filled these before going to bed!" Feeling even more shaken over not knowing what was going on, she looked out the side window over the sink. "Yes..." she thought out, feeling somewhat relieved that it had stopped raining. *"Though I know I ought to just get the girls up and go. It's late,"* she thought, going over to look in on them from the kitchen doorway, *"and they are sleeping soundly. I'll just go out and get some more,"* she continued, in the semi-darkness of the room, whereas the firelight from the living room offered little to no light to see by.

Doing so, she went over to the back door to open it. Once again, a cold breeze greeted her, as it crept up around her. "Great. You just had to go and do that again, didn't you?" she grunted, recalling now her first experience, while trying to pull her hand free of the doorknob, once again. "You know this is getting old. So, please... not now...!" she cried. "All I want to do is go out and get some more water. That's all. Just to get some more water. Okay...?"

Just then the door opened, and with a sigh she went out to get her water. As for the rest of the night, she felt as though someone was still watching her, as when she had first gotten there. *"But from where and why?"* she asked, knowing that sleep was out of the question.

When she did fall off to sleep, she dreamt of the same man, calling out to her, over and over again.

"Who are you...?" she asked in her sleep.

"Jessi_____!" he called out, letting his thoughts seep into hers. *"Please... help me_____! I need you_____! Please..., Jessi..., you can sense me...! I know you can.... Help me_____! I don't want to die_____!"*

Suddenly, waking from her sleep, her whole body shook with fear. "Oh, God... what is ha...happening to me? Never mind that. Why is this happening to me...?" she covered her mouth and sobbed quietly in near hysteria. *"Who are you? And why are you calling out to me_____?"* she asked, unaware she was doing it telepathically, as she pulled her blankets back up around her more, before looking over at her two daughters, still sleeping peacefully.

Then it happened again, only this time she was very much awake, when he whispered out to her, *"Jessi_____!"*

"What...? Oh, but no you did not just do that. And this," she gestured with both hands out around her, "This isn't happening. No. Uh, uh, it isn't," she swore, while shivering to the sudden oncoming chill in the air.

Getting to her feet, she added more wood to the fire, before sitting back down on her bedroll. "This is so freaking crazy," she cried, running a hand over her tangled hair. "What the heck is going on here?"

Taking that moment to look over at her watch she had set on the hearth earlier; it read four in the morning.

"Great," she continued, while getting up to pace the floor, then back to sit down on her bedroll again. Only this time, to pull her knees to her chest, to hug them, while staring off into the fire, hoping it would calm her down some. Though, finding how it hadn't, she found herself once again turning to the Lord in prayer. "Dear Lord," she groaned, "just why is this happening to me? Why am I having these dreams? And why am I now hearing him calling out to me? Who is he? And why me...?" she asked, just above a whisper.

Pausing for a moment, she went to clear her mind, when just then, for the first time since their arrival, she heard a sound coming from upstairs. "What?" she groaned again, only this time looking off toward the foyer. "Oh, no we don't. This has got to stop! I am not going to let these freakish sounds tear me up this way."

Grabbing her flashlight, she got up and walked out into the foyer toward the stairs, with every intention of be brave. Getting there, it was quiet. Not a sound was made, except the wind outside, and the rapid beating of her heart.

"Okay, girl, you can do this. It's just... a noise," she said, while trying to reassure herself. Meanwhile, feeling the coolness in the house, and the dampness of her T-shirt, she couldn't help but shiver once again, while standing at the bottom of the stairs, trying to bring herself to go up them. "This is crazy. I must be losing my mind. It's just the wind outside making that noise," she thought out loud, when turning back to go into the living room.

Then, she caught a glimpse of something, or someone moving across the hall upstairs.

"O...oh, my, G...God_____!" she cried out softly, in a shaky-like voice. Turning back toward the stairs, she gathered up all her courage to go up and check it out. Then, stopped and shook her head. "What am I doing_____?" she cried, looking back into the living room at her daughters. "I should just get them, and get the heck out of here! This is insane_____!"

Instead of doing that, with one hand resting on the banister, she laid her head on her forearm and waited. Waited for some God given sign for her to take the girls and go running out of there like some nut job that had just broken out of some loony bin, or march herself right on up those stairs to see what, God help her, waits for her to appear.

"Fine. I'll go up and check this out. But it had better not be some nut job waiting to off me, and then go after my girls. They will have hell to pay when I come back to haunt them, like this house likes to do to me."

Once upstairs, she listened intently, but not a sound was made. "This is so insane," she whispered uneasily. "Just forget it. I am not doing this," she groaned, throwing up her hands, as she was about to turn and go back downstairs. But then, out of the corner of her eye, she saw the door to the right move. At that moment, chills of panic ran up her spine, but still she found the courage to call out, "W...who's there?" she asked, when again there was silence, with the exception of the wind howling outside. "Fine!" she muttered, and turned to go back downstairs.

Then, she heard it. The same voice from her dreams, and shortly thereafter, now calling out to her. *"Jessi..."* he whispered softly. *"Please, don't go_____!"*

"W...what? Who are you?" she asked nervously, feeling her knees begin to shake. "And why are you calling me? Tell me, please...! And tell me how you know my name...?"

Still, no answer.

After giving it considerable thought, she pushed herself forward to go into the darkened room, to the right of the hall, to see who would be calling out to her. "Come on, girl, you can do this. Just go on in!"

And go on in she did, but not without feeling the pangs of fear knotting at her stomach.

Once inside, she quickly picked up on an old musty smell in the room, when calling out, yet again, "H...hello___! I...is their so...so... someone in here___?"

With the exception of what little moonlight peeked in through the clouds, she wasn't able to see much of anything. Even with the use of her flashlight, it was still hard to see when she had gotten halfway into the room.

At that moment, her flashlight started to act up. "Oh, God, no___!" she cried out, hitting it a couple of times, hoping to get it to straighten up.

Once she thought she had it, it had only come back long enough to see a few feet in front of her.

Then suddenly, she felt it, an eerie breeze pass her cheek. "P…please, if there is someone here, talk to me…!" she cried nervously. "If you don't answer me, I swear… I'm going to take my girls and leave this house."

"*No___!*" he thought to himself. "*I can't let her do that! Not when I'm so close to ending this nightmare of mine! I need her___! She's my only hope of ever setting my spirit free from this hell I've been in for the past two years.*"

Taking that moment, he focused all his energy on her flashlight, hoping to cause it to go dead, and then slammed the door behind her.

"What___? No___!" she cried, spinning around at that moment to see her only means of escape be cut off.

Making a blind dash for the door, she tripped over what seemed like a crate in the middle of the room. Falling over it, she hit her head on the floor, causing her to be dazed for a moment. When she attempted to get up, the room started to spin around her.

It was then she saw him for the first time, as he walked out toward her from the shadows of the far corner. "*Jessi___*" his voice came out in its spirit-like form, as he came closer to kneel down before her. His deep blue eyes, gentle, as he looked into hers.

"W…who are you?" she asked, noticing that gentle, yet crooked smile of his, as she tried not to collapse from the hit she took to the head.

"My name is Craig. And this," he indicated around him, "is my house! Are you all right?" he asked, when using his own gentle voice, while that same crooked smile found its way to her heart.

Not answering at first, she just looked up at him, wondering where she had seen him before. Just then, a ray of early morning sunlight broke through the clouds, finding its way into his room. As it did, it lit it up just enough for her to see him more clearly. Then it came to her, as the two slowly stood up, not once, taking their eyes off each other.

"It's you…!" she gasped, stepping back.

"Yes, it is!" he exclaimed, apologetically. "Hey, I'm sorry, but I really wasn't trying to scare you! I was just trying to get your attention."

"Oh, but you did. Get my attention, I mean. But why?"

"Well, when you said you would leave. I was afraid you would have. And then I would have missed getting your help!"

"M...m...my help? B...b...but..." she began. "Oh, my God___!" she cried, while taking another shaky step back. "I...I remember now. The dreams! I saw you in my dreams!"

"Yes, I know," he smiled sheepishly.

"B...but...but, you...you can't be here. You're... you're... dead! I saw him kill you."

"Yes. I'm afraid you did."

"Oh, God!" she cried, while suddenly feeling faint, "I...I don't understand! This can't be

h...happening to me."

"Jessi..."

"No___! This can't be___!"

"Why?" he asked, already knowing the answer.

"Because... that would mean, you're a...a...a..."

"Ghost?" he asked, with that crooked grin of his. "No, not exactly."

"What?"

"Here, take to take a seat on the crate, before you fall, and I will try to explain."

She did, and he went on.

"I'm what you might call a troubled spirit. It wasn't my time to go yet!" he offered, when looking away sadly.

Finding her words, she thought back to the dream. *'This ain't McMasters. You killed the wrong man...the wrong man...the wrong man...'* The voice echoed over and over again in her head until it hurt. "Oh, God, they were after someone else, weren't they?" she finally spoke up, as he turned back to face her.

"Yes, my friend, David," he exclaimed, shaking his head, while doubling up his fists. "And I wish to God I knew why?"

Just then, she had to place her head down in her hands.

Becoming concerned, he wished he could touch her. Instead, kneeling down, he raised his hand to her tangled hair. "Are you sure you're all right?"

"Yes. I'm just trying to understand, why me?" she asked softly, while rubbing the back of her neck.

With a small chuckle, he replied, "You seem to have the ability to perceive my presence here, when no one else can! Jess..." he offered, while placing a finger beneath her chin, when she looked up, feeling the tingling sensation it had caused, "I need your help. Please... will you help me?"

He sounded so desperate, as she looked into his pleading eyes. "But how?" she asked, losing herself in them for a moment, as though she could simply be washed away.

"I'll tell you, but not now."

"Why?" she asked, not realizing how late it had gotten.

"Your girls are awake and looking for you," he replied, while getting up to move over to the side window.

It was then she picked up on the fresh scent of his cologne. Stetson, to be exact. It was also then she caught a glimpse of his faded brown leather cowboy boots, as he continued to look out the window. *"Oh... how his legs look all so long and masculine. Even up through his back and shoulders seemed to hold that same strength,"* she went on, while thinking how he reminded her of her first love, standing there. As it did, the pain in her heart sank deeper.

Picking up on it, it had caused him to turn back to see the look of loneliness in her eyes, the eyes of someone he knew nothing about. "How did it happen?" he asked, catching her off guard.

"W...what?"

"This man you're hurting over."

"A car accident. He was killed several years ago in a car accident," she repeated, while fighting back the tears she kept buried most of the time.

"Sorry."

Getting to her feet, she went over to stand next to him. "The dream?" she asked, changing the subject. "It felt so real to me."

"Well it was real, to me," he returned, looking back out the window. "As for why it had affected you the way it ..." He paused for a moment to look back at her. Unsure how to tell her, so as not to scare her away, he had to think carefully.

"It, what?" she asked, sensing his hesitance.

"It was because I planted it there."

"Y...you what...?" she asked, as she began backing away from him again. While seeming a little frightened, she didn't know what to think. However, the thought to run like crazy did appeal to her.

Again, picking up her thoughts, he smiled, while taking a small step toward her. "I..." he began, only to be cut off.

"H... how..." she asked, when recollecting her first dream. "When I was at my parents' house, when the dreams began?"

"It wasn't easy at first," he continued to smile. "But after several attempts, I was able to reach your subconscious mind, while you slept."

"Oh, God!" She looked at the floor in front of her. "And now?" She looked back up at him. "What now?"

"In time," he returned. "In time I will tell you, but not just yet. You need time to absorb what has just happened here."

"Absorb?" she laughed, when just then, they turned, hearing voices coming up the stairs.

Turning back, he looked at her with a hint of panic in his eyes.

"Hey! It will be all right," she smiled warmly. "I'll help you. I promise." Turning to look away from those helpless eyes of his, she thought more to herself. *"That's once all this begins to sink in, of course."*

"And it will, Jessi. It will." He kept the thought from going out to her, as he just smiled down at her warmly.

With that, she turned back, before the girls could interrupt.

Before she could say anything, he held a finger to her lips. "Soon," he replied, as another warm smile crept across his face.

With a nod of her head, she smiled back.

Doing the same, he vanished, as the door began to open.

Chapter Five

"Here you are," Lora called out. "Are you all right?"

"Yes, I'm fine! What time is it?" she asked, realizing she no longer felt frightened by his presence. However, she was still a little confused on how she was to help him.

"It's eight thirty!" Lora grumbled. "What are you doing up here anyway?"

"I thought I may have heard something," she replied warmly, when catching a glimpse of him standing behind her girls.

"What was it?" Cassi asked.

She thought for a moment before answering. Though, looking up at him, he shook his head. "Well, uh… no!" she shook her head. "It was probably just a branch hitting the window! So what do you say we go downstairs and get something to eat. I'm hungry, aren't you?" she asked, moving out into the hallway.

"Yes," they both replied, following her.

Turning back, she saw him standing near the window again, looking at her with that crooked smile of his. And for a brief moment, she could have sworn she saw a ray of hope in his beautiful blue eyes, when she smiled back.

"Later, beautiful!" he whispered so that only she could hear. *"Later."*

"Yeah, later," she smiled.

After finishing breakfast, they packed the car back up for their trip home.

"Are we ready?" Jessi called out from the front door, while taking a good look around, before heading out.

"Yeah," Lora returned, while going out to the car to get in on her side.

"Let's get going then. I'm sure Ashley has been wondering where we are."

"Mom," Cassi called out from the back seat, "did you get my art pad and pencils?"

"Got 'em!" she announced, smiling to herself. *"Cassi and her artwork, what would she do without it? Lord, I couldn't imagine, when she is so good at it too."*

Shaking off the thought, she took one last look to make sure the fire in the fireplace was out, and the sofa-sleeper made back up. But just as she turned to head out to the car to leave, a feeling came over her. Turning at that moment, she looked back at the house, where in the same upstairs window she had looked at the previous night, she saw him, standing there, looking out at her. Though his expression looked lost, there was yet a ray of hope still in his eyes, as he continued to gaze down upon her, while she stood at her car.

"Please___don't forget me___!" he called out, reminding her.

"I won't forget. You have my word!" she thought back, though uncertain of what had just happened, as she went on to whisper her next response. "I am coming back, Craig, and soon!" she smiled up at him, hoping it would help to reassure him.

"Mom," Lora spoke up with a twisted expression on her face, while breaking into her mother's thoughts, "you aren't starting to like this place, are you?"

Looking in at her older daughter, she grinned, "Just think of it as an adventure!" she offered, when turning back to see Craig laughing.

"Emmm... and how handsome that smile of his is, even with that crooked grin whenever I see it," she thought fondly, but then stopped once she realized what she was doing. "Come on, girl, get a grip!" she scolded quietly, while getting into her car and heading out.

"Yeah, an adventure," Cassi was saying, while teasing her sister, who found nothing at all funny about any of it.

Meanwhile, watching from his bedroom window, as they left, he laughed, while propping one hand on his hip, and the elbow of the other arm on the window frame, while shaking his head. And for the first time since his death, he felt really hopeful.

As for the trip home, it was a quiet one, while she thought back to such an adventure. If only she knew where this adventure was about to take her.

Once back out on the highway home, her mind was also cluttered with the thoughts of what was really breaking her heart. And that was the expression in his eyes. *"He needs me!"* she thought to herself, while keeping track of the route back to the Inn.

Nearly an hour later, pulling into the drive of the old Inn, Jessi got out first, while calling back over her shoulder, "Girls... unload the car for me, will you? I have to run inside and take care of something."

"All right," they returned, looking at each other, before turning back to watch their mom run off into the Inn.

"What was that all about?" Cassi asked, following Lora around to open the trunk.

"I don't know. She wasn't like that at Grandpa's!"

"No. But oh well. Let's just get this stuff inside so I can get something to eat."

"Food, again?" she teased, while bringing out the rest of their things, before closing the trunk.

Meanwhile, just inside, Jessi went right into her office to write down the directions back to Craig's place, before she could forget. Afterwards, she placed the notebook back into her desk drawer, before heading down to their quarters, where the three of them lived in what used to be a basement, now converted into a two bedroom living area.

"Ms. Jessi?" Annie spoke up, startling her, when Jessi came walking out of her office.

"Oh, my Gosh," she cried out, placing a hand to her heart, "Annie____!"

"I'm sorry, dear! I was just in the kitchen, putting a few things away, when I heard someone coming in. And your father called awhile ago to see if you made it back all right."

"Yes..., well we ran into some bad weather, and had to take refuge in an old, abandoned farmhouse, about an hour south of here. The girls were pretty tired, so we chose to hold up there overnight," she explained, while stopping to look over the reservation book on the desk just inside the front door of the one hundred and ten year old, Victorian

Inn. Turning back, she went on. "If it hadn't been for the lightning, I would have called you guys on my cell phone to let you know what was going on!"

"Well, I'm glad to see you all made it back safely. Although, I should call Hank and let him know that he can park the Hummer."

"The Hummer?" she asked, looking puzzled.

"Oh," she offered, seeing her expression, "we were all getting worried about you. And last night's eleven o'clock news said a large tree had come down across the highway. There were also reports of broken glass and skid marks that only a set of car tires could have made."

"Oh, my…" she cried, going over to look out at her car in the Sunday afternoon light, "that was us. We had to skid off to the side of the road to avoid being hit by the tree."

"Oh, no… are you all okay?" she asked, seeing more to Jessi's expression than what was intended. Before she could ask, Hank came walking up onto the front porch, seeing the two of them standing there.

"Ms. Jessi, are you all, all right?" he asked thoughtfully.

"Yes, thank you," she returned, seeing that fatherly look on his handsome face. "Annie will fill you in on what all had happened. However, I'm going to have to call my insurance lady and get the car taken care of."

Looking questioningly to Annie, he started to ask.

"Yes," Annie returned, "it was her car they found the broken glass and skid marks from."

"And you're sure you're all okay?" he asked again, when turning back to Jessi.

"Lora has a few minor cuts and scrapes, but we're all right now."

"Good," he returned. "And now, if you're not needing me, I'll just be getting back to my chores," he explained, while turning to take his leave.

"Hank…" Jessi called out, as he was about to take the first step off the front porch.

Turning back, he looked up at her with that worried look still lingering on his face.

"Thanks for being so concerned. It's sure nice to have that around here. Which reminds me, how are the horses?"

"They're fine! I'll be going out in the Hummer to gather them up in a few hours to bring them back in to get settled for the night."

"Good."

Along with his background on horses, Jessi needed all the help she could get, with the old

Inn sitting on over one hundred acres of mostly woods, while running alongside beautiful Lake Michigan.

Turning back one last time, he called back to her, "Ms. Jessi. You're good people, and I wouldn't hesitate to go the distance to see to it that you are all taken good care of here."

With that, the two grinned sheepishly at each other, before he walked away.

"Well, I should be getting my chores finished as well. I have some things to do back home before I can turn in," Annie commented, while on her way back to the kitchen. "Oh, but should I prepare something for you and the girls, before I leave?"

"No, that's all right. We'll see you in the morning, if I don't see you before you go."

With a nod of her graying head, she was gone.

Later that evening, after her girls got settled in, Jessi went out into the backyard to do her nightly meditation, as she had always done in the past. This time though, was different. This time she was thinking of Craig and his situation.

Meantime, while walking out near the oversized white gazebo, feeling the breeze lift several strands of her hair, she whispered his name softly in the night air, before going on to think of other things that seemed to tie in with these unexpected feelings of sadness toward this man's troubled spirit.

Looking up at the night sky, as the small pillow soft clouds rolled by, she called out to her Heavenly Father in a prayer, "Dear Lord," she cried, "it's been so long since I have felt this way. Ever since..." she broke off just then, feeling her tears well up. "Of all times, why must I be feeling this way now? And why him? Of all people, Lord, why him...?" She knew His answer, before even asking the question. "Lord, did you send me to that particular farmhouse to help this...this spirit with his quest to free himself? And if so, why___? Why me? So I can say goodbye to him, like I didn't do with Daniel? You know how I felt for not saying goodbye to him. I can't do this again. I just can't go through that kind of pain, when it hurts me so… much."

Just as she turned to walk back to the gazebo, her prayer was interrupted when Lora called out to her. "Mom…, when are you coming in?"

"Soon. Why?"

"Have you forgotten, you were supposed to have called Grandpa?"

"Oh, Lord___!" she cried, running up to the patio doors of their walkout quarters, when the thought of her father crossed her mind.

Passing her daughter up on her way in, Lora shook her head, "You did, didn't you?"

"Lora…" she scolded, "I had nearly forgotten. That's all. But thanks for reminding me. I'll do it now."

"Well, someone had to. You haven't been the same since this morning," she commented, while closing the patio doors behind them.

"I have had a lot on my mind!" she exclaimed, hoping her daughter wouldn't pry any further. And once seeing she had given in and headed out of the living room to go to bed, Jessi gave out a silent sigh of relief.

"Goodnight, Mom," she called back frustratedly.

"Goodnight, sweetie," Jessi returned, while going over to her favorite recliner to put in the call to her father. While waiting for it to go through, she thought back to the look on Lora's face, *"Oh, Lora, I wish I could just tell you, but…"* Just then, her thoughts were cut short, when she heard her father's voice over the other end. "Hey, Dad!" she responded, while getting more comfortable, knowing she would be in for a lecture on why she shouldn't have worried them so.

And then it came.

"Hey, yourself!" he returned, sounding worried. "I was just about to send your brother out to look for you!"

"I'm sorry I didn't call sooner," she replied, while going on to fill him in on their trip home.

"Sounds like you had an exciting trip!" he commented after a lengthy summation on how the storm had taken its toll on them.

"That's an understatement if I ever heard one," she laughed, while shuttering out the chilling feeling of what all happened, before meeting Craig's spirit.

"Well, I'm glad you're all okay. I'll let you go now so that you can get some sleep."

"All right, Dad. And Dad, I love you both," she returned, while saying her goodnights, before hanging up to go in and check on the girls.

Seeing how they both had fallen off to sleep, she felt a sense of relief wash over her, while turning to head for her own bedroom. "Good, now maybe I will get a goodnight's sleep, too."

Though that night, and every night after, she was to discover a different dream, each time she would slip off to sleep. With them, she would call out to Craig, as she would feel his sadness playing over and over again in her mind, until she couldn't think of anything else.

Meanwhile, tossing and turning, she recalled his unique smile, and oh… how it had such an effect on her, as she whispered sweetly to herself, remembering how it made her shiver.

"Mmmm…" she smiled, while snuggling down into her pillow even more, while drifting even more into a deeper sleep, while replaying that smile over and over in her head.

Chapter Six

The next morning, Jessi had gotten up, bright and early, when Lora came walking into her mother's room, while Jessi was busy picking out something to wear. "Mom?"

"Yes?" she replied from the closet doorway.

"Who's Craig?" she asked, causing her mother to spin around, dropping a fresh pair of jeans at the mere mention of his name.

"W...where did you hear that?" she asked, while trying to hide her surprise, but failing miserably.

"So you do know him."

"Y...yes, but where did you hear that?" she asked again, while picking up her jeans, before going over to her bed to lay them out, along with a warm blue slipover sweater.

"You were crying out his name in your sleep last night."

"What___? No!" she cried. "Lora, we're not going to get into this right now. So why don't you go and get your sister up, while I grab a shower and get dressed. After all we have a lot of work to do today to get this place ready for our guests this coming weekend."

"She's already up, getting dressed!" she exclaimed, crying, as she stood her ground. "So tell me, who is he?"

"He...he's just someone I met recently," she explained, while fumbling for the right words to say, as she started for the bathroom with her change of clothes in hand.

Not satisfied, Lora refused to give up and followed her across the hall. "Then, why were you crying?" she asked more persistently from the bathroom doorway.

"Lora, aren't you supposed to be getting ready to work the front desk this morning?"

"Yes...!"

"Then get moving!" she was saying, when they both heard the phone. "I'll get that," she announced, passing her daughter in the doorway. "Just work on getting yourselves ready to go."

"Fine!" she agreed angrily, when turning to walk back toward her room.

Feeling bad that she couldn't tell her own daughter what was really going on, she called out to her hurriedly, "Lora…!"

"Mom…"

"I'm sorry. I just have a lot on my mind and…"

"I know," she smiled tearfully.

Fighting her own tears, Jessi hurried back off into her room to grab the phone on its third ring. "Hello!" she answered, wiping away at a tear that came.

"Hey lady, is everything okay?" Ashley, the closer of her friends asked.

"Yes. Or it will be."

"Good. Now, what time are you coming up?"

"I'll be right up, just as soon as I can grab a quick shower," she replied to the forty-two year old, who stood about five foot four, with dark brown hair and light brown eyes.

Thankfully, aside from herself, Ashley, too, was the levelheaded sort. Whereas Renee, built similar to their friend, though, Hispanic, was better known for her fun loving nature, while making life more upbeat for the three of them.

Thinking back to the day when all this started, Jessi and her two friends were sitting in the break room of their local Wal-mart Supercenter, where they met and started working together. "What do you think," Renee asked in her bubbly way, "we each put in our share and buy a lottery ticket?"

"That's fine by us!" Jessi and Ashley had agreed, while rubbing their aching feet.

"But what if we win?" Ashley asked, while slipping her shoes back on. "What then?"

"Well…" Jessi smiled, with a twinkle in her eye, "we do what we have always talked about."

Later, hearing they had won the jackpot, they were shocked. As for some time they talked of owning their own businesses. A Bed &

Breakfast for Jessi and her girls, and a Boutique and Coffee Shop for Ashley and Renee.

Deciding to call it 'The Serenity Inn' the three women celebrated their good fortune, and soon found the perfect place for it, outside their small town of Langley, Indiana, where Jessi had found a one hundred and ten year old, two-story, Victorian home in the country.

Within a few months, she had its basement remodeled into a two bedroom living area for her and her girls. Which included a small galley kitchen, a corner fireplace in the living room, and a set of glass French doors leading out into the beautifully landscaped yard. As for the rest of the quarters, aside from the two bedrooms, one which the girls share, there was also a generous bathroom with its garden tub. As for natural lighting, there were ample sized windows put in to make it seem less of a basement.

Then came the time for the Grand Opening. As the guests pulled into the driveway, the beauty of a large, white wood-planked front porch, which extended from one side of the Inn to the other, greeted them. On it were three sets of white iron tables and chairs to accommodate an outside breakfast that could be served on all those beautiful spring and summer-like days.

Upon entering it, the guests were first greeted at the reservation desk, located off to the left of the oversized, solid oak doorway, welcoming them warmly into the ample sized foyer, thus adding to all its warmth and decor.

However, the one thing Jessi found different about this Inn, was found at the front portion of the upstairs hallway. Another set of steps leading up to an attic that was rarely ever used. In it were two other bedrooms and a full bath, full of dust and cobwebs. However, it wasn't that, that caught her attention. The bedrooms could always be used perhaps at a later date, but until then, there in the back left corner was an area that held a mysterious feeling every time she went near it. Because of it, the attic was kept locked.

Meanwhile, finishing their conversation, Jessi and her girls headed upstairs to start on another workday after having breakfast.

"Hi, ladies," Jessi called out to her two friends, while walking into the Boutique, located across from the front desk, when leaving one of her girls to answer the phone, while the other cleaned rooms.

"Hi, yourself," Ashley greeted, while pouring a cup of coffee for her, and two cups of cappuccinos for Renee and herself. "Did you get any sleep last night?" she asked, knowing that something was up.

"No, not really," she replied, taking her cup, before going over to sit down to discuss the itinerary for the day.

"Do you want to talk about it?" Renee asked kindly, looking to their friend.

"Perhaps, but not now, we have so much to do, before we get busy," she replied, while staring down into her cup, before getting up to get a spoon from behind the coffee bar.

At that time, the two women simply looked at each other, but were not about to give up quite so easily.

When Jessi turned back to see their expression, she asked, "What?"

"Are you going to tell us why you couldn't sleep?" Renee asked impatiently.

Shaking her head at her friends' persistence, she tried changing the subject. "You know," she said playfully, "I was just thinking how nice it would be to set up some tables out on the front lawn. What do you think?" she asked, while taking a cautious sip of her hot coffee.

"All right, Jess," Ashley said scoldingly, "what's up? And why are you trying so hard to avoid the question?"

She shook her head and looked at them, until they got up to join her. "All right, I'll tell you. Lord knows I have to tell someone," she said, when finally giving in.

"Yes. Well now, that's more like it," Ashley stated, while they went back over to take a seats. "You don't just cry out in your sleep for nothing. What was the dream about that got you so upset?"

"And who is this Craig?" Renee added.

"What...? How did you know about him?"

"Sorry, lady," Ashley offered sympathetically. "Lora called me this morning just before you had gotten up. She was worried about you, when you started calling out his name in your sleep. She said she couldn't wake you, and called me to see what she should do."

"Oh, God, she shouldn't have bothered," she explained, while trying to sound casual, as she fiddled with a napkin on the table. "As it is this whole thing is so hard to believe!"

"Try us," Renee said, while patting her on the hand.

Glancing up at the clock, Jessi noticed they had an hour before they needed to open the Boutique doors for business. "All right, but I'll have to keep it short."

By the time the story was over, it was time to open the doors, as the guests of the Inn were already starting to arrive to do some shopping. As the day went on, everyone was so busy, no one had time to think much about anything other than what was going on around them.

Then finally, Renee spoke up, asking Jessi, who had stuck around to lend a hand, about her plans for the Fourth of July weekend.

"The girls will be visiting with my cousin's two girls, while I go back down to Crawfordsfield," she replied, not wanting to say anymore, when going over to pick up a few things that had fallen off the rack.

"Oh?" she was asking, when a short stout woman in her mid fifties, strolled in somberly, with dark brown hair pulled back in a tight bun.

Looking over at her, from the front window, while arranging some catalogs on a table, Ashley couldn't help but notice the woman's clothing looking worn and strangely made, from the long brown skirt, meeting just above a pair of black laced, high top shoes. The jewelry she wore set off her white blouse, which was nearly covered by an old, black tattered shawl that hung past her ample hips.

"Can we help you?" Ashley asked the woman who was looking around the room, as if searching for someone particular.

"Jessi Rae," the woman asked pretentiously. "Is she here?"

"Yes. She's standing over at the coffee bar, now! May I ask who wants to know?"

Just then, Renee walked up to join them. "What's up?" she asked, smiling at the two.

"This lady is asking for Jessi."

"Oh? What do you want with her?" she asked the stranger, puzzledly.

"I must speak with her. It is of a personal matter, and I do not wish to discuss it with anyone else," she stated, when walking off toward Jessi, while the others followed close behind.

At the coffee bar, Jessi was once again preoccupied with thoughts of the tall, handsome, troubled spirit, who needed her. Not seeing the three of them arrive she went on thinking to herself, when suddenly, her thoughts were interrupted.

"Are you Jessi Rae?" the woman asked with a mysterious undertone.

"Y...yes!" She turned around to see the stranger staring up at her. "What can I do for you?"

Just then, the stranger turned to look back at the others, and then back to Jessi.

Seeing she didn't want to talk in front of them, she suggested going to her office. "We can talk more privately there, if you would like."

"Jessi..." Ashley spoke up just then.

Assuring her friends, she left the Boutique, taking the mysterious woman with her.

Upon entering her office, she closed the door behind her and proceeded over to her desk, where an overstuffed chair sat nearby. "Please, have a seat, Ms...?" she pointed, walking around to take a seat behind her large mahogany desk.

"My name is not of any importance to you. I am here to tell you of a very serious matter. One in which you must not ignore."

Sitting back in her chair to study the stranger's face, Jessi asked her uninvited guest why she wouldn't tell her who she was. "Ms. whoever you are, I am not in the habit of having someone just walk in and demand to see me without knowing who they are. So unless you start..."

"Very well then," she cut her off, "if it's that important to you, my name is Doreen. I have been receiving some rather disturbing visions that concern you and a man whose spirit is troubled. He has been crying out to you in your dreams to help him, and he will continue to do so until you go to him. He needs your help, Jessi, as time is of the essence. So you must go to him, and soon, or he will continue to be troubled for yet another year until someone else can perceive his presence."

Jessi listened in awe, as she knew exactly what this woman was saying, when she then got up and walked over to the couch.

Taking a seat, she looked down at her open hands. "You're a...a psychic, aren't you?"

"Yes, I am," she answered, while getting up to go over and join her. "Does that bother you?" she asked, taking a seat next to her.

"Not really," she replied sadly, while bringing her, now, folded hands up to her chin to ponder over her next words. "I've been thinking a lot about him, ever since we arrived home the other night. What bothers me," she said, turning to face her visitor, "is having these dreams, and not knowing what to do. However, I am planning on going back out to see him."

"When?"

"This weekend."

"That is good."

Feeling unsure of herself, Jessi asked, while getting up to go back over to her desk, "But what do I do when I get there?"

"Follow your heart, Jessi. You have a gift."

"I what?" She turned back with a look of surprise on her face.

"Yes. You have had this gift all your life. It's been growing inside of you, waiting."

"Waiting for what?"

"For you!"

"For me? But why?"

"For you to mature!" she said calmly, before rising to her own feet. "And now the time has come," she added, taking Jessi's shaking hands, when coming over to stand before her. "It's time now for you to learn how to use it. Don't fight it, whatever you do."

"But, I…I don't understand…" she cried, shaking her head, as she was just about to pull away, when her caller lead her back over to the couch, to sit down again.

"Then let me explain it to you. From this point on, you will start to feel his pain. And soon, very soon, you will also encounter someone else who was once very close to him. Even his pain will be very apparent to you."

"Great!" she grumbled.

"Yes, well, you will also be going through a lot of changes, as well as some danger."

"D…danger…?"

"Yes, but the worst will be the one that changes the lives of all those who are closely involved. And Jessi, no one must try to attempt to change what is about to happen," she warned ominously. "And last, but certainly not least…"

"There's more…?"

"Oh... yes, don't be afraid. When his thoughts start to come through, you must relax and let it happen."

"But... if I can hear his thoughts, does this mean..."

"Yes, your mind is open to his. He will even know when you are in trouble."

"Oh, great...!" she thought, while getting up to walk over to open the door. "Doreen," she stopped the woman, as she started to leave. "Thank you for coming in. I'll get started right away on what we have talked about."

"Very well," her visitor said, while walking with Jessi out to her car.

After Doreen had gone, Jessi found herself standing out front all alone to think over their conversation. Turning to go back inside, she stopped short of the front porch, to find her two friends standing there, waiting on her.

"Get started on what?" Renee asked, puzzledly.

"On my uh... errands!" she exclaimed hesitantly, as she walked passed them in the doorway.

"Oh. I guess this means that we are not to know what's going on then." Ashley asked, sounding disappointed.

Stopping just inside, Jessi turned back to look out over the front lawn, as the sun was just about to settle over the horizon. At that moment, feeling lost in her own thoughts, she sadly replied, before going back into her office, "I...I'm sorry, it's just that I'm not so sure of it myself!"

"Jessi___!" Ashley called out, feeling bad for her friend.

Stopping short of the office door, she looked back partially over her shoulder. "Ash, really, I'm sorry, but I have a lot of paperwork to do. As it is, I'm falling pretty far behind."

"Sure. All right," she said, letting it go for that moment, when turning to go back into the Boutique with Renee.

"What do you make of that?" her friend asked, looking back, as Jessi closed the office door, and then the girls, who looked lost, as well.

"I don't know," Ashley returned, peering back herself. "But I will say this, this has me really worried."

"Us too!" Lora agreed quietly, while she and her sister went over to join them in the doorway of the Boutique.

"She'll be all right," Ashley replied.

"Sure she will," Renee added, while looking to her friend, knowing what was really going on. "We just have to give her some space, is all."

Chapter Seven

That afternoon, finishing on a mound of paperwork that had been piling up on her desk, it was time to take a break. "Well, that's all taken care of. Now to go and see what the others are doing," Jessi groaned achingly, while getting up to head over to the Boutique.

Walking in, she heard Renee's voice, "Well, its closing time!" she announced, seeing Jessi standing at the door. "What do you say we go out and get something to eat?"

"Sure. I'm up for it!" Ashley agreed, looking over at Jessi. "What about you?"

Walking over to the counter, she turned to them, "I'm going to have to pass on it this time. I wouldn't be much company tonight, anyway."

"Still thinking about what that woman had to say?" Ashley asked.

"Sort of."

Remembering Annie's last words, before leaving, Renee suddenly spoke up, "Hey, why don't we raid the kitchen? Annie said she left some extra food prepared in the fridge for us in case we had to work late!"

Jessi agreed, smiling, "I have to feed the girls, anyway," she explained, going over to the reservation desk, while her friends locked up the Boutique. "And since Annie left us the extra food in case we had to work late, why not!" After calling Cassi, who had gone downstairs to watch TV, Jessi turned to Lora, "Come on. It's slow. Let's go eat."

"Sure."

Going into the kitchen, everyone got out their own plates and silverware, while Jessi went to warm up the food.

"Mom," Cassi spoke up, walking in. "Can we sit out on the front porch tonight to eat?"

Turning to the others, Jessi asked, "Well, how about it?"

"Sure, and after today, the fresh air will do us all some good!"

Agreeing, they headed out to sit at their favorite table at the far corner of the porch.

"This place sure has been a madhouse ever since we opened nearly a year ago," Ashley commented, while taking their time eating.

"I was hoping it would," Jessi put in, seeing how tired her girls were getting. "And after we get through here, why don't you two call it a night. I'll have the front door locked, and the intercom on in case someone comes in late."

"I think everyone is already in for the night," Lora replied, tiredly.

"Good, but just the same, we still have a few vacant rooms to rent out."

"If you want," Ashley spoke up, "I can stay around to keep an eye on the front desk so you can get some sleep."

"Thanks, but you're going to have your own hands full with the shipment you two have coming in tomorrow."

"Oh, sure…! I had nearly forgotten!" Renee laughed.

After they finished eating, no sooner had they taken their dishes in, they heard the front door open, and then close, followed by the sound of the front desk bell ring.

"It's almost ten o'clock! Who could that be?" Lora asked.

"Don't know. But let's go find out," Jessi suggested, while heading back into the foyer ahead of them.

Walking in, she found a tall man looking to be in his late forties, with graying hair, standing at the desk. "May I help you?" she asked, walking around to the other side of the desk.

"I need a room," the stranger replied, his voice deep and gruff, as his icy blue eyes glared down into her green ones.

Causing her to feel uncomfortable, she looked away and opened the registration book to hand to him. "How long will you be needing it?" she asked, avoiding his glare.

"For a few days, or so. Will that be a problem?" he asked, signing in.

Not paying attention to what he had just asked, she found herself staring at his attire. With his long pale blue shirtsleeves rolled up just below his elbow, she noted his strong hands and forearms, as he finished signing in.

Realizing she hadn't answered, he repeated himself, while looking more intently into her eyes, as she went to blink back at him.

"No. No, of course not," she replied, when then the others became concerned about how this stranger was effecting her.

While continuing to study her and the others, Jessi went to get him his key.

Turning to hand it to him, it was then she noticed a pack of cigarettes in his shirt pocket, just beneath his dark blue padded vest. Seeing the familiar label, it read: Marlboro Lights 100's. *"Hmmm,"* she went on, while forcing the thought out of her mind, when giving him his key. "Room Two," she announced, just as their hands touched. At that moment, she couldn't help but find herself looking back up, and into the eyes of this rather tall, mysterious stranger, with his graying hair and rugged exterior. Thus, giving him the look of a man who had been beaten down in life, and hell-bent on getting even with whoever, or whatever caused him so much pain and anger. Yet, there was something else about his eyes, something strangely familiar. *"But what,"* she wondered, allowing her hand to linger a little longer in his.

Slowly, he took the key from her hand, while looking into her puzzled expression. But then moving on down, he caught a glimpse of her lips, as they parted under his watchful gaze. "Thank you," he said, picking up his bag to head for the stairs. But then, he stopped and turned back, catching her off guard. "One more thing, Miss uh..."

"Ms. Rae," she corrected, while subconsciously rubbing the hand that he had touched.

Seeing her reaction, as she acted as though she were busying herself, straightening up the desk, he grinned coyly. "Yes, of course. Will you be here in the morning?"

"Yes. Yes, of course," she stammered, while turning away from his little bit of humor at her expense.

Just then, out of the corner of her eye, she noticed for the first time the exact same pair of brown, leather, cowboy boots that she had seen before, but for whatever reason she couldn't place clearly on where.

At that moment, Lora spoke up, interrupting her mother's thoughts, as she started to tell the man that they lived there.

"Lora." Jessi stopped her, not wanting the stranger to know their business.

Looking at Lora, and then Jessi, he raised a suspicious eyebrow.

"Great. Does he suspect what Lora was about to tell him?" she asked, not remembering what Doreen had told her about her thoughts reaching out to a certain troubled spirit across the miles. Though, at that moment, it had brought a smile to his lips.

"Oh, Jessi...," Craig kept the thought from reaching her, *"if only you knew,"* he laughed to himself.

Just then, Renee interrupted them, "Hey, it's late, and we need to be going home now."

"Yes," Ashley agreed, seeing the intense look on her friends' face. "Oh, but we can stay if you think you'll need us."

"No, I'll be fine," she replied, while putting her arms around both girls. "We'll be fine."

Before walking her friends out, Jessi stood for a moment, watching the man turn to go up to his room. His long masculine legs and powerful upper thighs radiated through the faded blue denim jeans he was wearing, at the same time, accenting his narrow waist and hips even more. Then, after hearing the door to Room Two close, she turned to go out with her friends to their cars.

"Are you sure you're going to be all right?" Ashley asked. "I can always call home and tell them I'm staying over!"

"No, that won't be necessary. We'll be fine. I'll see you both in the morning," she called out, once they got into their cars, and waved goodbye.

After seeing them off, she was just about to turn and go inside, when out of nowhere, the wind picked up. And with it, she felt as though someone was calling out to her.

It wasn't her imagination though. For in the wind, the voice she heard was a man's voice. *"J e s s i___"* he called out, as if to warn her.

"Who's there?" she called back, while turning to see where it was coming from.

Once again she heard the same eerie sound, carrying in the wind, as it continued to call out warning her. *"Jessi___be careful___! Be___careful___!"*

"That voice...!" she cried inwardly, while looking around herself.

"It sounds so familiar. But…" Stopping, she waited a moment. When nothing happened, she decided then to go back inside.

As she started for the door, she caught a glimpse of a shadowy figure moving off to the left of the front porch. Having never felt more terrified as she did right then, to make matters worse, the front door opened, and Lora stepped out to see what her mother was doing.

"Lora____!" she cried out, making a mad dash to get her back inside, while taking the steps two at a time.

"Mom____!" Lora shrieked, seeing the look of horror on her mother's face.

"No time to explain…! Get back inside! And hurry!" she yelled hurriedly, while taking Lora by the arm.

Shoving her back inside, Jessi closed and locked the door as fast as she could.

"Mom____?" Lora cried out again. "What's going on?"

Still facing the door, while trying to catch her breath, all she could do was lean her head against its frame.

But then, at that moment, the stranger from Room Two appeared out of nowhere, to see what was going on. "Is something wrong, Ms. Rae?" he asked, his expression hard and serious.

"Wrong____?" she cried breathlessly, when spinning around to face him. "Just where were you a few minutes ago?"

"I was up in my room____!" he thundered back, while trying to control his own anger, with his eyes fixed on hers. "Not to mention, my window was open at the time I heard you cry out. You sounded as though something or someone had frightened you!"

"Something or someone *did* frighten me. Or perhaps I should say, terrified me!" she cried sharply, when going over to the desk to see who this stranger was. Finding her answer in the registration book, she slammed it shut, and turned to look back up at him. "Mr. Storm, is it? Just exactly who are you, anyway?"

"My name is Alex Storm. That's all I can tell you, at this time," he returned, sounding even more mysterious than before. "Now, Ms. Rae, tell me what just happened out there? And I want to know everything."

Not liking the way she felt being interrogated, she decided against arguing with him at that time, on account of her girls. "Fine. I'll tell you. I saw someone in the shadows just off to the left side of the porch," she nodded her head in the general direction, while trying to keep a grip on her shaky hands, not wanting him to know how frightened she really was.

"Would you mind telling me just what the hell you were doing out there, anyway?" he asked, while glaring down at her.

Just then, all attempts to control her temper had failed her.

"Oh... boy," Lora grumbled, while cringing off to one the side of the foyer, as her mother stepped forward to nail this man for his arrogance.

"Alex Storm, is it? Well, excuse... me, but where do you get off reading me the riot act? For your information, I was seeing my friends off," she snapped back, while the two continued to glare at each other until Cassi spoke up.

"Mom... what's going on?" she asked tiredly, when her mother went over to put her arms around both of them.

"It's going to be all right," she tried to sound reassuring, as she went on to explain what had happened.

"All right then. Stay here. I'll be right back," he ordered, while sounding so much like a cop, as he headed for the front door. Getting there, he opened his vest, not intending to reveal a service revolver while hidden away under his vest, in a shoulder holster.

But then as he turned back to say something, he was cut off by Jessi's sudden demand at what she had just seen. "Oh___, my___Lord___! Mr. Storm___" she nearly came unglued, "what on earth are you doing with a gun, and here in my Inn?"

"Ms. Rae..." he growled, "you'll just have to wait on that. For now, lock this door behind me like I was about to say."

"What..." she started, when she then saw how his eyes turned to a steely shade of blue.

"Do it, Ms. Rae. Just do it."

Doing as he said, she fumed, going over to lock it, after he went out onto the porch.

"Mom..." Lora spoke up again.

"Like I said, it's going to be fine. But for now, let's just go into the office and wait," she suggested, leading the way.

Once inside, the girls each went over to the sofa to get comfortable, while Jessi went over to the front window to pray.

"Mom, are you sure you should be standing there?" her girls questioned, concernedly.

"You're probably right," she chuckled nervously, and stood back a ways.

Meanwhile, having his back to the wall, Alex drew his revolver in case the shadowy figure was to show itself.

"Okay now, let's just see who we have here?" he growled quietly, while moving closely around the same side of the Inn, Jessi last saw the prowler.

Getting there, the coast was clear. But then, hearing something off in the distance, he knew their visitor must have had a car waiting down the road, from the sound of it.

"Damn!" he growled, hurrying off to try to catch what he could, before the car could get very far.

Doing so, he knew he could have just as well taken his vehicle to go after the person, but didn't want to leave these people alone in case their visitor returned. Though, once he got to the road, the car was too far to get a make off it.

"Great," he growled again, while peering down the road at its taillights. "And just who were you, anyway?" he asked, returning his revolver back to its holster, before heading back to the Inn.

Stopping short of the porch, a bad thought came to him.

"No..." he shook his head. "But if I'm wrong, to make certain our friend doesn't come back, I'll just stay out here a little while longer, walking the grounds to be sure."

And walk the grounds he did.

Chapter Eight

Back inside, there was still no sign of Mr. Storm after nearly an hour had gone by.

"Mom...?" Lora spoke up, sounding worried.

"Yes?" she asked, having gone back over to the window to look out.

"What could be taking him so long?"

"I don't know!" she replied, sounding worried as well. Then thinking, she turned back to ask, "Is Max still downstairs?"

"Yes!"

"Good. Let's go get him," she suggested, while heading for their quarters.

Getting there, Max, their German shepherd, greeted them joyfully.

"Hey, Max! How's my baby doing?" Jessi asked, giving him a big hug. "Do you want to come upstairs?"

He let out a soft bark and pulled away to head for the stairs.

Jessi laughed.

"Mom," Lora interrupted. "Can I stay down here? I'm tired and want to go to bed."

"Sure. What about you, Cassi?" she asked, while going over to check on the patio doors, before heading back up the stairs. "Do you want to go up with me, or stay down here?"

"No. I'll go up with you."

"Mom," Lora stated concernedly, "you should tell her what's going on before you guys go up."

Seeing concern on both their faces, she smiled reassuringly. "Our guest in Room Two is out checking on a possible prowler."

"Why him?" Cassi asked, wondering. "Why not call the police?"

"I think he is the police," she grinned, sensing something about him. "So, shall we go?"

"Okay, let's go then!" Cassi agreed, feeling somewhat at ease now hearing about him.

Stopping at the steps, just before heading up, she turned to their Rottweiler, Maggie, "Stay with Lora," she ordered.

"She will, Mom," Lora returned, patting Maggie on the head, before heading down the hallway to her room, on the left, next to the bathroom.

Upon reaching the landing, Max heard a sound out on the front porch, and right away headed for the door, growling.

"What is it, Max?" Jessi asked, going over to stand next to him.

Soon she had her answer, when there came a knock at the door.

"Mr. Storm... is that you?" she asked quietly.

"Yes," his voice came back sounding low, almost hushed.

Opening the door, she stepped back to give him room to come in. But then, he went to close the door for her.

"Did you see anything?"

"No, but I can't be too sure," he explained, as he turned back to face her. At that moment, he came to a sudden stop, spotting Max sitting next to her.

Not sure what he would do, Alex looked slowly to Jessi and asked, "Your dog?"

"Yes!" she returned with a knowing grin, while looking from Alex to Max, then back to Alex. Seeing that 'not too sure' expression on his face made her feel somewhat superior, even if only for a brief moment.

"He's a beautiful dog! Is he a pure bred and trained to obey you?" he asked, continuing to study the dog's reaction to having a stranger standing in front of him.

"Yes, and sort of," she grinned, watching him approach Max slowly.

"Hi, Max! Are you going to be friendly?" he asked, while slowly kneeling down in front of him.

Getting up, Max looked up at Jessi, and then at this man whom he had never seen before.

"Go ahead, Max, he's all right. I think!" she laughed.

Turning back to the stranger, Alex began running his hand lightly at first over Max's coat, before going on to ruffle it once he saw that Max wasn't going to bite his hand off.

Seeing how well Max and Alex were hitting it off, Jessi then asked, "Mr. Storm is everything really all right out there?"

Not getting up right away, he simply said, while giving more attention to her dog, "Probably, but for now I think I'll just call in another officer to come out and check on things a little more tomorrow."

"What do you mean… *another officer?*" she asked surprisingly, while glaring down at him. "Just exactly who are you, and why are you here at my Inn?"

"Ms. Rae," he glared up at her when he began to stand up slowly, so as not to alarm her dog. "Like I said, I am Alex Storm. Or perhaps I should say, Detective Alex Storm," he corrected, knowing they had already spoken before, on the phone, over another matter, which had ruffled some feathers.

"Detective?"

"Uh huh," he nodded. "Of the Crawfordsfield County Sheriff's Department. As for the rest. It can wait until tomorrow."

"Yes, it will have to!" she answered, looking a little rattled at hearing his response.

"Yes," he returned, while continuing to study her reaction. *'Really. Surely you remember who I am now!'* he silently grinned.

Going over to lock the front door, she closed her eyes to all that had just happened, as she just wanted that night to end, and none too soon.

"Well, Mr.…. Detective Storm," she turned back, "if you will excuse us. We are all a little tired now and need to get some sleep."

"Sure!" he agreed, while watching them turn to walk away. Not to mention, avoid anymore eye contact with him. Speaking up then, he broke the silence, "If you don't mind, though, I'd like to go around and check all the doors and windows first before I turn in."

"Is that really necessary?" she asked, stopping at the door to their quarters.

"Yes, until we know who your shadowy visitor was."

"Fine. Be my guest," she called back over her shoulder. "Or do I need to go with you?" she asked, while trying not to look back at him.

When she did, their eyes met, and once again something began to form in her mind, but still not quite within reach.

"No," he broke into her thoughts once again. "The two of you look pretty tired. I can handle it from here."

"Good," she returned. Though, just as he was about to walk away, she stopped him.

"Mr... I mean Detective..."

"Ms. Rae," he turned to cut her off, his eyes, almost warm and gentle, as he came face to face with her now, "starting tomorrow, call me Alex."

"Oh...? Why would I want to do that?"

"Because, I said so," he grinned sheepishly.

"All right...!" Forcing a grin on her tired face, she turned to leave him.

"Goodnight, Ms. Jessi," he teased, just as something clicked in her mind.

'That's it! It's his voice!' she said silently. *'There is something vaguely familiar about it!'* Turning back to face him, while he went to check the lock on the front door again, she asked, "Mr. Storm?"

"Yes...?"

"Have we spoken before?"

Before answering her, he looked up at the ceiling, grinning, while shaking his head at an earlier recollection he had of their conversation on the phone shortly after her opening.

Just then, her blood began to boil, when seeing his reaction. "We have, haven't we?"

"Once," he stated, turning to see her reddened expression. "And believe me, Ms. Rae," he smiled, "I won't ever forget it, either."

"Oh, my Gosh! You're the one who took my call!" she said, accusingly.

"Yes, I am," he returned sheepishly. "As I recall, you were rather upset with me."

"Upset?" her voice went up an octave or two. "You brushed me off, Detective

Storm!" she snapped back at him.

Coming back more defensively, he tried to restrain his earlier anger,

"Ms. Rae," he glared. "For your information, I was working on an important case that I couldn't quite put down."

'And won't, until...' he thought heatedly, just as his expression changed to one of great sadness.

Realizing that she had hit a nerve, she offered an apology. "I...I'm sorry. I didn't know that at the time. Well, if you will excuse us!" She turned, saying her goodnights.

"Goodnight, Jessi."

"Mom," Cassi spoke up for the first time, "is he really a cop?"

"Yes, sweetie," she answered, turning back to look at the man who came into her Inn, seemingly, out of nowhere, "he really is a cop," she replied, as she was about to close the door behind them.

"Jessi?" he called out, stopping her.

"What do you need now, Mr....." she stopped. "I mean, Alex?"

"Why didn't you tell me that you and your family lived here?"

With a raised eyebrow, she asked, "Why didn't you tell me you were a cop?"

"A Detective," he corrected. "Okay," he laughed, "but I'm still going to have to check your place, as well."

"Fine!" she smiled coyly. "But I should warn you, we have a Rottweiler, too."

Having said that, her smile broadened even more, as she placed a hand on the doorknob, and then lightly laughed at his amused expression, when he shook his head.

"Great! I guess I don't have to worry about you and your kids then!" he commented with a deep laugh, as he went around to check on all the remaining doors and windows, before going up to his own room to place a call to his old partner.

The next morning, while waiting on Jessi to arrive, Ashley and Renee were getting things setup in the Boutique for another busy day.

"Where is she this morning?" Renee asked, sounding worried.

"I haven't a clue!" Ashley returned, while walking over to the register.

Feeling uncomfortable about their friend running late, Renee stopped for a moment to look over at Ashley. "You don't think..." She stopped. "What I mean is do you think we should go and check on her?"

No sooner had she gotten the words out, Jessi came walking in, wearing a soft blue gauzy dress, and a heavy black cardigan sweater, while carrying a clipboard with her. Smiling, she asked, "Are we ready for another big day?"

Ashley and Renee stopped to look at each other, as Jessi went over to the coffee bar to pour them their usual concoction, before taking a seat.

"What?" she asked, turning to see their expressions.

"Where have you been?" Renee asked, sounding concerned. "It's nearly time to open the doors already!"

"Sorry, but I was in setting up a menu plan with Annie!" she exclaimed. "Oh, yes, and before I forget, I had to hire another girl for the front desk. Just to give us some extra help this summer, mind you."

"Oh? Do you really think we're going to be needing the extra help?" Ashley asked, going over to take a seat, while Jessi continued pouring their coffee and cappuccinos.

"Yes, and…" she said, while stopping for a moment to carry the cups over to the table.

Getting up to take hers, Ashley asked impatiently, "And…?"

Taking her seat, Jessi felt amused over how her friends were taking the news. "And…" she smiled, while cautiously taking a sip of her hot coffee, "she'll be here soon."

"Well…" Ashley went on, "do we get to know who this person is?"

"Yes, of course!" she was saying, when they heard a car pulling in. "In fact," she went to get up to see who it was, "here she is now!"

With a bright smile on her face, Jessi ran out to greet, yet, another old friend of theirs, while leaving the others behind.

"What on earth was that about?" Renee asked, looking puzzled, as the two got up to follow after her.

Arriving outside, Jessi ran up to a tall blonde haired woman, looking to be in her early thirties, with light blue eyes, wearing a long, tailored, pink summer dress. "Lisa!" she cried out, throwing her arms around her friends' shoulders.

Lisa, like the others, worked at the same Supercenter, until she moved away after her divorce.

Shocked now at who she was seeing, she cried out, as well, "Jessi, is it really you?"

"Yes, and are you in for a surprise," she replied, nodding her head back at their friends.

"I...I can't believe it!" she cried, seeing the others walking up to greet her.

"Well, believe it," Jessi said, turning to the others. "Well, ladies, meet the new girl."

"No. Lisa?" Renee cried out, running up to give her a hug.

"Renee? You're here, too?"

"We're all here!" Ashley spoke up, when coming up to give her a hug, as well, while Jessi's newest guest was looking out his window, watching the whole reunion unfold before him.

After a few more minutes of tear-filled greetings, Jessi interrupted, "I think we all have a lot of catching up to do. What do you day we go back inside to do it over some coffee and cappuccinos?"

"I'll say we do! Along with an explanation," Lisa added, smiling.

Once inside, Renee fixed Lisa up with her favorite 'Irish Crème' cappuccino when they went over to sit down at their table.

"All right, who's going to begin?" Lisa asked, just as they all began laughing.

"I guess that would be me," Jessi smiled.

"Yes, I guess it would be," Ashley stated, smiling over at her friend.

"Well..." she laughed, shaking her head, "it's like this, when I first saw Lisa's application on my desk, after Annie had gotten back from the Employment Agency, I was so surprised. However, I was on my way out to my folks' house for the weekend. So I had Annie fill in for me. Before leaving though, I told her not to tell Lisa who she would be working for. I also had to make sure the two of you weren't going to be here, either."

"Well, you sure kept that a secret," Lisa laughed, shaking her head in amusement.

"No kidding," the others chimed in, while going on to talk about other things, like their mystery guest, who showed up late the previous night.

"Hey, Jess," Renee spoke up, "why don't you tell her about you know who."

"Who is you know who?" Lisa asked curiously.

"Oh, just a certain troubled spirit she offered to help," Renee teased.

"Renee!" Ashley scolded. "Maybe she doesn't want him talked about so freely."

"Jess," Renee turned to her friend to apologize, "hey, I'm sorry. I didn't mean to make it sound so cad."

"No. And normally I would joke too, but…"

"Yeah, sure, maybe later," Lisa returned, while trying to offer her friend a kind smile. "It sounds kind of interesting."

That's an understatement,' Jessi thought to herself, while looking down at her watch. "Oh, my, gosh!" she cried, getting to her feet. "Hey, I hate to cut this short, but it's that time already, and I have a lot to do to get this lady whipped into shape if she is to learn anything, before we get too busy."

"Yeah, you're right," Ashley agreed, looking down at her own watch, before getting up to clear the table. "Lisa," she smiled, "glad to have you with us."

"Same here," she smiled, while turning to leave with Jessi.

"Yeah, same here!" Renee called out lightly.

Walking into her office, Jessi asked, "Are you ready to dive into your first day?"

"Yeah, sure! But first, what is this about helping a troubled spirit?"

Not seeing Alex on the front porch, having his coffee, he turned to look up at the mere mention of a troubled spirit, as Jessi went to close the door.

"What can I say? I promised to help him out, is all," she exclaimed, unaware she hadn't gotten the door closed all the way, when she went over to her desk to take a seat.

"But a ghost…? Where was this at?"

"Out near Crawfordsfield."

At that moment, Lora got up to go out to the front porch, leaving the front desk unattended. Taking advantage of her absence, Alex walked in, and went over to the office door to listen in on their conversation, while having already picked up on the word 'ghost'. Not hearing where, he thought to himself, *'Could they be talking about...'* He stopped and shook his head. *'No... they couldn't be...!'*

"What I don't understand is," Lisa went on, while going over to the couch to take a seat, "why do you feel you have to help him?"

"I really can't explain it. I just know that I have to do this. Not to mention, that Doreen helped to reinforce that feeling," she was saying, when she got up to join Lisa.

"A psychic?"

"Yes."

Just then, they heard a noise out in the foyer.

Turning back to face the partially closed door, Jessi asked, "Did you hear that?"

"Yes!"

Going over to the door, they both went out to see what it was.

"Did you see anyone?" Jessi asked.

"No! What do you think it was?"

"I don't know, but we might as well get back to why you are here," she suggested, while going on up to the front desk to open the registration book.

Joining her, Lisa looked over her shoulder to see the list of guests.

Meanwhile, out on the front porch, Alex's expression had paled. "Craig...?" he whispered to himself. "There's no way!" Stopping, he heard their voices coming from the foyer, as he stood close to the front door, trying to look nonchalant, as a few of the other guests were walking by, carrying on their own conversations.

"Who is this guy in Room Two?" Lisa asked, pointing to Alex's name.

"He's the one we were just talking about."

"And the couple in Room One?"

"A young couple from Michigan."

At that moment, the phone started ringing, and from then on the two dove into their work, having no more time to chat, while Alex left the porch to take a walk and think about what he had just learned.

Chapter Nine

After explaining the routine to Lisa most of the morning, Jessi decided to take a break out on the front porch, where Annie had left a cart of refreshments for everyone.

"What do you think?" she asked after taking in several calls. "Do you think you can handle this on your own?"

"Sure, I can!" she replied cheerfully, while stretching her arms up over her head, before getting up to push her chair in.

"You'll be fine. Ashley and Renee will be here to help you if you run into any problems when I'm gone."

"When are you going?"

"In a few days," she replied, while heading out onto the front porch, where she nearly collided into Alex on his way in.

"Excuse me, ladies," he smiled, while bowing his head. Looking at Lisa, he then turned to Jessi, wondering once again if what he overheard could be true.

"Oh, I'm sorry! Mr. Storm, this is Lisa. She'll be running the front desk while I'm out."

"Out?" he asked, with a slight edge to his voice. "Where?"

Surprised at the way he was asking, she fudged for a moment. "Oh, uh... just on some errands, is all!" she smiled.

"Errands..." he repeated casually. "You wouldn't by any chance be planning on going anywhere in or around Crawfordsfield, would you?"

"Why, Mr. Storm, have you been eavesdropping on our earlier conversation earlier?" she asked, thinking back to the noise they had heard.

"Your conversation? No!"

'I'll just bet,' she said under her breath. "Well, if you will excuse us, we were just on our way out to get something to drink."

"Of course!" he grinned slyly, while feeling he had succeeded in getting her goat up once again. At that, he turned back to head out to his specially equipped, black Chevy Blazer, with its tinted windows.

"Mmmm, interesting," Lisa grinned on their way out to get their drinks.

"What?"

"He gets to you, doesn't he?"

"He's just a stranger, that's all he is," she put in, while watching him move around to get a few things from his vehicle. Yet, still there was something about those boots of his that reminded her of someone, *'But who?'*

By four-thirty that afternoon, Jessi hung up the phone after taking in several more calls for the Fourth of July weekend. "What a day!" she commented, tossing the pen onto the desk, before leaning back in her chair. "How about another break?" she asked Lisa. "It's time for dinner, anyway."

"Sure! What about the others?"

"What about the others?" Renee asked, smiling, while walking across the foyer with

Ashley at her side.

"Are we ready to get something to eat?" Jessi asked, leading the way out to the front porch, when her daughters walked up to join them.

"Sure!" they all agreed tiredly.

Following her out to sit around their table, Annie had just brought out a cart of food.

Looking it over, Lisa commented, "Boy, this looks great!"

"Sure does!" Alex agreed, walking up.

'Great!' Jessi thought to herself, while feeling his powerful presence standing next to her. With a kind smile, she looked up, shielding her eyes with one hand from the afternoon sun, "Would you care to join us, Mr. Storm?"

With a slight grin, he raised an eyebrow at her continual use of his last name, and replied, "No thanks, I just stopped by to let you know that I'll be needing to see you shortly. For now, I'm just waiting on a phone call."

"All right!" she smiled politely, before returning to dish herself up a plate of food, when he turned to walk away.

Having no more than gotten half way to the door, his cell phone began to ring. Hearing it, Jessi couldn't help but wonder if it could be the extra man he was referring to the other night.

"Wow, what was that about?" Ashley asked, interrupting Jessi's thoughts.

"Oh, nothing really!" she returned, while still thinking of the other night. "He was just waiting to hear back from his old partner is all."

"His, what...?" Renee asked, when Jessi came back over to sit down with her plate.

"Oh, boy..." she grumbled, slightly, seeing the look on their faces.

Knowing she had to tell them something, Ashley cut in again, before she could start, "Jessi, what's going on?"

"Okay! I know I should have told you all, but..."

"But what?" she asked. "Did something happen last night, after we left?"

"Well... yes."

"What?" they asked.

"We thought we had a prowler," Lora spoke up.

"A prowler...?" they gasped at the thought of some unknown stranger roaming around out there in the dark.

Only it was Ashley who seemed the most upset over the news. "Why didn't you call me, Jess? You know I would have come back out to stay with you guys!"

"It was late, Ash, and I didn't want to worry you. Besides, we weren't alone!" she had no more said, when Alex returned to their table.

"I'm sorry, Ms. Rae," he spoke up, taking her arm, "but I really need to see you inside. Please!" he insisted.

"Sure!" she replied, feeling the strength of his grip, as she went to get up. Turning to the others, "I'll be right back."

"All right!" they nodded, while watching the two go inside.

"Now, what can I do for you?" she asked, turning to face him, just inside the doorway.

"That was the extra man I was telling you about last night. He's on his way out with some information. Do you have an extra room for him?"

'Huh, perhaps the stables, where I'm strongly considering sending you!' she thought, smiling. *'No, I couldn't do that to the horses,'* she went on to think for a moment longer.

"Ms. Rae... Jessi?" he persisted.

"Let me take a look," she replied, going to the desk to open the reservation book.

Seeing how she had an opening, she turned to pull her master keys off the peg, near the office door.

"Alex..." she was saying, when he shook his head slightly to clear his thoughts. "Detective Storm..., your old partner, when will he be arriving?"

"Soon," he stated, while trying to avoid looking directly into her eyes, when she turned to face him.

"All right, I'll just go up and make sure the room will be ready for him."

"Thanks," he replied, as she headed for the stairs. But then wanting to see this room for himself, he called out stopping her, just as she was about to take the first step. "Would you mind if I tagged along?"

"Sure! Be my guest!"

"Oh, but I thought I already was!" he grinned.

"Keep it up, funny man," she teased, while smiling at his odd humor. "Shall we, now?"

Arriving just outside Room Four, she unlocked the door to let him in. However, not realizing how close she was when turning back to face him, their bodies brushed into each other in the doorway.

"Oh, I'm sorry," she offered, while trying not to stand so close, when then noticing the scent of his after shave, and how she had missed smelling it on someone she loved long ago.

Picking up on the scent of her Vanilla Musk, it sent him back to a place he didn't want to go at that time. "No, I'm sorry," his groaned, clearing his throat.

"Yes, well, will this be all right?" she asked, when feeling her own body begin to betray her, as the scent of his aftershave reached out, taunting her senses. *'This is crazy!'* she thought, fighting off what his nearness was doing to her. *'What am I thinking? He is all wrong for me!'*

Shaking her head slightly to clear her mind, she went on to ask, "Alex, I…I really need to be getting back down to my dinner. So if this is all right with you, can we please go back downstairs so I can rejoin the others?"

"Yes," he nodded, looking into the room. "It's fine." Then looking across the hall at the other two rooms, he asked, "What about those two? Who's in them?"

"Room One has a couple from northern Michigan, and Room Three is vacant. Why do you ask?" she wondered, turning back to see the intense expression written on his face. "Alex, what's really going on here? It isn't just about some prowler, is it?"

"I'm not sure, just yet. And as I have told you, the man who is coming by has some information for me. Until he gets here, I won't know anything on what had happen last night. As for now," he began, when looking back down into her beautiful green eyes, while still feeling the enormous heat radiating from his own body at the sight of hers standing so close to him, "I'm afraid you will have to be patient just like me," he explained, when turning to look back toward the front portion of the hallway.

"I'm afraid, Alex, that I'm not one for being patient. Not when it comes to my Inn."

"I'm sorry," he returned, when noticing what might be another set of stairs leading up to an attic. "Jessi?"

"Alex?" she asked, while turning to see what he was looking at.

"What about those?" he nodded his head toward the front of the Inn. "Is that another set of stairs? If so, does that mean there's an attic in this Inn?"

"Yes, why?"

Not answering her, he asked, "Is there another way down from here?"

"No! Just the front stairs! Alex, why all the questions? Just what exactly is going on?"

"Hopefully nothing," he returned, while running one hand through his graying hair, the other resting on his hip, as his icy blue eyes grew dark with concern.

Seeing this only made her more determined to know what was going on. "Damn it, Alex, tell me! I have a right to know, for the sake of my kids! Not to mention, everyone else here!"

Shaking his head, he started to move away.

"Alex?"

"Jessi, believe me, for your kids' sake, I real hope nothing is going on. But if something was to happen, and I hope to God it doesn't come to that," he stopped gaze into her troubled eyes, "is there some place they can go? At least at night?"

"Yes, they can stay with Jo!" she replied softly, referring to her cousin. "Alex, damn it, I want some answers."

"I can't give you any!"

"You can't, or you won't?" she asked cynically, while turning away to close and lock the door to Room Four. After doing so, she turned to look back up at him one last time.

Seeing her angered expression, he just shook his head.

"Fine!" she fumed even more heatedly than before, when turning sharply on her heels to start for the stairs.

"Jessi!" he called out, stopping her.

Turning back, she snapped at him, "Alex, I won't allow for my friends, family or my guests' lives to be placed in any kind of danger. If things were to start to get out of hand, you will tell me. Do I make myself clear?"

"Very," he growled heatedly, while watching her turn back to descend the stairs.

That night a tall, distinguished looking, black, male, dressed nicely, in a black tailored sports jacket, arrived, wearing a pair of designer sunglasses.

Looking up, Lisa asked, "Good evening, sir. May I help you?"

"Yes, my name is..."

"Hey…!" Alex called out, cutting his old partner off from saying anything more. "I see you finally made it! What do you say to a cup of coffee? The Innkeeper has some made up out on the front porch."

"Yes, sure!" he agreed, leaving his things to walk back out onto the porch with Alex.

Hearing the commotion, Jessi came out of her office to see what was going on. "Was that Alex I just heard?"

"Yes. He took, I assume, his friend he had been waiting on, out on the porch for some coffee."

"Okay," she replied, while going over to look out at the man standing next to Alex.

"What do you want me to do?" Lisa asked, while coming around to join her.

"Go ahead and take his things up to his room. He'll probably be staying until his business here is over."

"Room Four?"

"Yes," she replied, while turning to go back into her office.

Doing what was asked of her, Lisa went around getting the master key, before picking up the suitcase and overnight bag, to head up to his room.

Meanwhile, out on the porch, Alex was pouring himself some coffee, while going on with their talk. "Man that was close. I don't want anyone to know why we are really here, unless it comes down to that. The owner of this Inn and her two daughters live here. So I want to make sure the place is kept secure at all times." He sighed. "Our so called friends out there are getting too close."

"Well, you're right about that. They are close. Closer than you think."

"What?" he nearly thundered, while turning to look back at the open doorway. Lowering his voice, he growled through clenched teeth, "Where?"

Sitting down first, Ted leaned forward to keep from being overheard. "Well, according to our source, they have informed me that Tony and his sidekick left Chicago sometime last night."

"Okay... so where the hell are they now?"

"You're not going to like this, Alex."

"Damn it, Ted..." he glared, seeing the look in his friend's eyes, "where?"

Reaching across the table, Ted took his old partner's arm.

"Ted...?" Alex growled.

He answered in a hushed voice, as he braced himself for a reaction that was sure to follow. "Like I said, Alex, they're close. Very close. In fact." He stopped. "They're... here."

Having no more than gotten the words out, Alex slammed his fist down on the table, before getting up to grab his poor, defenseless coffee cup. "Damn it to hell…!" he thundered, while hurling the cup out across the driveway, busting it up against a tree on the far side. "We're not ready for this!" he continued with doubled up fists.

"Yeah, well, that's not all."

Turning back to see his face, he asked, "What… now…?"

Filling him in on the rest of the news, the two sat talking for a while longer.

Chapter Ten

Nearly two hours had passed, when the two walked back in to find Jessi standing at the front desk, talking to her friends. Interrupting her to introduce his old partner, Alex cleared his throat, "Ladies," he said, turning to Jessi, "this is Ted Jones, my old partner, and friend, I had mentioned earlier."

"Mr. Jones!" Jessi exchanged nods with the man, before turning back to Alex.

"I'll be up getting him settled in if you need me."

"All right!"

Turning to head up the stairs, Alex stopped. "You did put him in Room Four, didn't you?"

"Yes, as you requested earlier." But then, sensing a little tension in his behavior, she asked, "Is everything all right?"

"Sure! Everything's just fine!" he returned, while trying hard not to show any reason for alarm. "If you will excuse us!" Stopping once again, he turned back sheepishly, "Oh, and Jessi?"

"Yes?"

"It seems I owe you a new coffee cup."

"O...kay...!" she replied slowly, wondering what that was about. Then it hit her, when noticing the expression on his face, as he turned to look back at her, before going on up to their rooms, this worried her.

After the two had started back up the stairs, Ashley left to go back over to the Boutique, while Jessi headed for her office. However, just as she was about to go in, two other men walked in, just then.

"May I help you?" Lisa asked.

"We need a room," one of the men spoke up, gruffly.

Upon hearing him, Jessi's hand froze just as she was about to open the door. *"Th...that voice!"* she cried. *"What is it about that voice?"*

At that precise moment, looking up at the top of the stairs, she noticed the angry expression on Alex's face, when he turned back to see the two men standing there. Quickly taking a step back away from the stairs to avoid detection, the look became even more intense.

"Okay, that was odd! What is it about these two men that would catch his attention? Yet, even I sense something vaguely familiar about the man's voice. But what?" she wondered. *"Oh, my God!"* she cried, while hurrying into her office, before closing the door behind her. "Oh, Craigwhat am I going to do?" she asked quietly, while leaning her back against the door.

At that moment, no matter what Doreen had told her, nothing could prepare her for what was about to come.

As she stood by helplessly, Craig's voice called back, startling her at first, *"J e s s i..."*

"W...what?"

"You must get Alex!"

"But why?" she asked, while continuing to keep her voice down, though it didn't seem to matter if she talked silently in thought, or openly, Craig seemed to hear her either way. But then what he said made sense. "Well of course, he's a cop!"

"He's more than that," he started to say, when she opened the door a little to call Lisa in.

"Yes?" she asked, leaving the two newcomers at the desk to go into the office, when Jessi closed the door behind her.

"Lisa, I don't have time to explain," she spoke quietly. "So will you, please, take our new guests out on the front porch for some coffee? Tell them…" She stopped to think. "Tell them I need a few minutes to check on their room first. I'll let you know when you can send them up."

"All right!" she nodded, and turned back to the door to leave, but then stopped to look back. "Are you all right?"

"I will be soon. And Lisa…!"

"Yes…?"

"Please… don't mention our other guests to them."

Seeing her worried expression, she agreed without asking, while turning to go back out to the desk. "Gentlemen," she announced, "shall we go out on the porch for some coffee first? The manager needs some time to check on your room before she is ready for you to go up."

"What the hell is she doing?" Alex growled quietly.

"Your guess is as good as mine!" Ted quietly returned, while watching Jessi come back out of her office, after waiting until the coast was clear.

Turning to Alex and his friend, who were about to turn away, she got their attention, and motioned them into her office, before they could get away. "And I mean now... gentlemen!" she ordered in a serious, yet, hushed tone. "And I will not take *no* for an answer."

Against their better judgment, the two hurried down the steps to her office, as she watched the front door closely, before going in and shutting the door behind her.

"Jessi, this is going to have to wait," Alex said firmly, when stopping just inside the door.

"No. This won't wait," she stated angrily. "I demand to know just what's going on here. And don't you dare blow me off this time with that, 'I can't say' crap," she nearly yelled, as his face reddened with anger.

Glaring down into her smoldering eyes, she met his glare head on, before going on. "All right, Alex, I saw the look on your face when that man spoke up. So, out with it."

"Damn it, Jessi, stay out of it!" he warned in his deep threatening tone, as his glare deepened down into her very soul. "This doesn't concern you!"

"Like hell, it doesn't...!" she shot back, while trying to keep her own voice from being overheard. "Those men out there are staying in my Inn, and from the looks of them, they are dangerous. At least the one named Ton..." She broke off suddenly, not wanting to explain how she knew his name.

"What did you just say?" he growled, taking her arm angrily, as she tried to turn away.

"Alex!" she cried quietly, as he forced her back around to face him.

"Out with it," he glared. "Just how did you know his name?"

"Alex!" Ted stepped forward to try to calm him down.

Putting up a hand to ward off his friend, he continued to stare down at her heatedly. "Tell me, damn it! Just how did you know his name?"

"I...I... can't!" she stammered, while trying to pull free of his intense grip.

"Fine!" He shoved her away. "Now who's being secretive?"

"A…Alex, I…" she tried, when Ted cut in.

"Jessi, what do you know about this man?"

Shaking her head sadly, "I don't think you really want to know what I know about him, or Harr…" She cringed, realizing once again what she had almost let slip out.

"What?" Alex snapped. "You know them both?"

"Yes! No! Well…!"

"Yes? No? Which is it?" he demanded.

"Oh, God, it's not in the way you would understand!"

"You're right," he thundered, "I don't understand, and I probably don't want to, either. Damn it," he groaned, throwing his hands up in the air as he turned, shaking his head with frustration, before going over to the window to look out at the two men on the porch, drinking their coffee. Glaring at them, he continued to groan angrily, only to himself for what they had done.

At that moment, she reached over to buzz Lisa on the house phone, knowing she would be able to hear it out on the porch.

"Yes?" Lisa came back.

"Please, show the two men up to their room."

"Yes, Ma'am."

"Alex," Ted spoke up in a rather concerned voice, after going over to stand next to him, "she should know what this is all about."

At that moment, while standing at her desk, she asked more softly, "Please, Alex, who are they, really? And, Lord…, please tell me why are they here?"

With his back still turned toward her, he began in a shaky, yet angry, voice, as he fought to control the emotions that had been locked up inside for the past two years. "They…" he started, as the words cut through him like a double edge blade, "k…killed… an innocent… man!"

"Oh?" she asked, feeling the pain tightening around her own heart. "When?"

"Two years ago," he explained, looking halfway over his shoulder, not wanting her to see him this way.

Hearing that, she knew she had to ask where, while feeling her hands gripping the side of her desk. "A…Alex…?"

"Jessi, I can't…" he began.

"A…Alex, please!" she stammered, afraid of what the answer would be. "Where did it h…happen?"

Alex couldn't bring himself to answer. Instead, Ted spoke up, seeing his friend shake his head. "Out at his place," he replied, turning to Jessi.

"His p…place!"

"Yes. North of Crawfordsfield."

Feeling her legs suddenly start to shake, she repeated Ted's comment.

"Yes, why?" he asked, seeing her face turn pale, while having to lean against her desk for support. Then with a puzzled expression on his face, he asked, "Jessi?"

Not able to answer him, she looked at Alex, while fighting to keep her head.

Even he noticed the strange sound in her voice, as he, too, turned to see the eerie look on her face.

Then the question she was really afraid to ask came out, "W…what w…was his name?"

"Alex," Ted spoke up thoughtfully.

"P… please, Alex…!" her voice continued to sound a little shaky, when a tear broke free, falling down along her cheek.

Moving in a little closer to study her strange behavior over what was said, he then recalled her earlier conversation with Lisa, *'It can't be that!'* he thought to himself. *'How would she have known who killed him?'* Then answering her question, "His name was…" he began, and then stopped, choking on his emotions, "Craig. Craig Matthews. He was… my nephew."

"C…Craig" she cried out, suddenly feeling faint, "H…he's your uncle…?" she cried, as she began to fall slowly to the floor, "A…Alex Storm… is your… un…cle"

Shocked at what he had just heard, he and Ted both rushed over to catch her.

Seeing that same expression, Ted watched as Alex held her in his arms, while looking down into her paled face.

"Oh, my, God…!" he groaned more to himself. "You were talking about my nephew!"

Meanwhile back at Craig's place, he was sensing what all was going on back at the Inn. *"Yes..."* he whispered out through the night air to his emotionally distraught uncle, while hoping he would be able to somehow reach his conscious mind, *"Alex..., she was talking about me...!"*

Meanwhile, back at the Inn, as Alex continued to cradle her in his arms, he called out to her repeatedly, asking her what she knew about Craig. "Come on, girl, wake up. Tell me what you know about my nephew..." he cried, pulling her up into his muscular arms even more, while trying to revive her.

"I...have... to... help him...!" she began, when coming around. "H...he needs me...!"

"Alex, she's..." Ted started, when Alex stopped him.

"Yes, I see that," he replied hurriedly, while the color began coming back to her.

Getting up to help him, Jessi opened her tear-filled eyes and looked at Alex first.

"What is it, Jessi?" he asked, fighting back his own emotions. "What do you mean; you have to help him? How? Did you know my nephew before he was killed?"

"Mmmm... yes...! No...!" she tried to explain, while getting up slowly with their help to be put into her chair.

"There you go again with this yes, and then no stuff. Which is it?" he asked frustratedly.

"Oh, God, it's not in the way you would understand..." she cried, covering her face to hide her own pain. "So, please," she begged, pushing herself up out of her chair to head for the door, "don't ask me anymore! I can't stay out of it. It's just too late!"

"What do you mean, it's too late?" he asked, stopping her, as she placed a hand on the knob. "Damn it, Jessi, I want to know just how you know my nephew, and I want to know now!"

Not wanting to look back to see his hurt expression, she felt the room about to spin once again. "Oh, Alex..." she began, when placing her head on the door to stop the spinning, "you wouldn't believe me if I told you."

"And just why wouldn't I?" he asked, coming over to stand in behind her, as he sensed that she was about to faint again.

"Because," she swallowed hard before going on, "it's all so hard for me to believe at this time. Besides," she turned then to still see that puzzled look on his face, "I made him a promise!"

With that note hanging in the air, she turned and opened the door, as he tried to stop her. To his dismay, she walked out, closing the door behind her.

"Damn it," he groaned heatedly, while slamming his fist into the closed door, when turning back to look at Ted, "she is going to get herself hurt, if not killed, if she doesn't stay out of this."

"What are you wanting to do now? Those two guys are bound to see you sooner or later."

"We've got to come up with a plan. Until then, we'll have to watch each other's back."

"And your, Ms. Rae?"

"As for her," Alex looked puzzled, "I'll have to dig a little deeper. I have got to find out what she knows, and just why wouldn't I believe her," he wondered, while shaking his head over her last comment.

"Alex, you heard what she said. She called out to Craig!"

"Yes, I heard. That's what has me so puzzled!"

As Alex began to open the door, he looked back at where Jessi had been standing when she said what she did. *Just what is her connection with you, Craig?* he wondered.

Walking out of the office, after making certain the coast was clear, they first stopped off at the front desk, where Jessi was talking about the Fourth of July bookings.

"Lisa, I want to try and keep room one available for larger families. As for four…" she stopped to look back at Alex. "I don't know what to say."

"Are you referring to our new arrivals?" he asked, getting in on the conversation.

"Yes, why?" As if she didn't already know.

"Where are they now?" Ted asked, going over to the front door to look out.

"They're up in their room!" Lisa offered, smiling up into his beautiful dark brown eyes, when he turned slightly back to study her for a moment.

At that time, an idea came to him. Stopping though, he looked over at Ted, and with an ornery grin, he shook his head, turning back to interrupt their conversation.

"Oh, no…" Ted laughed.

"Ladies," Alex smiled, "due to the surrounding circumstances, I want you both to meet your new desk clerk. He will be taking over the night shift in order to watch over things here," he announced, grinning, while going over to pat Ted on the shoulder.

"My what…?" Jessi cried quietly, while unable to believe what she had just heard. "How dare you come in here and think you can just take over like this. And without asking me first, before you go and do something like this…!"

"Jessi…" he began, only to be cut short.

"No, Alex. This is still my Inn," she snapped back quietly, before going on, "and no matter what the circumstances, I demand respect."

"Damn it, why do you have to be such a hard ass? I'm just trying to protect you and your family. I apologize for not discussing this with you first, but because of the circumstances, I would have thought that you wouldn't have minded an extra man on hand to watch over things."

"Well I…I…"

"Gosh darn it, those two men up there know me. But they don't know Ted. And while I am at it, I'll also be needing another place to stay until all this is over."

"And just what exactly did you have in mind?" she asked, placing both hands firmly on her hips, while continuing to glare up at him.

Not able to help but laugh at how she reminded him of a female rookie he had once fallen in love with, he grinned, "Your quarters will do nicely!"

"What…?" she asked, gritting her teeth, while fighting back a sudden urge to strike out at him. "Are you out of your freakin' mind…?"

"No!" he smiled. "What's wrong with that? The girls are going to be gone, and you'll be in and out a lot! So, why not?" he asked, studying her reaction for a moment, before giving her another slight grin.

"Oh… fine! But only for the weekend, and you'll still be expected to pay for being here."

"I wouldn't have it any other way!" he chuckled.

"Oh…" she groaned furiously, and turned away, while her mind went a hundred miles a minute. *"What on earth have I gotten myself into now?"* she asked, while resenting this man for coming in and taking over like he did. And now, all she wanted to do was to get away. *"But why should I, after all, this is my Inn!"*

"Ms. Rae?" Alex spoke up, barely touching a finger to her elbow, when she spun around to face him again. Seeing the angry expression still on her face, using his charm, he began to grin even more to melt her defenses.

It wasn't until then, she noticed a strong resemblance between him and his nephew.

"Give him a chance, Jessi," Craig's thought came through, as she began to look away.

"But..." she started.

"He's a good guy, Jess. He'll even put his own life on the line for the right person."

Seeing the look on her face change to one of distance, he wondered what was going on in her head at that moment.

"Jessi, what's going on?" Lisa asked puzzledly, when interrupting the awkward moment between the two.

"We have a problem," she replied quietly, while turning away from him.

"Is it those two men who just checked in?"

"Yes," Ted replied.

"Lisa, while I'm out for the next few days, Alex and Ted will fill you in on what's going on. For now, please excuse me."

"Wait!" she cried nervously. "I thought you weren't leaving for another day or two."

"I'm sorry, but something has just come up," she explained, having to force herself to look away once again, when she felt his icy blue eyes clouding up.

"Jessi..." Alex begged.

"No," she cried, knowing how she must avoid his hurt feelings that were radiating from those eyes of his. If he only knew, he would never understand how she had gotten herself mixed up in all this in the first place.

"Please, Jessi, no." He took her by the arm, while the look in his eyes pretty much said it all, when she looked back at him. "We have to talk," he spoke softly, but deeply.

"No, Mr. Storm, we don't have to do anything of the kind!" she exclaimed, pulling away.

"Are we back to that again?" he asked, while tightening the grip on her.

"What do you think?" she asked, not liking the way he was holding her.

"Please," he lowered his voice, "we need to talk."

It hurt to see him like this, knowing from the way he reacted in her office, Craig must have meant a lot to him.

Just as she was about to give in, Craig broke into her thoughts, *"Jessi,"* he whispered, *"tell him. Even if he doesn't believe you at first, he will, eventually."*

"Oh, Craig, he must have really loved you to be hurting so much!"

"We were as close as any two brothers could be, with the exception of him being my uncle that is!"

At that moment, she couldn't help but think of her cousin, Jodi Tate, who both had gone through their own pain of losing someone they had loved.

Fighting back the tears that threatened to come, she looked up at him with sympathy in her eyes. "Perhaps you're right, we should talk. Let's go back into my office."

Chapter Eleven

After closing the door behind them, she went over to stand next to her desk to think for a moment. *"Where do I start?"* she asked, sending a thought out to Craig.

Once again, he helped by sending her a soothing thought to help ease into the subject that would surely send his uncle right through the roof, and blurting out the fact that she had just met his nephew's ghost probably wouldn't have set well with him.

"Jessi," Alex spoke up in such a low tone, while coming up behind her to place his strong, yet gentle hands on her shoulders to turn her around to face him, "I have to know. Please tell me what this connection is that you have with my nephew, and how is it that you know both Tony and Harry. And while you're at it, tell me just where you are going, and why?"

Looking up at him, she saw the pain still lingering in his eyes, just like it was when she knelt down next to his nephew in her dream. Wrapping her arms around her waist, she looked down at the carpet between them. "Oh, Alex," she said in a small voice, before looking back up at him. "All right, I'll tell you. However, once you've heard what I have to say, you won't want to believe me."

"But, why…? Why wouldn't I want to believe you?"

Moving around him, she went over to sit down on the sofa, as he followed suit, by going over to an overstuffed chair to join her, before she went on.

"Oh, Craig… I can't do this. It's just too hard…!"

"You'll be fine!" he thought back to reassure her.

"But what if he doesn't…"

"Tell him. Tell him he was right all along about Abigail."

"Jessi?" Alex interrupted her thoughts.

Snapping to attention, she looked up at him. "Yes, of course!" she fudged, thinking how she was going to start. "All right," she began nervously. "You see, Alex, it's like this. I have this gift that I was totally unaware of until just before I had met your nephew's troubled spirit." Stopping, she covered her face. "No! No! No!" she cried, knowing how crazy it must have sounded.

"Say what...?"

"No... I can't do this! It's just too crazy!" she cried, hearing Craig roaring with laughter

"Yes, Jessi, you can! Try it again!" he laughed a little quieter now.

Getting up to move away, she stopped to look back down at him. "Jessi."

"Try it again...!" Craig whispered soothingly.

Biting down nervously on her lower lip, she groaned, "Oh, Alex, how can I just tell you?"

"Just tell me, then, damn it! Spit it out!"

"It's Craig..."

"Yes...!"

Dropping back down on the couch, she blurted it out anyway, "He reached out to me one night, a while back. It was in a dream I was having at first while at my parents' house."

"He what...?" he shot up out of his chair, scaring her as he began pacing the floor in front of her. "No way...! You're out of your mind if you think I'm going to swallow that," he nearly yelled again, while raking a hand through his hair.

"Oh, but, yes, Alex!" she exclaimed, putting up a hand to stop him, before she could lose her nerve. "And then again," she went on, "the day of that bad storm we recently had, when the girls and I had to find a place to stay. As it turned out, it was his place. Only this time, that night the dream had played itself out in my head. Come to find out, it was Craig's way of telling me what had happened to him!"

"So, what you're saying is that you saw his murder in a dream? My nephew's murder?"

"Yes."

"And Craig...? You saw him, too...?"

"After I tripped over a crate in the middle of an upstairs bedroom floor."

"Which bedroom?" he asked, at the mere mention of Craig's old room.

"The front room! Upstairs, on the right!" she explained, wondering why, as he took his seat again, though not for long.

When he shot back up out of his chair again, shaking his head, he walked over to the window to look out at the night sky. "Oh, God, girl, you have got to be out of your mind!" he repeated, while turning back to look down at her troubledly. "This is all just too hard for me to believe. Perhaps when you fell, you bumped your head and just thought you saw him."

"But it's true, Alex. I know what I saw. It was Craig!"

"Okay! What was he wearing?"

"A blue denim shirt that snapped down the front, with long sleeves rolled up just beneath the elbows, like yours!" she pointed. "And..." Smiling, she looking down at his boots.

"What?" he asked, following her eyes.

"His boots! When I first saw yours, I wondered where I had seen a pair just like them!"

"I bought these for him on his thirtieth birthday!"

"Those are his...?"

"Yes...!"

Feeling a sudden panic attack, Jessi covered her mouth.

"Jessi, are you all right?"

"Uh huh...!" she cried, trying hard not to think back to her dream, but thought fondly of the last time she had seen him. "A...Alex, there is something else I must tell you."

Walking over to sit down in front of her, he reached out to take her hand. "What is it, Jessi? What are you trying to tell me?"

Closing her eyes, she called out to Craig once again for his help.

"*T e l l... h i m...*" he whispered coaxingly.

Looking away for a moment to think, she then turned back. "A... Alex..."

"Go ahead."

Looking deep into his eyes, she swallowed hard. "We've talked."

"You what...?" he asked, retracting his hands.

Pushing forward, she explained, "Not only that, I can hear his thoughts, and he, mine."

"No." He shook his head. "This isn't happening!" he groaned, pushing himself back up out of his seat to go back over to the window. Turning back to face her, he asked, "How do you expect me to believe that my own nephew's troubled spirit is roaming around in his old house? And of all things, trying to reach out to you in a dream?"

Turning back to the window, he wanted to cry out that he didn't believe in ghosts or in troubled spirits. Instead, knowing that on several occasions, while he had stayed out at Craig's place, since his nephew's death, he had sensed there was something different about it. *'But what?'* he asked, going over everything that had happened during those visits, in his mind, as he had to wonder if what he felt was indeed his nephew's spirit trying to reach out to him. For instance, the fire in the fireplace had nearly been extinguished. The cologne up in his old room was fresh, not old or stale smelling. *Could it be?* he wondered, shaking his head.

"Alex," Jessi spoke up softly, "perhaps telling you this may help to convince you."

Turning back to face her, he saw a calm expression come over her. "What is it, Jessi? What could you possibly tell me that would convince me, otherwise?"

"Go on," Craig urged. *"Tell him. He'll know then you're telling the truth."*

Taking a deep breath, she looked directly at him. "You were right all along, Alex. Abigail was all wrong for him."

"W...what" he began, when suddenly feeling his knees begin to buckle, as he leaned heavily against the window frame. "What did you just say?"

"Yes, Alex."

"It can't be!" he thought out loud, when turning back to look out the window. "Craigyou have been there all this time? Then it was you!"

"Yes, Alex, it was me," he repeated, keeping the thought from reaching out to his uncle.

At that moment, in a voice only to be heard by himself, Alex went on sadly shaking his head, "At the house, you were messing with the fireplace, and then again with the cologne! Oh, my, Godyou were trying to tell me" he choked back on his emotions, "y...you were there!"

"Oh... yes, Alex," Jessi got up to join him, "he was there," Stopping, she placed a loving hand on his shoulder, as he turned to look back at her, "and he still is!" she smiled.

Telling him everything she knew about his nephew, she conveniently left out where she was going.

"Now you know everything!" she exclaimed, before turning to leave.

"Not everything!" he said, grabbing her wrist.

"Alex!" she protested, while attempting to pull away.

"You haven't told me where you were going!" he groaned. But then seeing her tears, he slid his hand up her arm, causing a small spark between them, when his fingers inadvertently brushed against the side of her breast.

Causing her to tense up unexpectedly, caused her to question what had just happened, *"Why on earth would his touch do this to me?"* she thought, while forgetting for a moment that Craig could hear her, as she attempted to pull away, not liking the confused feelings she was having for this arrogant man, standing in front of her. But then, feeling her struggles were futile, she gave up and told him. "All right!" she turned to look up into his eyes. "I'm going to keep a promise."

"Jessi, please!" he pleaded. "Stay out of it!"

"I can't do that, Alex, it's too late!"

"Why, Jessi?" he asked, glaring down into her eyes, his breath hot against her skin, causing her to close her eyes, as he leaned in closer. "Why is it too late?"

"Because," she cried, feeling the light sensation of his mouth starting to cover hers, and with it came the sensation of her own saliva, as it built just beneath her tongue. The feeling one would get while anticipating a kiss, "b…because, I c…care… about…" she began, only to be cut short, when he claimed her lips, while bringing her body up into his embrace.

"Oh… Alex…" she groaned, pulling away after what seemed like an eternity, when the kiss had finally come to an end, "I care about him!"

Suddenly, hearing her words, he pulled back, looking into her clouded eyes. "And I don't?" he asked, gripping her upper arms.

"Alex… I didn't mean it like…"

Cutting her short once again, he growled, "Damn it, he was my nephew. We were like brothers, Craig and I. This should've never happened to him."

"I know that," she cried back, feeling his fingers biting into her flesh. "God, Alex, they were after his friend, not him!"

"But how..." he stopped, thinking back to what she had told him. "The dreams? Of course, you saw him get killed in your damn dreams!"

"Yes, and after..." she stopped, when he suddenly let go, to go back over to the window.

Turning back to look at her, he nearly yelled, "What? What were you going to say?"

Looking frightened for a moment, she went on, "Harry went over to pick up his wallet, and when he saw the name in it, he told Tony they had the wrong guy."

Running his fingers through his hair, Alex looked beaten. "Now Tony is back to finish the job he screwed up!"

"That must be why his spirit is so troubled! He wasn't supposed to have died!"

After all the dreams she'd had of Craig, she was beginning to discover she was having feelings for him, as well. And now, all she could think of was to go to him.

Turning to leave, she walked over to the door. Before walking out, she turned back to look into Alex's troubled blue eyes, as he turned back to see her go. "Craig needs my help, Alex. I have to help him."

"So, you're going ahead with it? No matter how much danger you're putting yourself into?"

"Yes, Alex."

"Jessi..." he groaned helplessly, when she left the room to go down to her quarters and pack her daughters things for their stay at Jodi's, as well as her own for her stay at Craig's.

As for the rest of the night, to Jessi's relief, Alex didn't bother her anymore, but instead, had Ted go up and get his things to stay in the office.

Chapter Twelve

The next afternoon came before anyone knew it, and with the other two men having gone into town, while Jessi was at the front desk helping out, Renee came walking out of the Boutique with Ashley. "How about some lunch, before you go?" she suggested.

"Sure, just let me see to my girls first," she agreed, while turning to close the office door.

Stopping, she saw it. Having been so preoccupied all that morning, she hadn't noticed Alex's things tucked in between the front wall and the sofa.

"What?" she thought quietly, when at that moment, knowing Craig would hear her, it didn't matter to her, as she went on wondering why Alex's things were in her office. *"He must have slept in here last night, instead of coming downstairs, but why?"*

"Jessi." Craig came across, not so unexpectedly this time.

"Craig?"

"Yes, Jess," he returned. *"Alex is one of those decent kind of guys. He knows when to leave a person alone."*

"But I feel so bad for him!"

Not hearing Ted walk up behind her, he spoke up softly, seeing her expression, "Ms. Rae,

Alex didn't want to bother you. He knew you were upset over everything that's been going on here. So he had me to bring his things in here for the time being. As for your girls, they're in the dining room, now."

"Is Alex..." she started, when turning to look up at his old partner.

"Yes, and he's talking to them, while they're waiting on their ride to pick them up."

Turning back one last time, before closing the door, she thought, *"Oh, Craig... I just hope I know what I'm doing."*

Closing the door, the four of them headed into the dining room. Upon their arrival, her heart suddenly felt even more saddened at seeing him sitting at the end of the large oak table. Yet it was his nephew she was helping, and what she was doing was important to her.

Then their eyes met, she felt a sudden urge to turn and run. Instead, she pushed the feeling aside, while going over to sit down with her girls, hoping that if she could simply ignore him long enough to get away, she would feel a lot better. But that wasn't going to be easy, when she could still feel his eyes on her from time to time, throughout lunch.

"Mom?" Lora spoke up, causing her to jump.

Looking up to answer her, she saw his raised eyebrow. *"Oh, great, did he see that?* she wondered, when turning back to her daughter. "What is it, Lora?"

"Karen is on her way. Can we go out and wait for her?"

Jessi's cousin, not able to come herself, was sending her best friend and business partner to pick the girls up.

"Are you two through eating already?"

"Yes."

Looking over to Alex first, as if he were going to stop her, he nodded his approval.

"All right, but stay on the porch," she instructed, as her girls got up to leave the table.

"We know! Alex told us!"

"Oh...?" She looked back, only to see his encouraging grin, and knowing she was probably feeling as bad as he was, she smiled softly in return.

"I didn't want them to be alarmed in case one of us had to take action if any one of those guys made a move."

"Alex, no...! They wouldn't!" she sounded frantic, while trying to hide her fears from the others, but failed miserably.

"Jess, I wouldn't let anything happen to them, or to you as far as that goes," he offered, while reaching out to touch her hand.

Then it happened again, the feel of his touch suddenly sent waves of sparks through her veins. *"Damn it, why is this keep happening?"* she asked, while pulling her hand away to thank him. "I'm sure the two of you will try your best, but it still doesn't help what I'm feeling, or take away the bad memories of seeing..." She stopped, when seeing how everyone was looking at her.

"Yes, well I have my own memories to deal with," he groaned, speaking more privately to her now.

"I'm sorry, of course you do," she replied sadly, while looking down at her hands.

"Jess..." he began, and then stopped, knowing this wasn't the time or place to go into it.

After lunch, everyone got up to go out on the front porch, while Alex helped Jessi bring up her things. "You're really going, aren't you?" he asked, stopping in the middle of her living room to study her troubled expression.

"Yes, and I'm taking Max with me," she replied, picking up her suitcase.

"Here, let me get that for you," he offered, taking her suitcase from her hand.

"Thanks."

"Sure. And as for you taking your dog, I'm glad, but won't you please tell me where you're going?"

"I think you already know the answer to that," she replied, while heading for the stairs.

"Jessi," he turned, watching as her back stiffened, "I could stop you, you know?"

"Alex...!" She turned back to protest.

"Yes, Jessi. If I choose not to let you stay there, I could stop you, as I am the executor of Craig's place."

"Would you really do that? Would you, knowing the connection we have? Would you really stop me from going out there to help him?"

"No, I couldn't. But still, I wish you weren't going!" he exclaimed, when taking his free hand to pull something out of his pocket.

"What's that?" she asked after he sat the suitcase down to pull a silver key off its ring.

"It's the key to his house," he grinned. "You might as well use it. It's better than having to climb into a window every time you go out there."

"You're right," she smiled, thinking how high the windows were at the side of the house.

"It wouldn't be easy for me to do that. Not when it was Lora who climbed in, in the first place."

"That had to have been interesting!" he laughed, thinking of his nephew's expression, while walking up the stairs with her.

Out on the front porch, Ashley and the others were waiting, when the two walked out. "Jessi," she spoke up with concern written over her face, as she and the others walked over to join them, "when are you coming back?"

"In a few days. If you have any problems I'll have my cell phone with me. The number is in on my desk in case you don't have it on you." Just then, hearing the familiar sound of Karen's car pulling in, Jessi saw the familiar smile on her cousin's, best friends' face.

"Mom! Karen's here!" Cassi shouted happily, when seeing the woman drive up.

"Yes, I see that! Okay, you girls have my number. Call me...!"

"We will!" they said, while giving her a warm hug, before leaving.

"Lora..." Jessi looked to her worriedly.

"Hey! I'll call you. I promise."

"You had better!" she'd nearly cried, while returning her daughter's hug.

Watching, them getting ready to pull out, she felt at a loss until Alex interrupted her.

"Jess?"

"What is it, Alex?" she asked abruptly, while not turning to look up at him, as she went on out to put her cooler into the trunk of her car.

Following her out to her car, he stood back watching, as she placed the oblong container into the trunk. At that moment, seeing her from a whole different side, while unable to keep from admire her shapely hips, not to mention, her long legs, she turned back to face him. Doing so, he caught a bead of perspiration rolling down between the fullness of her breasts, which had then partially appeared when a few top buttons worked their way loose on her white blouse. *Damn...* he groaned, while trying hard to shake the sensual thoughts from his mind, *I can't be thinking about this, not now,* he scolded himself, so as to concentrate on more important things. At that time, clearing his throat, he pleaded with her one last time, "Please, tell me you're not going out to the old farmhouse."

"I can't do that, Alex," she told him, while calling for her dog.

"Jessi…"

"Alex, no."

"All right, if I can't change your mind, at least call me when you get there to let me know you made it all right," he groaned, handing her his cell phone number. "I mean it."

"I will. I promise," she offered, turning as Max excitedly ran up to get into her car. Looking back, she saw Alex's concerned expression, as she got in behind the wheel. "Alex, please be careful."

"I'll do that, and I expect you to do the same."

With that said, she pulled out of the driveway before the other two men could return to see him standing there. Though, with everything that had been taking place, since her return from her parents' place, she needed the time to get away and think things through.

"Oh, Max…" she groaned after forty-five minutes of driving at a comfortable speed, "how did things get so out of hand?" she asked, when soon after, arriving safely at the old farmhouse.

While letting her dog out to run, she went up to the front door, while pulling out the key

Alex had given her. Smiling, she slipped it into the lock and turned it. "Okay…!" she sighed at first, when feeling a little uneasy after taking her first few steps into the house. Once inside, she noticed right away how dark, damp, and cool the place felt to her. "Mmmm…" she smiled nervously, "perhaps if I do some cleaning, it will help pass the time, while listening to some music."

Doing so, she went back out the car to get everything she would need, before setting up her battery-operated tape player to put in one of her favorite tapes.

Walking back in, she gave the door a soft kick with her foot to close it, before making her way into the living room, where she went to sit her things down on the sofa. "Boy," she sighed heavily after straightening back up to have a look around the place.

Unaware that Craig was watching from the entryway, he had a big smile on his face, while she went on to see what all she had to do in order to make this place even halfway livable.

"Okay, Matthews," she mused, after putting on some music, before heading into the kitchen, "where would you keep your broom and rags?"

Walking in quietly behind her, it wasn't long, before she found what she was looking for, when she turned to go back into the living room with a song on her lips. But then as one song ended, another one began, one that she loved even more. At that, she started singing to it, when turning to see that awesome grin on his face, as his eyes lit up at what he had seen in hers. "Oh, Lord, Craig! Don't do that!"

"Sorry, but you looked like you were having fun!"

"Yes, well…" she turned, scolding herself for allowing his unique smile to get to her,

"Great. Gosh darn it, girl, what are you thinking? For God's sakes, he's just a spirit!"

"What…?" he teased, knowing just what she was thinking.

"Oh… it was nothing!" she fibbed, while giving the rag, she was holding, a toss in his general direction. "Hey," she returned, changing the subject, "would you mind if I took out the broken pieces of glass in that window out in the foyer?"

"You don't have to do that!"

"I know, but I would really like to."

Smiling, he told her where she could find some wood to cover it with.

After getting through carefully removing the pieces of glass, she took his advice and went out the back door to the old woodshed, where she found some boards. While there, she remembered the well that stood next to it.

"Thank goodness for that, I could sure use a bath right about now," she smiled, while looking down at her watch. "Oh, no…! Craig" she gasped, while running back into the house, "why didn't you tell me it was so late?"

"I wish I could, but, well…" he grinned, shrugging his shoulders.

Laughing, her face turned red. "Sorry, I forget that spirits don't have any concept of time. It's just that I was supposed to have called your uncle when I got here. If I don't, he'll think that something had happened." Although, the thought of Alex getting mad made her smile, until she recalled the steely look in his eyes, and how they scared her.

"No…"She shook her head, "he would really be pissed, if he had to come out here, just to find out nothing was wrong," she concluded, while looking up at Craig, when they both started laughing.

"Pissed…?" he asked, laughing.

"No…?" She continued to shake her head.

"No," he too shook his head, "that would be an understatement."

"Uh, yes, I kind of thought so," she grinned, wrinkling up her nose, while going over to sit down on the sofa to call him. While there, she noticed a shiny piece of metal on the floor at the edge of the sofa. "What's this?" she asked, picking it up. "Is this what I think it is?"

Going over to join her, he saw metal she was holding. "Yes, it's the medallion he gave me just before I was killed."

"Oh? How did it wind up clear over here?"

"It must have fallen off when…" he broke off, as the memory of what happened stung.

Getting up, he walked over to the fireplace, while she continued to look over the piece of jewelry. Suddenly, thinking back to one of her past dreams, she recalled seeing him falling back onto the floor. *"Oh, my, there was something shiny flying from around his neck as his arms flew out to the sides. It was this!"* she cried sadly. *"The medallion must have fallen off when…"*

"I fell," he finished.

Looking over at him, she could feel the sadness wash over her. "Your hand must have caught it, and broke the chain!"

"Yes."

Turning it over, on the backside was an inscription, which read: *To my nephew, C. M. from A. S.* "Craig Matthews," she read out loud, "and… Alex Storm!"

No sooner had she said the words, Alex's voice sounded out on his end. "What about Craig?" he asked abruptly, while down in her living room, looking out the patio doors at the evening sky.

"Oh, hello, Alex!"

"Jessi…" he growled.

"It's nothing…!" she exclaimed, while sticking the medallion down into her pocket, "I just called to tell you I made it all right."

"But it's after six! What the hell took you so long? And what about Craig?"

"It's nothing, Alex. I just lost track of time, that's all."

"Damn it, Jessi," he yelled so loud, even his nephew could hear him when she held the phone away from her ear to avoid going deaf, "you can't keep doing this! And it certainly isn't a laughing matter."

"No, Alex," she ripped back into him defensively, "it isn't. And in addition, I am not thrilled about those two men staying at my Inn, where no one, it seems, is safe anymore."

"I'm sorry about that, but I have no control over where they choose to stay. Now," he changed the subject, "did you see anyone around when you got there?"

"Just a farmer."

"How do you know it was just a farmer, and not someone else?"

"Because, Alex, he walked out to his tractor, and started it up to plow his field. What do you think?" she fired back sarcastically, when seeing an amused look come over Craig's handsome face, as she shook her head in an amusement, as well.

"Okay," he returned, hearing her sharp wit, "just be careful, and call me first thing in the morning, or if you need anything at all. I don't care what time it is. Do you hear me?"

"Yes… I hear you! Now, about the Inn, how are things there?"

"Pretty quiet. Our friends are up in their room now."

"Good, because I need some time alone," she returned, looking back up at Craig, as he walked over to the front door.

"I sure hope you know what you're doing!" he stated, while breaking into her thoughts, when Craig turned back to see her warm expression on him.

Clearing her throat, she asked, "W… what did you say?"

"Never mind," he shook his head, while turning away from her patio doors to go into the kitchen, where he found her coffee pot and filters, "just tell me, how are you surviving out there without any utilities?"

"Surviving?" she smiled. "Well, there's the well out back, and I have my camp stove to cook on, along with the fireplace to keep me warm!"

"Well, I guess," he commented, letting out a small chuckle at how she did things her way, "just like another stubborn woman I know."

"Oh…? Why, Alex, are you feeling left out?" she teased, as Craig also started laughing.

"No…!" he returned, with a much deeper chuckle, then. "Hey, before I get off here, do you need anything, anything at all?"

"No, I packed plenty for the weekend, and Max seems to be quite content out here."

"That's good, just don't forget to check in with me in the morning," he reminded with a teasing threat to his voice. "If you don't, I'm coming out there, and I won't be all that nice about it either when I get there."

"Yes, sir…!" she teased in return. "Well, I had better be going. I need to get cleaned up, and call my dog back in."

"All right. Oh, before I forget, you have a new groundskeeper. You know, just to watch over things around here for a while, that is."

"Fine! We will talk about that tomorrow, Mr. Storm."

"I figured as much," he teased, just as Ted came down to go over some plans to increase security around the Inn, now that things were getting more intense. "Goodnight for now, Ms. Rae. We will talk more later." he laughed.

"Oh, great, I'm looking forward to it," she returned, loving her sense of humor with that arrogant jerk, as she hung up.

Noticing that Craig had already vanished, leaving her alone to think out loud, she went over to the door to call for her dog. "A groundskeeper?" she laughed. "Alex? Now that's funny! And when I get a hold of him, he will pay for causing me so much grief."

After calling her dog, noticing how it was still somewhat light out, she turned to head back into the living room.

"Good, just in time to go out and wash off most of this dirt and grime, before calling it a night," she continued to think out loud, while going over to get out a large towel, some soap, and shampoo, before heading out back through the kitchen to get washed up.

Reaching the well, it was then she noticed that not too far from the well was a man-made shower, covered in vines. "Well, what do we have here?" she asked, going over to check it out.

Finding that it was still in good use, she decided to try it out, unaware that Craig was now standing at an upstairs window, at the back of the house. While there, he looked out over the yard, when his gaze soon fell upon the shower, where she was now stripping off her things, one by one, before stepping in under the cold, running, water to allow it to work its magic over her tired and aching body.

Meanwhile, feeling the effects of the water running over her, taken by surprise at just how beautiful she really is, he felt an ache go through him, wishing that he could be with her, holding her in his arms, kissing her soft gentle lips, and yes, even making love to her. The sort of things he had been robbed of for nearly two years, now, because of his so-called best friend. *"Oh... Jessi...!"* he thought to himself, as she turned to rinse out the shampoo from her hair. Just as she did, it caught his attention, when seeing the fullness of her breasts, as her nipples hardened under the cold running water, and how it brought back old memories of his own past, when he and his late wife used that very shower, the shower he had built himself.

As she continued to run her hands over her body to rinse off all remaining soap, he went on visualizing the two of them together, kissing one another, and as their kisses deepened, so had their passion.

"Oh... lady..." he groaned, as the scene continued to play out, with him lifting her up into his arms, before pinning her body up against the shower wall. There, Jessi would wrap her legs around his narrow hips, while bringing her arms up around his broad shoulders to cling to his ever passionate desires, as he plunged within her, something she hadn't felt in so long. "If only we could," he thought out loud, as he turned away to lean against the window frame. "Oh, Jessi, if only you knew what seeing you like this is doing to me," he cried out sadly, while looking off to one side of the back room, where he had some old pieces of furniture still waiting to be refinished.

Meanwhile, coming to a sudden stop, she too realized what she was thinking. *"But how can that be? How can these thoughts feel so... real, and yet..."* she breathed, closing her eyes, while running her fingers through her hair, "Oh, Craig..." she cried out in a soft whisper-like voice, not realizing he had heard her.

At that moment, turning to look back at her, as she did the same, she cried, seeing such deep pain and sadness in his eyes.

Chapter Thirteen

"Oh, Craig...!" she cried, as he continued to look down over her beautiful body.

Meanwhile, aching with desire to have her for himself, he cried, as he was about to turn away, *"But how...?"*

Feeling so overwhelmed by what has happened, she called out, telepathically, stopping him, while feeling the same desire he had for her, as she turned away to cry some more, "What's happening here...? And how... how can this be happening...?" she asked, while taking a hand to wipe some water away from her mouth, before reaching for her towel to wrap around her.

With a shiver, upon returning to the house, she was caught off guard, when he came up behind her.

"Jessi..." he spoke up softly.

"Craig..." she cried out, spinning around, "stop that!"

"I...I'm sorry!" he laughed, "I didn't mean to scare you. And as for..." he stopped to look deep into her eyes. "I shouldn't have been watching you like that."

"No, I'm sorry," she, too, laughed with a blush of the face, when turning away. *"Oh, Lord, could it be? Had he..."*

"Picked up your thoughts, while out there?" he asked, as she turned back to look up at him. "Yes." he smiled warmly. "And yes, I think you're very beautiful."

Suddenly, feeling hot all over again, she changed the subject, as she turned once again to avoid his glistening blue eyes, as they penetrated down into her very soul. "Well..." she smiled shyly, "like I said, I should be the one apologizing, not you."

"What on earth for? You didn't do anything wrong!"

"Oh, but I did! It's just that I felt so grubby after all that cleaning," she explained, while gesturing toward the living room.

"Yes, well, the house looks pretty nice, thank you!" he exclaimed, smiling down on her, when she did turn back to look up at him.

"Oh, Lord," she continued to cry, when looking once again at that beautiful smile of his, *"why is it that every time I see it, I feel the heat rise up within me? And yet,"* she stopped, *"at the same time his eyes would light up. Does he know the effect his smile has on me? And if so, can he really hear my every thought?"*

"Oh, yes, Jessi, I can," he replied, but only to himself, when he couldn't help but notice how she was looking a bit nervous, as she wrapped her arms around herself more to secure her towel. "Nervous?" he asked, grinning.

"Nervous? Me?" she laughed. "No… but I really should go on in and get dressed."

"Oh, but don't do it on my account," he teased warmly.

"Yeah, well, just the same," she laughed even more nervously, as she turned to go into the living room to get out her change of clothes. While there, she thought back to the shower, not thinking he would hear her.

Smiling, he had, while sending her out a message from the kitchen doorway that would no doubt bring her to a sudden stop, *"Oh, but, Jessi, the feelings are becoming quite mutual! If only you weren't so darn beautiful…"* he broke off, when she turned to look back into those pain stricken eyes of his, as he blocked the next thought from going out to her. The thought of how he ached at the mere sight of her beauty, as she stood there with the towel loosely wrapped around her now. The thought of what he had been robbed of.

"Craig…" she began, knowing he was thinking about something, but of what, she had no clue, "please, tell me what I can do to help you ease this pain you're going through."

"If you only knew," he smiled back, while shaking his head. "Go and get changed, we'll talk when you get back."

"All right," she replied, heading for the bathroom with her burgundy sweats in hand. While there, she continued to ponder over what had taken place out in the shower, while having been such a long time since she had felt such passion. Meanwhile, leaning against the sink, she cried out quietly to God, asking why it had felt so real. But then stopping, she suddenly felt the heat return to her veins. "Oh, Lord, this is insane…!" she groaned, pushing away from the sink to hurry into her clothes, before returning to the living room to find Craig sitting on the hearth.

"Feeling better?" he asked, when turning back to see her walk in.

"Much!" she returned, while going over to her cooler to get out some fresh fruit, before getting comfortable on the sofa. "This friend of yours. David?"

"Yes."

"How long were the two of you friends?"

"Since birth, you might say. We grew up together, like our parents did, until I went off and got married."

"To Abigail, this wife you mentioned before?"

"Yes," he replied, sadly, while looking down at his hands. "She died two years before I was killed."

"Oh, I'm sorry! What happened?"

"A semi truck lost control on an icy road, hitting her car head-on. The only good thing that came out of it was knowing that she didn't have time to feel anything."

"Oh, Lord, that still had to have been awful!"

"It was."

"What was it like? Your lives, that is, before the accident?"

"Funny you should ask. What had started out like a fairy tale romance went downhill from there."

"Downhill?"

"Yes. She wanted to move back to the city."

"But why, when it's so beautiful out here?"

"Not when I spent a lot of time away!" he exclaimed, resting his elbows on his knees.

"Away?"

Seeing her puzzlement, he grinned, "I'm a contractor, or I was before all of this," he indicated with a wave of his hand around him.

"You must have spent a lot of time away then."

"Yes." His expression changed, as he got up to stoke the fire. "When I returned, all I had found of hers was a note saying she loved me, but couldn't handle the country life anymore."

"Had she already…"

"Filed for a divorce? Yes."

"Was there…"

"Yes," he cut in, "she met him one of those times I was gone. They had planned to be married just as soon as the papers went through," he groaned, raking a hand over his dark brown hair, "Damn it, Jessi," he turned back, swearing, "she never made it back to town that day!"

"Oh, Craig…!"

"How could I have not known just how unhappy she was out here?"

"You couldn't have!" she offered, as he went over to the front window to look out.

"Damn you, Abby, why?" he cried. "Why couldn't you have just told me how unhappy you were? I would have done anything to have made you happy!"

"Craig…" Jessi got up to join him.

"Jess, she hated it out here! She hated it. And I never had a clue!"

"That's a shame. The country can be a beautiful place to live for the right couple."

"For the right couple?" He turned back to look at her. "And you…? What about you?"

Smiling, she looked around the dimly lit room. "I grew up in the country, along with one brother and two sisters! I've always loved it out here."

"What a shame!" he grinned, going back over to the fireplace.

"Why? What do you mean?" she asked, following him.

"Nothing."

"No, really, what did you mean?"

"She hated it, and you…" he turned away grinning, before telling her more about his earlier days with David and his uncle, not to mention, Jarred, his cousin who had also hung around the three of them.

Then, he came to the day of the shooting. Getting up, he noticed how she was beginning to get cold, as the fire had died down some. "I have some old blankets up in my closet if you need one."

"Sure, that would be nice, since I had only brought this lightweight quilt with me."

Getting up to get one, she headed up to his room and found the closet he was referring to, when she went over to open the door.

"Well," she smiled, seeing the selection she had to choose from.

Finding one that had specifically caught her eye, she reached in to get it. "This has to be his favorite," she smiled, while taking that moment to smell it. "Mmmm… it even still has his scent on it!" she smiled, while smelling it again, before pulling out a few more.

After getting out what she thought she would be needing, she closed the door and headed back down to the living room.

Upon her return, holding out the one blanket that smelled the most like him, Craig turned to see it in her arms along with two others. "I see you chose my favorite!" he smiled broadly.

"Oh, I thought so! It smells like a man who had used it a lot."

At that, they both began to laugh.

"Craig," she interrupted, "not meaning to put a damper on the evening, but what happened that day when those men showed up here?"

Turning to stare off into the flames, he didn't answer right at first, but then the words started coming out slowly at first. "My truck… it wasn't running very well that morning. So I caught a ride into town to borrow David's. At the time, he was out in his garage restoring an old car Alex had given him. Tossing me his spare set of keys, I asked if he wanted to go along. But he said he had a lot to do, before he could quit. So we talked awhile longer, before I got into his truck to leave. As I did, I had just turned back to see him run off into his garage. I didn't think anything of it at the time, until I saw the dark blue sedan pulling up behind me."

"The dark blue sedan?" she asked, remembering the one in her dream.

"Yes, and yet there was something about the men in the car that bothered me."

"Like what?"

"I didn't know at first, but then I got to thinking, and after taking the next couple of corners, I knew then I had seen them before, but I couldn't remember where. By then, remembering, it was too late. Looking up in the rearview mirror, I saw that they were still following me."

"But who were they?"

"Someone David had hung around with. When it hit me where, all I could think of was to try and shake them off my tail."

"I guess you weren't too successful," she replied, looking sadly into his eyes.

"No, they caught up with me out here. I had just pulled in and got out of the truck to run into the house, when they pulled up behind me. Before I could say anything, the bullet rang out. When it hit, I couldn't believe what was happening, as I fell to the floor. It must have been then that one of them realized they had the wrong guy."

"Yes, Harry, when he went over and picked up your wallet!"

"Yes, I kind of thought so," he replied quietly, while glancing down at his open hands, before looking back up at her. "They left me here to die, Jessi! To die!" he sounded so hurt then, as he got up to walk around the room, shaking his head in disbelief.

"What can I do now to help?" she asked, as he came over to sit next to her.

"Go to him. Tell him he owes it to the both of us to come out here. Jess, I have to know why they were really after him."

"All right, I'll go first thing in the morning!"

With a slight smile, seeing how sleepy she was getting, he got back up, turning to her, "Good, and seeing how tired you're getting, we'll talk tomorrow. So get some sleep."

"All right," she agreed, snuggling down into bed, after having made it out earlier. "I am tired," she added, taking in the scent of his blanket, as she pulled it up around her shoulders. And with a yawn, she closed her eyes and soon fell asleep.

"Sweet dreams, pretty lady," he whispered softly, while bending down to lightly kiss her forehead. Standing back up to look down on her, while she lay sleeping peacefully, he noted how soft her brown hair swept over her pillow. At that, his thoughts returned to earlier ones. "Somehow, I will find a way to feel you in my arms. If only just once..." he broke off, hearing her call out to him in her sleep. "I'm right here, Jess. I'm not going anywhere. I promise."

And promise, he did. For staying by her side most of the night, if only to imagine taking in the scent of her perfume, Musk, he found himself wanting her even more. Though that wasn't going to be easy, for he needed someone to step into so that he could be with her. *"But who?"* he asked. Then a thought came to him. Not what he had originally wanted, but perhaps it would work just as well.

That night, planting a pleasant thought in her mind, whereas she wouldn't keep having dreams of him getting killed, he created a dream of his own, with a beautiful wooded setting, and a babbling brook running through it. At the end of the path she would find him, standing with one hand reaching out to her. *"J e s s i..."* he whispered softly in her ear, in order to reach into her dream-like state of mind, *"c o m e...t o m e!"*

"Mmmm... Craig?"

"Y e s."

Walking up to him slowly in her dream, she reached out, taking his hand. "I can almost feel you!"

"I know, but it won't last long."

"Why...?"

"It takes too much out of me."

"Oh, Craig... what's happening to me? How..." she began, when looking deeply into his eyes, as he slowly lowered his lips to hers.

Closing her eyes to receive his warm and passionate kiss, it had finally come, and along with it, came the heat that would surely rise up in her veins as his arms pulled her up even tighter into his embrace.

Moaning out loud, he knew he had succeeded in touching her very soul with that kiss, as his own spirit soared with pent-up pleasure, while wanting her, wanting her now. "Oh, Jessi, I want you so... much!" he groaned, running his hand over her tummy, then up to where her sweatshirt ended so he could gain access to her voluptuous breasts. As he did, with every breath she took, he could almost taste them. And then it happened, as he went to capture one of those luscious swells, reality hit, and when it did, it hit very hard. "Damn..." he swore, pulling away. "Oh, God, how I want her!"

"Mmmm... Craig... please don't stop!"

"I'm sorry," he whispered, looking back down at her, and how he ached to have her. Just to touch her, to caress her. But he couldn't. Not this way. And hating not to be able to do what he had in the past, he simply rose up on one elbow and looked lovingly down on her sleeping face.

Waking to feel her hot tears running down into her hair, she asked what happened, when looking up to see his expression change.

"I can't do this to you, Jess. Not this way."

"Not unless..."

"I could really feel you and smell you, and yes.... God help me, taste you," he groaned even more, as she rolled over onto her side, not wanting him to see anymore of her tears.

Taking his hand, he lightly brushed it over her hair, as she felt the tingling sensation of his touch. Rolling back over onto her back, she remained there until she drifted back off to sleep.

"Oh, Lord, why..." he asked, while continuing to lie there, watching her sleep, when even then, she would cry out to him from time to time. "I'm still here. Now sleep, pretty lady. *S l e e p...*"

Chapter Fourteen

The next morning, the sound of her cell phone woke her out of a deep sleep. Reaching over, she picked it up tiredly, "Hel...lo...!"

"Well, it's about time you answered your phone." Alex's voice sounded a little upset on the other end.

"Alex... you woke me out of a beautiful dream, you jerk!" she complained, rolling over in bed, as she continued to moan.

"Sorry about that, but do you have any idea what time it is?"

"Yes... it's time for me to change my n...number..." she yawned, rubbing her tired eyes.

"Very funny. It's after nine!"

"Is that all?" she asked, seeing Craig walking toward her, smiling. Returning his smile, she sat up, tossing back the blankets, while allowing the feel of his deep blue eyes to wash over her, as it caused her to blush.

"Ms. Rae," Alex interrupted, "you were supposed to have called me first thing this morning. When I didn't hear from you, I began to worry."

"Alex..."

"No. Jessi, I told you if I didn't hear from you, I would be coming out, and if I did, you wouldn't like me when I got there."

"Oh...?" Thinking of his reaction, she laughed quietly to herself. *"And just how mad would you be, Captain Storm?"* she thought. But then shaking it off, she ran her fingers through her tangled hair. "Well, Alex, I'm still alive and well. Thank you for your concern. Besides, I have somewhere to go later today."

"Where?" he demanded in a thundering tone.

"Alex, I told you before, I made a promise, and I plan on keeping it."

"Even if it means risking your own life in the process?"

"What do you know about promises, Alex?" she asked, not knowing the pain her question was going to cause the two men in her life.

"I know more than you think I do," he growled with a hint of pain in his voice. Even Craig's expression changed, knowing what his death had caused his uncle.

"Alex..."

"No, you listen to me. I made a promise of my own to my nephew, damn it! I swore I'd catch those men who did this to him."

"I did too," she returned softly, as a tear found its way down her cheek.

"Jessi, these men are dangerous, Belaro especially. He doesn't care who gets in the way, as long as he gets his job done. So tell me, what are you going to be doing today, and where?"

Hesitating, she looked up at Craig.

"I can't protect you out there, Jess, but he can, if you'll let him. So please, tell him where you're going, and be safe."

"All right."

"All right, what?" Alex's deep baritone voice echoed over the phone, while causing her to quiver.

"I'm going to see David, is that all right with you?"

"McMasters?"

"Yes, Alex, David McMasters."

"Damn it, Jessi, I'm warning you! Stay out of this now, before you do get hurt, or worse yet, killed!" he yelled so loud, that even across the room, Craig looked a little upset at first.

"No, Alex," she yelled back, while getting up to gather her clothes to go and take a shower. "I told you, it's too late! I can't stay out of this, and I won't. So deal with it, because I am!"

"Damn it, Jessi! You're out of your league with these two. Just tell me what you're going to do, and let me handle it."

"Alex, no, it's not that easy!" she tried to explain, and then abruptly changed the subject. "Listen, I've got to go."

"All right, fine, if you feel you must do this, then you're not going alone."

"Yes, I am!"

"Like hell you are," he yelled, hanging up.

"Lord, why does he have to be such a hardhead?"

"Because he is just trying to protect you, Jess," Craig put in, stopping her at the back door, before she could head out to get her shower.

Turning back to see his concern, she smiled, "What could possibly happen? If he's keeping an eye on them, I should be perfectly safe going over to talk to David!"

"Yes, but if you don't tell him what you're planning to do, he won't know if you're in danger or not! You can't trust those men, Jess. Like Alex said, they're dangerous."

"All right, I'll talk to him. But keep in mind I want to help you. You need me, or this hell you are going through will never end."

"I know, and yes, I do need you. But that was before I knew those men were back. Now things have changed, and I don't want you getting hurt. So promise me, you will start including my uncle in on what you're going to do."

"All right! I will!" she said, turning to walk out, but then paused a moment. "Craig?"

"Yes?" He forced a smile on his face.

"Seeing the pain in your eyes…"

"Jess…"

"No!" She stopped him. "There's something else I must tell you about this gift of mine."

"What is it?" he asked, already knowing what she had discovered.

"For some reason…" she began, not knowing how to say it.

"You can feel it too, can't you, as well as what my uncle is feeling?"

"Yes!" She looked surprised, but knew she shouldn't, when it came to him. "It hurts, Craig. It really hurts."

"Jess…" He looked apologetically.

"No, I can't stop. I have to do this. I have to!" she exclaimed, when turning on her heels to hurry out to the shower, before Alex could get there, and stop her from going to David's.

After getting a quick shower, she rushed back in to dress. Before heading out the front door, though, to see David, Craig gave her one last warning to be careful.

"I will," she replied, looking at her watch, "but I had better be hurrying and not all too soon, either," she smiled, when seeing how it had been at least forty minutes since their phone call.

Saying her good byes, grinning, he understood why she wanted to get out of there so fast.

His uncle had a reputation of being a hardhead about a lot of things.

Meanwhile, down the road, having passed a mailbox not far from Craig's house, Jessi read the name printed in bold letters on the side, **"The McMasters' Place"**. Hmmm… I wonder if that could be any relation."

Soon the answer came to her.

"Yes, it's David's parents' house," Craig responded.

"Oh…?" she smiled, unaware that David was there at that time, helping his father out in the field. But then something else came to mind; it was also the house she and her girls passed up on the night of the storm! Turning her car around, she headed back to the house.

As she pulled into the driveway, up near the house, she spotted a woman with graying hair sitting under a tree, looking through a photo album.

Getting out of her car, the woman got up to greet her.

"Mrs. McMasters?" Jessi asked politely.

"Please, call me Rose."

"Yes, well, my name is Jessi Rae. My girls and I had to take shelter in Craig Matthews' old place last week, when we had that bad storm!"

Extending her hand, Rose took it, smiling. "Yes, I know who you are! Alex called a while ago to tell me you would be spending some time there."

"Oh, did he now?" she smiled warmly. *"Why, Alex Storm, what else are you going to do to make sure I don't get in trouble?"*

"Yes. He mentioned something about needing some time away from your Inn!"

"To put it mildly, yes, I've been needing to get away for awhile, due to some unexpected tension."

"Honey, there are a lot of places you could have picked. Why on earth would you want to stay in that old place, when it needs an awful lot of work done on it?"

"I know it does. It just so happens I love old farmhouses. They have so much character about them, don't you think?" she asked, thinking fondly of the owner.

"Well, you're right about that! Craig, the former owner, did have character. But doesn't it bother you that he was killed there?"

"I'm aware of that!" She thought sadly. "It's just that, somehow, I feel a connection when I'm there."

"You've seen him, haven't you?"

"Craig?"

"Yes!"

"Well…" She stopped to think whether or not she should tell her.

"You can tell me! I'll believe you!"

Jessi smiled. "Yes, I have, but he looks so sad, too, at times," she returned, when looking back off toward his place. "And when he does, it really breaks my heart to look into those eyes of his, when he is hurting."

"Oh, my…" she cried, interrupting Jessi's thoughts. "Ms. Rae, I have made some freshly brewed tea. Why don't you come and join me so we can talk some more."

"I'd love too, Mrs. McMasters."

"Rose…, please…, and I'm David's mom," she explained, while leading the way over to a few lawn chairs, under a large shade tree, in their front yard.

"Well, in that case, Alex has already told you who I am."

"Yes, he did, but I would like to hear more about you and this Inn of yours."

"There's so much to say!" she replied, taking a seat. "You would really love it there."

"Yes, I imagine so. But here, let me show you something," she suggested, changing the subject back to Craig's old place, while picking up one of the two photo albums she had sitting on the table next to her. Turning it to the page where Craig, Alex and David were standing near a tractor, she asked, "Can you tell me which one you think is Craig, and which is David?"

Looking it over, Jessi knew right away. "Though I have never seen David, I can tell you now that this is Craig," she pointed, while going on to look at the other two men, when a smile came to her lips.

"What?"

"That one!" she announced, laughing at their funny expressions. "That's Alex!" Then turning her attention to the guy standing next to him, she nearly cried, dropping the book. "Oh, my, gosh, is that…" she asked, staring at the two guys next to Alex.

"What is it, Jessi? What do you see?"

Covering her mouth, she finally answered, "They do look a lot alike. It is so uncanny, but…"

"But what?"

"It's that smile of his that tells them apart!"

"What about it?"

"It's crooked!" she smiled, while tracing Craig's lips, lightly, with her fingertip.

"Oh, my, this is wonderful!" Rose cried, while taking the book from Jessi to close. "My husband said that I just wanted to see him. But I knew somehow he was there."

"And did you, ever see him, that is?"

"No, not like you have. But I know he's there!"

"And David, did you tell him?"

"No. I have tried to get him to go over with me, but he won't. And ever since Craig's death, he avoids that place."

"Where is he now?" she asked, turning back to see a red pickup truck she hadn't noticed before, until now, sitting in the driveway, next to the garage. Looking at it more, it looked an awful lot like the one in her dreams. Then suddenly, she felt a sickening feeling in the pit of her stomach. "Oh…, my Lord…!"

"What is it, dear?" Rose asked, looking over at her son's truck.

"I…is that his truck?" she asked, getting up to go over and have a closer look at it.

"Yes. Yes it is. Why?"

Coming around to the driver's side door, Jessi stood back a little, and closed her eyes. At that time the dream suddenly came flooding back, as she remembered seeing Craig drive up to his place in that very truck. Shortly thereafter, it all happened again, with the sound of the gun going off, shattering Jessi's thoughts, when Rose reached out quickly to take her arm, as she began to waver in her tracks.

"Jessi…?" Rose cried out, frightened over what was happening in front of her. "Jessi?" she cried out again, snapping Jessi out of her trance.

"Rose...?"

"Yes, dear, I'm right here," she returned, while placing an arm around Jessi's shoulders.

"Are you all right? What just happened to you? You looked as though you had seen a ghost!"

"This truck...!"

"Yes, dear, it's David's! And at this moment, he's out in the field with his father. But he will be coming in later for dinner! Are you sure you're all right?"

"Yes. Yes, of course," she was saying, while attempting to shake the sudden feeling of queasiness from her. *"Lord, Doreen,"* she thought, *"you never told me that I would be having visions, or how sick I would get when they would come!"*

Then, without warning, Craig called out, *"Jessi... are you all right?"* he asked, sounding concerned about her sudden reaction to seeing the truck he had driven that day.

"All right?" she cried. *"Craig, why didn't you warn me that David still had this truck...?"*

"I didn't know it myself, until now."

"I'm sorry? I didn't know?"

"Yeah, well, never mind me. Are you all right?"

"Yes, I am. Just give me a moment to catch up with my stomach!"

Feeling Craig's laughter, she stood more erect, while taking in some air.

"Jessi," Rose spoke up, seeing the color coming back to her pretty face, "why don't you join us for dinner? Besides, you don't look as though you feel that well. You shouldn't be alone."

"No, I really shouldn't intrude."

"Nonsense, we'll have plenty. Which brings me to my next question."

"Oh...!"

"Just how have you been getting by without any power over there?"

"I came across some oil lamps earlier, and I have my camp stove, along with the fireplace and the well out back!" she blushed.

"Well, Alex was right, you are a survivor," she replied, when they both started laughing.

"In that case, if the offer still stands, I would like to change my mind and take you up on your invitation. But if I'm going to be staying for dinner, I'll need to run back to the house for a minute. It seems that I have left my cell phone behind."

"Would you like some company?"

"Sure, that would be great!" she smiled, while turning to head for her car.

"You know, it isn't all that far. What do say we walk?"

"You're right, it's too nice out to be crammed into a car. Let's go then."

On their way, neither one noticed that Alex had driven by, while they were looking at David's truck. Meanwhile, down the road a way, he backed in, off the road, next to Allen McMasters' truck, so not to be detected if anyone drove by.

"Okay now, Ms. Independent," he smiled, while getting out his binoculars to watch the two, knowing why they were heading over to his nephew's place, "I'll give you just enough time to get there, before I start calling your cell phone, that you had so kindly left behind."

Chapter Fifteen

On their way, Rose told Jessi all about how happy Craig was, only to have it all taken away. "He was so excited about getting his first house. And in his line of work, it didn't seem to matter that it needed a lot of work done on it. He was actually looking forward to it."

Not saying anything, looking over at her, Rose became concerned, when seeing some tears building up in her eyes.

"What is it dear? Did I say something to upset you?"

"No, of course not. I was just remembering the pain in his eyes when he cried out just before he died." Suddenly aware of what she had just said, it was too late for her to take it back, when Rose took her by the arm to stop her.

"Say what...? How did you know that?" she cried. "No one could have known how he felt at that time."

"Oh, Lord!" she cried, looking away.

And then it came, *"Jessi..."* Craig whispered, *"it's all right. Tell her."*

"But..."

"Tell her."

Seeing that far away look come over her, Rose turned to look up at Craig's place, now that they were getting closer. As she did, she wondered if somehow he were reaching out to her.

Before she could ask, Jessi spoke up, interrupting her thoughts, "I suppose," she hesitated a moment, "I should tell you what I meant by that."

"No," She turned back to stop her. "I think I already know. You were just talking to him, weren't you?"

The look on Jessi's face gave her away.

"Oh, dear, Lord. You were, weren't you?"

"Rose, it's not something I can just explain away, without taking a chance that it may sound totally ludicrous. Alex has even questioned me on it."

"Alex knows…?"

"Yes, and I'm not all that sure he really believes me."

"Then tell me…!"

"Rose, it isn't that easy!"

"Jessi, Craig was like a part of our family. He practically grew up with David."

"Yes, I know."

"Then tell me. I won't doubt what you have to say, no matter how crazy it may sound."

"All right!"

Walking up through Craig's front yard, she told her about the dreams she had had. By time she was finished, having reached the front door, she stopped and turned around in time to see the expression on Rose's face.

"Oh, Lord, girl… how awful that must have been for you."

"It was!"

"In that case, he needs you, Jessi," Rose returned, while placing a hand gently on her shoulder. "You have the gift!"

"Yes, so I've been told. I just never expected to…"

"To what?" Rose asked. But then she saw it written on her face. "Oh… Jessi… are you falling in love with him?"

Slowly turning back to look at her, while unlocking the front door, she bit her lip, "I know how this must sound. How can I fall in love with his spirit, when someday he'll be gone?"

"Oh, Honey, it's only natural you would care for him! He was such a good person when he was with us!"

"Oh, Rose, it's much more than that," she explained, while going on in to get her phone, "I can also feel his pain. And, God, does it hurt to see him so sad."

"Then how can you do this?"

"It's something deep down inside me that draws me to him. I can't explain it. I just know that I have to do this."

"Jessi, changing the subject, is there someone in your life right now?"

"You mean a boyfriend?"

"Well, yes!"

"If there was, none of this would be going on."

"Well, then…" she hesitated, when Jessi's phone interrupted her.

Going over, Jessi picked it up. "Hello!" she answered, having a feeling it would be Alex.

"Jessi, where the hell have you been?" he asked, acting as if he were really upset. "I have been calling you for the past hour! Which brings me to ask, why didn't you go to David's like you said you were going to?"

"Alex, would you please… stop! I've been visiting over at his parents' house, with his mother. And the reason why you didn't reach me was because I left my phone behind."

"I know."

"You what?"

"I found it when I stopped by, looking for you."

"You were here? Why didn't I see you pass by Rose's place then?"

"You probably would have, but the two of you were looking so intently at… David's… truck…" he slowed at the last couple of words, recalling the description of what had taken place in her dream, knowing that it was the same truck his nephew had used that day, nearly two years ago. "Damn, Jessi, I'm sorry!"

Not hearing anything back from her, he knew, seeing the truck must have had some kind of impact on her.

"Jessi," he asked softly, "are you all right?"

"Alex…"

"Jess," he cut her off, by changing the subject, "the reason why I'm calling is to let you know that those men are out roaming around right now. Had of you went to David's they might have wondered if there was any connection between the two of you, and I was afraid you could have gotten hurt had they seen you there. So, please be a little more careful when you're out in the open like that."

"You've made a good point there! But really, I'm a big girl!"

"Yes, so I've noticed!" he chuckled.

Just then, Rose cut in, "Jessi, let me talk to him."

"Sure!" she replied, handing her the phone, before walking off into the kitchen.

Upon getting there, she heard Craig's soft, gentle, voice reaching out to her. Turning to see him, she saw the look of concern etched on his face. "I know what you're thinking, and yes, he's made a good point in letting me know that those two men are out running around. But I'm not used to having someone move in and take control of things."

"Yes, Jess, but he means well."

"I know he does," she returned, while going over to stand next to him at the sink. "But can't he be a little less controlling?"

He laughed. "Alex...?"

"No...?"

"N...o," he chuckled, shaking his head. "We are talking about my uncle, here. A man who is always use to being in control. So just try to be patient with him. Together, we want you to be safe, both here and out there. And since I can't be out there to protect you, he can, if you will let him. Besides, I don't want to see you end up like me. It isn't fun. So mind my uncle."

"Do I have to...?" She played as if she were pouting.

"Yes," he ordered lightly, with a warm smile on his face, just before vanishing, when they heard Rose coming their way.

"Jessi, are you all right?" she asked, walking in.

"Yes, I'm fine," she smiled, while still leaning against the counter.

"Good. I called my husband to let him know where I am, and that we'll be home after we go shopping."

"Shopping...?"

"Yes. Which reminds me, do you have a bathing suit, here, with you?"

"No, I didn't think to bring one. Why?"

"To go swimming, of course!" she exclaimed, with a coy smile on her face, while taking Jessi's hand to leave. "We'll have to go back and get my car of course so we can run into town. Oh, and by the way," She stopped just outside the door to add, while Jessi was locking up, "Alex says that he will be joining us later."

"Oh, yippy!" she thought, walking out off the porch, when then, she felt Craig looking down at her from his bedroom window. Looking up to see him smiling at her, while shaking his head, she smiled back, *"All right, all right, I'll behave...!"*

Later, in town, Rose and Jessi went to two different department stores, before finding her a decent bathing suit to wear, yet it was a little daring.

"I like this one," Rose announced with an ornery smile, while holding up a black shiny one piece.

"Why that one? It's, it's, it's so revealing!"

"Well, let's just see how it looks on you, before you decide."

"All right, but if I were to get it, I will also be needing something to go with it."

"Sure, I saw just the thing back over a couple of aisles. Why don't you go on in and change, while I go and get it for you?"

"Sure!" she replied, while watching Rose go off to get what she needed. Once she had gone, turning, Jessi went into the fitting room to change into the suit Rose had picked out for her. "This is crazy," she thought out loud, while slipping out of her clothes. "But, at least, it will be fun to go swimming."

It wasn't long before Rose returned with a black, fishnet, tunic, when she found Jessi standing in front of the fitting rooms' mirror.

Seeing the sleek, black suit, with its plunging neckline and its high cut thighs, Rose commented, going up to her, "Why, Jessi, that looks really sharp on you!"

"It sure does!" came a deep male voice out of nowhere.

Hearing it, Jessi spun around to find Alex standing there, his icy blue eyes fixed on her. As they did, they soon began to move slowly over her finely shaped body, back up to where her full, ample breasts were barely covered by the shiny, black material, while leaving a lot to be seen from the front mid-section, as well as the sides. "Alex…" she cried out in surprise, "what are you doing here?"

"Well, I had to pick up a new pair of trunks to go swimming in, too!" he exclaimed, while looking back up into her warm, loving eyes, before finding his gaze return to the fullness of her breasts, causing her nipples to respond as the warmth of his gaze penetrated the material.

Feeling herself heating up at the sight of his rugged good looks, she blushed, while taking the black fishnet top from Rose to cover herself with. "Alex, please…" she cried, wrapping her arms tightly around herself.

"Well," he finally spoke up, "she's right, you do look great!" he returned, swallowing hard at the mere sight of her, as well as the material that had barely covered her, leaving a gap at the sides where he could just as well reach in and start caressing those luscious swells if he wanted to. *Damn…* he growled inwardly, while trying to shake off the last thought, but finding it growingly difficult to look away.

"Why, Alex…" Rose spoke up, smiling, "are you feeling all right?"

"I feel f… fine. Why?" he asked, while still attempting to shake off the erotic thoughts that continued to plague him.

"Your face, it's turning awfully red, dear," she laughed, as he was finally able to turn away.

"Well, uh, if you'll excuse me, I had better be getting dressed," Jessi commented, while going back into the changing room.

After seeing Jessi going into one of the booths to change, Rose turned back to Alex, "Alex, dear?"

"Yes?" he returned, clearing his throat.

"She's quite beautiful, isn't she?"

"Rose…!"

"Now, I know she isn't anything like your rookie, but she is available."

Oh, but that's where you're wrong! She is a lot like my rookie! He smiled at the thought of Beth Lamb, his little rookie, back at the academy, a few years ago, just before Craig's death. Having been told that they weren't permitted to have a relationship between the cadets and their superior officers, he still wondered to that day how the department knew about them.

Meanwhile, coming back out after trying on a few other suits she had picked out, Jessi noticed that Alex had already gone, when Rose walked up. "Have you decided on which suit you will take?"

"Yes, it looks as though you were right!"

"Great! Now let's get these paid for and get back to the house."

On their way out to the car, Rose turned back to Jessi, who was checking her watch, "Jessi, how do you feel about Alex?" she asked, while going around to open her car door, after taking her keys out to unlock it.

"In what way?"

"I think you know!"

"Rose, Alex is a very handsome man, but the feelings are simply not the same!"

"How do you know, when you haven't gotten to know him that well. Why don't you just give it some time and see where it could go?"

Not giving her a response, Jessi just thought of more pleasant things on the way back to Rose's place.

Upon arriving, Jessi spotted Alex's Blazer right away, parked next to David's truck. As for Rose's husband, Allen McMasters, he had already gotten the grill going for their cookout, when Rose announced their arrival, while taking Jessi through the house, and out onto the patio. "We're here!" she called out cheerfully.

Following Rose out, Jessi saw a large, in-ground, pool, surrounded by a number of chairs, and a grill, where the men were all standing. Spotting Alex right away, wearing a pair of snug-fitting blue jeans and a white tank top, she couldn't help but notice how beautifully tanned and muscular his torso was. As for David, even though he looked a lot like Craig, he was missing his muscle tone and sexy smile, while wearing a pair of cutoffs and a light blue tank top. That's when she turned to look off toward Craig's place, and smiled. *"He does look so much like you standing there!"*

"Yes..." he returned, when David's father broke into their thoughts, just then.

"Ladies," he called out, in his swim trunks, while flipping burgers and steaks on the grill, "did you find what you were looking for?"

"We sure did!" Rose smiled, while going on to introduce Jessi to her husband and son. After which, she turned to Alex, "Dear, why don't you show Jessi where she can change. I'll be in shortly."

"Sure!" Taking her hand, he smiled, "Shall we?"

"All right!" she agreed, while following him back into the house.

Once inside, she sent out another thought to Craig, *"Oh, Lord, Craig, she isn't doing what I think she is, is she?"*

"Jess," Craig smiled warmly, *"Rose has always been one for matchmaking. Just ride it out and have some fun with it."*

"But I'm not..." she began, but then stopped, once they reached David's old room, where she turned to Alex.

Seeing her expression, he knew before she could say a word. "Jess, before you say anything, I know what you're thinking! And that doesn't surprise me," he laughed. "What did you tell her?"

"Oh, Alex," she broke off, turning away, "why does it have to come to this?"

"Jess," he offered, reaching out to her to hold her.

"No! It's not that I don't find you to be quite handsome. I do, but…" She was saying, when turning back in his arms to see his expression change. "Oh, Lord, Alex, I can't. Besides, we fight a lot."

"I know," he said sadly, looking into her eyes. "And you're right, we do fight a lot. It's just that I'm trying to protect you, Jess. That, and I know it's Craig you care about right now. But what's going to happen when he's finally able to rest? What are you going to do then?" he asked, as David and his mother walked into the room at that moment.

"Alex," David spoke up, curiously, "what's going on?"

"Oh, it's just a lover's quarrel," Rose interjected, when seeing the pain in both their eyes, while going over to take Jessi by the hand. "Come on, girl, let's get you ready."

Chapter Sixteen

Still puzzled over what he had heard, David followed Alex back out, longing to know what was really going on between them. "Alex, what about Craig?" he asked more persistently.

"I'm sorry, David, but this isn't the time or the place to tell you."

"To tell me what?" he asked, at just the mention of his best friend, whose death he had been blaming himself for all this time.

"We've had to reopen Craig's case. It seems that your head has a price tag on it again."

"But how...? It's been nearly two years!"

"You ought to know the answer to that! Besides, as you know, I've never stopped looking for the man who had killed my nephew, and do you remember Ted Jones, my old partner?"

"Yes!"

"Well, it seems that he has picked up some rather interesting information concerning this man, or men I should say."

"Alex, no...!" he cried, looking back at his dad.

"Yes, David. You know damn well I'm going to stop them! But it would sure help to know why they were after you in the first place. So out with it. Tell me what went down back then, and tell me now," he growled quietly, so not to be heard by David's father.

"Alex, I can't. Not now."

"When, David? Just when the hell are you going to tell me?"

"I will. Just not now!"

"We don't have a whole lot of time here. Time is running out as it is. I have to know what went down back then, and I have to know soon."

"And, this, Jessi? What does she have to do with it?"

"What do you know about her?"

"I saw her car over there this morning, while I was coming out to give dad a hand."

"I can't explain that just yet. However, I'm trying to keep her from ending up like him. But I have to say, neither one of you is helping matters."

"Oh, what do you mean?"

"It seems that she, too, made him a promise, as well as I did, but as for anything else, I'd rather not..." he stopped abruptly, when Rose and Jessi walked out onto the patio.

At that time, both turned to see her in her bathing suit, while covered by the fishnet tunic.

"Boy, Alex," David gloated, while staring holes right through the woman standing next to his mother, "you must really hate your job."

"Yeah, well it's a hard job," he laughed, grinning at the thought, "but somebody has to do it. And it might as well be me."

"Hey, how about a swim?" Rose asked everyone.

"Sure," Allen returned. "Food won't be done for another half hour."

"Well, girl, what do you think?" Rose laughed, looking at Alex and David, who couldn't take their eyes off her.

"Hummm..." she turned to whisper something in Rose's ear.

"Oh," Rose returned, smiling, "what did you have in mind?"

At the look on their faces, David was getting a little curious. "Mom, what are you two planning?"

"Oh... nothing!" she fibbed, while turning back to Jessi, who at that moment held a sweet smile on her face. "Sounds like fun," she agreed, looking back. "But what about their clothes?"

"Oh, well, what can I say, they had time to change," she continued to smile, while slowly and seductively removing her robe, while watching David's eyes nearly bug out of their sockets at the mere sight of her suit. Not to mention, seeing how he had to swallow hard on the sudden arousal her half-naked breasts were causing him, when he grabbed onto Alex's arm.

"I'll trade you jobs anytime," he gulped, watching as she began to walk casually over to the pool with his mother.

"I just bet you would!" he laughed, looking right into her eyes, at the same time catching a glimpse of her soft voluptuous breasts, as the sunlight gently kissed upon them, especially when she lightly ran her fingers over the outer edges of the skimpy material that barely covered them. *Damn you, Jessi,* he groaned inwardly, while following her fingers around the outer swells of each breast.

Seeing what she was doing to him, she leaned in to whisper something else to Rose, "I'll take Alex, if you'll take David!" she suggested, while wanting to pay him back for the little trick he played on her earlier with her cell phone.

"All right!"

Strolling over to check out the water, she pretended like she was just minding her own business, when he walked up to join her.

"Don't you look nice," he commented, while looking warmly into her eyes, as she turned to look up at him.

"Really, Alex?" she asked sweetly, while still smiling up at him, when she went to carefully maneuvered herself around to place his back toward the pool.

"Yes," he returned, as she then slowly raised her arms up to pull her hair back into a ponytail holder.

Watching, his eyes drift down to where her breasts nearly brushed up against him, she moaned playfully, "Mmmm... Rose," she called out, while turning slightly to be sure to brush into him, "I think he looks a little hot, don't you?" she asked innocently, as she slowly brought her hands down to make her next move.

Unaware of Jessi's hands coming down to his narrow waist, he smiled down at her, while loving the feel of her body so close to his.

"He sure docs!" she grinned, just as Jessi gave Alex a hard shove back into the pool.

"What? Jessi!" he roared out, falling backwards into the cold water. As his body hit, the sound it made brought on a roar from the sideline.

Seeing this, even David roared with laughter at Alex's expense.

"What are you laughing at?" Rose asked, as she tried her best to throw her son in.

"Momdon't you dare!" he cried out, struggling to keep from losing his balance.

Seeing that Rose needed her help, Jessi went right over to give her a hand. However, by sheer accident, his hand landed between her breasts, before she could succeed in pushing him in.

Realizing what he had done, he turned a deep shade of red.

"David!" she cried out, pretending to be offended.

"B…but it was an accident!"

"Yeah, right…!" she laughed, giving him a hard shove into the pool.

Turning then to laugh with the others, she and Rose congratulate each other while they watched the two guys come climbing out of the pool together.

"Hey, you guys, you kind of look wet!" Allen called out, laughing.

Seeing the look on Alex's face, when he climbed out first, she knew she was in deep trouble, especially as he slowly unfastened his jeans to pull them off, along with his wet tank top.

Noticing her reaction in doing so, Jessi's eyes fell upon the magnificent swell beneath the new, black swim trunks he was wearing.

Oh, yes… he grinned, seeing how he had her full attention, as he walked up slowly to take her arm. "Why, Ms. Rae, it looks as though you could use a little cooling off, as well," he said in a rather deep, yet, unnerving tone, as he swept her off her feet. When he did, his left hand landed just beneath her breast at the outer side of her suit. *Oh, God, woman,* he groaned achingly, when their eyes met. But before he could look away, his gaze fell upon the fullness of her lips, as they parted beneath his gaze. "Oh… Jessi," he whispered, as he realized he was no longer able to fight his desire for her, when he found himself, suddenly, claiming her lips.

Oddly enough, she began to respond, when thinking about Craig holding her in his arms. And as their tongues began caressing one another, the heat between them began to escalate.

"Mmmm…" she heard herself moan, while taking in more of his desire for her. But then suddenly realized what she was doing, she cried, pulling away to look up into his smoldering eyes, "No…! What am I thinking? Alex…"

"Oh, God, Jessi, I'm sorry! I don't know what got into me!" he offered, while looking deep into her eyes. "If it were anyone but Craig," he growled quietly, "I would have taken you from him right here and now."

"But…"

"I know, damn it to hell."

"Oh, God, Alex, you are so… incredibly handsome, so much so that it drives me crazy to even look at you, sometimes. But I feel so drawn to him. I know that must sound really strange, but he has that affect on me."

"Yeah, I know," he laughed, hearing her words.

"Alex… it's not funny!"

"I'm sorry, but you might say, it runs in the family!"

"Oh, Alex," she suddenly found that she, too, was able to laugh.

Just as quickly as their touching moment began, it came to an end, when David interrupted, "Alex, are you just going to hold her, or are you going to throw her in?"

"Well…" he warned with a playful smile, "I have to put you down!"

"Yes… but…" she began to squeal, before turning it into a full out scream, as she clung to his neck tightly. Doing so, she refused to let go, while causing him to fall in with her.

Coming up, they both heard everyone laughing.

"Hey, Alex…" Allen called out, "how could you let her do that to you again?"

"She wouldn't let go!" he called back, laughing along with them, while helping her over to the side of the pool.

"You're darn right I wouldn't. I'm not stupid!" she laughed back, while splashing water up at him.

"That's for sure!" he grinned back down at her. "But let me give you a little warning, Ms. Rae," he whispered, when coming up closer to trace her bottom lip, as it began to quiver, "I am only human. So if you don't want to get something started, then don't, and I repeat," he growled, looking down at the fullness of her breasts, "don't wear something that is going to cause me to want to do more than just…" He stopped then to look back up into her eyes. "I can only take so much teasing," he groaned, while causing her to catch her breath, as his thumb went in through the side of her suit to find a hardened nipple.

"I…I got your m…message," she groaned, while fighting from closing her eyes to his slow torturing caress.

"Are you sure?" he asked, pulling her in even closer into his embrace, until she could feel his hot breath against her face.

"O...oh, yes. Loud and clear," she whispered, while letting out a slight whimper, as he went to pull his hand away.

"No more toying with my hormones?" he warned, as she looked up into his stormy eyes.

"No, no more teasing," she returned, when feeling his lips coming back to lightly taste hers. "A...Alex, p...please...!"

"All right," he smiled, "I guess that goes for me too, huh? Just remember, you are so damn desirable. Don't make me regret changing my mind."

"I...I'll try to re...remember that," she shivered against the molten desire of his body.

"All right, you two," Rose laughed, seeing the chemistry build between them. "If you're through now, the rest of us would like to take a swim!"

Taking that moment, as everyone got into the pool, Jessi went over to talk to David about Craig. Before she could start though, he had a few questions of his own. "You and Alex look pretty close. Are the two of you involved?"

"Not in so many words, no."

"Oh?"

"David, I didn't come over here to talk about Alex. I came to ask if you think you will ever go back over to Craig's place again?"

"Yeah, sometime," he replied, while sadly looking away. "Jessi, is it?" he asked, looking back to see her nod her head. "It wasn't supposed to have happened to him."

"I know. It was you they wanted."

"Well, you're half right. It was actually Tony who wanted me, not Harry."

"What do you mean?"

"Harry is in too deep. Tony had already warned him."

"And you?"

"I didn't want any part of what he was. I tried to tell him that."

"Then what?"

"I..." he looked away quite suddenly.

"David," she said, grabbing his arm to turn him back to face her, "you have to tell Alex. He has the right to know what happened!"

"I know. It's just that…"

"You two were close once?"

"Yeah."

"Alex still cares about you, but now it's time for the truth to come out. Craig's spirit has to rest!" she cried quietly. "It's been almost two years now."

"I know, but…" He stopped, as he felt the pain of his guilt returning, "I can't do this…" he groaned, turning away to get out of the pool.

Looking over to see the look on Alex's face, she shrugged helplessly, while going after David to offer her apologies. "David…" she called out in a hushed-like voice, while coming up, as he turned to offer her a towel, "I'm sorry, I didn't mean for you to get upset."

"I've been blaming myself for a long time now. And the thought of going over there, well…"

"Think about it, please…!"

Looking back at the others, he nodded his head sadly.

Later, when everyone was about to get out, David gave Jessi a hand up, before going over to get her another one of their large towels. "Do you really believe his spirit is roaming around over there?" he asked, looking back toward Craig's place.

"Aside from what little I've said, where did you hear that?"

"Mom was talking to dad about it. Then Aunt Sue and Uncle Bob told them about the seminar they went to last year. It dealt with things like Craig's spirit, and how he had a score to settle, before he could ever rest."

"Well, you're right about that!"

"Jessi, Alex said that you made him a promise."

"Yes, I did!"

"Then you've seen him…?"

"Yes, several times! He talks about the two of you a lot!"

"Really?"

"David…"

"Hey, you two!" Rose interrupted. "Come and eat!"

"Yeah," David nodded, while turning back to take Jessi's hand.

Before going, though, she had to tell him about Craig's message. "David, wait!" she said, pulling him back. "There's something else you need to know."

"What?" he asked, still standing along the edge of the pool.

"I have a message for you."

"From Craig?" he asked, somehow sensing it could only be from him, since Jessi had been seeing him lately.

"Yes, he said that you would understand?" she explained, while leaning in to whisper something in his ear, "I owe you."

"What? No!" he yelled, as she pushed him in.

At that moment, feeling Craig's laughter clear from his house, she also laughed, as David resurfaced. "Sorry!" she continued, while covering her mouth.

Shaking the water out of his hair, he came climbing out of the pool, laughing, with her help, "Craig, you bastard!" he growled quietly, and then more privately, he whispered, "Tell him I'll be there."

"I will."

While the two wrapped up their conversation, Alex was on his cell phone with Craig's father, while having their own private discussion. "So, what you're saying is, all I have to do is, go up to his old room and call out to him?"

"Yes, and if Craig is truly there, he will need someone to help him do what he's unable to in the state he's in."

Looking off toward Jessi, he thought quietly to himself, *Perhaps this is what she needs, since she has really come to care for him.*

"Alex," Bob interrupted, "from what you have told me about her, she must really believe that he's there."

"She does," he returned, shaking his head. "And so it seems that I'm beginning to think so, too!"

"Then go, and do exactly what I told you. If anyone can do it, it would be you."

"Why me?"

"Because the two of you were so close."

"Like brothers, Bob. Like... brothers."

After ending their conversation, Alex went over to join the others, when Jessi looked up to see his saddened expression. "Are you all right?" she whispered thoughtfully.

"I will be soon!" he grinned, knowing what he had to do, when they got back to Craig's. "What do you say we dive into this wonderful food? I'm starving!"

"Now that sounds like the Alex we all know and love," Allen laughed, while passing him the plate of steaks.

Chapter Seventeen

Shortly after they had finished, Alex and Jessi said their goodbyes and followed each other back to Craig's, where he checked the house out, before letting her in.

"Looks all right," he announced, holding the door open for her, before going in to build them a fire.

With a puzzled look on her face, she asked, tossing her things over onto her suitcase, "What are you doing?"

"Just building a fire. Why don't you go on over and relax. I'll be right back."

"Fine, but if you don't mind, I would like to get myself a shower and put on some fresh clothes first."

"Fine. Yell if you need me. You know, if you hear something out of the ordinary!"

"Yes, I know, and don't worry, I'll have Max nearby to keep an eye on things while I'm cleaning up."

"Good," he replied, as he left to go up to Craig's room, as she went over and switched on her radio before going to shower and change into something warm.

Meanwhile upstairs, Alex closed the front door before calling out to his nephew. "Craig…" he began, while feeling a little odd, "I know you're here. Bob told me all about your troubled spirit, and Jessi too! She tells me she has been seeing you. She cares for you a great deal, Craig. She must, or why would she put her life on the line for you? And if I know you," he swallowed back on his building emotions, "you probably care for her, too. So here it is. What I'm about to offer is going to sound kind of strange, but then I've done some pretty strange things in the past! But this," he went on, while going over to the window to look out. "I understand that a spirit can enter another person's body for short periods of time to do things that they can't normally do, otherwise. So here I am, and she's downstairs." Stopping, he shook his head in disbelief over what he was about to say. "Man… this is got to be really crazy! What the hell am I doing? If it were anyone else, I wouldn't do it."

"*T h e n w h y d o i t a t a l l?*" Craig's voice came back, startling his uncle.

Spinning around upon hearing it, he cried out, "Say that again!"

Sounding more human now, Craig asked again from the shadows of his room, where Alex was unable to see him just yet, "Then… why… do it?"

"Craig" Alex shook his head, "is that really you?"

"Yes," he returned, moving to the center of the room, though still unseen by his uncle.

"Why then, can't I see you?"

"It takes too much out of me! But soon, I promise."

"Craig, Jessi needs you."

"Yes, I know. And I…" He stopped to look away.

"Then go to her."

"What are you saying?"

"This is your chance to be with her for however long you need."

"Alex…"

Knowing what his nephew was about to say, he interrupted. "Yes, Craig, I'm offering myself, so that you can be with her. Though she is really a special lady, it's you she wants. So do it for the both of you."

Once said, he waited a few minutes for Craig to digest what he was offering, before going back down to Jessi.

"All right." Craig conceded.

"What do you want me to do?"

"Go back down to her, I'll be there shortly."

"Craig?"

"Don't worry, Uncle," he laughed, "I hear it doesn't hurt much once you get used to it."

"Sounds as though you've done this before."

"No. You're my first."

"Great…!" Alex laughed along with his nephew, before leaving his room.

Arriving downstairs to the sound of soft music playing in the background, Jessi was back, curled up in her warm sweats, by the fire, while Max laid sleeping nearby. "Jessi," Alex walked up, holding out his hand. "May I have this dance?" he asked warmly.

"Alex..." She looked up from the sofa. "We shouldn't. Not if we don't want things to get out of hand again, like before!"

"Let me be the judge of that," he said, taking her hand anyway.

"Alex...!"

"Hush now, and close your eyes," he whispered in her ear, as his arms circled her. "Try to imagine it being Craig dancing with you."

"But..." She hesitated, while feeling the warmth of his embrace engulf her.

With that, there was something in the way he held her, which caused her to relax. As she did, another beautiful melody began to play. Soon after, things began to happen, as Craig's spirit entered into Alex's body, causing him to sway just a little, it was now Craig's turn to hold her in his arms. "Oh, Jess," he whispered softly against her fresh scented hair, "I've wanted to hold you like this, ever since I first saw you laying on the floor up in my room."

"Craig?" she asked, slowing her steps, not knowing whether or not to cry, or to faint just then from hearing his voice.

"Yes, Jess, it's me," he swallowed hard, while looking down at her, as she pulled back.

"But, how..." she asked, too afraid to look up into his eyes, at that moment.

"Alex! He's allowing us this time together."

"A...Alex? Oh, Lord!" Slowly she looked up into what was once his uncle's icy blue eyes, only to see something vaguely familiar in them now. "Craig?" she cried, unsure now what she was seeing.

"It's going to be all right," he whispered, before claiming her trembling lips. As he did, he pulled her up into his arms even more, as though to merge their souls together in that moment. "Oh, Jessi," he groaned, as their kiss deepened, and as it did, so did the heat of their passion, as it began to sear through their veins, causing her to put her arms up around him that much more.

Pulling back once again, she had to see for herself that all too familiar smile of his, as it then turned into a deep passionate desire for her.

"Oh, Jess... I want you so... much!"

"Oh, God, Craig, tell me this isn't a dream!" she whispered, while gazing up into his, now, deep blue eyes, as she started feeling his hands sliding up under her sweatshirt.

"No, Jess, it's real," he whispered, while backing her slowly to the sofa.

At the realization of what was taking place in front of her, she reached up to tuck her fingers in through his hair, before bringing her lips back up to meet his with so much of her own pent-up hunger, when he brought them slowly down onto the sofa, where, with her help, he started pulling off his uncle's clothes, along with hers, so that he could really make love to her for the first time.

"Jess!" he groaned, running his tongue over her soft, silky-like neck, just before moving down to much more pleasurable things, since the first time he saw her out in the shower.

Meanwhile, bringing her legs up around his, she too groaned, wanting him as he went on suckling one of her perky blossoms, while bringing her up into the erotic sensation his touch was causing her. And even though it was his uncle's body, Craig's spirit, with its electrical current, sent tingling sensation through her body, though not enough to hurt her, as they continued bringing their love to much greater heights.

"Oh... Craig...!" she shivered, while feeling the erotic sensation on her senses, until she couldn't take it any longer.

Bringing himself back up to take her hands, he brought them up to just above her head. As he then positioned himself, until she felt the power of his arousal pressing up against her passageway, when it began.

"Jessi..." he called out, looking into her steamy eyes, with the same need in his own.

"Yes, Craig. Now...!" she cried, biting her lower lip, as he plunged within her a part of his uncle that she wasn't quite ready for. Though for a detective, his manliness was quite enhanced, and yes, very powerful, as he drove it in even harder with each passing moment.

"Oh.... God..." he cried out, plunging in deeper and deeper.

Crying out as well, she was consumed with more pleasure than she had ever known before. "Mmmm…" she moaned, feeling his desire building higher and higher, as she clung to his hands that still held hers captive over her head.

Stopping for a moment, after hours of rolling from one side of the sleeper to the other, first one on top, then the other, using her hands, she raised them to pull her hair up out of her face. Doing that, he saw by the firelight the richness of her true beauty, as the flames flickered off her now glistening flesh. "Oh, Lord, Jess, I never in my life knew it could be like this. Why do you have to be so… beautiful?" he groaned, catching sight of her perspiration, as it rolled down between her bosoms.

"And you, so handsome!" she smiled, while coming back down to capture his lips with hers, before he rolled her over onto her back to savor the sweetness of her breasts one last time.

"Mmmm… I don't ever want to stop," he moaned, running his fingers lightly over one of her nipples, "but…" he began, when he suddenly felt the draining of his spirit start to hit him.

Getting up, he nearly stumbled, when right away it brought her up to his side. "What is it?" she asked, frightened that something was gravely wrong. "Is it…"

"Yes, I'm afraid so!" he replied, while bent over weakly, and at that same moment, looking so sad just then.

"Oh, Craig!"

With her help, she brought him back up to stand before her.

Looking into her saddened eyes, he felt the same pain in his own. "I wish I didn't have to go, but I do!"

At that moment, looking back to see the mess they made of the bed, they both laughed. "I guess we should get cleaned up first, before Alex was to know what I have done to him!"

"Are you sure you have it in you to do that?"

"I have to," he smiled, "if I ever want to ask him to do me another favor again!"

"You mean…"

"Yes, Jess, if it's possible!" he smiled warmly, while touching her lower lip with the same finger Alex had used on her earlier at the pool, when at the same time, picking up on her thoughts. "Jess?" he called, seeing how she seemed to go on thinking.

Meantime, recalling Alex's desire, she shook it off, replacing it with something funny.

"Jess?"

"Yes, of course," she agreed, smiling at the promise she had made him, "he would be a little surprised."

Knowing what it was all about, he grinned, shaking his head over his uncle's demise with such a beautiful woman to torment him, when all of this was over. Yet, at that moment, he was beginning to regret when that time would come.

Quickly showering and pulling on some fresh clothes, they went back in to lay down after fixing up the sofa.

"Jess?"

"Yes?"

"Tell Alex I said thanks!"

"I...I will. I promise," she smiled, as he slowly tilted her chin up to kiss her warm and gentle, yet trembling lips goodnight.

Holding her close, until it was time for him to leave Alex's body, he left her to dream of their love, while making it easier for him to pull away, when the time came.

Shortly afterwards, Alex woke to find her curled up next to him, sleeping peacefully. Grinning at the sight of her soft brown hair tussled out across his chest, he stayed there, falling back off to sleep with his arm around her shoulder.

Chapter Eighteen

The next morning, when the sun came up, he got up slowly so as not to wake her, to head into the kitchen. On his way, seeing her dog lying comfortably by the fireplace, he motioned for him to follow.

"Are you hungry, boy?" he asked, going over to put on a pot of coffee, before heading out to his Blazer to bring in some more food, where as breakfast that morning consisted of ham, eggs and hash browns.

Meanwhile, not long after, Jessi woke to the aroma of food cooking. When she started to get up, suddenly, she felt weak. "Alex..." she called out, as she sat there for a moment longer. "A...Alex..." she called again.

Deciding not to wait any longer, she slowly got up to walk over to the kitchen doorway.

"Hey there, sleepy head!" he greeted, yet with his back toward her.

"A...Alex..." she began, when things suddenly began to go dark around her.

Turning off her camp stove, he turned around to see the expression on her face. "Jess... what's wrong?" he asked, looking concerned.

"I...I don't... know...!"

No sooner had she said what she did, she suddenly went limp.

Dropping the spatula, he rushed right over to catch her. "Jessi..." he cried out, sweeping her up into his arms to carry her back into the living room. "Come on, girl, don't do this to me!"

Arriving at the sofa, he carefully laid her down, while checking her over.

"Jess, talk to me! Tell me what's wrong!" he cried, looking up at the ceiling. "Damn it, Craigwhat have we done to her?" he groaned, filled with concern, when not hearing a car pull up out front, as the sun's reflection bounced off its windshield long enough to briefly blind him.

"W...What...?" he growled, snapping out of his thoughts to go for his service revolver, he kept tucked away in his boot.

With his gun in hand, he went over to look out the front window. To his relief, Rose was bringing Sue and Bob by to see Jessi.

"Thank, God," he groaned out a sigh of relief, while heading for the front door.

Putting his revolver away, he opened the door just as they walked up.

"Bob, thank God you're here!" he cried, grabbing his arm. "It's Jessi. She's fainted."

"Where is she?" he asked, as Alex led the way back into the living room.

"She's in here."

"Sue, go and get my bag, please," he ordered, while going over to sit beside Jessi. "What happened?"

"I was fixing breakfast, when she woke up and came into the kitchen. She didn't look well, so I asked what was wrong! She had no more than said, she didn't know, when she fainted!" he exclaimed, looking on worriedly, as he stood by, watching Bob examine her.

Hearing him say something about his cooking, Sue teased her brother, when she came back in with Bob's medical bag. "Alex, you probably scared her with your cooking! It's a good thing Bob's a doctor!" she laughed, as he gave her a half-baked frown, while shaking his head.

"Alex," Bob interrupted, "on a more serious matter, did you do what we talked about?"

"Yes, last night when we got back. I built a fire, while she went in to get a shower and change. Afterwards, I went up to Craig's room. God, Bob..." He stopped, as the look on his face was filled with emotion.

Seeing this, everyone thought he was about to cry.

"What?" Bob asked.

"While up there..."

"Alex..." Sue spoke up.

Turning to look into his sister's eyes, a smile came over his handsome face. "He spoke to me, sis! I had no more than said, 'why am I doing this?' Then suddenly, out of nowhere, he spoke up, asking me why I was!"

"Craig…?" Bob asked, going to stand back up to face him.

Nodding his head sheepishly, Alex broke down, about to cry. "The process though, took place here."

"Oh, my…" Sue covered her mouth to shed her own tears, as Rose went over to comfort her, "he really is here?"

"Yes, and Jessi's been here to help him, it seems," Alex went on.

Looking Alex over, as well, he asked, "How do you feel, both physically and mentally, that is?"

"A little drained, but fine! Why?"

Turning back then to look at Jessi, he shook his head. "She shouldn't have been affected by the change!" he exclaimed, puzzledly.

"Mmmm…" Jessi moaned, as she started to come around.

"Jessi…?" Rose called out, coming around to the other side of the sofa. "Honey… it's me, Rose McMasters. Can you hear me?"

Opening her eyes, Jessi looked around the room, first to see Rose, and then Alex, as he came up behind her. Turning then to see a stranger standing nearby, she blinked a few times to try to clear her head.

"How do you feel?" the man asked, looking quite similar to his son, only much older, as she opened her eyes again.

"Wh…what?" she asked, looking frightened.

Seeing her startled expression, Alex spoke up right away, "It's all right. This is Craig's father!" he explained, referring to the man now taking a seat next to her.

"He's also a doctor!" Rose added, smiling.

"The name's Bob Matthews! And this here is my wife, Sue!" he pointed to the woman who was coming up to stand next to him, with dark brown hair like Craig's, and eyes to match.

Looking at the two of them, she could see where Craig had gotten his good looks.

"I'm also Alex's older sister," she went on. "As for his gray hair though, that he has gotten from our father."

Smiling, Jessi found it easier to relax around them, while Bob went on checking her over.

"So now," he went on to ask, "just how are you feeling?"

"A little tired, but really hungry!" she exclaimed, while trying to sit up.

"Well, if you will allow me," he was saying, while reaching down into his bag to pull out a Glucose Meter to check her blood sugar level, "I'd like to check on a few minor things to find out what caused you to faint. Starting with telling me what you were feeling just before you did!"

"I felt oddly weak!"

"Mmmm…" he returned, pulling out a pair of reading glasses to see by, before pricking her finger.

"Ouch!" she flinched.

"Jess, are you all right?" Alex asked thoughtfully.

"Yes. I just hate needles, is all."

"Sorry, young lady, there's no other way to avoid doing this," Bob offered, while placing a sample of her blood on a test strip, before inserting it into the meter.

"Bob?" Alex spoke up.

"It'll take a few seconds, before we know anything. Until then, Ms. Rae, have you been eating well and getting enough sleep?"

"Yes!"

"Oh…" Sue spoke up, "Alex tells us you have been under a great deal of tension lately."

"More than I'd like!" she acknowledged, while frowning up at Alex.

"Well now, what do we have here?" Bob spoke up again, reading the results.

"Bob," Alex asked impatiently, "what is it?"

"According to this, it's only natural she would be feeling weak! It seems here that your blood sugar is pretty low, my dear. To be exact, seventy-one!"

"What?" the others gasped.

"Yep!" he returned, putting his instruments away. "And if by chance you're not eating regularly, you need to start, or you'll make yourself sick!"

"Don't worry about that, she has a big breakfast waiting on her now!" Alex announced, feeling relieved that what had taken place the other night wasn't the cause of her fainting.

Giving her a warm smile, he headed for the kitchen to warm it up.

Meanwhile, Rose shook her head, looking down on Jessi, "Sweetie, you had us worried!"

"I'm sorry!"

"Is it true...?" Sue asked, knowing all about Jessi's gifts from Alex. "Do you really have a connection with our son's spirit?"

"Alex...!" She looked to him, when he poked his head around the doorway.

"I told them all about it the other day."

"Then, it is true?" Sue asked again, while covering her mouth, tearfully.

"Yes..." she replied slowly, "yes, it's true!"

"To add to it," Alex went on, while coming back into the room with her food, "when things are going on back at the Inn, she'll be staying out here from time to time."

"Why on earth for? The house needs a lot of work, and well..." Sue couldn't go on.

"We do appreciate what you're doing here," Bob went on in her place, "knowing that our son's spirit will finally be able to rest once all this is over, but surely there are other places you could stay, while the investigation is going on!"

"Sure," Rose spoke up, "you can stay with us, if it's anything to do with wanting to be close by!"

"Th...thanks, but..."

Seeing her saddened expression, Rose went to place an arm around her shoulder. "Oh, honey, things will be all right. You'll see."

"Will they?" she thought sadly to herself, while taking her plate of food from Alex.

"Jessi," Bob spoke up, concerned about her reaction to what had just been said. "I know you feel you have to be here in order to help him. And mind you, we do appreciate what you're doing here, but your health is important too. And in time everything that you are going through is going to be, well..." He stopped to find the right words to express his own sorrow. "Well, it's going to take some time to get over. So try to remember now you have some friends here who will try to help you out."

"You sure do!" Rose added, while giving her a little motherly hug, before having to go.

Looking down at his watch, Bob added, while getting up to leave, as well. "Call me if you're not feeling any better. And get plenty of rest."

"I will," she returned, thanking him.

"Hey, I'll be right back," Alex replied. "I'm just going to see them out."

"All right."

Outside, Bob turned back to see Alex coming up behind them. "Take care of her. She has to start taking it easy, before she winds up in the hospital over this."

"I will," he replied, turning to his sister, who reached up to give him a hug.

"Thanks, sweetie!" she smiled tearfully.

"I loved him, too, sis!"

Not saying anything, she just went over to get into their car.

Waving goodbye, from the bottom step of the front porch, he returned to check on Jessi.

Once inside, he saw that she hadn't taken a bite of her food. "Hey, what's wrong?" he asked, sensing her sadness. "You're not eating!"

"No, I guess I'm not."

"And why not?"

"Because, there's something I have to tell you."

"Oh...?"

"It's about Craig!"

Alex's eyes grew dark with concern at the mere mention of his nephew, when he came around to sit next to her. "What about him?"

"He wanted me to thank you."

"For what?"

"For giving us this time together. It meant a great deal to the both of us."

"I'm glad I could be of help!"

Looking down on her plate, he got up to go into the kitchen to get his own.

Joining her, they ate in silence, with the exception of talking a little about what had happened, starting with the conversation, which had taken place between him and his nephew.

"You must have felt pretty good about that," she commented.

"Well... sure!" he laughed.

"What?" she smiled up at him.

"Oh, I was just wondering how you felt when you first heard him calling out to you!"

"Oh, you mean once I got passed his pranks with the back door, and the water jugs! And then to top it all off, his running his fingers up my back, and to my neck, while I stood at the front door to say a prayer, before turning in for the night! That?" she asked, toying around with her food first, before finishing. "I felt like grabbing my girls and getting the heck out of here!"

At that, they both cracked up laughing, while finishing their meal.

"Mmmm... how did you learn to cook like this?" she asked, savoring the last bite.

"Are you sure you really want to know?" he asked, looking into her puzzling eyes, as she slowly put down her fork. "Craig showed me a few tips on how to use certain herbs!"

"Really?" she asked, getting up slowly to go into the kitchen.

"Yep! He was the chef in the family, next to Allen McMasters, that is!"

In the kitchen, she went to get herself a drink of water, while talking about other things, when Alex walked in behind her. "I never realized," she went on, "just how much I could really care for someone after my first love was killed several years ago."

"Oh?" he asked, surprised to hear such a thing coming from a beautiful woman as her. "How did it happen?"

"A car accident," she replied, while turning away to fight back the sudden rush of tears.

"I'm sorry to hear that!" he offered, while placing his strong, yet gentle hands on her shoulders to comfort her. "About last night," he went to ask in a more subdued tone, as she went about gathering up their dishes to wash them.

At that moment, dressed in an oversized, well-worn, white t-shirt and baggy sweats, while standing at the sink bare-footed, Alex caught his first glimpse at how the chilling air in the house caused her nipples to harden, as she turned to get the spatula off the stove. It was then, too, that he noticed how their dark pigmentations were nearly visible through the thinning top. Whereas in the other room, she had had the blanket pulled up around her the whole time. And now, finding it rather enticing to his growing taste buds, he was beginning to find it hard to look away so as not to catch her attention.

"Alex…?" she turned, interrupting his thoughts, so that he could finish telling her what he had started to say.

"Oh, huh, about last night, was it what you hoped for?" he asked, while going on to offer his help with the dishes, to pass the time, not to mention, to get his mind off her breasts.

"Better than that," she went on smiling, while unaware of the torment she was causing him, "it was the most wonderful night I have ever had, thanks to you," she said, when reaching over to give him a hug, as one of her breasts brushed into his arm.

Feeling it, he tightened up at what it was doing to him. "What happened?" he went on to ask, while fighting down the oncoming arousal she was causing him.

"We had been dancing, and before I knew it, we were…" She stopped suddenly at what she was about to say, when blushing, she swatted him on the arm with the dishtowel. "Alex… that's personal."

"Really?" he laughed, noticing how, whenever she moved, her breasts, since not wearing a bra, would move as well, and yet, stirring even more heat through his groin. "But it was with my body!" he went on teasingly, while swallowing down the saliva that was building in his mouth for her luscious breasts.

"Yes, well…" She backed away slowly, while unable to resist teasing him even more, "don't remind me!"

"What…?" he barked, when she tossed the towel down on the counter, before making a mad dash out the back door.

Hot on her heels, he went after her, tossing down his own dishtowel, as well.

Meanwhile, catching up with her out near the woodshed, he tackled her to the ground, rolling her over onto her back, while laughing all along.

"Alex…" she laughed uncontrollably, as he continued to look down into her smiling face.

"You just said it was wonderful!"

"Well… yes…, I said Craig was wonderful!" she laughed again, as he began tickling her.

"You little brat..." he roared, reaching up with one hand to tickle her side, as she rolled around to try to get away.

"Alex...!" she cried out, laughing.

"Oh, no you don't, you're not going to get away that easily," he continued, unaware that she had worked her t-shirt up passed her hips, to where he'd been tickling her around the waist.

Just then, rolling back over onto her back, laughing, his hand slid up under her shirt, purely by accident. As it did, finding the softness of one of her breasts, she suddenly caught her breath, as she laid her head back to look up into his, now, stormy eyes.

Looking down to see what he had done, he saw how her voluptuous swells were pressing against the thin material of her top. *Oh, God...*he groaned, swallowing even harder, when the urge to kiss her consumed him, as he looked back up into her smoldering eyes. And yet, as if what happened the other day hadn't been bad enough, he knew better than to try it again. "Damn it, Jess, why do you have to be so damn desirable?"

"I...I..." she began with great difficulty, while feeling the temperature rising in herself, when at that moment, all she could think of was to reach up and kiss him.

Yet for him, the mere thought of having one of those luscious mounds in his mouth, he cursed himself, as the muscle along his jaw line flexed repeatedly. By then he found it increasingly difficult to stop, as his thumb reached up to run itself over her taut nipple. "Damn it to hell, what am I thinking?" he swore, hating himself for what was going through his mind.

Getting up at that point, he shook his head angrily.

"Alex..."

"No, I can't do this to you," he groaned, turning back to face her. "I care too much about you to hurt you like this. But God help me, Jess, you are so damn desirable."

Feeling slightly ashamed of herself, she sat up, pulling her knees to her chest to help cover her modest body. "I...I'm sorry, Alex, I wasn't trying..." she began, while hiding her shame now, she dropped her head down to her folded arms.

"Oh... Jess," he went back over to hold her, "I know you weren't trying to get anything started here."

"Oh, Alex, last night…" she cried, "what happened between Craig and I, was so… incredibly beautiful. And yes," she went on, looking up at him now, "it was through your body that it was made possible."

Finding it in him to smile, he said, holding her loosely, "Well, in that case, I'm glad that I could be there for the two of you."

"Oh… you can say that again!" she thought, feeling slightly embarrassed, when she turned away to hide what she was thinking. "Alex, I don't think either one of us knew that it was going to happen. It just did!"

"How…" he began.

Sensing what he was about to ask, she turned back to face him with a blush on her face.

"That good?" he asked, smiling down at her, as he traced her bottom lip with his thumb, while causing her to quiver once again at the feeling it gave her, both the previous day and again last night with Craig.

"Oh, Lord… what is it with these two men?" she questioned herself, quietly.

"Jessi," he broke in on her thoughts, "where is Craig now?"

"He said he was nearly drained, and that he may not be here this morning when we had gotten up!"

"I guess it took a lot out of him to be with you?"

"Yes."

"Well, it's getting late," he changed the subject, "we had better be getting back to the Inn pretty soon. Can you drive, or should I take you with me?"

"I'll know better after I get dressed," she replied, noticing what she was still wearing.

Getting to her feet, she ran off into the house to get what she would be need to grab a shower out back, while Alex called Ted.

Getting there, she gladly slipped out of her things, before turning on the water, as she gave some thought to what she and Craig had had the other night. *"Mmmm…"* she moaned her delight in feeling his power reaching areas, which had, by no means, been reached before.

Chapter Nineteen

Finishing with her shower, she came back inside, wearing a blue cottony summer dress, with her hair nicely pulled back in a loose ponytail, to find Alex on the phone with Ted.

"We're on our way. How are things there?" Alex was asking.

"It's been pretty quiet, so far."

"Good. I guess then I had better be putting my disguise on, shouldn't I?"

"You had better!"

"All right," he laughed, seeing the look of puzzlement on Jessi's face, "we'll see you in a few hours."

"Okay," Ted returned, hanging up.

"Ted?" she asked, putting her things together to carry out to her car.

"Yes. He says everything has been pretty quiet."

"Good!" she grumbled, fighting with the catch on her suitcase.

Coming over, he offered her a hand, "Here, let me get that for you. They can be really cantankerous when they want to be!"

"Sure! Thanks!" she appreciated, while backing away to give him room.

"There you go," he grinned, giving the catch a firm nudge, when hearing it snap shut, before picking it up to carry out for her. Doing so, she went to get the cooler. "No," he called back, seeing what she was about to do, "I'll get that in a moment."

"You know, I'm not completely helpless!"

"Yes, but why push it? This time away was to give you a break! So take the help when you can!"

"You're right about the break, but the helping part," she sighed, while going over to pick up a smaller suitcase, to carry out after him, "well, that isn't always so easy, when I have had to do things for myself for so long. And I don't want to find myself having to depend on it, when it's not always around!" she concluded, once they got to their vehicles.

"I can see your point there. But why do I get the feeling that, at some time in the past you had gotten use to having the help, but then something went wrong?"

"Because it did. It was called a divorce."

"Oh, I knew that!" he grinned, taking her case, before going back in to get her cooler.

"So now," she asked out in the bright sunlit morning air, "what's this about a disguise?"

Taking a look around before answering her. Once he saw the coast was clear to tell her, he had to fight back an urge to laugh, "I'm your new groundskeeper!" he announced, before stopping by his Blazer first to get out his things to change into, before getting her cooler.

"Oh, this ought to be interesting," she thought, while going back in to have a seat, while he went into the bathroom to change.

Returning to the living room forty-five minutes later, he looked completely different. His hair and eyes, having been so much lighter, were now brown, while wearing wire-rimmed glasses. Even his voice carried a different pitch, when asking how he looked. "Well?" he grinned boldly.

"Alex, is that really you?" she laughed.

"No, ma'am! The name's Jake Green, your new groundskeeper."

"Great!" she teased, catching sight of Craig, laughing as well, from near the staircase.

"Well, if you are about ready to go, I'll just get my things, along with your cooler here, and put them out into our vehicles."

"I will be right out," she returned, following him to the front door, when he stopped to turn back.

"Is everything all right?" he asked, seeing that growing look of hers whenever it had something to do with his nephew.

"Yes...!"

"Craig?"

"Uh huh! How did you know?"

"I can see it in your eyes. Where is he?"

"The staircase."

"Jessi..." Alex looked to her questioningly, when worried his nephew may have known what had almost took place earlier.

"It'll be all right," she assured him.

While trying to smile, he turned to go out to his Blazer. "Take your time," he called back, "after putting this stuff away, I'll be out here with Max, until you're ready to go."

"All right," she smiled, watching him, as he walked off the front porch, before calling out for her dog.

Seeing the two hitting it off after getting their things put into their vehicles, she turned back to go into the living room. "Craig?" she called out.

"Right here, beautiful!" he called back from the kitchen doorway, while smiling his one of a kind smile at her.

"Hey...!" she attempted a smile.

Seeing how she wasn't smiling as brightly as usual, he began to wonder. "What's wrong?" he asked, picking up on bits and pieces of her troubled thoughts.

Not answering right away, she went over to sit back down on the sofa.

"Jess, it has to do with Alex, doesn't it?"

Trying hard not to cry, she simply nodded her head, when looking back up at him. The look on his face though, wasn't all that surprising. "You know, don't you?"

"About the pool, and then again out back? Yes. Although, the scene leading up to out back was pretty funny!" he laughed.

"But the pool? Knowing what happened there, you still wanted to be with me?"

"Jessi," he laughed, to set her mind at ease, "Alex is only human, and so are you! I..."

"Craig" she cried out, stopping him, "I know what you are... and..."

"The feelings are mutual," he replied, knowing what she had been feeling all along. Looking away, though, he went over to stand at the front door to watch his uncle. "Jess, he's not such a bad guy, once you get to know him."

Coming up behind him, she too, watched, as Alex let Max chase after him, while holding onto his ball. "Yes, and he's really good with Max, and my girls, as well, but," she shook her head, "not now!"

Turning back, he still held that lopsided smile of his, while bringing one back to her face, when she conceded to allowing herself to do so. "Things will work out. You'll see."

"So I've been told."

"Oh...?"

"Yes, your parent's. They were here earlier with Rose. Oh, and before I forget, David will be here sometime. I just don't know when."

"Good, then finally I'll get some answers," he replied, looking back out the door.

When he turned back to see her saddened expression still lingering, he stepped away from the door. "Come, close your eyes," he whispered, looking into them warmly.

"Why?" she asked, moving away from the door to lean back against the entryway wall.

"Just do what I've asked!" he smiled, while coming around to stand in front of her.

Doing so, he lightly ran his lips along the side of her neck, causing a trail of tingling sensations along the way.

"Mmmm..." she murmured, feeling the rest of her body warming to his mystical touch.

"I've often wondered what would happen if I would have tried that," he whispered softly in her ear, before going on.

"I could have told you after what had happened last night."

"It didn't hurt you, did it?" he pulled back, looking concerned.

"No," she smiled up at him. "It was quite exhilarating, to be honest!"

"Huh, really?" he smiled, thinking only to himself.

"What?" she asked, unable to pick up on his sudden mood change. "Craig... what are you up to?"

"You'll see, just close your eyes again," he told her, smiling, as he went back down to nuzzle at her neck a little while longer.

"Craig!"

"*T r u s t m e*" he whispered eerily.

Once again, after seeing that awesome smile of his, she did as he asked.

"You'll surely feel something now, but don't be afraid."

"Craig!"

"H u s h."

Once again she felt the sensation at the side of her neck, and then suddenly it had increased, as he put more effort into his thoughts. By then, he was able to move her hair back off her shoulder with his hand. And although he couldn't taste the sweetness of her neck, he found the ability to leave a reminder of his desire for her.

By then she began feeling a slight burning sensation at the base of her collarbone, when she let out a soft cry, while trying not to wince at the pain.

Placing her hands out to the side, to press up against the wall, behind her, he pulled back slightly, and happily smiled, at his handiwork.

"What?" she asked, curiously, while opening her eyes to see his smile.

"You'll know soon enough," he laughed. "Let's just say, you won't be able to forget me, while you're back at your Inn."

"I could never forget you," she smiled back up at him, when hearing Alex start up his Blazer, when they both turned to look out the front door.

"Well, I guess this means we have to go now."

"Looks like it," he smiled sadly.

"See you soon?" she asked, turning back to see a saddened expression on his face.

"I'll be here!"

"Craig..." she stopped.

"Yes?"

"Even without your uncle's help..." she smiled, leaving the rest for him to pick up on.

Grinning his crooked grin, he nodded his head. "See you, beautiful!"

"Yeah, see ya!" Smiling, she turned to go before he could see her own tears escape her.

However, when she cleared the front porch, seeing her tears as she walked out to get into her car, Alex asked, "Are you all right?"

"Yes," she fibbed, while forcing herself to look back at the house one last time, wishing things could have been different for the two of them.

Arriving back at the Inn, Jessi went straight into her office to get started on her mound of paperwork, when shortly after, came a knock at the door. "Come in!" she called out.

"Jessi…" Lisa called in, opening the door, "Doreen is here to see you!"

"Thanks, Lisa," she replied, while getting up to go over to the door. And even as tired as she was, she greeted Doreen with a warm smile, as Lisa returned to the front desk to wait on a new arrival. "What do you say we go out back for something cool to drink?"

"All right!" the woman dressed in a long dark skirt, tan-colored blouse, hanging out past her hips, tied with a rope-like belt and shawl, replied, while following Jessi out onto the front porch, where Jake was painting the porch swing.

"Jake," she spoke up, introducing him to her. "We're going out back to have something to drink. Would you join us, please?"

"Sure thing, Ms. Rae, I'll be there shortly," he grinned, tipping a finger to his temple, as the two women walked off the porch.

Arriving at a nice shady area, where Jessi found Annie sitting a pitcher of lemonade and two glasses on a table, she smiled, while going over to lend a hand. "Annie, how did you know?"

"I was just putting out some cool refreshments for the guests, when she walked in. Lisa said she was here to see you."

"Thanks. Oh, and Annie," she called out, as she was just about to turn away, "I'll need one more glass for Jake. He'll be joining us shortly."

"He'll probably have his own glass with him then," she returned pleasantly. "He was the first to pour himself a glass when I brought the cart out."

"All right, then," she returned, with a light laugh in her voice, before turning back to her guest. "Please, have a seat," she offered, while going about pouring them both a glass of lemonade, before taking a seat opposite of her. "Is everything all right?"

Taking her glass, she nodded her head, and then looked around, before saying anything. "Though I should ask, how have you and your handyman, 'Jake', been?"

Turning a light shade of red, she smiled, "I can't fool you, can I?"

"No, but it will work for awhile on your other guests."

"What can you tell me about them?"

"The one named Tony is the bad one. But then you know that. As for the other, Harry? He's full of regrets, and wants to stop, but Tony has threatened him. Be careful, Jessi, Tony hates Alex, and since the two of you have grown so close, he won't hesitate to go after you to get to him." She was saying, when Alex walked up to join them.

Leaning inwardly, Jessi asked, "Does he know that Alex is here?"

"Does who know I'm here?" he looked at the two of them, and asked suspiciously.

"He suspects it," Doreen replied, ignoring his superiority. Then, turning to him, she added, "Though he isn't aware of who you really are in your disguise, just yet!"

Seeing the expression on Jessi's face, he turned back to Doreen, after listening to what she had to say. "What's going on here?" he demanded, glaring down at her.

"Doreen, can I tell him?"

"Yes, he'll want to know this, and more."

"There's more...?"

"Oh... yes, a lot more. You must not try to change anything concerning Craig, and or David's fate. Craig must handle the score with these men on his own, and David must be there at the farmhouse, when the time comes. The two of you will be there, as well. And Mr. Storm," she was careful not to say his name too loud, "Tony wants your head," she warned, "no matter how he goes about getting it."

"Alex..." Jessi spoke up, sounding frightened, "Tony plans on going after you, even if it means hurting me to get to you."

"He won't get anywhere near you," he growled, putting a protective arm around her, to comfort her, "I'll see to that. Even if it means staying in your quarters, until this is all over," he went on to assure her, before turning back to the woman who knew more than she ought to. "Ms. Doreen, just who are you, and how do you know so much about this information?"

"Alex...!" Jessi attempted to cut him off.

"It's all right!" she replied, turning back to Alex. "Mr. Storm, people don't believe in what I am. However, you may decide otherwise, after telling you what I have to say."

"Why the hell is that?" he asked sarcastically, while taking the seat next to Jessi.

"Alex, please, hear her out first, before you're ready to judge her."

"All right!" he agreed, while looking to their visitor, skeptically, "just what could you possibly say that would convince me to believe otherwise?"

Doreen studied him for a moment, before going on. "Mr. Storm, I see that you have most recently experienced a spirit encounter, haven't you? With your nephew, Craig, I believe, so that he could be with the one he loves, even if only for a short time. And Jessi," she turned, looking deeply into her eyes, "you are about to go through some changes that will involve Craig, David, and even you, Alex," she turned back to study him once again. "Watch your health, Jessi," she warned, looking back at her, before getting up to leave.

"My health?" she questioned, as she and Alex stood to see her off.

"Yes."

Leaving them standing there alone with so much on their minds, Jessi finally spoke up, after seeing the last of their guest, "Alex...?"

"Yeah, right here," he offered her a shoulder to lean on, seeing how she much needed it.

"I'm really scared!"

"I know you are. And for what it's worth, so am I!" he exclaimed, while turning to hold her. "God, Jess, I'm sorry, too, that this has to be happening here at your Inn."

"Why?" she asked, looking back up at him thoughtfully. "I was already involved, before you got here."

"Yes, well," he began, while looking down into her tear-filled eyes. *Oh, God... I can't keep doing this,* he groaned, catching himself feeling vulnerable toward her, once again. "Jess," he pulled away, yet taking a hold of her hands instead, while wanting to avoid anymore possible temptations, "we had best be careful out here in the open. It's just not safe anymore with Tony lurking about."

"You're right," she agreed, while trying hard to smile, when looking down on his strong, well manicured fingernails. "I suppose I had better be getting back to my office. I have so much work yet to do, before turning in."

"Are you going to be all right?" he asked, when she began to pull away.

"Yes, sure!" she grinned, looking back to see his genuine concern for her written all over his handsome face.

"Jess," he called out, before she could get too far, "I have a few things yet to do. Afterwards, I'll be stopping in to speak with you later."

"All right."

Chapter Twenty

Later that evening, after talking with Ted about some of their new plans, Alex went down to see Jessi in her office, as he had said he would, to discuss what their plans were going to be. "Jess," he spoke up, closing the door behind him, before approaching her desk.

Stopping just short of it, he saw something he hadn't seen before at the base of her neck.

"Yes, Alex?" she asked, looking up from her pile of paperwork, when seeing his puzzled expression. "What is it, Alex?"

Coming around to take her hand, he pulled her up to examine the area just to the left of her neck. "Well, what do we have here?" he grinned mischievously, while running the back of two of his fingers down under her collar to touch the area.

Flinching at his touch, she pulled back with a hint of pain on her face. "Ouch… Alex, that hurts!"

"Yes, I imagine it would! Question is where did it come from? It wasn't there earlier this morning, back at Craig's place!"

"I don't know what you're…" She stopped quite suddenly and turned away, while recalling something Craig had told her, just before they left. *You'll see soon enough, he smiled.* Turning back to Alex, she looked surprised.

"Is there something you want to tell me?" he grinned.

"I don't know! What does it look like to you?"

Raising an eyebrow, he frowned.

"Alex…?"

"Have a look for yourself!" he continued to grin, while taking her over to a mirror hanging near the door.

Stopping, Jessi look at Alex first, then into the mirror. "What? I don't see anything!"

Coming around to stand behind her, he brought his hand up to slip her collar off to one side, while innocently pulling a button loose on her blouse in the process. "There," he smiled at the reddened area at the side of her neck, where earlier she recalled the searing pain Craig had brought to her.

"Oh... my... gosh...! He did do this!" she cried, blushing at the hickey left on her neck.

"You say Craig did this? When?" he asked puzzledly. "It wasn't there this morning."

"No. But it was this afternoon, before we left. I didn't know it at first. I mean after all, he's a spirit. How can a spirit do this?"

"Yes, and once again, I ask, how?"

"I can't answer that. We were just talking, and he bent down to see what would happen if he kissed me. Before I knew it, things started to happen!"

"I can only imagine!" he teased, thinking about his nephew.

"Yes, well, that, and then some," she laughed.

"What else?" he joined in on her laughter.

"Nothing, really! It was the way he felt when being so close to me..." She stopped, remembering the electricity she had felt when he kissed her.

"Well...?"

"It was all so tingly!" she smiled, before going on. "Alex, Craig doesn't have the abilities like we have. To feel, or smell, or even..."

"Taste?" he asked. "He can't taste you, is that it?"

"Yes, and he really hates that," she said sadly, while running her hands lightly over her breasts, thinking back to a dream he had planted in her mind the night before, after having cleaned a few rooms of the house. At that moment, she crossed her arms over her chest.

"What?" he asked caringly, sensing more.

Smiling, she looked up at him in the mirror. "It was in this dream I had the night before. He somehow created it in my mind. And in it, he was standing at the end of a beautiful trail, holding his hand out to me..." she drifted off.

"Jessi..." he said, coaxing her to go on, when she turned to look away. "What?"

"I could almost feel him, when we touched. And then..."

"You kissed?"

"Uh huh!"

"That had to be interesting!"

"Oh… it was! Though, it wasn't the same for him. He felt he had to have more. Not able to really feel me or…"

"Having his other senses?" he asked, while avoiding the 'T' word.

"Yes. It really hurts him, Alex!"

"I can imagine."

"But before that, in the shower…" She broke off suddenly, not having told him quite so much about the day before when she was suppose to have called him upon her arrival.

"Jessi…! What about the shower?" he asked, when raising a suspecting eyebrow.

"After I first got there, I did some cleaning around the place. Going out back to wash off,

I found…"

"The man-made shower?"

"Yes."

"What happened?"

"Nothing at first, but then we both found ourselves thinking the same thing, only I was alone. He was up in the back bedroom, looking out over the yard."

"Seeing you down in the shower must have triggered some memories!"

"He told me about Abigail, and how she had died."

"You said though, the two of you were thinking the same thing. About your first love?"

"No…" she laughed, "though that would have been much safer!"

"Oh… then… what?" He toyed around a little, while seeing her blush.

"We were thinking…"

"Well…?"

"Alex…! Okay! We were thinking about making love. But I had no idea why, or even how it had gotten started. It just happened! I felt as though he were really there, in the shower with me, that is. Lord, it felt so…"

"Good…?" he grinned, humorously.

"Oh… more on the lines of…"

"Fantastic?" He laughed at seeing her expression.

"Yes, a lot like last night!"

"Are we back to that again?" he groaned playfully.

"Oh, Alex…!"

"What…?"

"Last night, when he, you…"

"Craig," he smiled thoughtfully.

"When he was making love to me, I felt a tingling sensation on my…"

"Nipples?" he smiled.

"Yes, Alex. On my… nipples."

"Oh, yeah? Well we are breast men, Craig and I! It's only natural that he went for yours!"

"Oh…?"

"Well, face it, you have some pretty great looking ones there!" he grinned, looking down at them then.

"I'll keep that in mind!" she laughed. "Alex," she turned, "you really need a girlfriend. You know that?"

"Yeah, well," he groaned, turning her around to face him, "I'd rather not get into that subject," he replied, while fastening the button that had come loose.

Doing so caused her nipples to harden at the mere nearness of his hands.

Stopping to admire them, she cleared her throat.

"Mmmm… they do have a way of easily perking up, don't they?" he teased.

"Yes, and especially when your nephew's around."

"He's one lucky guy, Jess."

"Yes. I just wish…"

"What?"

Turning away to hide her sadness, once again, he turned her back to face him.

"We can't…"

"Can't what?" he asked puzzledly.

"Well, when we kiss, there isn't the same sensation, as what he can do to the rest of me. There's no…"

"Tingling?"

"No. There's no intensity like what..."

"We shared?" he laughed.

"Both you and Craig, the other night. It was so warm and filled with so... much..."

"Passion?"

"Am I being awful for feeling that way?"

"No."

"I really miss that in my life."

"Yeah, me too."

Turning, Alex headed for the door to leave.

"Hey... just why did you come in here?"

"Oh, damn... it was to tell you about a plan we came up with. What do you say we meet down in your quarters to go over them?"

"Sure! Just let me tell Annie to have our supper brought down there."

"All right, I'll get Ted and head on down."

After seeing to their supper arrangements, Jessi grabbed her two friends, while leaving Lisa to watch the front desk. "We shouldn't be too long. Ted will fill you in when he gets back."

"All right."

Turning then, they headed down to her quarters.

"Mom?" Lora spoke up, when Jessi walked in.

"Yes?" she asked, while taking a seat.

"What are we going to do?"

"We're going to act as though nothing has changed!" she exclaimed, while looking calmly from her daughter to Alex, and then to Ted.

"That's a good idea!" Ted agreed. "Those two men have been quiet so far."

"But in case they decide otherwise, I have called in for more help," Alex added, while standing near the French doors.

"Oh?" Jessi returned with a raised eyebrow.

Knowing better than to cross her after their first encounter, he smiled, "If that's all right with you. I thought perhaps you could use the extra help in the Boutique and kitchen?"

"Ashley? Renee?" she turned to her friends first for their thoughts on the matter.

"That sounds fine with me!" Ashley agreed.

"All right, Alex, bring them in! I'll fix up the extra rooms in the attic for them."

"No, I'd rather you didn't. I'll work on the attic, myself."

"You sure you want to do that?" she asked.

"Yes." he smiled.

"All right, I'll take you up later to show you around."

Nodding his head, he turned to the others, "Are we all settled on this then?"

"Yes," Lora laughed, when Annie arrived with an armload of food. "Now let's eat," she continued, when surprising her mother, as it was usually Cassi who was always hungry.

But then her bubble burst, as Cassi cried out, letting them know she was hungry too!

At that time, everyone had gotten up to give Annie a hand.

"When will this help be coming?" Jessi asked, while breaking the silence, before being seated around the table.

"Sometime tomorrow," Alex replied.

"That doesn't give us much time then, does it?"

"Just how bad is it?" he asked.

"Not too bad! Mostly some cleaning and a few repairs! There's already some furniture up there. So they should be all right for now!"

"Good, and no one is to know that the new help are police officers. Is that understood?"

"Sure, but what do we do with them when they get here?" Ashley asked.

"The same as you would have anyone do. Make up a schedule, but keep it light so they can be ready to move if they have to!"

"Man…" Renee spoke up, "all this sounds so dangerous!"

"Well," Ted looked over at his friend.

"We hope that it doesn't get that way," Alex returned, while looking to Jessi and her two daughters. "In the meantime, we'll do our best to keep the situation safe for everyone here."

"I hope you can!" Jessi put in worriedly.

Chapter Twenty-One

After dinner, Ashley and Renee went on home, while Alex and Ted went up to Jessi's office to iron out a few last-minute details.

Meanwhile, getting ready to go out to do her nightly meditation, Jessi headed for her patio doors. "Cassi, in case Alex wants to know where I am, tell him I went out to meditate."

"Okay, Mom," she replied, getting ready for bed.

"Mom...!" Lora called out from the hallway, sounding worried. "Take Max with you!"

"Well, Max, what do you say?"

"Rrrr...uff," he returned with a soft bark and a wag of his tail.

"Okay, boy, let's go."

Preoccupied with so much thought of all that had been going on around her, walking around under the moonlit sky, Jessi wasn't aware of someone watching her from behind a large group of bushes, off near the family room side of the Inn.

"Mmmm... Max, it's such a beautiful night out!" she whispered softly, while reaching over to pet her dog, as a breeze caught her long, flowing, brown hair, to blow it back away from her face, as she went out farther into the backyard to meditate a little while longer.

Meanwhile inside, Alex was just about to wrap up things with Ted, when he headed for the door. "Well, I'm out of here," he grinned.

"To see if Jessi is ready to go up to show you the attic?"

"Yeah."

"All right, just let me know when you're ready for me to stand guard."

"Sure thing."

Leaving the office, Alex suddenly stopped, when having a bad feeling something was about to go wrong. Looking out to see that Tony's car was still there, the feeling hung over him like a wet cloth.

"Hey," Ted spoke up, while coming out of the office, behind him, "what's wrong?" he asked, seeing his old partner's expression.

"I don't know!" he exclaimed, looking up toward Tony's room, and then down the short hall toward Jessi's quarters. "Something just doesn't feel right." Turning back to his friend, he held out a cautious hand. "Stay ready, I may be calling on you."

"You got it."

Heading quickly to Jessi's quarters, Alex found the living room empty, and right away went straight for her room.

"Jessi…?" he called out, while knocking at her door. "Jessi?" Not getting an answer, he thought quickly to himself, *Okay, where could she be?* he asked, looking across the hall at the open bathroom door. "Lora…?" he then called out.

"Yeah…?" she answered sleepily, while coming out to see what he wanted.

"Your mother, where is she?"

"She went out to meditate like she always does about this time of the night!"

"Damn it," he growled, heading back into the living room.

"Alex…" she called out stopping him, "she has Max with her."

"All right." Still not feeling all that comfortable about it, he headed for the patio doors, anyway.

Meanwhile, out in the semi-darkened yard, just about the time her mystery man was getting ready to make his move, Alex walked out to join her. "Ms. Rae…?" he called out, using his alias' accent, from the backside of the Inn, while trying to focus his eyes on the dimly lit yard. "Ma'am…?"

Before she could answer, Max picked up on a strange scent, and right away began to grow. Hearing this, Alex spotted her right away with her dog, and ran out, while pulling out his service revolver. "What is it, boy?" he asked, approaching them. "Do you hear something?" he asked, while focusing on the same set of bushes Max was growling at.

Not altering his position any, Max continued to grow, as the hair on the back of his neck stood out.

"Jessi, how about you?" he whispered just audible enough for her to hear him.

"No, not a thing, but Max must have!"

"All right," he replied, while continuing to stay focused on the bushes, while reaching inside his padded vest for his two-way radio, "Ted," he called out in a low, yet audible voice only he, Jessi and Ted could hear.

"Yes?"

"I need you, buddy! Get out here. But be careful when using the north side of the Inn. Our visitor is on that side, behind some bushes, not far from the family room doors."

"On my way."

Turning back to Jessi, Alex ordered her to stay in the gazebo for cover. "But stay low, while I go to check it out. Will you be all right doing that?"

"Yes, I think so!"

"All right, then. You ready, Max?" he asked, seeing that she had gotten to the shelter all right, before heading out on foot to check out the situation.

"Alex..." Jessi called out in a whisper, before he got very far, "be careful!"

"I will," he called back, following after her dog.

Leaving her there all alone, in the growing darkness, as the moon went in behind some clouds, she began to feel scared. For whoever it was had made their getaway, while dropping something, when they took off, upon hearing Alex and Max coming up.

Meanwhile, it wasn't very much longer when he returned, empty-handed, that Jessi called out, not thinking to use his alias, while sounding frightened, "A...Alex..." she cried, hearing someone approaching the gazebo. But then hearing the panting of her dog, she let out a sigh of relief.

"Right here," he called back, coming up to check on her. "Are you all right?" he asked, while pulling her into his embrace.

"I am now!" she returned, feeling the warmth of his arms encompassing around her, just before pulling away. "Alex, I think whoever it was dropped something in the bushes, when they ran off, hearing you coming!"

"Damn...!" he groaned, when turning back to the bushes, just as he heard someone coming up on foot. "Ted, is that you?"

"Yes. Is she all right?" he asked, running up to join them.

"Yes, she's fine. Did you see anyone?"

"No, not a soul. But that's not to say I didn't hear them, when I got to that side of the Inn," he replied, while looking around. "I heard what I thought to be footsteps, running out away from the place, I went out, just as you were coming up."

"Jessi may have heard whoever it was drop something over around the bushes. Stay with her, in case they circle around."

"Are you going back over around the bushes to find whatever it was they dropped?"

"Yes."

"You've got it," he returned, while keeping his own service revolver handy.

Stopping, Alex turned back to her dog, "Max, protect her," he commanded, just before running off.

"Rrrr...uff!" he returned, circling around her legs to take a protective seat.

Dropping to her knees, she hugged her dog.

"We'll catch him," Ted offered, sensing her fears.

"Will you?" She kept the rest of the thought to herself, while waiting for Alex's return.

Once again, the wait didn't take long, when he came back with something in his hand.

"What was it?" Jessi and Ted both asked.

"His gun!" he announced, turning to his friend, "I want this sent to forensics for fingerprints, and then have it cross-matched with the bullet they took from Craig. I have to know if it's the same gun."

"No problem," he replied, placing the thirty-five magnum into an evidence bag he had brought with him. "Alex?"

"Yeah?"

"You don't think it was Tony, do you?"

"My guess," he looked to Jessi, thinking back to something Doreen had said, "yes."

"Alex…" she cried, covering her mouth.

Going down on bent knees, he placed his arms around her, to hold her close.

"Alex," Ted spoke up once again, having a bad feeling, "if it was…"

"My cover may have been blown?"

"No…!" Jessi spoke up.

"What?" the two asked closely.

"You weren't using your normal voice when you came out! Max and I both heard you sounding like Jake at the time."

"You're right! But just the same, let's just hope he didn't hear me talking to Ted over the radio then, either."

"Yeah, I hear you. So what now?" Ted asked.

"Take it a day at a time. But just in case it wasn't blown, let's be a little more cautious."

"Yeah, right," he agreed, when turning to head back up to the Inn, to call and have the gun picked up.

"Well, now," Alex turned to take Jessi's hand to head back toward her quarters, "let's get you back inside."

"No, wait…!" she called out after taking a few steps off the gazebo to pull away. "I'm sorry, but I came out here to pray, and I really need to speak to God now, for all of us here and away, if you know what I mean."

"Fine, but I'm not going far," he replied, letting go of her hand to walk off a little ways toward the Inn to give her some privacy.

"Thanks, I won't be long."

Turning away herself, she crossed her arms securely around her waist as she looked up into the heavens.

Meanwhile, looking back over his shoulders, he watched, as she went on praying in a very soft whispery-like voice, one such as an angel would sound like. *Oh, Lord,* he too prayed, while hearing bits and pieces of her own, *what is it about her?* he asked, totally blown away by her dedication to their heavenly Father, and yet, at the same time, the love that poured from within her for his nephew was so rich and powerful. *Where does that kind of love come from?* he asked, looking heavenward.

After having finished with her meditation, the two walked back into the Inn together.

"Are you sure you're all right?" he asked, turning to her just inside the living room doorway, once they were closed and secured for the night.

"Yes," she replied more calmly now, as she headed for her small galley kitchen.

"Good...!" he nearly yelled, taking her by the arm to turn her around sharply to face him. "Then would you mind telling me just what the hell you think you were doing out there alone, and why I wasn't told first?"

"For crying out loud, I had Max with me," she screamed back, while jerking away at the same time.

"Darn it, Jessi, he's a great dog, but he isn't going to keep you from getting shot. So just when are you going to start listening to me?"

"Well, for your information, I didn't get shot. So take it easy."

"I will when all this is over. Until then, don't go out anymore by yourself, unless you tell me first!" he glared.

"All right! Fine! You made your point!" she cried, rubbing her arm from where he had a hold of it. "Now can we just go to bed? It's late and I have work to do in the morning."

"The couch?" he asked, unable to resist the sudden irony of her comment.

"Yes, Alex, the couch," she glared back, before going to get him a pillow and blanket.

Afterward, returning to her room, she closed the door behind her in order to get ready for bed.

"Jessi?"

She heard his voice just then from the other side of her door.

"Alex... goodnight!"

"Very well, goodnight!"

With her head leaning back against it, she stood for a moment, before going on to get changed. Afterwards, she quietly slipped out to check on her girls.

"Mom?" Lora sat up in bed, when she heard her mother walk in.

"Yes?"

"Is Alex staying down here, with us, tonight?"

"Yes, and from the looks of it, he'll be down here for quite awhile."

"I'm glad," she replied, sounding a little frightened.

"Lora, everything is going to be fine, you'll see. Now get some sleep, tomorrow is going to be a long day."

"All right."

Turning to leave, she looked back once again, while feeling bad for what her girls were having to go through.

"Lora?"

"Yeah?"

"I'm sorry."

"For what?"

"For all you two are going through."

"Mom, Alex and his friend are going to protect us. We'll be all right!"

"Sure we will," she smiled, feeling proud of her daughter now for being so brave. "Now, get some sleep. I'll see you in the morning."

Chapter Twenty-Two

The next day, as Jessi had said it would be, was just that, busy. Showing Alex the attic, he pointed back at the right hand corner, and asked, "What's down there?"

"The bathroom?"

"Uh huh…" he thought, while going into the room to the left of the staircase.

"What is it, Alex?"

"This wall!" he pointed out, looking at the back of the room. "Why is it so shallow compared to the other room, across the hall? It looks like there should be another room up here."

"There may have been once, but…"

"But…?" he asked, seeing something in her expression that worried him.

"Well, it's hard to explain!"

"Try me."

"At times when I'm up here alone, I get a feeling of sadness in certain areas of the attic!"

"Like where?" he asked, when she turned to walk back out into the hallway.

"There," she pointed at the back section of the attic, when he walked out to join her.

Checking it out, he went back to stand in between the bathroom doorway on the right and a blank wall on the left. Shaking his head, he turned to go on into the bathroom, where he found an old claw-foot tub, an old sink, and a toilet. "Do you know if these work?" he asked, going over to the sink first.

"I'm pretty sure they do, but they probably need to be run for a few minutes to get all the air and rust out of the lines."

Doing just that, he started by turning the cold-water faucet on the sink first, and then the tub. At that, with all its moaning and groaning, the pipes let out their rebellious sounds of coughing and sputtering, before allowing the water to run clear.

Turning them off, he moved over to see about the old fashioned toilet, with its free-standing tank. "Well now, how about you?" he grinned, giving the old white porcelain a gentle tug, while using the chain on the right side of the tank.

With a steady flow of its water, the old girl seemed quite happy to be working again.

"Did you hear that?" he asked, turning to Jessi. "She said thank you!"

"Yeah, right...!" she smiled, while shaking her head, as they turned to head back out into the hallway.

Stopping once again, he looked directly at a wall in front of him. "This must have been where there was an extra room at one time," he commented, while looking over the area from ceiling to floor.

Not getting an answer, he looked back to see Jessi's face go pale. "What is it?"

Suddenly, picking up on the most overwhelming feeling she had ever known possible, tears began streaming down her cheeks. "A... Alex...!" she cried, heading toward the stairway.

"What is it? What do you see?" he asked, feeling as though he should be doing the same, while going right over to stand by her side.

Looking back at that same moment, he had to wonder if he might have missed something she may have seen.

Closing her eyes, she turned away. "It wasn't of this time!" she whispered eerily.

"What?" he asked, turning her to face him.

Pulling free of his hold, she hurried down the stairs with him hot on her heels, only to be met up by Ted, who had just arrived outside the attic doorway.

Seeing the expressions on their faces, he asked hastily, "What is it?"

"No time to explain. Just lock it up, and meet us down in her office, as quick as you can!" he ordered, tossing back the keys.

"Sure, but…" he called back, just as they reached the other set of stairs to continue on down to her office.

Shaking his head, Ted turned back to look up at the hall overhead, wondering what that was about. "Okay, Alex, what has gotten into you?" he grumbled, while closing the door to lock it, before heading back down to see what was going on.

Meanwhile, arriving safely in her office, Alex closed the door behind them. "All right, now that we have gotten clear of the attic, what the heck just happened up there?" he asked, while going over to take a seat across from her, as she sat huddled on the sofa.

"I don't know…! But I know this much, these gifts I have are really starting to scare the b'jesus out of me."

"You saw another spirit up there, didn't you?"

Shivering, she shook her head, "It was more like a ghost of a spirit. As if saddened by the great loss of a loved one, but so many years ago."

"So much for the attic, then!" he grumbled, looking down on his partially folded hands.

"No."

"What? But, I thought…"

"No! As I said, it was so long ago. And it had only scared me to see it for the first time, is all! She…"

"She? Our ghost is a she?"

"Yes, she."

"All right, so what you're saying is the rooms can still be gone over and made usable?"

"Yes. As for the likelihood of someone else seeing this isn't so likely."

"Okay…!" He pondered the thought for a moment, when there came a knock at the door.

Going over to answer it, to his relief he saw it was only Ted. "Good, come on in!"

"Sure. Now will someone tell me what the heck that was about?" he asked, turning back to Alex, once inside.

"First, how would you like to give me a hand?"

"Doing what?"

"Fixing up a couple of rooms," he laughed, seeing the look come over his friend's face.

"The attic?" he asked puzzledly. "After the way you two had just left there…! For crying out loud, if I were a betting man, I would say something or someone had been chasing you down the stairs…!"

"Yeah, well, I can't go into it now, but yes, the attic."

"Yeah, but…"

"Sorry, pal, but I really can't explain just yet. I do, however, have to get those two rooms up there ready, and quick, for our two undercover officers, who will be arriving later today. So Can I get your help?"

"O…kay…! But that doesn't give us much time!"

"No, it doesn't."

"Well, in that case, will we be needing anything to supply these two rooms with?"

"No," Jessi explained, looking up at them. "The rooms are both supplied with everything imaginable, including antique hair brushes, combs and hand mirrors to go with the other antiques left behind by the original owner. Not to mention, everything my cousin brought over in the way of antiques to give the place a sense of belonging!"

"Great," Ted commented, when turning to the door, "I'll just go up and get changed, and be back down to help get what all we'll be needing to get started."

"Sounds good," Alex returned, looking back to Jessi, once Ted made his departure. At that moment, he let loose of his laughter, "So much for just seeing my nephew!"

"Yeah, and speaking of nephew," she smiled thoughtfully, "you don't have any more out there, do you?"

"Not like Craig, you mean?"

"No, but I guess that means you do, huh?"

"Yes, and he wanted to be a part of this investigation, but…"

"Apart?" She looked confused.

"He's my new partner. His name is Jarred Stanton. Lieutenant Jarred Stanton, my other sister's boy."

"Why wouldn't you let him help you?"

"Because, losing one nephew was enough. Besides, we were wrapping up another case, when some new information came up on this one."

"Oh, I see!"

"Well," he turned to leave, "I had best be getting started, before they get here."

"Alex…" she called out, stopping him. "These two officers, what are they like?"

"Beth," he started on first, thinking of her fondly, "she's a terrific girl. You'll fall in love with her, when you see her."

"Oh?"

"Yes. And as for her, I want her back in the kitchen, working with Annie. And Terri," his face grew angry, "put her up front in the Boutique. She's pretty tough, and can handle anything."

"Huh, including you?" she wondered, by the look on his face.

"Jess…" he started, when sensing what was on her mind, "she isn't…" He stopped abruptly, when feeling his temper getting the better of him.

"Alex, I…"

"Listen, if I don't get started…"

"Yes. Go, and have fun," she said, turning her sense of concern into one of humor.

After seeing him off, she went over to see her two friends, before getting back to work.

Hours later, the two undercover officers arrived.

"Hi, we're here to see Ms. Rae!" the tall blonde, looking to be in her mid-forties, spoke up first, while announcing themselves to Lisa, while the shorter, more wholesome-looking girl, in her late twenties, with strawberry blonde hair, and baby blue eyes, stood back from the reservation desk to have a look around.

"Who shall I say is asking?" Lisa asked guardedly.

"It's about the job," the other spoke up sweetly.

"Okay…!" she replied, liking that one right away, when turning to knock on Jessi's door.

Hearing the knock, Jessi got up to answer it, "Yes?"

"There are two ladies here to see you?" Lisa questioned.

"Oh, gosh, yes. Ted must have forgotten to fill you in!"

"Well, slightly!" she teased, while going back to wait on a couple, who were getting ready to check out.

"Sorry!" Jessi smiled, before turning to Alex's female officers. "Ladies, please, come in. I'm Jessi Rae, the owner of this Inn," she explained, while closing the door behind her, before returning to her desk.

"Thank you," the tall blonde returned, while going over to take a seat near the desk, as the other did the same. "Captain Storm sent for us."

"Yes, I know. Now, which one of you is Terri and which is Beth?"

"I'm Terry, and this," she pointed, coldly, "is Beth."

Noticing now what Alex was trying so hard not to say about this particular woman with dark blonde hair and a cocky attitude, gave Jessi a bad feeling. As for Beth, a more simpler, yet sweeter person was just like he had described, was the kind of girl anyone would love to have around.

Starting with Beth, she asked, "How do you feel about working in the kitchen? Nothing too heavy or too dirty, that is. He wants you at the back of the Inn. And as for you, Terri," she turned to look at the blonde, "you're to be in the Boutique, where you're best suited to watch the front end of the Inn."

"That sounds fine!" Beth replied, happily. "Will he be here, as well?"

"Yes, but you won't be referring to him by his name. He's known here as Jake Green, our groundskeeper."

"Yes, of course, we were told about that, before coming out," Beth replied, smiling.

"I figured as much," she smiled back, before turning to see the smug look on Terri's face, as the woman began to gloat. "Is there something you care to share with us?"

"Oh, just that that sounds like the perfect job for him," she replied even more smugly.

Not liking her remark, Jessi looked at Terri, feeling a sense of hostility toward her. "Ms..." she started up heatedly.

"Shaw," Terri spoke up, looking all so proud to be working alongside him.

"Have you known him long?"

"Oh... yes...!"

Getting up from her seat, Jessi walked out around from behind her desk. "Ladies, let me make one thing perfectly clear. You are here to do your job, and nothing else. This..." she stopped to glare down at Terri, "means no messing around with the help, Police Officer, Detective, or otherwise. Is that clear?" she asked, while continuing to glare at her.

"Yes, ma'am!" Terri returned, while looking back up at her sarcastically.

"Ms. Shaw, I mean what I say. I will not have it here at my Inn. And if you so much as try it, I'll have you out of here, before you know what hit you." At that, she walked over and opened the door. "Shall we meet the others now?"

Getting up to walk out, passing Jessi in the doorway, Terri turned and glared back at her.

"Ms. Shaw, let me give you a little warning, I am not one to be reckoned with."

'Oh, we'll just have to see about that,' Terri gloated, while following along over to the Boutique.

"Oh, but we will," Jessi picked up on her attitude, while arriving at the Boutique, where she called out to her friends, while trying hard to force a smile on her face, "Hi, ladies! I have someone here who would love to learn about the shop."

"Great!" Ashley returned, while pouring Jessi a cup of her usual. "How about the two of you, coffee, tea, or cappuccino?"

"Ahhh… cappuccino sounds heavenly!" Terri exclaimed, while sitting down at the table where Renee indicated.

Meanwhile, seeing right through her friends' artificial smile, Ashley walked over to speak to her more privately, "Girl, I can see from the way you walked in here that you don't like this particular one. Heck, I can see why, just looking at her!"

"You noticed it too, did you?" she asked, sounding surprised to hear her friends' assumption so early.

"How could we not?" Renee asked quietly, while coming up to join them at the coffee bar, while leaving the other two to wait.

"I don't understand! How did you two…" Jessi began.

"Jess," Ashley cut in to explain, when seeing the look of confusion on her friend's face, "we heard her in the foyer, when they first arrived."

"Not to mention," Renee added, "Lisa came over to tell us about the speech she overheard you telling them, about education in the work place! So, of course, we had to check it out for ourselves!"

"Well, you probably think I'm crazy, but I don't like her."

"That's quite obvious! Now, the question is, what are you going to do about it?" Ashley asked, looking back over their shoulder at the smug-faced woman, waiting on her cappuccino.

"Keep her busy," she replied, while pouring only Beth's tea, as she had asked for in her quiet little voice.

"Sure, I can do that!" Ashley smiled, while handling Terri's drink to her, herself.

"Good," Jessi returned, while walking over to give Beth hers, before taking a seat to talk over their agenda.

After a short visit, Jessi got up to show Beth where she would be working.

"Ms. Rae, Alex said that I would really like working with you. And a part of me wanted to say something earlier, but I thought not."

"Because of Ms. Shaw?"

"Yes," she replied sadly, when reaching the kitchen door. Stopping, she looked up at her unofficial new, boss.

"What is it, Beth?" she asked, seeing the girl's expression change.

"Terri," she began. "I'm sorry about the way she spoke to you. She can be a…"

"Bitch?" Jessi asked, smiling. "I know."

"Yes, well," she blushed timidly, "Ted said that Alex didn't ask for us, and especially for Terri. They, or I should say, he hasn't cared for her for some time now."

"Oh…? And you, how do you feel about him?"

"A…Alex? He…he's my superior officer!" she stammered quietly. "We're not permitted to get involved with each other!"

"Oh?" Sensing something in her manner, Jessi wondered what it was, but chose not to ask at that time. Instead, she changed the subject, "Well, Beth, as for Annie, you will love her, as she is really sweet and motherly. It'll even be like working in your own kitchen at home!"

"Really?" she asked, with a gleam in her eye.

"Yes. Yes, indeed," she laughed, while walking on into the kitchen. "Annie…" she called out, closing the door behind them, "this is Beth. She'll be helping you for a while. I had also told her just how mothering you are."

"Oh… Ms. Jessi," Annie blushed.

"Well, it's true! And now if you'll excuse me, I'll go and find Jake to see if your quarters are ready yet."

"Ms. Rae!" Beth spoke up, stopping her at the door. "Thanks!"

With a warm smile, Jessi gave the girl a hug. "Alex said you were really sweet. He was right. You'll do just fine here."

With that, she said her goodbyes and left them to go up to the attic.

Chapter Twenty-Three

She walked into one of the two front rooms to see him working hard without his shirt. Sweat was rolling off his glistening back.

Clearing her throat, she asked, "How are things going up here?"

"It's just about finished!" he exclaimed, when turning to look up at her from across the room. Seeing that all too familiar look on her face, he knew something was weighing heavily on her mind. "Have the two new ladies arrived?" he asked, sitting back on his booted heel.

"Yes, and you were right about Beth, she's great for the job."

"Uh, oh…!" He somehow sensed trouble in her tone, as it changed right away.

"Alex…?"

"Jess, if it's about Terri, she would like to think we still have something going on, but there isn't. She's not my type."

"Oh… and just what is your type?" she asked nervously, knowing what his answer was.

Turning to look directly at her now, the expression in his eyes caused a sharp pain to her heart. "Do you even have to ask?" he groaned, while tossing the hammer off to one side, before grabbing up a rag to wipe away the beads of sweat from his forehead.

"No! But are you sure that she would be good at her job?"

"She's the best. I'll talk to her about her actions later."

"Well…!"

"Jessi…!"

"Alex," she grumbled, "okay, so, yes, I already told her that she is to keep her personal life out of here."

With a humorous laugh, he grinned at the mere thought of Jessi putting Terri in her place. "Yeah, well, I'm sure she really liked that!"

"Alex…" she interrupted his private little joke, as she went to walk over to the window, at the side, to look out, "I don't like someone coming here under false pretenses."

"No, I guess not, but really, Jessi, what is it?" he asked, going over to put his arms around her waist from behind. "What's really got you so on edge?"

Leaning her head back against his hot, sweaty chest, she simply added with a worried look on her face, when she turned in his arms to look up at him, "I'm just worried, is all. I need to know that she is going to be professional about her job."

"Jess…" he breathed in her sweet-smelling perfume, as he went to pull her up into his arms, only to comfort her, when their eyes locked.

Just then, their peaceful moment came to a crashing halt, when Terri and Ashley walked in on them.

"Well, excuse… the interruption!" Terri beamed heatedly at the two.

"Damn it, Terri… what the hell are you doing up here?"

"Well, obviously not what you're doing."

"Meaning…?" He glared at her, as if wanting to kill her where she stood.

"You heard me."

"That's what I thought, damn you, anyway. Now, before I have you reassigned to another case, clean up your attitude, now, before I change my mind."

"You wouldn't dare!" she glared back heatedly. "You know that I'm the best there is."

"That may be true," Jessi interrupted, while still in Alex's arms, " but you have exactly three seconds to change your way of thinking, or I will have your butt escorted off my property, as you were warned earlier," she glared right back at her.

"You can't do that. Alex is my boss, not you."

"Sergeant Shaw," Ted spoke up authortively speaking, as he made his grand entrance into the room, after hearing all the commotion from down the short hallway, while working on the bathroom, "that didn't sound anything like police business to me. It sounded more like a jealous female, and I, as your other superior officer, don't like the way you sounded just now. Now," he continued, eating it up, while seeing Alex's heated glare, "do I have you escorted out of here myself, or do you change your attitude? Oh, and yes, you will take orders from Ms. Rae, or get the hell out of her Inn," he ordered.

Fuming, Terri turned back to Alex, "You haven't heard the last of me yet. I'm darn good at what I do, and you damn well know it, too."

"Shaw…" he growled back heatedly. "Leave it alone! It's over between us, you got it?"

"No, it ain't over, not by a long shot."

"It is as long as you're both here in my Inn," Jessi glared at the two of them. "Whatever you've had with him, you will not start it up again here. Do I make myself clear?"

"Very," she replied, staring holes right through her, before turning back to glare at him.

"Oh, and if you're wondering, your room is across the hall," Jessi informed her, seeing that this room was the prettiest of the two, and no doubt, was perfectly suited for Beth.

"Fine," she growled, as Jessi turned on her heels to leave the three to go back downstairs with Ashley at her side.

On their way, Ashley asked, "You really don't like her, do you?"

"Is it that obvious?" she asked angrily, while turning to her friend, when they reached the main floor. "And, no," she lowered her voice, cautiously, in case Tony or Harry were around to hear them, "there isn't anything going on between Alex and I."

"Then what was that I saw upstairs?" she asked, pointedly.

"I was upset!" she exclaimed, while walking on back into the Boutique.

"Are you sure that's all there was to it? Jess, I've seen the way he looks at you. That man up there is in love with you, girl!"

"Ash…" She stopped at the coffee bar, to turn back to her friend, "darn it anyway, I know he is, but…" She broke off suddenly, unable to take any more of what was going on around her. "I can't do this." She threw up her hands, and headed for the door. "If you will excuse me, I have a lot of work to do in my office."

"Jessi…!"

With the next few weeks going by quietly, Jessi kept herself busy in her office, meeting only with her friends and spending time with her girls. And when she wasn't doing that, in the quiet seclusion of both her room and out, she carried on back and forth with Craig, when things had gotten a little hairy, and even when they weren't. Still they longed to be together, and on those occasions Alex would slip off with her from time to time to play the all-so-willing middleman, or just simply see to it that her visits were safe, before returning to the Inn to take care of bigger matters.

Then, one bright and beautiful June afternoon, Rose and Sue dropped by to see her and the Inn.

"How have you been feeling?" Rose asked, going into her office to give her a warm hug.

"I've had better days," she replied, shaking her head.

"Well, just try to take it easy and let some of the others help out once in awhile."

"That's what they've been doing lately. Besides, it isn't so much the Inn that has me rattled, it's that…that…" Jessi was about to say, when she looked up in time to see Terri come walking out of the Boutique. "What the heck…?" she groaned, while walking over to the front window to see the blonde going over to get chummy with Alex.

"What is it?" Sue asked, going over with Rose to have a look. "Lord, Rose, isn't that…"

"Yes, it is."

Fuming over what she was seeing, Jessi turned on her heels to head out of her office for the Boutique. "Ladies, if you'll please excuse me. She's been warned not to do this here at my Inn. And now I have had it with her!"

"Oh, no," Sue groaned, "I have a feeling we're about to see an epic battle between those two."

"You're right. We had better see what we can do to stop it, before anything happens."

Arriving just inside the Boutique, Jessi snapped at her friend, "Ashley, just what is she doing out there?"

"She never said! She just walked out!"

"Well, we'll just have to see about that," she hissed, heading for the front porch, where Terri was still cozying up next to Alex.

"Jessi, no!" Sue called out, stopping her in the foyer. "She isn't worth it. Just let my brother take care of her, himself!"

"How? She is nothing but a tramp, and has been ever since she got here!"

"Well, she is that!" Rose agreed, knowing more than she was letting on.

"What...?" Jessi turned back, hearing what she said. "What do you mean by that?"

"Just that!"

"Rose, out with it. I have no time for games here," she lowered her voice at seeing a few guests coming down for coffee.

Taking Jessi back into the Boutique, the three of them went over to join the others, before delving into Terri's past, while being sure to keep their voices down.

By the time the story was nearing the end, Jessi and the others were horrified.

"He what?" she asked.

"I'm sorry!" Rose exclaimed. "It all happened pretty much around the time of Alex and Beth's breakup! You see, he and Beth were getting really close after her Rookie training."

"That in itself is a whole other story," Sue laughed.

"But this one. What happened?" Jessi asked.

"Rumors have it, that Terri had it bad for my brother. And seeing him growing closer and closer to Beth, well," Sue shook her head miserably, "Terri wouldn't have it, and turned them in. Not long afterwards, he went out to see Craig, and well..." The pain at that moment was simply too much for her to go on, when she broke off, fighting back the tears of her son's death.

"Sue...?"

"Jessi... that was when..." Rose too was finding it hard to say the words. "Oh, Lord, honey... that was when he found him... dead! Craig had been killed sometime earlier that day.

The two had plans to work on..."

"Craig's truck?" she finished, knowing he had been having trouble with it.

"Yes, and the pain of losing both Beth to the departmental rules, and then Craig," Rose went on, "well, it was simply just too much for him to handle."

"And Alex's relationship with Terri?" she asked, "Didn't he know she was the one who turned him in?"

"We're not sure on that," Sue spoke up. "From what we heard, he lost it one day, while investigating Craig's death. He was even up for suspension if he didn't pull it together, and fast."

"Which brings us to what we were just telling you. We think Alex had turned to Terri, while he was staying out at Craig's place," Rose put in shamefully.

"How did she know he would be there?"

"She had been watching and waiting to catch him at his lowest moment, and knew she would find him there. And since he wouldn't allow anyone else to handle the investigation leading into Craig's death, well....!"

"Not even his new partner?" she asked knowingly.

"No," Sue offered, sadly, "he didn't want the same thing to happen to Jarred. In fact, he had even submitted a letter of recommendation to get him taken off the force after it happened."

"And then…" Ashley chimed in.

"Terri, she took full advantage of the situation," Sue explained, shaking her head.

"And after that, we would see them out there together from time to time," Rose went on.

"Yes, but Alex told me he had nothing to do with asking her to come out there," Sue offered firmly. "That was his and Beth's place to go, once in awhile, to visit with Craig."

"Beth knew Craig?" Jessi asked wonderingly.

"Not that way. She was all Alex's girl," Sue smiled.

"Until Terri butted in," Rose ended.

Turning now to see how Terri was running her hands over Alex's chest, while reaching up to try and kiss him, the look on his face was serious, and yet, not seeing Jessi, now standing in the Boutique window, he wasn't able to prevent her from lashing out at them.

"That does it!" she nearly yelled, going out to the reservation desk to grab the phone. "Since he won't get her out of here, I will."

"Jessi…" both Lisa and Ted spoke up, seeing her angry expression, "what's wrong?"

"It's that piece of trash you call a police officer," she glared quietly at Ted.

"Jessi, please…" Sue spoke up quietly from behind, "you have good cause to be mad, but not at my brother! So please, try to remember what we just told you! It's Terri you should be upset with, she's bad news!"

"You don't have to tell me that. But at the same time, he should have put his foot down in the first place, and not agreed to let her come out here," she replied heatedly, while putting in the call to his Commanding Officer.

Just then, turning to see someone coming down the stairs, Lisa and Ted grabbed Jessi's arm to warn her upon seeing Tony and Harry coming down to have coffee out on the front porch.

"Great," she grumbled, nodding her response, as she hung up the phone.

Seeing how things were about to get a little hot around there, Ted went out to get Alex.

Meanwhile, out on the front porch, Alex was busy himself, putting Terri in her place, when Ted walked up, taking him by the arm, "You have got to get in there, and right now," he whispered.

"What's going on?" he asked, seeing Tony out of the corner of his eye.

"It's Jessi, she was just about to call you know who, and boy, is she ever…"

"Let me guess, pissed?"

"Oh… yeah."

"Damn it," he growled, shoving Terri off to the side to go in and see what was going on.

Turning just as he cleared the front door, Jessi snapped heatedly at him, while at the same time, knowing that Tony wasn't too far off, she kept her voice down to a minimal roar, "She has been warned, and now I want her out of here, you hear me? Or you are all out of here, that goes for your pals out there, as well," she pointed.

"Like hell…" he growled quietly, while grabbing her by the arm. "Damn it, Jessi…"

"No, Mr. St…" She stopped abruptly at what she was about to say. Instead, glaring back at him, she tried jerking her arm free of his grasp to turn and head for the kitchen in order to put some distance between them. In doing so, all attempts to break free failed when he tighten his grip on her.

"Alex," Ted stepped in quietly to try and pull them a part. Ease up on her, buddy."

"Sure, when she learns to let me do my job, and not before then," he continued to glare, until he saw what it was doing to her.

As for Jessi, feeling the pain biting into her arm, she pushed passed it and refused to back down as well. "Damn it, Alex, just do it. Get her out of here now, or else."

"Damn you, woman, I won't be threatened. I'll…" he began, when suddenly Ted cleared his throat quietly at seeing Tony at the door, drinking his coffee.

"Man… we've got company…!" he warned.

Looking slightly over his shoulder to see Tony for himself, Alex dropped his hand. "All right," he growled through tightly clenched teeth.

Seeing Tony as well, Jessi merely stared Alex down, while thinking of what to say next. *"Damn it to hell,"* she swore more than usual, *"what now?"* she asked, angry that he didn't get rid of Terri in the first place. Now it was up to her to do it, as she bit down on her tongue, before going on. "Mr. Green," she pointed venomously at the woman, now, standing behind him, while the others stood by watching, "get rid of that tramp, now, or you're fired," she returned, even more heatedly. Then lowering her voice to a near hiss, she added, "Do it, or get the hell off of my property. Oh," she pointed behind him, "and take her with you. Do I make myself clear?"

"Very," he growled beneath his breath, as she turned to walk off into the kitchen. "Damn her, anyway!" he went on.

"No, little brother," Sue glared at him, "damn you."

"What…?" He shot around to look at his sister.

"You heard me. She's right, and you know it."

"Sue… damn it, stay out of it."

"No, I won't." Turning, she went after Jessi, with Rose following right behind.

Growling even more heatedly, he doubled up his fists at what all was going wrong around him, before going after her himself.

Meanwhile, having just gone into the kitchen after her, Sue called out, closing the door behind them, "Jessi, I know how it must look, but..."

"But nothing!" she turned back, tearfully. "I can't stand seeing her like that."

"Yes, honey, but remember what Bob told you!" Rose spoke up worriedly. "You have to start taking it easy!"

"And I assure you, it wasn't my brother's doing!" Sue added, while going up to offer her support.

"I know that! It's just that I have had it with all this investigation, and that... that tramp," she swore. "Sue, I'm not out to get rid of him, just her!" she whispered, pointing out toward the foyer. "If he doesn't get her out of here, I'm..."

"You're what?" he growled, storming in through the kitchen door to grab her arms and shake her. "Damn it, Jessi, what the Sam hell was that all about?"

"You know damn well what that was all about. I saw her all over you, and I warned her what would happen if I saw her carrying on like that here at my Inn. And now, I want her gone! You hear me...? I... want... her...out of here!" she yelled, while trying to pull away from his brutal grip, once again, without any success.

"You listen to me," he glared hard at her, not seeing the look on the others faces, as he did. "First of all," he gritted his teeth, "she came on to me, I didn't start it. And secondly, why the hell would you care when your heart belongs to someone else?" he glared down at her with so much built-up anger, more at himself than her, for wanting someone, who couldn't be had, after going through it himself.

"That's enough, little brother. Stop it, now!" Sue cried out, while trying to pull him away from her. "You're hurting her!"

Letting go, he walked over to look out the back window for a moment, when seeing Beth, as she stood frozen next to Annie, at the sink. The look he then saw on her face was one of hurt. Seeing that, he shook his head sadly, before looking deep into her baby blue eyes.

Even at that, Jessi knew for herself that he must have been feeling pretty bad. As seeing the hurt expression etched on his face over Beth's own saddened expression, when she tried to offer some sort of solace to ease his pain, "Oh, Alex... I just wish that it wasn't... so..." She then stopped suddenly in mid-sentence, when turning to look at Sue, then

Rose, and then back at Alex. When at that moment, the room began to spin around her, like it did back at Craig's place. "A...Alex... I..." she cried out, feeling herself about to fall.

"Jessi..." Sue cried out as well, when she too saw the color drain from her face, when she started to fall slowly to the floor.

Turning just in time to see what was happening, Alex too, called out, as he rushed right over to catch her, "Jessi...! No!"

Quickly sweeping her up into his arms, he took her over to a nearby chair.

"We're going to need some water over here, please," Sue requested to Annie.

"Come on, Jess," he continued to call out to her. "Come back to me, please...!"

"Alex," Beth came forward with the cool washcloths in hand.

"Call Ted in here, please, Beth!" he returned, while taking them from her.

"Yes, sir," she replied, quietly, as she turned to head for the door.

"Beth..." he spoke up, stopping her.

"Sir!" she held her position, when turning back to him, while still hurting over what she had just heard.

"I...I'm sorry you had to hear that."

"Alex," she spoke freely, while looking to the others, "it was almost two years ago. I've had to put it all behind me, as you did! So please..." She broke off, while fighting so hard not to cry, as she still felt the pain of what they were forced to give up.

Chapter Twenty-Four

Leaving the kitchen, it wasn't long before she returned with Ted coming in ahead of her. "Alex, I'm here," he called out from the doorway, with Terri not far behind.

Seeing Jessi in Alex's arms, he looked down at his old partner's face.

"Check on our friends, will you? I need to get her downstairs," he ordered. "And as for you, Officer Shaw," he glared up at her, "pack your things now, before I do something I might regret. What you did was unforgivable, and you will be severely reprimanded for it. Now, get the hell out of my sight. You make me ill."

Doing so, Terri turned and left, as Ted returned to announce that the coast was clear.

"Let's go," he told them, as Ted took the lead.

Following right behind, Alex still looked in all directions for Tony.

Upon their arrival, Lora and Cassi were both alarmed at what they saw.

"Mom…!" Lora cried out. "What happened to our mom?" she asked, as Alex carried her on into her room.

"Girls, she'll be all right," Rose offered, taking them aside, while Sue called her husband, to explain Jessi's situation.

"Bob," she spoke up as soon as she heard his voice, "it's Jessi, she's fainted again."

"That's not good. I'll be right there. Get her vital signs, while you're waiting."

"All right, dear," she replied, while hanging up to go into Jessi's room, after the girls had shown her which one it was.

"Sue...?" Alex asked, sounding worried, when she walked in, seeing him sitting next to her, while holding tight to her hand.

"Bob's on his way."

"Good! Any idea what caused it this time?"

"You would know better than any of us!"

"All the tension going on around here?"

"That, and Terri. What were you thinking, Alex? Just what were you thinking?"

"Sue," he nearly barked back, "she was not my choice. I had nothing to do with either one of them being here. The Commander made that choice. Damn him, anyways! As if I don't already have enough to worry about."

"And Beth...?" she asked. "Did you give any thought to how she would feel, seeing you working with the woman you had gotten involved with so soon after your breakup?"

"You want to shove that knife in a little deeper?"

"Alex..." she began, when Jessi started to coming to.

"Mmmm... Craig!" she cried out softly. "Craig... I need you!"

"Oh, my... God..." she looked shocked. "Alex?" she asked, hearing her son's name being called out. "Up in the kitchen you said her heart belonged to someone else?"

"Yes."

"Are we talking about my son, here?"

Seeing her expression, he looked away, frowning.

"Alex...?"

"Yes. It seems the two of them, for some godly reason, have fallen in love. And it scares me to think what is going to happen, when they have to say goodbyes. Lord, Sue," he looked back up at his sister, "she has already lost one man in her life, because of some accident!"

"And now..."

"Yes. And now."

"Craig!" Jessi cried out again, opening her eyes.

"No, Jess, it's me. It's Alex!" he called back, looking into her tear-filled eyes, just as they started streaming down her cheeks.

"A...Alex?"

"Yes," he returned, coming around to hold her in his arms.

"No! Leave me alone! Please... just leave me alone!" she cried even more, while trying to push him away, but couldn't. He just sat there, holding her even tighter, while refusing to let her go, as his own tears began to fall down his ruggedly handsome face.

"Jessi, please don't. Terri's gone now!" he whispered through her soft hair. "And, God, I am so sorry I didn't send her away sooner." He went on blaming himself. *What the hell was I thinking? I should have never agreed to the Commander's suggestion, and allowed her to come here.* He continued scolding himself. "This would have never happened if I would have found another place to stay."

"Alex," Sue spoke up sharply, while trying to ease her brother's mind some, "aside from what went on between the two of you, you had no idea she was going to behave this way."

"Oh... but I was wrong, and now the two women I care about most seem to be getting the raw end of the deal."

"Alex..." Beth spoke up, just as she walked in on their conversation, "you had a lot on your mind, when we had to break it off. And finding Craig the way you did." She looked away.

"Beth..."

"No, Alex. You see, I wanted to be the one to console you, but Terri came to me and said it wouldn't be wise. It would only serve to get you into that much more hot water with the Commander! And I didn't want that to happen, so I had to stay away!"

Looking to his sister, Alex's face turned an even deeper shade of red, hearing Terri's part in what had gone down between him and Beth. "Terri...?" he growled.

"Yes, Alex," Sue spoke up, "she obviously had it bad for you, and wanted Beth out of the picture."

"Then it was Terri who turned us in..." he growled heatedly, while looking back at Beth, who then went over to stand next to his sister.

"Yes," Sue cut in, while placing an arm around her shoulder, and taking her hand in hers.

"Alex..." Jessi spoke up, becoming more and more aware of her surroundings, while getting in on the tail end of their conversation.

"Jessi..." Sue called out, smiling, "you're going to be okay, and Bob's on his way. So try to relax until he gets here," she added, while leaving the room to get her another cool washcloth.

"What's wrong with me?" she asked puzzledly.

"We're not sure yet, dear. When Bob gets here, hopefully we'll know something then," Rose put in

"Oh, Craig... where are you?" she cried out telepathically.

Having been a few days since she had heard from him, her wait was soon over, when his warm sounding voice came through, *"Jessi... I'm still here,"* he returned. *"I had to build my strength back up."*

"Oh, Craig, I need you!" she cried out again, while closing her eyes to try and focus on his face.

"I wish I could be there for you, but..."

Not able to finish what he was about to say, his father walked into her room to check on her condition.

"Well, what do we have here?" he asked, walking over to Jessi's bed, when Beth turned to excuse herself, and go back out into the living room to wait.

"Bob..." Alex started in.

"Alex, you're better off waiting with the others, while I check her over. Besides, it could be awhile before we know anything."

"I can't. It's my fault she's like this."

"That may very well be. But for now, please go and wait with the others, while I do what I have to, to see what's wrong here."

Doing so, it seemed like hours to Alex as he worriedly waited for Bob to finish his examination on Jessi.

At that moment, Rose cleared her throat, while indicating to Beth, who had been standing, sadly, looking out the patio doors.

Nodding his head, he went over to see how she was holding up. "Beth..." he murmured softly, as she turned to face him with tears streaming down her cheeks, "Oh, God," he groaned, pulling her into his warm embrace, "I am so sorry! I never wanted any of this to happen to you. Damn it, anyway! Not when I..." He stopped, as his own tears took over.

Not saying anything, she threw her arms up around his shoulders, and cried quietly into his chest, while feeling his warm embrace consume her. But just as he was about to pull back to gaze down into her loving eyes, they heard the door to Jessi's room open.

Turning, they all got up to see Bob walking out, looking worried.

"Bob, what's going on?" Alex asked, while dropping one arm down from her waist.

"Well, it's a combination of things," he explained, while taking out a pad of paper from his bag. "First of all, there's this woman police officer that you agreed to bring out here."

"Bob…" Rose spoke up, clearing her throat.

Looking up at that moment, he stopped when he saw Beth standing off to one side of Alex. "Oh, Beth, I'm sorry, I didn't…"

"No, that's all right. I'm sure that whatever you have to say won't matter much now that she is gone. All I care about now is Ms. Rae. Is she going to be all right?"

"Yes," he replied, turning back to Alex, "As for you, Jessi can't handle any more of this stress she is being put through. Because of it, she hasn't been eating like she should. Secondly, she needs a lot of rest. And the only way that's going to happen is to get her away from here until this case is over."

"I can't agree with you more!" he returned, all too happy to get her out of there.

"Well," Rose spoke up, smiling at her daughters, "she and the girls can stay with us until this is over!"

"Thanks, Rose," Jessi spoke up, when emerging into the living room with Sue by her side. "I appreciate what you're offering, but it won't be necessary. It's just that I'd like to spend some time out at the farmhouse alone, and maybe even get the girls to stay out there with me from time to time. And if Alex wouldn't mind," she turned to look over at him, "I would really like it to have Beth join us, as well!"

"Are you sure?" Beth asked.

"Yes. Alex?"

Feeling somewhat odd about the situation of having Beth and Jessi both out at the farmhouse at the same time, he ran a free hand through his hair thoughtfully.

"Alex, please!" Beth smiled warmly.

"All right."

"And Rose, as for your offer! I would like to come by with the girls, if that's all right?"

"Jessi, you can come by whenever you wish!" she exclaimed warmly.

"Jessi, please feel that you can come by our house, as well," Sue spoke up, thoughtfully.

"And don't forget," Bob added, "you have to get some rest and eat well!"

"Oh, she will," Alex grinned coyly, "since I'll be staying at the farmhouse with them."

"Great," Jessi laughed, "and just where are we going to get extra air mattresses for everyone to have a place to sleep?"

"That's not a problem," Sue offered. "We've got two full-sized ones at home!"

"And I've got one you can use, as well!" Rose added.

"Well," Alex turned to give her one of his warm smiles, "you know that I'll have my bedroll fixed up on the floor near the fireplace to keep the fire going on those chilly nights!"

"Which reminds me," Bob asked, "did you ever get the utilities back on?"

"Yes," Alex returned, "about a week or so ago."

"Good! Now seeing that everything is all taken care of here, I'll just be on my way," he announced, while heading for the stairs. "Oh, and Jessi, you do have a beautiful place here."

"Thank you," she smiled, as Sue walked her husband up to the front door, to leave.

Chapter Twenty-Five

"Jessi, just where do you think you're going?" Rose fussed, when she got up to head for the stairs. "You're supposed to be getting some rest!"

"I can't! I have to get caught up on my paperwork, before I can even think about going anywhere. And then I have to get the girls ready."

"Why not just take the work with you, and do it out there?" Alex asked, while still standing next to Beth. "As for the girls, I'm sure they can get their own things together after lunch."

"I'd rather not. And as for the girls, they're pretty much packed already!" She smiled back, thinking how much they're going to like it out there. *"Well at least Rose's house,"* she grinned quietly to herself.

"Alex," Beth asked, "are you sure you're okay with me going?"

"Yes, I don't want you up in the attic alone with Tony so close by to hurt you."

"Alex... I can take care of myself!"

"What was that?" Jessi started in laughing at hearing Beth's rebuttal. "I don't believe it!"

Smiling broadly at him, she shook her head teasingly, when he turned back to look into her warm, sparkling eyes, and laughed, while shaking his head.

"Well, what do we have here?" Sue asked, returning to Jessi's living room.

"It seems that Alex has met his match!" Rose laughed. "Only it seems to have happened to him twice now."

"Yeah, just when things were finally starting to get peaceful in my life," he continued to laugh right along with the others.

"Oh, you poor, baby," Jessi and Beth both teased.

"Yeah, I got..."

"Alex!" Sue chimed in, shaking her head at him.

"Well, ladies, shall we go back upstairs now?" Jessi asked, when leading the way, while leaving Alex standing there looking puzzled.

"Where are you guys off to?" he asked.

"The Boutique!" she smiled.

Going along with them, he stopped off at the front desk to talk to Ted, while the others went on into the Boutique to talk quietly over their plans, while staying at Craig's.

"Oh, Ted," Jessi turned back, smiling, just outside the Boutique doors, "before I forget."

'*Oh…no,*' Alex thought, seeing that look on her face.

"I have a job that needs taking care of."

"Yes, ma'am?" He tried hard to hold a straight face.

"Jessi…!" Alex growled warningly.

Ignoring him, she went on, "Please escort my groundskeeper out onto the front porch, and explain to him that he has been given a second chance, and if," She turned to Alex, while cocking her head to one side, and grinned, "he wants to keep it, don't screw it up this time."

"Sure thing, Ms. Rae," he grinned, hauling Alex out by the arm.

Stopping short of the front door, Alex turned back with a funny smirk on his face, but then seeing the look come over Beth's, he groaned, "Oh, no… not you too…? No… Beth…!" Shaking his head, he groaned once again, while looking back to Jessi, "You're really loving this, aren't you? No," he corrected, "the two of you are really loving this?"

"Uh huh!" Beth laughed quietly.

"Definitely," Jessi smiled. "Oh… yeah, definitely."

Turning, she and Beth proceeded into the Boutique with the others, while Ted took Alex out on the front porch to get some coffee. There, he took great pride in reprimanding his old friend, while also noting that Tony and Harry hadn't left yet.

"Jake," he spoke up, seeing Tony over near the coffee cart, before going on over, "you could have really screwed up here. But since you have chosen wisely, and got rid of that girl, Ms. Rae has deemed to give you a second chance. Now all I can say is don't screw it up for yourself. She really likes your work, and wants to keep you on. But she will throw your butt out of here if you ever dare to bring that girl back here again."

"I won't be doin' that no more. She weren't worth losin' my job over."

"Good, cause Jake...!"

"Yeah?"

"You've got a lot of work to do to prove your trust again. And I can't think of any better place to start, but with the stables," he hid the grin of loving his job even more, from the others, while going on to get their coffee, when Tony had taken a few steps away.

"No... the stables?" he growled quietly, seeing just where Ted was going with this.

"Yep! It seems Hank's back has been giving him some trouble. And he needs the manure hauled out right away. So finish your coffee and get on down there, he's waiting on you."

Growling even more under his breath, he looked back at Ted with contempt in his eyes, and downed his coffee quickly.

Smiling to himself, Ted turned to head back inside, while calling out over his shoulder,

"Today, Green! Today!" he finished, while laughing quietly, when the phone started ringing.

Shaking his head miserably, Alex looked back in through the Boutique window to see Jessi and Beth hitting it off. Seeing it brought a silent smile to his face, as he turned to head for the front steps, but not before stopping to look in at his friend, while mouthing the word 'Bastard', before walking away.

Grinning back, Ted went on to take, yet, another call for the Fourth of July weekend.

Meanwhile, sitting in the Boutique, Lora was asking what they were going to be doing out at the old farmhouse. "Nothing personal, but that place is really spooky!" she complained, not knowing Sue was the previous owners mother.

"Lora..." Jessi scolded. "It isn't spooky! It was just dark and mysterious looking!"

"Well you won't have to stay there all the time," Rose spoke up. "We have plenty of room and tons of movies to select from. Not to mention, a big pool out back to swim in!"

"Really?" Cassi cried, excitedly, at the invitation.

"Sure!"

"Oh, girls," Jessi spoke up warningly, "before we go too far, you should know, sitting next to you is the mother of the guy who lost his life in that house, his house to be exact. So please, show some respect."

"I'm sorry," Lora spoke up, "I didn't know!"

"That's because I haven't told them, yet," Jessi explained, after looking to her friends.

"Girls," Sue spoke up apologetically, "it's okay, the house has been sitting there empty for nearly two years. And the kids around there haven't been very nice, breaking out a few of the windows. But thanks to Alex, their parents have been heavily fined."

"Yes," Rose added, "and too, Craig was a great guy, if you had have known him!"

"Craig…" Lora looked to her mother puzzledly. "Wasn't that the name of the guy you said you had just met shortly after we got back from Grandma's last month?"

"Yes," she blushed, looking at the others, all but Beth, who hadn't heard the story yet.

Seeing inquiring eyes looking upon her, Jessi knew, one day, she would have to sit down and talk with those who hadn't already known about Craig's troubled spirit. Then too, she wondered, would her girls pick up her gift, as well.

After another hour of visiting, Sue and Rose had to go.

"We hate to leave, but it's getting late," Rose replied, while carrying her things out to the front desk. "Make sure you call, when you arrive, so we can have another cookout."

"I will!" she returned, while seeing Alex standing at the desk, when Sue walked over to say goodbye to him.

"Hey, don't worry too much about her, we will all help take care of her so you can concentrate on other things."

"Good, because time is running out. I can feel it," he announced, when turning to see Jessi's expression change.

"No" she mouthed the words, when turning to head for her quarters.

"Jessi…?" the others called out, stopping her.

"I…I'm sorry! If you will excuse me!" she called back, while choking on her emotions, "I think I'll just go on back down to my quarters for a bit, before starting on my work."

"Sweetie, are you all right?" Rose asked.

"Yeah. Just tired."

"Okay!" she smiled, while going up to give her a hug, before walking out to their cars.

"Well, I should be going too," Beth spoke up, while heading for the kitchen, to talk to Annie, before getting a few of her things together.

Nodding his head, warmly, Alex turned back to his sister. "What am I going to do, Sis? Jessi loves him!"

"Give her time."

"Time. Right," he groaned, looking back toward the door that led down to her quarters.

After seeing them off, he went back out to the stables to keep an eye on things.

"Mom, how long are we staying out there?" Lora asked, while coming down to get her own things ready.

"A few days or so," she replied, tiredly, while walking into their kitchen.

"What are you going to be doing while we're there?" Cassi asked, while bringing out her suitcase.

"Oh, I'll be out walking the grounds, and checking things out. You know, like we did, when we found the Inn! That, and visit with Rose and Sue!"

"What if those men show up out there?"

"You won't have to worry about them showing up," Alex explained, while coming down to join them. "I just called to have some extra men added on. There will also be another man put out here, as well. In any case, you will be safe at all times. Besides, Max will be there with us," he smiled down on him. "Isn't that right, boy?"

Panting his reply at the mere mention of the farmhouse, Jessi smiled, "I think he really loves it there! *Or is it,*" she thought, smiling, *"the former proprietor that you like?"*

Later that afternoon, when the all clear was given, Ted went down to get Jessi's things along with her girls'. "Are we all ready?" he asked, standing at the bottom of the stairway.

"Yes," Jessi replied, coming into the living room.

"All right." Taking a few of her suitcases, the two headed back up, while filling her in on what was going on. Stopping at the top of the stairs, he turned back, just as he was about to open the door, "Alex wanted me to tell you that his men are here, and already at work."

"And the ones out at Craig's? Are they there, as well?"

"Yes, at least four of them. So you and your girls should feel pretty safe out there."

"Thanks."

Heading on out to put their things into her car, Ted saw that Tony's car was still there, "Ms. Jessi!" he spoke up, stopping her.

"Yes?" She stopped to see the look of concern on his face, when he went to tuck one of her cases up under his other arm in order to reach out to her.

Taking her arm, he spoke quietly, while leading her over to Alex's Blazer. "He has asked that I put your things in with his."

"Oh?" she asked, worriedly, when seeing Tony's car parked not far from the Inn.

"It's all right," he offered reassuringly. "They're out horseback riding, at this moment. That's why Alex isn't here with us now. He's out in the stables keeping an eye on them with a pair of high-powered binoculars."

"Ted, he is…"

"Yes," he smiled warmly. "He's being careful."

"Good," she replied, just as he went to place her things in the back of the Blazer, right beside her daughter's things, "I'll just give him a call if that's all right, and let him know we're almost ready."

"Sure, that shouldn't be a problem. I'll just be up getting Beth's things for her, as well, while you're doing that. Oh, and if it's all right with you, would you mind if we just put your car in the garage? Alex will probably want you and the girls to ride with him as well."

"And Beth? What about her?"

"She will more than likely take her car. We'll know more when you guys get ready to leave."

"All right. See you later."

Heading back inside, while Ted went up to Beth's quarters, Jessi went around the front desk to call Alex on the intercom.

"Jake?" she called out, using his alias.

"Yeah?" His voice came back loud and clear.

"Can you talk?"

"Sure! What's up?"

"We're all loaded, and Ted is up getting Beth's things now."

"What are you going to do, until I get done here?"

"Work on some of this paperwork, so I won't have to take it with me."

"All right, I shouldn't be too long. They're coming back up the trail now."

"All right. Should I tell him? He said something about putting my car in the garage while we're gone."

"Yes, so he can get it done before they see it."

"Ok."

Ending the conversation, she stood there for a moment, feeling concerned, while Lisa continued handling the guests, as they were checking out.

"Ms...." one of them spoke up, asking for direction.

"Jessi?" Lisa turned to ask, "Jessi?"

"Yes. Yes, what is it?" she asked, snapping out of her thoughts to give her full attention to the couple standing at the desk.

"The airport," Lisa repeated. "They're wanting to know where the nearest airport is."

"Twelve miles up the Interstate, on your right."

"Thank you," the man smiled, as he bent down to get their suitcases.

Seeing them out, Jessi turned back to Lisa, "If anyone asks, I'll be out back talking to Beth, while waiting on Alex to get done."

"All right! Oh, but what about Ted? You were saying something to Alex about telling Ted something."

"Darn... that's right!"

Hearing him coming down the stairs, while talking on his cell phone, she waited to interrupt him.

"Yes, she's right here," he said, stopping at the bottom of the stairs.

"Alex?" Jessi asked, smiling.

"Yes. He says you were about to tell me about the car situation. I'm going out now to take care of it, along with getting Beth's things put into her own car. Do you have the keys handy?"

"Yes." Running off into her office, she was back in no time, handing him the keys. "Take good care of her. She's my baby," she smiled.

Smiling back, he hurried off.

"Good," she continued to smile, while turning to walk off toward the kitchen. "Now to get Beth and go out back for our talk."

"Are you sure that's safe?" Lisa asked, after her.

"Yes, Alex will be there shortly," she called back over her shoulder, before reaching the kitchen door.

Walking in, Annie looked up from the sink, seeing her tired expression, "Aren't you feeling any better?" she asked.

"Just tired, is all. Not to mention, I still have a lot of paperwork to do, before we can go."

"Well, sounds like you have your work cut out for you."

"Sure seems that way," she agreed, turning to Beth. "Would you mind joining me out back for some iced tea?"

"Sure! Annie?" she turned to ask.

"Go ahead," she replied, smiling, "I've got things covered here."

"Thanks, Annie, you're the greatest," she cried, giving her a big hug, before going off to the refrigerator to get out the cold pitcher of tea and two tall glasses.

"Shall we?" Jessi smiled, while taking the two glasses with them.

Shortly after getting their drinks poured, the two had just sat down to take a break, when

Alex walked up to join them.

"How are things going?" he asked, taking the seat between the two.

"Fine," Beth replied. "How are our friends?"

"From the looks of it, they're having some fun first, before going after David."

"Great," she had no more than said, when Jessi lowered her head to look into her glass.

"Jessi," Beth looked over to see her saddened expression.

Shaking off the feeling, which came over her, Jessi got up to walk over to the gazebo that sat in the middle of the backyard, near a set of lilac bushes. As she did, her long, pink, summer dress, and brown hair, trailed softly behind her in the afternoon breeze, creating a softer side of her, as Alex got up to join her.

Placing his hands gently on her shoulders, he lightly massaged them. "I'm sorry, Jess," he offered softly in her ear, "I wasn't thinking."

"Alex, I know we're running out of time," she cried, placing her hands over his, as she turned slightly to look back at him over her shoulder, "but I just don't want to be reminded of it."

"I know. It's not that easy for me, either! I just wish..." he was saying, when Beth looked over to see two figures walking up from the stables toward them.

"Heads up, folks!" she warned, when coming up to nudge Alex in the side. "We've got company coming our way!" she nodded slowly toward the stables.

Catching sight of them, he dropped his hands down to his sides, as Jessi placed a smile on her face. "Gentlemen!" she greeted, as they walked on by. "Did you enjoy your ride?"

"Yes, ma'am, we did!" Harry spoke up, smiling, though Tony held a scowled-like look on his face, while looking up at them standing there.

Seeing this, she pulled out all her resources and continued to smile warmly, "Good, I'm glad to hear it," she nodded her head, as they passed on by. "Jake," she then turned to snap him out of his heated glare, "as I was saying, would you and Beth please set up a few more tables out front for tomorrow?"

Quickly picking up on her lead, he replied, "Yes, ma'am, we'll get right on it."

"Thank you," she nodded, smiling, as Tony and Harry disappeared from sight.

"Smooth!" Beth laughed quietly.

"Wasn't it, though?" Jessi winked at her two companions.

Grinning back down on her, he shook his head in approval, "You did well, Ms. Rae."

"Yes, well the look the two of you were giving each other, I thought you were going to get into right then!" she groaned on their way back up to the Inn.

"I wanted to, but then..." he shook his head angrily.

"Not the right time?" Jessi offered, sympathetically.

Looking to her, he nodded his head.

"Alex," Beth spoke up, just as they were about to walk inside, "what's next?"

"We'll be heading out in a little while. Are you ready to go?"

"Yes."

"Good! Until we get back, I'm leaving Ted in charge."

"All right, then, I'll see you both later," she replied quietly, once inside the kitchen, while watching them head out into the hallway.

Stopping just outside the kitchen doorway, he turned to Jessi, "What about you?"

"Well, I still have some paperwork to do!"

"All right. After I go see Ted, I'll join you."

"Okay!"

After watching him head up to Ted's room, she went on into her office, and closed the door behind her. *"Boy, what a day,"* she thought with a heavy sigh, while looking at her watch to see what time it was getting to be.

"Heavy day?" Craig asked, surprising her.

"And then some!" she returned, while going over to her desk to get started. *"Oh, and by the way, you're going to be getting some company for a few days."*

"Oh...?"

"Yep! My girls and I are coming out, along with Alex. Oh, and Beth is coming out, too!"

"Beth, too?" he laughed.

"Uh huh!"

"Jessi?"

"Hmmm...?"

"Are you all right?"

"I've had better days! Your dad wants me to take it easy, until this passes. I just hope you don't mind us all coming out so soon?"

"No, it'll be fun!"

"Craig...what are you planning?"

"Nothing too scary!" he laughed softly.

"Good! Now if I don't get any of this done, I'm going to be having to bring it with me."

"Just don't push yourself too hard."

"*I won't,*" she replied, while pondering over what she was going to get started on first.

Chapter Twenty-Six

After an hour of working at the pile of bills and receipts, Alex walked in, closing the door behind him. "Hey, lady, you're looking pretty tired there!"

"I am! But I have to get all these bills and receipts recorded, before I can even think about leaving now!"

"No you don't!" he announced, coming over to pull her away from her desk.

"Alex... what are you doing...?" she rebelled, "I can't think about stopping right now. I have too much to do, as it is...!"

"Oh, but you can!" He stopped to look firmly into her tired eyes.

"Oh, I can, can I?" she asked, seeing a slight glimmer in his own. "All right, just for the sake of argument, why?" she asked, propping a free hand on her hip.

"Bob said you're not to overdo it. So you are going over to the sofa and lie down!"

"Alex... I don't have time to lie down. If we're going out to the farmhouse tonight, I've got to get this done, and now!"

"But you don't seem to quite understand! I'm not giving you a choice in the matter. *You* don't have to, because I can do it for you," he smiled broadly, once they reached the sofa.

"What?" she cried. "But how? You don't know the first thing about this...!"

"It can't be all that hard! Besides," he laughed, "I majored in accounting in college!"

"Oh, great," she conceded to his odd way of getting the message across, "and if you're really good at it, you could always come to work for me!"

"Not a chance, lady," he laughed, as she went to lie down.

Watching as she fell off to sleep, once her head hit the pillow, he went back over to work on her books. And like he thought, they weren't hard to do at all.

Waking a few hours later, he was just getting ready to wrap things up, when seeing her stir. "Are you feeling any better now?" he asked, leaning back in the chair to stretch out his long legs, before getting up.

"Yes," she replied, while getting up slowly to walk over to her desk.

"Good, because we're all done here!" he pointed with a spread of his hands over the desk.

"Really?"

"Yep!" he exclaimed, getting up. "So if you're ready, it's getting late, and we really need to be getting on the road, if we're to get there at a reasonable hour."

"All right."

"Oh, that reminds me." He stopped short of reaching to the door.

"What?"

"Why don't you wait for me here, while I go and let Ted know we're about to head out. Oh, and thanks for not giving me any grief about going with me in the Blazer, while Beth drives ahead in her car. It's just that I have a bad feeling they may try to follow one of us. If they do, more than likely it would be me. Then again, even you! In that case, I'd rather be in control of the wheel. As for Beth, I would doubt they'd go after her, when it seems to be us they're interested in."

"Sure! All right, if you feel that strongly about it," she agreed, without a protest.

"What..." he asked, sounding surprised, "no argument?"

"Oh, I'm sorry, did you want one?" she smiled up at him.

"I can't believe it!" he shook his head, laughing.

"Alex, I'm not always... What did you first call me?"

"Hard ass," he grinned boldly, before walking out to the front desk.

"Alex!" Ted spoke up quietly, when seeing his friend coming out. "Are you ready to go?"

"Yes, just as soon as I get the others. Oh, and our friends, how are they doing?" he asked, looking around.

"They just went up to their room a few minutes ago."

"Good, cause I'm going to be needing you to stay with Jess, until I get back."

"Where are you off to?"

"To do a security sweep."

"Are you going out to check on their car, as well?"

"I was planning on it! Why?" he asked, while checking out his service revolver.

"Oh, but not without back up, you're not!" Beth called out quietly, as she and the girls walked up, after first checking out the hallway, before bringing them up.

"In that case, how about the two of us go on the rounds, while she stays with Jessi and her girls? That's if you don't mind?" Alex asked, when turning to Beth.

"I don't mind!"

"Good, and until we get back, stay in there so I know where you're at."

"You've got it, boss," she smiled up at him, before taking the girls into the office.

"Beth..." he began, but then shook his head at her warm smile, before heading off.

Meanwhile, going around to check out the place, Alex turned back to his friend, "What's the news on Shaw?" he asked quietly.

"She won't be a problem to us anymore."

"Oh? How's that?"

"The Commander has her assigned to finding bail jumpers from our county, and then she'll be buried under a ton of unsolved files, until they are cleaned up."

Slapping him on the back, he laughed, "Good job, old partner."

"Well you know she was pretty pissed, when she was told to leave. I just wanted to make certain she wouldn't be causing you any trouble on your cover."

"Yes, and how in the hell did I allow myself to get mixed up with a woman like that?"

"You know the answer to that. She has had her eye on you for years."

"Damn, why her though?"

"Who knows?" The two continued on in silence, while the others waited it out back in Jessi's office.

Meanwhile, turning to Beth, while going over to take a seat on the sofa, along with her tired girls, Jessi commented on how it was going to be so nice once they got out there.

"Are you sure you really want me to go with you?" she asked, looking a little sad at the amount of time she would be spending with Alex, not to mention, back out at Craig's old place, after what had happened there.

"Yes," she smiled, while putting an arm around her girl's, when Cassi went to lay her head on her lap. "Besides, Sue said you used to go there with Alex, when Craig was still alive."

"Yes," she began, frowning at the happier memories, just then. "All right. Besides, it would be nice…"

"What would be nice?" Alex interrupted, when he and Ted walked back in.

"Oh, I uh…" she started, when hearing the sudden undertone in his voice. Feeling nervous, she looked down at her hands, before answering. "I was just about to say how nice it would be to go back out to Craig's old place after all this time of being away from there!" she explained. But when looking back up to see his grin, she found herself smiling warmly at him.

"It has been awhile since we've been out there together, hasn't it?" he asked, while turning back to the door.

"Yes. Too long."

Seeing this, Jessi's matchmaking mind started ticking away. *"Hmmm…"* she smiled quietly to herself, *"just maybe this trip might prove to be even more profitable than expected!"*

"More than you think," Craig smiled back.

"Ted," Alex spoke up, bringing Jessi's mind back to what was going on around her, "you are in charge, until we get back."

"Don't worry about a thing, just keep your eyes open out there, both of you," he added quietly, while walking them out.

"We will," Alex turned back, grinning, at the thought of having both Beth and Jessi out there together.

Once they got to their vehicles, Beth spoke up quietly, when breaking into Alex's train of thought, "Do you think Tony will try to follow us?"

"I don't know," he replied, when turning back to see one of his other men come walking up onto the porch to join Ted.

Looking like one of Jessi's handymen, Frank Peters, a tall, husky, man, in his late forties, stood relaxed next to Ted in the doorway, while trying not to look like a cop.

"What is it?" Jessi asked, while turning back to see Alex's expression.

"Nothing, I was just making sure your new handyman was doing his job," he replied, while turning back to open her door for her. "Max, come on, boy!"

Once everyone was ready, Beth headed out first, taking the lead, while Alex watched in his rearview mirror, once they passed an unmarked car that sat up the road a ways, tucked back amongst some trees.

Wanting to make certain it was one of his own men, ready to move if Tony decided to follow, his question was soon answered, by the flash of the man's headlights, indicating his readiness. "Good," Alex commented, under his breath, while turning back to watch the road ahead of him.

Meanwhile, back at the Inn, still keeping a lookout, Ted and Frank caught a glimpse of something moving off in the darkness. "Frank, stay here and keep an eye on that area out there," Ted ordered, when turning to go back in to get Jessi's other dog.

"Where you going?" he asked.

"To get Maggie!"

"You got it!" he returned, not knowing Ted was referring to Jessi's other dog, who had spent a great deal of time with Alex, while working with her.

Upon his return, Ted asked, holding the Rottweiler back, "Where is he now?"

"Just on the other side of those bushes, not too far from their car," he returned quietly, while nodding his head over in the general direction.

"Well, Maggie, it's show time! Let me see what all you have learned, since your training, okay, girl…!" he grinned, while removing her leash. "Go get'em, girl. Protect!"

And protect, she did, as she picked up on his scent, and right away ran out onto the front lawn, growling, as their trespasser took off running in a different direction from his car.

Seeing that, Frank turned to Ted, while trying to hide his amusement, "Should we call Alex to let him know what's going on?"

"Yes, but I'll do that, while you stay out here and watch over the area," he ordered, while turning to go back inside. Stopping at the doorway, he paused a moment to think.

"What?" Frank asked.

Looking back at him, he grinned, "Oh… just thinking!" he smiled, while turning then to look up toward Tony's room, "I think after calling Alex, I'll just go up and check on friends, claiming to have seen a prowler outside, of course!"

With a nod of his head, Frank went back to his post to give Ted some privacy. "You do that," he grinned mysteriously. "You just… do that."

Meanwhile, it didn't take long when Alex's voice came on the other end.

"Alex, it's me," Ted spoke quietly, as he went on into Jessi's office, closing the door behind him.

"What's up?" he asked, turning off onto Highway 94.

"One of our friends was heading for his car, but Maggie changed his mind at the last minute."

"Oh… yeah…!"

Hearing Alex laugh, Ted went on to let him know that he was going up to see which one was still there. "You know," he concluded with a slight chuckle of his own, "just to make it look like we were protecting the property, of course."

"Sounds good. Let me know how it goes," he ordered, while looking over at Jessi, sleeping peacefully in the seat next to him.

While driving to his nephew's place, he heard Jessi's soft cries, as she called out to his nephew. Shaking his head, he wondered. *What is it, Jess? What are you and my nephew talking about now,* he grinned, when looking then in his rearview mirror to see her daughters sleeping, as well, in the back seat, along with Max.

Snapping out of his thoughts, the forty-eight year old detective heard his partner's voice on the other end of the line, telling him to hide his vehicle well. "Just in case they decide to take a midnight drive, after all."

"I'll do that. Just let me know right away if Tony and Harry do decide to take that drive."

"Sure thing."

After hanging up, Ted headed up to Tony's room. Once there, knocking on their door, Harry called out, thinking it was Tony. "Is that you?" he asked.

"No, sir, it's the desk clerk!" Ted announced, while playing his undercover role well. "I just wanted to let you and your friend know that we have been having troubles lately with prowlers. Is your car locked up for the night?"

"Yes. Yes it is!" he replied, sounding worried, as he went to open the door.

"And your friend, is he here with you now?" he asked, glimpsing into the room.

"No," he replied shortly, while attempting to close the door, but then couldn't, when Ted put out his hand to stop him.

"Well, for his sake, I sure hope he's not outside! We've just turned the Rottweiler loose to chase off a prowler," he went on, while taking a step into the room.

"Yeah, well I don't know where he is! He just said he's going out for awhile."

"Okay, but while I'm here, Ms. Jessi has asked that I check on your balcony doors, just to make sure they're still locked, that is. Her insurance company says that the balcony is in need of repair. And if someone were to get hurt on them, she could be in serious trouble. And if that were to happen, everyone here, who cares about her, would be pretty upset, since she has been a pretty terrific boss to us all, you understand?"

"Yeah, well I can see she's a real nice lady and all, but really, you don't have to do that. They're locked all right!"

"Harry, is it?" he asked, noticing his nervousness, as he got closer to the doors.

"Yeah, I...I'm Harry!"

Turning the knobs, Ted looked back to the man shrinking off to one side of the room, "These doors aren't locked!"

"B…but…"

"I'm sorry, sir, but they have to stay that way," he announced, while taking out his hand radio to call one of the groundskeepers. "Travis?" he spoke up, hearing his voice.

"Yes?"

"This is Ted. Run up a padlock, would you, please? We have a repair in Room Three for you to take care of."

"I'm on my way."

"Great." Turning back once he had gotten off the radio, he saw right away how Harry's face had gone pale, just then. "Harry," he began, while putting the radio back inside his vest pocket, "did Tony go out through these doors?"

Knowing he couldn't avoid the truth any longer, he admitted to it, "Yes, he did, but…"

"But what?" he asked sternly, while looking right into the man's eyes.

"I don't know!" he cried, when turning to look the other way.

'Well now,' he thought quietly to himself, while taking out his cell phone to call the police, *'I think we have our prowler.'*

"Sheriff's Department! Troy speaking!"

"Yes, Troy, this is Ted Jones, out at The Serenity Inn. I'm standing in for Ms. Rae, while she and her family are out of town on business."

"Yes, sir, what can I do for you?" the dispatcher asked, recognizing Lieutenant Jones' voice, as well as the nature of the case they were working on.

"It seems we have a prowler loose on the grounds. Will you send out a car right away to check it out?"

"Yes, sir, I'll have one out there as soon as possible."

"Thank you," he returned, ending the call, while turning back to Harry. "Well you might as well have a seat, Harry, as I'll be seeing to the repair in order to make sure it's done right."

"Man… I told him not to do it, but he is so hell bent on getting that…that… cop!" he muttered out, realizing he had said too much, when he felt Ted's eyes boring down on him. Attempting to say no more, he walked over to look out the balcony windows.

But that didn't stop Ted, while pretending not to know, "What cop, Harry?"

"I…I didn't mean it the way it came out."

"Sure you did! In fact, it'll even be our secret. I promise," he offered quietly, while going over to close the door behind him.

"Why should I trust you?" he asked, darting around to face him.

"Am I a cop, Harry?" he asked, coyly. "In that case, do I even look like one?"

"Well, no…!" he shook his head.

"Okay then, I don't have anything better to do! So out with it. Who is he after, and why?"

"Man, he would kill me, if I tell anyone."

"Well, Harry, the way I see it, how does he know that you haven't?"

"All right! All right! But you didn't hear it from me. You swear?" he cried, walking back over to sit on his bed.

"You got it, bro! Now spill it. Who is this cop that your friend is after?"

"First of all, he ain't my friend, and secondly, it's that Alex Storm!"

"Captain… Alex… Storm…?" he asked, acting surprised.

"Yeah, that one."

"Man, he's one mean mother. He got me for drug dealing four years ago. What's his beef with Tony?"

"Tony killed his nephew," he explained, while getting up again to go back over to the window. "Now I ain't saying no more," he grumbled, when stopping short to look back at Ted. "And I mean it!"

"That's cool, dude! Just one more question though, and I'll drop it."

"What?"

"Does he know where Storm is now?" he asked, in hopes to find out if his friends' disguise had been blown or not.

"He thinks the cop is real close, and he don't care what he has to do to get him. Even if it means hurtin' Ms. Rae to do it."

"Damn… why her? What does she have to do with him? She doesn't even trust cops, much less like them!" Ted said, crinkling up his face.

"We saw her at that old farmhouse, where Matthews was killed!" he exclaimed, while coming back over to sit down.

"So! Maybe she likes that place."

"But Storm was there too!"

"Yeah, well, haven't you thought that maybe she wants to buy it? After all, from what she has told us, he has control of his nephew's property. Perhaps she had a meeting with him about buying the place."

"I never thought of it that way," he was saying, when Travis showed up to fix the door.

Letting him in, Ted turned back to show him the repair, before going on with Harry.

"I'll have it done in no time," Travis returned, while taking out his tools.

"Thanks. And now, Harry," Ted turned back, lowering his voice, "about Tony, just maybe you might want to tell him that piece of information. You know, to protect Ms. Rae, that is."

"Yeah, well…" Harry chose then to clam up, knowing Tony's temper the way he did.

And from that point on, the two remained silent, while watching Travis work on the door, when making certain no one would bother it again.

"Well," the groundskeeper said bluntly, when finishing up, "no one had better mess with these doors now!"

"Thanks, Travis," Ted returned, walking him to the door, once he had gathered up his tools to leave. "I'll be down shortly."

Nodding his head, he turned to leave.

"Well, Harry," Ted turned back to one very nervous man, still sitting quietly on one of the double beds that occupied the room, "you sound like a good and honest sort of person. So try not to follow Tony in his footsteps. And if you really care about Ms. Rae, tell me if and when he plans to go after her. Again it will be our secret. I promise," he added, as he went to close the door behind him.

"Hey…!" Harry called out, stopping him.

"Yes…?"

"I don't want to see anything happen to her either! She's a real nice lady! And what happened to Storms' nephew shouldn't have happened. But it did. And I'm real sorry about that!"

"You're right about that," he agreed, feeling the anger build up inside over what his old friend went through, "it shouldn't have happened. What I read about the guy, was that he was just an innocent bystander. His death was the cause of a mistaken identity."

Looking even more frightened, Harry asked, "What are you going to do about it now that I have told you?"

"What can I do? It happened years ago. Besides, I gave you my word," he smiled, leaving the room.

Going back down to wait on the police, Frank asked, "The balcony doors?"

"Yes," he replied, looking broken up.

"What else?"

"Just some bad news, is all. Though, while I was up there, I'd also put in a call to have an officer come out and check out the grounds. And two, it's no secret that she knows Alex now."

"Oh, but how?" he asked, knowing what had happened to Alex's nephew.

"They were seen together last weekend out at Craig's old place," he explained, while going over to the front door to watch for the patrol car.

"Great! Now what?"

"We wait!" he explained. "We just… wait."

And wait, they did.

Chapter Twenty-Seven

"Here they are now!" Frank nodded toward a patrol car, coming up the drive.

"Good," Ted replied, going out alone to talk to them.

"Ted Jones?" one of the two young officers asked, while getting out of their car.

"Yes."

"What's going on?"

Filling them in, he left out Harry's end of the conversation, while wanting to keep it just between him and Alex.

"What would you like for us to do, sir?" they asked, in a much lower tone.

Turning to see where Frank was, he looked back at the two men standing at the ready, "Give him a hard time, but don't haul him in. Alex and I have plans for him."

"All right, we'll get right on it, and then have a talk with his friend, as well."

Nodding his approval, the two went off in search of Tony, while he went back inside to call Alex.

Once again, it didn't take long to answer, while not wanting to wake Jessi or her girls.

"Alex, it's me again," Ted announced, closing the office door behind him, while Frank remained standing out on the porch, lighting a cigarette.

While there, the man acted all so nonchalant about things, while taking a puff off his cigarette. As he did, looking up, he saw Tony across the road, ducking in behind some trees to wait out the search. "Well, well, well, so you're still lurking close by, huh?" he grinned, while reaching down casually for his radio to key the mic. "Well we can't be having you hurting an innocent woman or her girls now. No, the boss wouldn't like that," he added more settledly.

"Alex," Ted interrupted, "hold up, we may have something."

Doing so, Alex listened in on his own two-way radio, hoping Beth was doing the same.

Meanwhile, turning back to his radio, Ted asked, "What do you have?"

"It's Frank. We have company right across the road from here. And Ms. Rae's dog has just come back."

"I copy that. Keep an eye on him, I'll be right out," he ordered, turning back to Alex. "Did you get that?"

"Yeah. Beth?"

"I got it!" she returned, while slowing down to make their turn down Craig's road.

"Go for it, Ted," he ordered deeply.

"Gotchya."

Hanging up his cell phone, Ted headed out to the front porch. "Guys…" he called out quietly over his radio to the other undercover crew, including the two young patrolmen, "make your move, but let our men in uniform do the apprehension. Just cover him if our target tries to pull out another gun."

"You heard him!" one of the other officers called out over his end. "Let's hit it!"

Before long, the ground was full of activities, leading up to Tony's capture, which hadn't taken long.

Bringing him up to the front porch in handcuffs, he glared at Ted heatedly. "What's the meaning of this? I was just out getting some fresh air."

"Sorry, sir, but we've been experiencing trouble with prowlers here lately, and you were reported having been seen out on the balcony by some of the guys out walking the grounds. And furthermore," he pointed up toward the man's room, "those doors up there are to remain locked. You were told that by my assistant clerk when you checked in."

"So! What do you plan to do about it? Call your boss? I'll just tell her what I think of her rules."

"Well then perhaps, Mr. Belaro, a night in jail might help to open your eyes, and with any hope, start showing some respect for such rules. After all, they are placed here for your own protection."

"Sir," one of the uniformed officers asked, "are you wanting to press charges against this man?"

Looking down at Tony heatedly, as much as he wanted to put him behind bars, he and Alex needed him out to catch him at what he came there to do.

"Sir?"

"Well," Ted continued to glare down at the man, while hating him with every fiber of his being, "are you going to leave the doors up there alone? And as for Ms. Rae, I am in charge of this place, when she is unavailable."

"Fine," he growled. "I'll leave them alone."

"All right, let him go," he ordered, having heard Harry open his door to eavesdrop on their conversation. And keeping to his word, Ted didn't say anything about their conversation earlier, when sensing his fears. "Oh, and Mr. Belaro," he added in Harry's defense, with a slight grin, kept only to himself, "as for your friend. Next time he decides to lie to me about you're not going out through those doors, he's out of here, right along with you. Do I make myself clear?"

"Very," he glared back after the cuffs were removed.

"Good. I'm glad we understand each other," he bowed his head in gesture to saying goodnight. But then seeing Harry out of the corner of his eye, he knew for sure Tony scared him badly, as he slipped off quietly into their room. Meanwhile, after seeing Tony head that way, Ted held up a hand to Frank and the other men, while quietly going up after him, to listen in on their conversation.

Not hearing any potential problems coming from the other side of their door, he went back down to take the group out onto the porch for some coffee.

"What now?" Frank asked, when a few of the other men walked up quietly to be filled in.

"Stay close by, all of you. And stay alert. Marcose," he turned quietly, when seeing him looking ever so powerful with one strong capable hand holding a near empty cup of coffee, the other resting on his hip.

"Cover the back and side area of their room?" the man concluded with a broad grin.

"Yes. And Chase," he turned with the same grin, "I want you with him."

"Yes, sir," he said, putting down his cup, after downing his coffee.

"Are you finished with us, sir?" the two young patrolmen asked.

"Yes, but stay in the area in case I need you."

"Yes, sir."

"Frank," Ted turned back to him and another undercover officer, who looked fit to be a real groundskeeper, "I want the two of you out here on the front porch. Talk like you know what you're doing, and mention Hank's name, or any of the others, like you're pals," he murmured, while looking in, and up the stairs for any signs of trouble.

"Sure thing," they agreed, taking a seat.

"And Maggie," he bent down to instruct Jessi's dog to stay with them, "keep guard over the area. All right, girl?" he ordered, patting her shoulder lovingly.

With a soft bark, she turned back to Frank, but then stopped, as he glanced down at her. "Rrrr..." she began growling, as she started backing away.

"What is it, girl?" he asked, when suddenly feeling alarmed.

"Oh, uh..." Frank stopped quickly to think. "She, uh, probably smells Belaro on me, is all," he laughed nervously, while staring down at her.

"Yeah. Sure!" Ted agreed questioningly. *But then, you weren't anywhere near the guy, when they brought him up,* he questioned, while studying his reaction to the dog. "Well, in that case, I'll just leave her out here with the two of you anyway, while I go and put in another call to Alex. He'll want to know what's going on."

"Sure!" Frank agreed, while holding still, until Ted left them alone.

"Man, she sure doesn't like you!" Ted heard the other officer say, while standing just inside the foyer.

Hearing that, while puzzled over Maggie's reaction, Ted, once out of sight, darted off to one side of the doorway, holding up a finger to Lisa, who hadn't gone home yet.

Picking up quickly on his warning, she acted as though she were simply taking in more calls, while quietly watching, as he continued to eavesdrop on their conversation.

"Yeah, well," Frank stated, "like I said, she probably smells the guy on me."

"Yeah, right," the officer laughed, "and I know better that that!"

"You know nothing of the kind. And if you were smart, you would just keep your mouth shut, and let us pros handle this guy."

What...? The look on Ted's face went grave at what he had just heard. *Is this just my imagination, or is this cop dirty?* he wondered, while slipping off quickly into Jessi's office to call Alex. Stopping first, though, he pulled Lisa up off her chair to go in with him.

"Ted..." she began frightenedly, once inside the confines of her friends' office.

"Not a word," he murmured, while placing a finger to her lips, before going over to the window. While there, he muttered his frustration, while putting in his call to Alex.

Meanwhile, picking up sooner than Ted thought he would, Alex heard his friend over the other end. "What happened?" his asked quietly, while keeping an eye on the road.

"It was Tony, like we thought it might have been, and he went out the balcony doors. However, they're padlocked now."

"Good."

"Yeah, well, that's not all."

"What...?"

Not wanting to say anything just yet about his suspicions, concerning Frank, he went on to tell Alex about his and Harry's conversation, "He knows, Alex. Tony knows."

"Knows what?"

"The connection, between you and Jessi."

"What...? But how?"

"You were seen last weekend out at Craig's place with her."

"Damn..." he growled, when it suddenly hit. "Wait a minute. Just how did you get him to tell you that?"

"I told him I wasn't a cop," he laughed, seeing Lisa's reaction, as well.

"You... what...?" he asked, laughing over the phone.

"I told him... I wasn't a cop!"

"I'll be damned," he roared.

Meanwhile, after filling Alex in on everything that was going on, he added, "Take care of yourselves out there. Tony is pretty mad. So there's no telling what he will do now."

"Damn straight! Besides, we're too close to nailing him now to see it all go up in our faces."

"We'll get him, Alex, God help us, we'll get him." Ted replied, just before hanging up.

Turning into Craig's driveway, Alex pulled around back to park it in next to Beth's car.

"Well, here we are, safe and sound!" he announced more to Max than to the others, who were still sleeping soundly in their seats, while he went to shut off his vehicle, before opening his door. Turning to Max, he ordered him to stay, while he went in to check out the house. "I won't be long," he smiled.

Doing so, Max jumped up into his seat, while Alex went up to talk to Beth first.

"Would you mind staying with them, too, until I get through checking out the place?"

"No, not at all!"

"Good. Max is watching over them, too, while they're asleep."

"That doesn't surprise me. And about Jessi, she's been really running herself ragged here lately, she needs her rest."

Looking back at Jessi, he grinned, "Yes, and now it's time she gets it," he agreed, when turning to smile back at Beth, before heading up to unlock the back door.

Once inside, after turning on the kitchen light, he went over to the counter, near the refrigerator, to find a note from his sister that read:

Hi little brother,
Thought you guys would enjoy some extra groceries, so Rose and I went out and picked up a few more things. Make sure she eats well and gets a lot of rest, and call me in the morning, we have plans for you guys.

Love ya,
Sue

"Great, sis!" he laughed, while going around checking out the rest of the house, before returning to get the others.

"Is everything all right?" Beth asked, when he walked out, heading for his vehicle.

"Yes," he replied, opening the front passenger door first to get Jessi. "So what do you say we get them inside first, before getting the stuff unloaded?"

"All right!" she returned, while giving him a hand with the girls, when he went to gather Jessi up in his arms.

"Come on, boy," he called out to Max, prior to giving the door a kick of his boot to shut it, before heading back inside.

Once there, the light from the kitchen began to wake Jessi. "Mmmm... Alex...?" she murmured, while lifting her head to look up at him tiredly, "Are we here already?"

"Yes," he returned softly, as he looked down into her sleepy face. "Can you stand on your own okay, or should I take you on into the living room and lay you on the sofa?"

"No, I can stand!" she replied, looking around the kitchen, while he went to set her down. Seeing the box of groceries sitting on the counter, she asked, going over to them, "What's this?"

"It seems Sue and Rose went and did some shopping for us. Is anyone hungry?" he asked.

"Sure...!" they all smiled gladly.

"Mmmm... I wonder if there's any fruit?" Jessi mused, as she and Beth joined in, giving Alex a hand.

Seeing how there was, he smiled, while finding a wide variety of them, and even some snacks for the girls. Laughing, he announced, "Looks as though we have everything anyone could possibly want! So, if it's all right with you ladies, how about I go out and get our things unloaded, while you take care of things in here?"

"Beth?" Jessi turned, smiling.

"Sure!"

While the two took charge of the food, the girls gave Alex a hand. Though, at his insistence, they stayed inside and received their things to carry into the living room.

"Mom, where do you want us to set up the air mattresses?" Lora asked, seeing three of them sitting beside the sofa, when going into the living room to set her things down.

"Alex?" Jessi turned, hearing him walking back in.

"Just between the sofa and where my bed roll will be. Beth will be on the other side of the sofa, near the corner."

"Near the corner?" Beth asked puzzledly.

"Yes," he instructed, while going into the living room to show them what he was talking about. "As you can see, the corner would be the best place for you, as it's out of the way of the entryway. So if someone was to come in through that way, you could take them by surprise."

"Alex…" Jessi began concernedly, when nodding her head toward the girls.

Smiling, he shook his head reassuringly, "Not to worry, I have a couple of guys assigned to watch over them. They'll be meeting them later. However, as far as their mattresses concerned, there are two other rooms upstairs, aside from Craig's old room, if they want to stay up there?"

"Thanks," she returned his smile. "Girls, what do you think?"

"I… don't know," Lora replied, shaking her head. "What if…"

"No," Jessi knew what she was thinking, "you'll both be quite fine up there. Besides, this isn't the time he comes out… usually," she teased.

"Mom…, that's not funny," Lora frowned.

"I know, sorry. But just the same, why don't you two go on and take your mattresses up and pick out a room."

"What choices are you giving us?" Cassi asked, tiredly.

"The room second to the right of the hallway, or the back room, while you're waiting on the food to get ready. Both rooms are pretty nice."

"Okay," they agreed, doing so, while waiting on the food to be ready.

"And now," Alex turned back to go into the kitchen, "how's the food going?"

"Slow," both women replied, when going back in with him, while the girls took care of the air mattresses.

Turing back to see just how tired Jessi looked, he grinned down at her, "Why don't you go on back into the living room and get yourself comfortable, we can handle things from here," he turned to Beth and continued to grin.

"Are you sure?" she smiled.

"Yes. Now go," he suggested, while giving her a gentle shove out of the kitchen.

"Fine," she smiled tiredly, while retreating over to where she had left her sweats behind earlier, in the corner, near the fireplace, "and while I'm at it, I think I'll just go and get changed too!"

"Sure! Take your time!" he added, from the kitchen doorway, while watching her move around to get her things, before heading off toward the bathroom.

Looking back to see him standing there, looking all so powerful, she couldn't help but think how there was something about him that reminded her of Craig, while standing there. *"Oh, Craig..."* she cried out longingly, before breaking free of her thoughts to turn and walk away.

Watching him, watching Jessi, Beth couldn't help but admire the compassion he felt for her. "Hey, how about I give you a hand with this?" she offered warmly, when he turned back to get started on their food.

"Sure!" he smiled, when she went reaching across him to grab the bag of apples, while he pulled out a couple of plates from the cabinet.

"Just like old times, huh?" she commented, when getting a whiff of his manly scent.

"Yes, only..." he slowed his reach to look away.

"Oh, God, Alex... I'm so sorry!" she cried, bringing herself to stand in between him and the counter to place her arms around him. As she did, he too dropped his arms down around her waist. "I wanted so much to be here for you, but..."

"I know," he began, as he went to close his eyes to the smell of her fresh scented hair, when once again they found themselves holding each other. *Oh... sweet, little Beth,* he groaned, as he allowed his hands to run down to the small of her back. "By the way, Sergeant Lamb," he pulled back to look down into her warm, caring face, "I hear that congratulations are in order."

"For what?" she began, when remembering. "Oh, my promotion! Thanks!" she laughed.

"Yes, well..." he struggled with his words, while still fighting hard to control the burning desire he had buried inside for her. *Damn it to hell,* he growled, *how am I ever going to be able to put her behind me, when we are having to work so closely together?*

"A...Alex..." she cried, remembering, too, what they once had.

Not replying, he tried harder to keep his head cleared of such thoughts, since they had never consummated their relationship. Swallowing hard, he went on looking deep into her glistening blue eyes. "Yeah, well, I uh... was just wondering what your plans were now that you have earned your stripes?"

"Detective training!" she returned, when giving him one of her all knowing smiles, while knowing how much he still worries about her.

"God, you're really going ahead with it then, aren't you?"

"Yes, Alex, I am," she informed him sternly, while feeling his arms tighten around her.

Meanwhile, having decided to grab a shower, since the rest of the utilities were turned back on by Alex, after closing the bathroom door, Jessi leaned against it and closed her eyes for a moment. "Oh Craig..." she cried out quietly, "I need you so... much! Where are you...?"

Getting no answer, after a few moments had passed, she pushed away from the door to get her shower over with. Yet, while there, allowing the water to run over her tired body, she turned unknowingly to look out through the clear shower curtain. It was then she was pleasantly surprised to see him sitting on the sink, grinning back at her.

"Hi, beautiful," he smiled richly, while bringing on a chill to her senses.

"Hi, yourself!" she returned, while reaching over to turn off the water, before stepping out into the cool room to get her towel.

"Did you miss me?" he asked, hoping to cheer her up a little, while going on to admire her beautiful body.

"Yes, I sure have!" she whispered, while trying hard to ignore her sudden awareness, as his gaze dropped down to her voluptuous nipples, as they started to perk up. "Oh, Craig..." she groaned, feeling the heat of his desire on her body, "I wish we could hold each other for a little while. I have really missed feeling your arms around me."

"Don't you mean my uncles?" he teased.

"Craig...!"

"Sorry. And yes, I wish we could, too, but..."

"Alex has to approve of it, before you can just slip in and take over?"

"Yes, and then with the others here..." he smiled, while nodding his head over her right shoulder, at the closed door.

"Yes, well, I'll figure something out. As for Alex, I'll ask him after we get settled in."

"Until then..." he placed a kissed finger to her lips, "I'll see ya later."

"Yes, later."

After finishing up in the bathroom, she went out to find the beds already made up, and an area fixed up near the fireplace for Alex.

"Ask me what?" he grinned, knowing she had been talking to his nephew all along, while the others were all in their beds sleeping, except for Beth, who was now curled up on her air mattress, reading a book.

"Alex..." she nearly cried, seeing him standing near the kitchen doorway, after having just shut off the light.

"Sorry, but what were you about to ask me?"

"Why don't we..." she pointed back off toward the kitchen.

Leading the way, he went in ahead of her, while switching the light back on so she could continue filling him in on her conversation with Craig.

"Did you hear everything that was said?" she asked, once they could talk more privately.

"No, just the last part," he grinned boyishly.

"You must think I'm crazy."

"No. Though Bob told me that only certain people have the gift to perceive a spirit's presence, I couldn't help but laugh. So, what does he want this time, as if I don't already know?"

"Oh, Alex..." she began, only to turn away to hide her feelings.

"Ah... I see! He wants to spend some time with you, is it?"

"Just to hold me for a little while. I really miss him, Alex!" she cried, while turning back to gaze up into his caring blue eyes.

"I know, you were crying out to him earlier in your sleep."

"Oh, Lord, Alex, I'm sorry!"

"No, don't be. Love comes in all shapes and sizes, as well as forms," he laughed.

"Yes, so it seems! Does this mean..."

"Yes, later, when I know it's safe," he offered, while smiling down on her gentle face. "But be easy on this old body, won't you?" he whispered, while not wanting Beth to know what it was all about, just yet.

"Oh, Alex..." she continued to smile, while picking up on his concern for Beth. "About Craig and I! To keep things private between us, why don't I take an air mattress up to stay in his old room, so you or Beth can have the sleeper sofa?"

"Are you sure you really want to do that?"

"Yes. Besides, it'll be fun! I guess."

"All right, but I'll take it up for you."

"Okay," she replied, while reaching up to give him a warm hug. "Thanks, Alex."

"Yeah, right," he grumbled playfully, "just what I wanted before my birthday."

"Oh? When is your birthday?"

"Next week."

"Why, Alex…" she teased, "you're getting older!"

"Don't push it, lady," he warned playfully.

"Yes, sir," she smiled, when he turned to walk out of the kitchen.

Stopping in the doorway, he smiled at the sight of seeing Beth having fallen off to sleep on her air mattress. Shaking his head, he turned back just enough to tell Jessi that they had better be calling it a night, too.

"Yes, you're right, we should!" she smiled at the fond look on his face, when he saw Beth all curled up on her mattress.

"Looks like I'll have to put her in where you were going to sleep?"

"Oh, but no… she looks so peaceful lying there. Why don't we just wait until morning to change the sleeping arrangements?"

"Because we only have the three air mattresses," he returned.

"Oh," she had forgotten, while going over to offer him a hand, after gathering up a few items of food to take up with her.

Reaching Beth's side, he knelt down to ease his arms in under her body to slowly gather her up against him. "Here we go, sleepyhead," he murmured, while carrying her over to the sofa, where Jessi had pulled back one of her own blankets, after taking Craig's off to bring upstairs with her. Once he had laid her down, he went back over to get the air mattress. "Ready?" he asked, turning to carry it up for her.

"Yes."

Shaking his head on the way out to the foyer, he asked again, "Are you sure about this?"

"Yes, Alex, I'm sure!" she replied, taking the steps ahead of him.

Once they got to the doorway of Craig's old room, walking in ahead of him, she sensed Craig's presence right away.

"He's here, isn't he?" Alex asked, seeing the warm expression come over her face, when he too felt the charge in the air from his nephew's presence.

"Yes," she smiled, as he looked around the dark and musty room, before closing the door behind him.

Taking the air mattress over to lay near the front window, the two soon had it made up, before taking his place on it next to her.

"Jess? He will return me, this time, back down to my bedroll, won't he?"

"Yes, Alex," she chuckled. "Especially with the others here, now."

"Good," he grinned. "Then I guess I'll just be saying my goodnight's for now so that the two of you can be together."

"Don't you mean morning?" she laughed once again, while pointing to her lit up watch.

"Oh, Lord, you're right!" he groaned, seeing that it was already one in the morning, while still wearing his shoulder holster, when laying back to look up at the ceiling. "Jessi?"

"Yes, Alex?"

"What are you going to do when all this is over?"

"I don't know!" she replied, feeling the hurt of the words, when turning over onto her side, to cry quietly into her pillow.

Just as he drifted off to sleep, Craig stepped in and turned Jessi back to face him. "Oh…

Jessi," his voice came across warmly, while sensing her tears, "I'm so sorry for causing you so much pain," he murmured, while pulling her even more into his arms.

"Craig…" she cried even more, while wrapping her arms around him, where together they cried each other to sleep.

Chapter Twenty-Eight

Just before daylight, Craig had to pull away, when his time in Alex's body was nearly over. Before going, he went down to the bathroom to get her a cool washcloth for her eyes. Coming back, he crawled in beside her. "I love you, Jess," he whispered softly in her tear-dampened hair, when going on slowly to lightly kiss her lips. When he did, she responded, causing their kiss to grow to where they would have to fight to control their desire for one another.

"Oh, Craig!" she cried, fearing their time was about up, sooner than she had thought.

"It's going to be okay," he offered with that crooked smile. "We still have time, yet."

"I'm glad!" she returned, tracing his lips with trembling fingers, until he went to reclaim them again.

Closing her eyes though, to welcome what was supposed to be one last kiss, came a fire, which housed so much passion, it set both their hearts and spirits aglow, before returning Alex down to his bedroll.

After several hours went by, Alex woke to find the others still sleeping. "Mmmm…" he groaned, getting up to go into the kitchen. Once there, he went over to start up her camp stove, before putting on some coffee. "Hey there, boy!" He turned to see Max waiting by the back door. "Do you want to go out for awhile?"

Excitedly, Max jumped up on him, panting and wagging his tail.

"All right," he laughed, taking that moment to go out and grab some clothes he had left in the Blazer.

Afterwhich, heading for the man-made shower, he thought how nice it would be to use it instead of the indoor shower. "Oh, man…

this is great!" he groaned, after turning it on and stepping in to tilt his head back and wash off.

Meanwhile, inside, Beth was waking up, thinking she heard someone in the kitchen. Getting up, she went in to check it out. However, to her surprise, there was no one there, just the coffee pot on, getting hot. "Hmmm, that's strange! I thought someone was just in here."

Seeing how wrong she was, going over to the back door, she walked out into the bright sunlit yard, not hearing the outside shower running. Walking out a little further, with her mind going back to earlier days, she came upon the area where Alex was about to step out.

Turning as he did, she gasped, covering her mouth at the mere sight of his well-endowed manliness, and all its glory. "Oh, my, Lord..., Alex... I'm sorry!"

"Beth...!" he cried out, as well, though not offering to cover himself at that time.

"I...I...I was just coming out to uh... to uh..."

"Look for me?" he grinned, while toweling off some of the water from his face.

When she didn't answer, he followed her gaze down to his manhood, which seemed to have caused an arousal. Looking back up to see her eyes glaze over, and her face turn a scarlet red, it dawned on him how they had never been intimate. "Oh, that's right," he spoke up, smiling, "you never saw me this way before, have you?"

Swallowing hard, she shook her head, "N...n...no, I haven't."

Offering to wrap the towel around his narrow waist, he reached out to take her arm. "Come on, let's get back inside, before the others wake up."

"What...?" she cried, when pulling back to stop him, "You can't be serious."

"What do you mean?"

"D...don't you think you should put on some clothes first?"

Looking down at himself, he laughed, "You're right, I had better be doing just that!"

Turning back to grab his jeans, he dropped his towel to slip them on.

Doing so, Beth turned away quickly to avoid any further embarrassment.

"Okay, now that that is done, are we ready?" he asked, grabbing up the rest of his things to carry back inside.

Looking back slowly, she was relieved to see he was looking more presentable. "Yes."

"Beth, it's all right, you know? It's just a body!"

"Yes, but one I've never…" she stopped.

"Seen before?" he grinned.

"Alex, please…!"

"All right," he returned, seeing how she truly was bothered by it.

Returning back to the house, he went right in to get their coffee poured, before going up to Craig's old room to check on Jessi. While there, he wanted to go through the old crate of stuff he had almost forgotten about.

"What are you going to be doing this morning?" she asked, standing at the counter, while watching him pour their coffee.

"Go up and look through that crate of Craig's to see what all he has in it! And you?"

"Get things straightened up a little, and then I'll probably come up afterwards to see some of those things, as well. If you don't mind, that is?"

"No, I'd like that." Taking two of the cups of coffee with him, he turned back and smiled, "See ya in a little bit."

Returning his smile, she went back into the living room to make up her bed, while the girls slept in a little while longer.

"Alex…?" she called out, before he had gotten half way up the stairs.

"Yeah?" he stopped to look back down at her.

"How did I get on the sofa?"

"I put you there, when Jessi decided to sleep up in Craig's old room. Which reminds me, did you sleep okay?"

"Like a baby. Thanks."

With a grin, he was off to hit the old crate, while she went around tidying up the place, before getting herself dressed.

Meanwhile, up in Craig's room, while walking in to check on Jessi, he smiled, seeing how she was still asleep. "That's it, you go right ahead and sleep," he murmured, while going over to set their cups down next to the crate, before opening it. As he did, he saw a wide array of things his nephew had collected over the years. "Well, well, well, what do we have in here?" he asked, laughing at some of the things he came across. When then, he saw it, a picture of him, Craig, and David, standing by Rose and Allen's grill. "Wow, what's this?" he asked, looking it over, more closely, when there in the background, he noticed a man standing off to the side of the McMasters' house. Turning the picture over to see when it had been taken, he was shocked. "Two years ago? On my birthday?" he questioned, as he went on to read it aloud.

July 3, 1998
Alex's 47th Birthday
Alex, Craig, and David

"Damn! I've got to get this blown up!" he growled a little too loudly, when accidently waking Jessi.

"Mmmm... Alex...!"

"Hey, there, didn't mean to wake you."

"No, that's all right, I should be getting up anyway. But what were you just talking about? Get what blown up?" she asked, opening her eyes fully to the smell of coffee in the air.

"This," he said, getting to his feet to show her the picture. "Take a look and tell me who you think the guy in the background is."

Rubbing the sleep from her eyes, she asked while sitting up on her air mattress, "Where?"

"Right there," he pointed, holding the three by five picture out for her to see. "Behind David, see him?"

"Yes, that looks like..." she focused a little harder. "Tony...?" she questioned, when looking up to see the hard look on Alex's face. "But what was he doing there?"

"I don't know, but you see it too, don't you?"

"See what?"

Turning, they both saw Beth walking in, just then.

Handing the picture to her, he helped her to stand up slowly.

"Are you all right?" he asked, seeing her waver a bit.

"Yes, just getting my sea legs from standing on this air mattress, is all."

"Alex," Beth spoke up, interrupting them, when she saw the same thing they did, "you're right, you'll need to have it enlarged to prove anything."

"Let's go downstairs then and call the station," he suggested. "I'll have the lab come out and get it."

"Have you called Sue yet?" Jessi asked, while bringing up the rear.

"No, I'll do that first to see if she has the negative," he replied, when stopping at the top of the stairs to collect his thoughts. "Beth, Jessi, this proves beyond a shadow of a doubt that Tony was around."

"Alex," Jessi spoke up, "you already have his gun! What more proof do you need?"

"I want to nail him, Jessi, and hard..." he growled.

"Alex, honestly, I know how you must feel, but..." she began sadly, when remembering the night she first saw Craig's old crate.

Looking to her worriedly, he asked, reaching out to take her arm, "Are you all right?"

"Yes, I'm fine! Just thinking about how I tripped over that thing a month ago." With a laugh, she added, "That's when..." Stopping, she looked back at Beth.

"That's when what?" she asked.

"Jessi..." Alex spoke up.

"Beth," she stopped for a moment, "there's something I really must..."

"Jessi..." he cut her off again.

"Alex, I have to!"

"Well, it sure would be nice to know what's going on!" Beth laughed shyly.

"Jessi... are you sure you really want to do this?"

"Yes, Alex, I'm sure."

"Yes, but everything?"

"To a certain degree, yes."

"All right. But how about after we go and see what Sue and Rose wants first?"

Seeing how bothered he was by it, she agreed. "Well in that case I'll go and get the girls up so we will be ready to go."

"Sounds good. Beth," he turned, "you coming down with me, or going in to see about the girls with her?"

"Jessi?" she asked.

"It's up to you!"

Thinking it over, Beth chose going downstairs with Alex to see what else she could learn about that day.

Meanwhile, after the two went on down, Jessi went looking to see which room her girls had taken. Upon sticking her head in the second door next to Craig's room, she was right to guess that one, as the girls were beginning to stir when she walked in.

"Hi, mom…" Cassi moaned. "What time is it?"

"It's still early yet, but Alex is wanting to see what his sister and Rose were planning for us today. That, and I didn't think either of you wanted to be left here alone. Not saying Alex would have agreed on that."

"No, that's o…kay…!" Lora grinned. "Though I didn't have any trouble falling asleep, I'm still not ready to meet any troubled spirits yet."

With that, they all laughed, while bringing attention to those downstairs, when they headed that way after grabbing a change of clothes.

On the way down, Jessi asked if they wanted to grab a shower out in the man-made one.

"Are you kidding…?" Lora asked, wrinkling up her nose at the idea.

"No! It's really quite nice, once you get use to it. And it's totally private. No one will see you, not even from the air."

Looking to her sister, she shrugged. "Well?"

"If you stand guard while I'm in there?"

"Yeah…! What did you think I would do? Go out to the street with a sign, charging admission? Duh…!" Lora replied, rolling her eyes.

Jessi laughed, walking into the living room, where Beth was sitting on the made up sofa, while the girls grabbed a few towels, shampoo, and some soap, before heading out. Stopping though, they told Alex what they were going to do.

"That's fine, but come straight back in when you're both done."

With a nod of their heads, they went out the back door, calling Max to go with them.

Meanwhile, having put in the call to his sister, he watched the both of them from the back doorway, until they reached the shower, where they stepped into the enclosure to get changed. Coming back around to check on Jessi and Beth, the two threw a pillow at him and laughed.

"Funny," he laughed, while waiting for his sister to pick up.

"Yes, we kind of thought so," Jessi laughed with her cup of coffee in hand.

Turning at that moment, he saw the girls playing with Max, instead of taking their showers like they had planned. But then, and not too far off in the tree line was one of his men watching them. *Good,* he thought quietly, when hearing his sister's voice on the other end. "Hey, Sis!" he went on, while going into the kitchen to talk more privately.

"How's Jessi been feeling?" she asked, while going over to get comfortable on her sofa.

"She's doing pretty good."

"Good. Have you all eaten yet?"

"No. Why?"

"We were just getting started with breakfast. Why don't you bring everyone over?"

"Sounds good."

"Oh, and Alex," she cut in, "if she's drinking coffee, take it away from her. She isn't supposed to have caffeine anymore."

"Oh, great! I might as well give her a loaded gun, she's not going to like hearing that!" he laughed, when coming back in to take Jessi's cup, while shaking his head *no* at her. "Yeah," he went on, "we'll be right over!"

Hanging up, Jessi looked hard at him. "What was that all about?"

"It seems like we've been invited over for breakfast, then lunch at Rose's. She also said no more coffee for you," he went on laughing.

"What?" she hollered at him. "Alex... you know how I am without my coffee. And if by chance you have forgotten..." she laughed, when turning at that moment to see Craig standing off around the corner, doing the same.

"No, that's all right, I remember," he groaned, playfully, while heading for the back door to make good on his escape, if she were to come after him.

Stopping, he turned back to see her shaking her head. "You are so in for it," she threatened, with her usual warm, smiling face.

"Good, at least it's only a threat. I can handle them!" he roared, while going on out to his Blazer. "Girls... does this mean you're skipping the shower for now?"

"That's for sure...!" Cassi squealed. "No one told us it had only cold water...!"

Laughing, he told them how that was good for their circulation.

"Thanks, but no thanks," Lora replied. "I don't think you would want to hear just how loud we can scream when going through that."

"No. Nor would you want to see just what would happen if my guy out there in the tree line would have to come running with his gun drawn, thinking you were in danger...!" he roared, seeing the same from his guy, when the man reared his head back with laughter.

"Yeah well it wouldn't have been a pretty sight for any of us," Lora groaned, playfully.

"No, I don't imagine it would at that. So now, if everyone is ready, let's go have breakfast at my sister's, before going over here to the neighbor's house!" he called out, turning to Max. "How about you, boy? Are you coming or staying?"

"Rrrr... Rrrr..." Max replied, while bounding over to jump all over his best buddy.

Turning back to see the look on Beth's face, he laughed, "I guess he's coming with us!"

"You think?" she too joined in on the laughter, along with the girls, when they came up to the Blazer to get in, while he went to open their door for them.

Going back into the living room, Beth asked Jessi if she was ready.

"Sure, just give me a minute," she said, while holding up a silent hand to Craig, and asked, "What about the girls?"

"They're already out in the Blazer with Max."

"All right, I'll be right out," she replied, when Alex came back in to check on them.

Seeing Jessi's warm, smiling, face, he didn't have to ask. "Shall we?" he turned to Beth. "We'll be out back waiting!" he grinned back at her.

Once they had gone out, Jessi called out softly to Craig.

"Right here!" he spoke up from behind her.

"Hey, there!" she was saying, when Beth came walking back in unexpectedly to get something she had forgotten, while the others remained outside waiting on them.

"Jessi..." she spoke up, just as Alex came up from behind to stop her.

Though, he was too late, when they both stopped abruptly, when seeing Craig standing near the fireplace.

"C...Craig" Alex cried, tearfully, thinking he would never catch sight of his nephew's spirit. "Oh, my... God!" he spoke up again, while staring right at him. "I...I can see you! I...I mean, that really is you, isn't it?"

"Yes, Alex, it's really me," he replied, still smiling, when he then looked to his favorite adopted sister. "Hi there, Bethany!" he teased, being the only one allowed to call her that.

"Oh, LordC...Craig!" she broke down crying, as her knees were about to give way, when Alex went to hold her to him for support.

"Yeah, squirt, it's me."

"Oh, my goodness, I...I...I c...can't believe it!" she stammered, as the tears began streaming down both their faces.

"Oh, God, Craig..." Alex continued, while stopping long enough to lean back against the doorway for added support, "I am so sorry! I had no idea what had happened, until it was all over with. And finding you... here..." he broke up over the memory playing back in his mind, "was the worst nightmare, come true for me. Why" he cried, wanting to go to his nephew and just hold him, but knew that he couldn't. "God, why did it have to be you?" he asked, angrily.

"I want to know the answer to that question as much as you do. But first, you must help Jessi. Keep her safe for me. Don't ever leave her alone, Alex. Please, promise me you won't ever leave her alone."

"I promise, she'll always be safe."

Turning back to Jessi, "And you," he grinned, knowing her temperament, "behave yourself out there, and mind my uncle," he ordered, while smiling down at her.

"Yeah, right! The day she listens to me...!" Alex roared, thinking of someone else standing right in front of him. "She, and a lot like someone else we know," he hugged onto Beth snuggly, "are two of the most stubbornness women around."

"Yes," Craig laughed along with him, while looking back at Beth, "they sure... are."

"Well, if the two of you are done picking on us, we have to get going!" Beth and Jessi both laughed.

Turning to Craig, though, Jessi smiled up at him. "We'll be back in a little while."

"All right. Have fun!" he smiled, tipping his head at her.

"Craig..." Alex turned back before he could vanish.

"Yeah?"

"I will be seeing you again, won't I?"

"Count on it, Uncle," he grinned coyly. "Besides, I'm going to have to talk to you anyway and..." he turned to Jessi, lovingly.

"Yeah, I sort of thought so, you dirty dog," he laughed.

"I love her, Alex," he turned back. "God, how...I...love...her..." he choked back on the last few words.

"I know, bro. I know."

Tearfully, they said their goodbyes, as Craig slowly faded away before them.

Walking out, Alex was full of sadness, as he walked over to get into his Blazer.

Doing the same, Jessi and Beth both joined him.

"Alex?" Jessi spoke up first.

"I'm all right. Let's just get over to Sue's. She'll probably have breakfast ready when we get there," he replied, looking to Beth, who was seated in between them, as she looked up at him, half smiling, though with tears still lingering close to those blue eyes of hers.

Looking off to one side, Jessi knew she would be hearing about it later, and not when the girls were around.

Chapter Twenty-Nine

After arriving at his sister's, Sue had shown the girls into the family room to watch TV, before preparing their breakfast. Meanwhile, Alex made himself at home, in the kitchen, to talk to his sister, while in the living room, Beth and Jessi stayed behind so Bob could check Jessi over for precautionary measures.

"Well, you're looking pretty good! How are you feeling?" he asked, while putting away his stethoscope.

"Not too bad!" she smiled.

"And you, Beth? Alex tells us that you've gone off to get your stripes! How did that go?"

"It was hard, really hard," she laughed, with a slight blush to her cheeks. But then, they all turned, when hearing Sue cry out from the kitchen.

"Alex! No!"

"Well, I guess he told her!" Beth turned to Jessi and smiled.

"Uh, huh!"

Getting up to see what the commotion was about, Sue came rushing into the living room to tell her husband what Alex had just told her. "Oh, Bob, I know you will want to hear this," she continued tearfully.

"Hear what?"

"Bob," Jessi spoke up thoughtfully, when seeing the broad grin on Alex's face, "if it's what I think it is, you might want to sit back down first."

Doing just that, he looked on anxiously, "All right, I'm sitting! What is it?"

"Bob, I saw him! We saw him!" Alex corrected, while pointing back and forth between himself and Beth.

"Who?"

"Craig…!" Beth exclaimed, cheerfully, as hers and Alex's tears broke free once again.

"At the house?" he asked, looking to Sue, and then Alex.

"Yes," Alex went on, while taking a seat, on the arm of the couch, next to Beth and Jessi.

"Doctor Bob," Jessi interjected, "he's still with us! Maybe not in body, but in spirit, and he can hear your thoughts! All of you! As for Alex and Beth, they just happened to get lucky and see him for themselves!"

"I can see why," Sue smiled, "Craig and Alex have always had a special bond between them, and Beth…" she smiled.

"And Beth," Bob added warmly, "she and Craig had also taken on a special bond."

"Oh?" Jessi asked, not knowing everything about the two of them.

"Jess," Alex went on to explain, "Beth had lost both her parents in a car accident. From there, she went to stay with her Grandmother, until the woman fell ill. At which time she had to send her to a convent, where she remained until she joined the force!"

"The convent wasn't so bad, though! Reverend Mother told me that my calling was out in the real world and that…" Suddenly, she couldn't go on.

Sensing there was more, Jessi placed a caring hand on hers. "It's okay," she smiled, "we can talk later if you would like."

Smiling back, "Thank you," she returned. "It's nice to know that you and my adoptive brother have this connection with each other."

"Your adoptive… brother?"

"When they met, Craig kind of adopted Beth as his little sister!" Bob offered with a warm nod of his head, seeing how it all was affecting Beth with his son's state of being.

"Jessi," Alex interrupted, "just before leaving the house…"

"I know," she smiled, feeling Craig's love through his uncle, "I can feel it, too!"

Shaking his head, she reached over with her free hand to take his, thoughtfully.

"Well…" Sue cried. "Is anyone going to tell us?"

"Shall I?" Alex grinned.

Knowing what it was, Jessi nodded her head softly.

"He says," he began, "that he loves her. And if I know my nephew, it's pretty deep."

"Oh… honey…" Sue came over, along with everyone else in the room to offer their sympathy for what she was feeling, when she looked away sadly.

At that point, Jessi couldn't hold the tears back for what she too felt for Craig.

"If it's any consolation," Sue went on, "we all felt his presence there, too, every time we went into the house. And then when Rose told me that you were staying there from time to time, I thought you must be out of your mind!"

"That was, until Alex told us the rest of the story!" Bob added.

"Sue, I never asked for this gift," Jessi went on. "It just came to me. I think it all began the night before I met your son!"

"The dream Rose told me about?" she asked.

"Yes."

"Jessi," Bob returned, "we're all grateful for this gift you have. And with it, Craig can be happier now, knowing that the two of you are there to help ease his pain. Aside from that, just knowing that these men are going to pay for what they did to him."

"Oh, but no…! Bob…" she explained, sadly, "Craig has to handle these men on his own! Alex can only be there to protect those from Tony!"

"But, I don't understand! Why on earth not…?" he asked, not remembering what all they covered at the seminar.

"Bob, she's right," Alex went on to explain, "Craig was alone when he died. And now, he has to end this nightmare alone."

"Oh, my…" Beth sighed, understanding now what they were trying to say.

"Oh, that's right!" Bob recalled, shaking his head. "I remember now, we covered that at the seminar last year."

"Well, I've heard enough," Sue interrupted. "If no one has lost their appetite yet, how about some breakfast?" she asked, while getting up to head for the kitchen.

"Toast and oatmeal will be fine for me," Jessi replied, thoughtfully.

"Same here," Beth put in.

"All right. And how about you, Alex?"

"Whatever you fix," he replied, quietly, while getting up to walk into the kitchen.

"What, the human garbage disposal doesn't care?" Sue laughed. But then seeing the look on his face, when he passed her by in the doorway, she became concerned.

"Alex," Jessi got up to go after him, "are you all right?"

"No, not really," he replied, standing at the patio doors, while looking out over the backyard, at the birdbath, that was surrounded by a few shade trees, he and Craig helped to plant.

"Thinking about Craig?" she asked, placing a gentle hand over his broad shoulder.

"Yes. God, Jessi, I can't explain how I really feel, when there he was, standing right in front of us. I could have reached out and touched him," he said, reaching out his hand, as if recollecting the memory of wanting to touch his nephew. "Though, I know you can't touch a spirit, can you?" he asked, looking down into Jessi's gentle green eyes, and wanting so much to hold her. But with Beth there, he knew it was best not to, since he still cared so much for her too.

"No, but you got more than that. You had him inside you, more than once!" she whispered, as a warm smile touched her lips, right along with his thumb, when he went to trace them.

"Yes, I know," he replied, smiling at the mere thought of what his nephew has with her. Their relationship, though, so deep, and so passionate, it seared with so much fire. *God, Jess, what is going to happen when all this is over,* he wondered, while shaking his head suddenly.

"What is it, Alex? What were you just thinking?"

"Nothing. Just thinking," he replied, and turned away.

"All right everybody, let's eat!" Sue announced, while setting the table.

While eating, the conversation was kept light. Though afterwards, they all headed over to Rose and Allen's for a late cookout, and some good old fun in the pool.

Everyone, except David and the girls, was excited to hear about Alex and Beth's experience.

"That must have been quite a shock for the two of you?" Allen laughed. "Although, I've had my doubts about things like that happening. But hearing about it now…!" He shook his head.

"Yes," Alex agreed. "It was quite a shock."

"Well, how about we join the youngins' in the pool, before it's time to eat," Allen suggested, while getting to his feet.

Getting up as well, Alex agreed, while he and the others stripped down to their suits, having changed into them earlier, knowing they would be going swimming.

Seeing Jessi in a different suit, he grinned, "I see you decided to heed my warning!"

"Well, I couldn't exactly show up Beth's suit now, could I?" she pointed back to where Beth was standing.

Seeing her in a simple, nevertheless, pleasing number, he was still thrown, when Jessi shoved him back into the pool, yet again.

"Nice going!" the crowd applauded her.

"Well, I couldn't have done it without Beth!" she announced, when Alex came up for air.

Hearing that Beth was the ringleader this time, he looked up at her mischievously, before heaving himself up out of the pool, nearest to where they were standing. "You…?" he growled playfully, while walking up to take her by the wrist. "Haven't you learned better than to do that to your commanding officer?"

"Oh, God" she cried out, when attempting to brake free, when feeling his hands come up around her waist to pull her up into his arms. "Alex, no!" she cried out, as he pulled her into the pool with him.

Coming up, she was still screaming at him, while still in his arms.

"Girl!" he laughed, when he then kissed her passionately, just to cut her off.

But then, once they parted, he wiped the water from off his face, when no sooner had he, she splashed it back up at him. "Alex!" she screamed. Only she wasn't playing, as she was truly upset with him, over their kiss, when hating the memories it brought back to her.

"What…?" he asked, seeing her frustration.

"How…" she started to cry, as she turned, angrily, to get away from him.

"Beth…? What…?" he asked, while reaching out to pull her back, but missed catching her arm. Then seeing Jessi along the sideline, he calling out to her, as well, when seeing her mixed expression at what had just happened.

Seeing how worried he looked, she knew he still felt strongly toward Beth. And why not, she was a real jewel, and she liked her. "I'll talk to her," she offered, when breaking out into a caring smile, to set his mind at ease.

"Thanks," he smiled sadly, while watching her walk over to join Beth at a far table.

"What happened?" Bob asked, while joining him in the pool.

"I think I upset her with that kiss!"

"By bringing back some deeply imbedded memories?"

"Yeah."

"You've got to be a little more careful! Memories like what the two of you shared are still, yet, sensitive for her."

"She isn't the only one," he groaned, looking on sadly at the two of them.

Having joined up with Beth, while the others went on swimming, Jessi was just about to say something, when Beth cut her off. "Please…" she cried, turning away, "it's okay!"

"Is it?" she asked, going around to take a seat in front of her." Beth, I saw the way the two of you were looking at each other. You still love him, don't you?"

"Yes, God help me, yes I do! But…"

"Departmental rules?"

"Yes! But how…" she cried in surprise, when looking back into Jessi's eyes, as Jessi reached over to take her hand.

"Sue and Rose told me."

"Oh…? But then what am I to do…?"

"Enjoy the time you have with him!" she smiled, while thinking about Craig.

"And you? What about you?"

Pulling away sadly, it was Beth who took Jessi's hand this time.

"I love him!" Jessi began to tear up.

"Craig…?"

"You thought it was Alex…?"

"Well…?"

"Oh, Beth…!" Jessi knew then she was going to have to tell her about the three of them.

"What? What is it?" she asked, sensing something really deep.

"Oh, Beth, there is something I have to tell you. But not here. And not now."

"About Alex?"

"Yes, and it also involves Craig in a most beautiful way."

"Oh, Lord, Jessi," she cried. "Please… tell me…!"

"I will…" she sighed heavily, not knowing where to start, "but it isn't quite that easy!"

"Please…! Try…!"

Looking back at Alex, Jessi stood, pulling Beth with her. "Come with me."

"Where are we going?" she asked, gathering up her clothes, when she remembered to grab her service revolver, and radio, that she was to carry on her at all times, other than the pool and shower, of course.

Following Jessi over to Rose, who was now stepping out of the pool, Jessi called back over her shoulder, "I'll tell you in a moment. Rose?" she called out.

"Yes, dear?" she returned, grabbing her towel.

"If Alex wonders where we went, tell him…" she stopped to see Beth's radio. "Tell him we'll be right back. We're just going over there to talk more privately," she explained, while pointing off toward the woods, where she noticed two of Alex's men standing by.

"Rose, tell him I'll have my radio on me," Beth added. "If he needs me, call me."

"All right."

"Are we ready?" Jessi asked, taking the lead.

"Sure!"

Spotting Marcose and Baker right away, Marcose asked if everything was all right, when they walked up.

"Yes," Beth returned, looking puzzled.

"Alex called this morning to have Brandon and I watch over the area," he offered, turning to Jessi. "He also thought your girls would like to check out the place, while they're here."

"And there's a lot to check out, too!" Baker added, while looking off toward the pool, when Jessi's older daughter got out to dry off her long, light brown, hair. Unlike her younger sister, whose hair was more along the lines of a reddish-brown, with blue eyes, whereas, Lora had eyes like her mother's.

"Baker?" Jessi spoke up, seeing where he was looking.

"Yes, ma'am!" he snapped back. "Sorry, but is that one of your daughters?" he pointed.

"Yes." She couldn't help but to laugh.

"Baker..." Marcose spoke, sternly, "put your eyes back in their sockets. We're here to work, not flirt."

"Yes, sir," the tall, twenty-five year old replied, while running a hand through his dark brown hair. And with the most deepest of blue eyes ever seen, stole one last look at her daughter, before turning away.

Turning back to the others, Marcose, an average height, well built, detective, in his early forties, cleared his throat, "Ladies!" he then smiled his gorgeous smile.

"Yes, well," Beth smiled at the two, "we were just going for a walk, but not too far from where Alex could still see us. Stay close by in case we need you."

"Sure thing," he replied, while hanging back some with Brandon, so she and Jessi could still talk privately, and not be overheard.

Arriving at an area where they spotted a creek running through it, Jessi went over to take a seat on a fallen tree, along with Beth.

"Ms. Jessi..." Beth spoke up, wondering why she felt a need for privacy.

"Beth, knowing Alex as you do, you know how finding Craig the way he did was really horrible for him?"

"Yes, I do!"

"Well, Alex blames himself for not being there, when Craig was killed. And now..."

"He wants to do whatever he can to make up for it? Yes, I know that! And he is! He's going after the men who had done this to him."

"Well, yes, but somehow, he feels that doing that, isn't enough."

"Then what? What are you trying to tell me?"

"Oh, Beth...!"

Telling Beth what she could, once she had finished, Beth was filled with both admiration and envy, as she smiled back. "You are so lucky to have that kind of love," she cried, unaware that Alex had been standing off in the trees listening for some time now.

"Then you're not upset?" he asked, walking up quietly.

"Alex...!" they both cried, when looking up to see him standing there.

"Beth?" he asked again, while looking at Jessi out of the corner of his eye.

"Well" she laughed nervously, "upset? No! However, it does sound like something out of a paranormal love story!"

"Thanks!" he smiled over at Jessi, as a feeling of relief came over him. "And now, how about we go back and join the others, before they start talking about us."

"And just what would they be saying?" Beth asked innocently.

With one raised eyebrow, he watched her blush at what he was thinking. By then the three began to laugh, while heading back, talking about how lucky they were for having nice weather for the swim.

After spending more time in the pool, Jessi, once again, got Alex, when he least expected it. "Ooops...! I'm sorry...!" she laughed along with the others. "I would have thought by now you would have remembered not to trust me!"

"Oh... but I do trust you," he laughed, coming up out of the pool, while using the ladder this time. "Just you wait until I catch you," he warned, clearing the last step to go after her with a playful look of contempt in his eyes.

"Alex" she laughed, dodging in behind both Allen and David for protection.

"Now, Alex," Allen laughed along with his son and the others, "you don't really want to hurt this poor girl, do you?"

With his hands resting on his narrow hips, while fighting back the laughter, Alex grinned mischievously. "Oh, but of course not."

"There, now, Ms. Jessi," Allen turned to look back at her, "he doesn't really want to hurt you!" he laughed, stepping aside to allow Alex just enough room to grab her wrist.

"Allen" she screamed, "I thought you were my friend!"

"Sorry, dear, but Alex is much stronger than I am. And he may consider me to be harboring a felon!"

"Alex! No!" she continued to cry out, as he swept her up off her feet, and up over his broad shoulder, to carry her off to the pool.

Trying futilely to get away, he growled humorously, "Oh, no you don't," he continued, while getting even closer to throw her in.

"Sue…! Rose…! Beth…! Girls…! Help me…!"

With that having been said, in one fell swoop, Alex had her cradled in both arms, while grinning down at her smiling face. "Give it up, pretty lady, you're not getting rescued by any of them," he laughed. "So take your punishment like a good little girl."

"Wrong… dear little brother," Sue spoke up, while walking up with the others in tow.

"Oh… and you think you can stop me?"

"No!" she smiled, looking off toward David.

"No…!" David cried, shaking his head.

"David…!" Sue shot him one of her warning looks.

"Fine," he conceded, coming to Jessi's rescue.

"Oh, but no… now that's not fair…!" Alex laughed, as David walked up to stand in between him and the pool.

At that moment, Beth and Sue took Alex's arms, David reached out to take Jessi away from him.

Feeling as though they had succeeded, they, all but Alex, let down their guard.

"David, David, David," he laughed. "Now, what have I told you about putting yourself in between me, and…" He stopped to smile triumphantly.

"Oh… shit!" David cried, and, as if in slow motion, looked behind him, as Alex heaved both, his sister and Beth into the pool, while knocking David off balance, as well.

As David, too, fell in, Alex reached out in time to catch hold of Jessi.

"Alex!" she cried frantically, as he brought her back into his arms, laughing at the look on her face.

"Didn't think I would catch you, did you?" he continued, while all along Allen manned the video camera from the sidelines.

"No! But what are you going to do with me now?" she asked, seeing that all knowing look of his.

"What would you have me to do?" he grinned warmly, as he felt the heat of her body so close to his. As if that weren't bad enough, his lips were so close to claiming hers, once again.

"Alex, no…!"

"Don't worry, I won't be trying that again. Well, at least…" He stopped to set her down slowly, while looking upon her full and supple lips.

"Alex…!"

Looking back into her glistening eyes, he grinned, while tracing a finger over her nose. "Jessi, I care deeply for you. You know that. And you know I want to be there for you when…"

"No, Alex, please…" she cried, pulling away, "I don't want to hear that!"

"Jessi," He stopped her, while still having a hold of her wrist, "Beth and I," he spoke low, seeing Beth out having fun with the others. "You know we can't. No matter how much I still care for her, we can't ever get involved as long as we work together."

"Oh, Alex…!"

"Jessi, I won't push you, I promise. Just keep it in mind."

"Very well, I will!" she promised, when reaching up to give him a light kiss on his lips, before the others got out of the pool to eat.

"Looks like we're in for a storm tonight," Allen commented, when seeing some lightning off in the distance, while setting his camera aside to eat.

"Sure does," Alex agreed.

"Well so much for nice weather," some commented, while hurrying to fill their plates.

"Yes, and we better be getting back to the house, as soon as we get through here," Alex added, when thinking of his men. "I don't want to get caught out in this if it were to hit anytime soon. Not to mention, the extra men I have walking the grounds to keep an eye out for Tony."

"Well, in that case, how about letting the girls stay here tonight?" Rose suggested. "We have some movies picked out just in case they were able to!"

"Mom," Cassi spoke, "can we?"

"Alex?" Jessi turned back to see what he had to say.

"Hold up a minute," he returned, while pulling out his radio. "Marcose? Baker?"

"Here!" Marcose called back.

"Where are you?"

"Not much more than a couple hundred feet away, why?"

"Bring it on in here."

"Same place?"

"Yeah. And Marcose…?"

"Yeah?"

"Come up through the woods."

"Gotchya."

"Your men?" Allen asked.

"Yes."

"How many do you have over there?" David asked.

"Enough to stop Tony!"

Just then, two men came walking up out of the woods, in jeans, a plaid shirt, and tennis shoes. One wearing a shoulder holster, the other not, but both carrying radios in case of trouble.

"Girls," Alex grinned at both Lora and Cassi's captivated expressions, "these are your body guards. Marcose, Cassi. Baker, Lora. When you're out, let them know what you want to do. They know the grounds pretty well now, and know just how to get you back to the house safely."

"Wow…" Cassi cried, "a Marco Sanchez wanna-a-be!"

Grinning back, Marcose bowed, while taking her hand to kiss it.

"Yeah, and look what I get stuck with," Lora grinned, "a guy with his very own set of swimming pools for eyes."

Coming back, Baker said, smiling, "Care for a moonlit dip, meanness?"

Blushing, she turned to her mother, "Do we have to have these body guards?"

"Yes," she returned, while smiling at how Officer Baker's ego was being deflated.

"Mom…?" Cassi spoke up again.

"Yes, the two of you can stay."

Chapter Thirty

After getting through with lunch, Alex announced their departure, when getting up to walk Jessi and Beth around front to the Blazer, while David and the girls followed along. "David," he turned, giving him a big brotherly hug, "keep in touch, okay?"

"I will," he replied, sheepishly. "When are you guys heading back to the Inn?"

"Monday," Jessi tossed in.

"All right, I'll call you tomorrow then."

"Great!" he returned, reaching for his door

"Alex," Jessi placed a hand on his arm to stop him, "what about the crate up in Craig's room?"

"You're right!" he agreed, turning back to David, just as he was about to walk away. "Hey, bring your truck by tomorrow, would you?"

"S...sure, but why?"

"I could use your help moving some things out of the house."

"Sure, a...all right!"

"Girls..." Jessi turned to say her goodbyes, "have fun, and if you get uncomfortable, call me. I'll come and get you."

"All right!" they returned, while watching them get in to leave. "See ya later!"

Waving goodbye, they pulled away, leaving them with their bodyguards to watch over them.

"They'll be fine," Alex smiled, seeing Jessi's concern, as she watched her girls in the side mirror. "Besides, Rose and Allen have a lot of movies, and David is a whiz at video games."

"Oh? In that case, it's David I should be worried about."

"Why?" he asked, picking up a hint of humor in her tone.

"Cassi! She has run the best of the best into the ground shamelessly!"

Laughing along the way back to Craig's place, Jessi brought up the subject that she and Craig had gotten into about how the three of them pretty much grew up together.

"Yeah," he answered slowly, while looking around for signs of Tony, "we did, until I left for college."

"Do you think David's relationship with you has changed since then?"

"What are you saying?" he asked, turning sharply to study her for a moment.

"I think I know!" Beth exclaimed. "His getting into trouble with those men!"

"Then you're saying that it's my fault for what had happened to him?"

"No! Sometimes a younger person attaches themselves to someone older. It's sort of like a security blanket to them, until the blanket is taken away! Once that happens, they have to find something to replace it!"

"But I don't understand! Why not Craig? He was his best friend!"

"That's just it," Beth offered. "He was his best friend, and the same age!"

"Alex," Jessi went on. "Rose told me that Allen worked a lot, so David looked to you. And when you went away..."

"He turned to Tony_____?" he swore, slamming his fist on the steering wheel. "Damn him! Why Tony? Why not someone better than that?"

"Because he was angry at you for leaving! You see, Alex," Jessi added, "to David, you were the better person."

"In that case," he asked, sounding hurt, "what do I do now?"

"Well," Beth suggested, "when he comes by tomorrow, spend some time with him."

"In fact," Jessi added, "go through the crate together, before he takes it and some of the other things with him! Which reminds me." She snapped her fingers. "Would you mind if I had the old furniture in the back room? Jodi is a whiz about refinishing stuff like that."

"Jodi?"

"My cousin, in Ripley! She has an Antique Shop there."

"Sure. I think Craig would really like seeing them get finished. As for David, yeah, I like the idea of going through the crate with him. All right, we'll do that!" he agreed, when pulling to a stop, in behind the house, before getting out, to go around and open the door for them. "I just have one question. How do you two know these things?"

Looking to Jessi, Beth smiled brightly. "It just comes to us!" she laughed.

"And it helps to do a lot of meditating to cleanse the soul!" Jessi added with a gleam in her eyes, as she walked past him to go into the house.

"Smart lady, isn't she?" Beth smiled, while standing off to one side, when he went to close the Blazer door.

"Yes, just like someone else I know," he grinned down at her. Unlike Jessi, Beth was just a little shorter and slightly smaller through the breasts.

"I like her, Alex," she smiled.

"I'm glad," he returned, while going around to the back end of his vehicle to let her dog out. "Come on, boy!" he laughed, holding open the hatch.

Once inside, Alex asked if anyone were hungry, while going over to get himself an apple.

"No," Beth replied, while going in to get out her I. U. sweats for the night, while Jessi took out a pair of Michigan sweats.

"It's going to get pretty chilly," Jessi announced. "How about building a fire so we can roast some marshmallows Sue had given us?" she suggested, while tossing Alex the bag, before going on into the bathroom to change.

"What will you think of next?" he laughed, while taking care of the fire.

"Oh, and Beth…!" Jessi called back. "If you'd like, why don't you continue using the sofa-sleeper?"

"You're going back up to Craig's room to sleep?" she asked.

"Yes."

"Sure! All right!"

Later that night, not hearing much out of the storm they had been expecting, after having their marshmallows, Jessi headed for the front porch to meditate. However, something told her first to let Alex know. "Alex…" she turned back, seeing the two of them sitting on the hearth, going over some plans for the next few days.

"Yeah," he looked up, seeing her standing at the door.

"I was just about to go out on the porch to meditate, would you two like to join me?"

"Count me out," Beth replied, while getting up to go over to the sofa. "I'm just going to read for awhile, before turning in."

"Alex, how about you?"

"I'll be right out," he said, getting up, while smiling down at Beth. "Enjoy your book!"

"Oh, I will, Boss," she teased.

Going out on the front porch, after closing the screen door behind them, Alex went over to get comfortable on the front steps, alongside Jessi. Whereas Max laid quietly at their feet, while letting out a soft grunt, before falling off to sleep, only to dream of chasing rabbits through the woods.

Sitting there quietly for a while, while listening to the breeze as the wind picked up, Jessi spoke up first, seeing the heavy dark clouds moving in even closer now, "I guess we're in for that storm like Allen said we were!"

"Yes, it sure looks like it," he agreed, while paying more attention down the road than the sky itself.

Meantime, hearing a few muffled barks, and a couple of whimpers coming from her dog, Jessi simply shook her head. "He must be dreaming again."

"W…what?" Alex asked, while tearing away from what he was doing, to hear the tail end of her comment. "Oh, Max. Yes, he seems to be chasing after something in his dream!"

Just then, the two caught sight of the first serious streaks of lightning scoring across the sky, when Jessi jumped nervously. "A…Alex" she cried, shivering.

"Hey," he turned back, sensing her fears, "are you all right with this?"

"D…does it show that much?" she asked, smiling cowardly at yet another flash of lightning, which had nearly blinded the two, when it was soon followed by the deep, harmonic sound of thunder, rumbling the ground beneath them.

"Yeah, well, I would say you're sure to be a good candidate for a padded cell in the next hour or so!" he laughed heartedly, while placing an arm around her shoulder, to bring her over a little closer to him, in order to comfort her.

"Alex, please… no" she cried, pulling away.

"What's wrong?" he asked, seeing the changed expression on her face. "Is it Craig?"

"Mostly! And…" she turned to get up and walk out off of the porch, not knowing about his earlier conversation with Beth, while she was in changing.

"Jessi…! Don't…!" he yelled, jumping up to stop her, while looking up and down the road for any signs of trouble.

"Alex!" she shrieked, while jerking back on his grip, when at that moment, Beth came running out to see what was happening.

"Alex?" she called out, while resting her hand in behind her back, where she kept her service revolver tucked away in its waistband holster.

"It's okay!" he called back, holding up a hand, when he saw her standing at the ready. "Jessi, I'm sorry!" he offered, yet, with his free hand still reaching out to her.

"Sorry?" she nearly yelled, until she saw the look in his eyes. Knowing something was up, she slowly began shaking her head, "No! No! Oh, God, Alex, please tell me…"

"No, Jessi, it's not going down yet. I just didn't want you to wonder off too far from the house, that's all…!"

"Is it?" she asked, looking to the two of them. "Is that really it? You just didn't want me to go too far away…?"

"Damn it, Jessi!" he began, when Beth spoke up in his defense.

"Jessi, we just didn't want to take any chances out here at night. Really!"

"Jess, please… I'm sorry!" he said regretfully. "But it seems that Tony has been casing the place for the last couple of weeks! And yes, I should've told you sooner, but…" He stopped to look more deeply into her eyes, as he waited for her next reaction to come flying out at him.

Then it came. Backing away slowly toward the front door, Beth moved aside as Jessi continued to glare resentfully at him, while shaking her head. Meanwhile, waiting for just the right words to surface, and they did, she screamed at him, "Oh, my, God, and you knew...? You knew all along, and didn't say anything?"

"Yes."

"And just when were you planning to tell me this? Damn you, Alex" she swore, shouting at him, "I'm not a child!" she cried, storming back into the house, while slamming the screen door behind her.

"Damn it, Jessi, for God's sakes...!" He started in after her.

"Alex..." Beth spoke up softly, stopping him at the door.

"Don't remind me," he growled, looking down at her. "I know what you're going to say. That I did the same thing to you."

"Yes. And I, like Jessi, didn't take too kindly to it, either."

"But damn it, I was only trying to protect you!"

"Yes, but give us some credit. We can protect ourselves to a point if we have too!"

"Yeah, well, what do I do now? I didn't want to upset her! After all she was supposed to be out here getting some rest! Damn it, anyway!"

"Give her some time. She'll come around."

"Great, two smart women," he broke down laughing, when suddenly Beth cried out.

"Alex?"

"Yes?" he asked, when seeing her attention advert itself to something across the road.

"The men?" she asked, seeing a huge bolt of lightning hit off in the distance, across the road. "Where are they to go to get in out the storm...?"

Seeing what she had, he replied, "They have a large camouflage tent to get into. As for the guys watching the girl's, Rose will be putting them up for the time being."

"Good!"

Standing out on the front porch a little while longer to listen to the oncoming storm, Alex turned to take Beth back inside, after hearing the rain start to come down. "Come on, boy...!" he turned back to call Max in.

Upon hearing them walk in, Jessi went right up to Craig's room to be alone, while outside the rain kept cascading itself against the house.

"Hey, there!" Craig spoke up, while coming around to join her in the darkness of his room, after she had gone over to open the window, and drag the crate over to sit on it.

"Craig…?" she turned to look up into his beautiful face. *'I really need you.'*

"Are you sure?" he asked, picking up on her most intimate thoughts.

"Oh, Craig, I'm so scared about what is to come, but yes, I have never been more certain!" she murmured, while getting up to slip out of her sweats, while bringing his attention to her beautiful body, as a flash of lightning lit across her smoldering eyes.

That night the storm outside wasn't nearly as bad as they thought it would be, though inside, the storm that took place in that room boiled up between them, as their passion lit up in volume, or at least the electrical current between them did.

By morning, Jessi had cooled off some over the argument that took place the night before, and was ready to go for a walk with Alex, while waiting on David to stop by and get the things Alex needed him to get.

"What are you and Beth going to do when David gets here?" he asked, throwing a stick out for Max to chase.

"I don't know, maybe go out for another walk!"

"Jess, about last night, I'm sorry. I really didn't want for it to turn into an argument between us."

"If you really mean that!" She stopped for a moment to look up at him. "Then stop treating me like a child!"

"I'm not trying to…!" he exclaimed, frustratedly, while going over to lean against a tree, while folding his arms across his chest, and propping a foot up against its trunk, to think over what all has happened, since running up against her.

Seeing his expression, she walked over and stood in front of him, while at the same time, close enough to feel the heat radiating from his body. "Alex, I know you're trying to protect me. Believe me, I'm grateful."

"Jess..." he stopped in mid-sentence, when seeing her standing so close, and feeling what he did for Beth, he just wanted to reach out and take her into his arms, like he had once before.

But now, torn between the two, the look in his eyes deepened at the way the sunlight danced off her hair. *Damn you, Jessi, why do you have to be so beautiful?* he groaned inwardly.

"Alex..." she began, when realizing what she had done just by coming up to stand so close to him. Backing away, she apologized, "I'm sorry."

"Why?" he asked, putting his foot down, as she turned away.

"Because, I just shouldn't have done what I did just then."

"Jess," he spoke softly, while coming up behind her to place his hands gently on her shoulders.

"Alex, no...!" she cried, shrugging free of his hands, when feeling the warmth of his touch radiating through her very soul.

"Jess!"

Feeling aggravated at herself for spring out at him, yet again, she tried to think of something to excuse her action, just then, but couldn't. "No, let's just forget it," she said, looking back up at the house. "Besides, we should be getting back, David's probably there, wondering where we are."

"Yeah, you're probably right," he agreed, while wondering what has been getting into him lately. Just then, his thoughts were cut off by the sound of a truck pulling up next to his Blazer, and being only a few yards away, he was able to see who it was.

"Hey, David...!" Beth spoke up, while coming out to greet him.

"Where's Alex?" he asked uncomfortably.

"Right here," Alex spoke up, while coming up the pathway with Jessi at his side.

"Well, what's this stuff that you needed my help with?" he asked, once he had gotten out, closing his truck door behind him.

"For starters, that crate up in Craig's old room, along with a few other thing that belonged to him. However, whatever you don't want out of the crate, I'll keep, and the things in the back room goes to Jessi's, cousin's place, in Ripley," he explained, while the two headed inside.

"That's fine, besides, it'll do me some good to go through that old crate anyways. That, and I kind of miss the old junk," he replied, while following behind.

"Alex," Jessi spoke up, bringing his attention back to her and Beth, while standing at the kitchen doorway, "how about we bring the two of you up some iced tea in a little while."

"Sounds good! Yell if you need any help!" he replied, turning back to smile at the two of them, before going on up.

"Oh, we will," she added warmly, when seeing the gleam on both their faces, before turning away.

Once the guys had gone into Craig's room, the two could hear the laughter over some of the things they had found in the crate, and hearing it was like music to their ears.

"Sounds good, doesn't it?" Beth asked, while going over to get out some glasses.

"Yes," she replied, not seeing Craig leaning against the counter, until he spoke up so that only she could hear him.

"Hi there," he laughed, seeing her reaction.

"Craig…!" she mouthed the words so not to draw attention to herself, while Beth poured the tea. Before she could go on, turning to say something, Beth saw the expression on her face.

"Jessi, are you all right?"

"Yeah, just thinking about the guys upstairs, is all," she lied.

"Oh… are you so sure it isn't the one down here, you're really thinking about?"

"Beth…?" Jessi spun around in surprise.

"Well…?"

"You can't see him, can you?"

"No, but I can sure tell your heart rate jumped a notch or two," she laughed. "He's here, isn't he?"

"Yes."

"Good! You two have a nice chat. I'll just get these right up to the guys."

"I can help!"

"Nope. Got it already," she smiled gleefully, as she turned to head for the staircase.

"I'll…" Jessi stopped to look back at Craig. "No, we'll be right up," she smiled warmly.

Laughing when she saw that crooked smile of his after Beth had taken the glasses up, she turned back, "You know if you keep doing that, I'm likely to be joining you on the other side."

"You wouldn't like it. It gets pretty lonely over here."

"Yeah, I know what you're saying." She turned sadly to look away. "It can get pretty lonely over here, as well."

"It wouldn't if you would let Alex..."

"No, not Alex. Not with Beth still feeling the way she does about him, and he about her."

"Jess," he started to reach out to her, but forgot he couldn't, when she walked over to open the back door. "I'm sorry. This whole thing wouldn't have happened if I'd have just left you alone." *Damn...* he thought only to himself of his own pain, had he not have reached out to her. And now, the feeling of not having her in his life at all was beginning to be too much to bear.

Turning away, he started to vanish as Jessi was just about to turn back to say something. But then, seeing him start to fade away, she cried out in a hushed-like voice, before he could go too far, "No! Pleasedon't go. Please! I need you, Craig."

"Jess..." he began to murmur, when turning back at that moment to see her tears, as they found their way down her cheek. "Oh, Jessi!"

"Please, don't leave me!"

"I won't," he spoke softly, while forcing a smile to his face.

Agreeing to drop the subject of his uncle for now, they talked of other things, while she poured her own iced tea, before going up to see how the others were doing.

"How was last night?" he asked, seeing her cheeks blush at the mere mention of their unique passion shared up in his room.

"It was wonderful!" she laughed, while taking a sip of her drink, in order to avoid those beautiful blue eyes of his that were now fixed on her smile.

"I didn't know whether or not it would work, but..." he stopped, as she fell back against the sink. Picking up on her alarming thoughts, he rushed over to her. *"Jessi, what is it? What were you just feeling?"* he asked telepathically.

"The memory of last night!" she explained. *"It had just went right through me, like..."* She gasped, feeling it hit her again.

Taking in a deep breath, she set her glass down to focus on what just happened to her.

"Talk to me!" he spoke up worriedly. "Tell me what had just happened!"

"It was as if last night had just repeated itself again and again. Only it was in a more condensed form this time!"

"Perhaps we should be a little more careful when we try it again," he suggested, while looking directly into her eyes, and feeling her passion flow from out of them. *"Oh God, woman, you are so..."* He stopped, and surprisingly turned away out of fear of what he too was feeling at that moment. "We should be going up to see how they're doing," he suggested, while changing the subject to a much safer one.

"Yes, you're right!" she blushed once again, as she took her glass of tea and headed for the stairs, while he followed along.

Once outside of Craig's old room, he had only made himself visible to her, so as not to scare David. *"Shall we?"* she looked back on him telepathically.

With a nod of his head, they walked on in.

"Well, how are we doing!" she asked, seeing the mess on the floor.

"Great!" Alex said, turning to look up at her.

Seeing her paled expression, he jumped up and took her off to one side of the room to ask if she were all right.

"Yes, I was just..." She stopped suddenly to look over David's right shoulder to where

Craig was now standing, looking so sad at all the things spread out on the floor, when at that moment he started shaking his head.

"I see!" Alex followed her gaze. Not able to see his nephew for himself, though somehow he could sense his presence there in the room. And why not, the people he loved most were all there, but his parents and David's.

Changing the subject, they saw David's expression had changed, as he turned to look up at them. By then they knew he had started to suspect something.

"We were just about to come downstairs with this stuff," Alex pointed to the half filled crate.

"Oh, all right, but don't forget the things in the backroom, as well.

I would like to get it over to Jodi's to have her check them out, and see what she can restore!"

"I hear you," he returned, going back over to pick up some of the things, as he turned to look up at Beth. Nodding his head over to Jessi, the look he gave was in the way of concern.

Nodding back, she walked over to take Jessi's hand. "Come on, let's get out of here and let the guys have some more fun," she suggested, while heading out into the hall with her glass.

"Sure!" she agreed, looking back at Craig, while he smiled and nodded his head.

"Go. Have a nice talk," he grinned.

"All right!" she smiled back quietly.

"Beth..." Alex spoke up, stopping them, "make sure the guys know where you're going to be, and carry your radio, as well."

"But I thought they were still over at Rose's?"

"No. I called them back, because of..." he nodded quietly over to David.

"Sure!" she returned, while seeing how David was still preoccupied with other things.

"Have fun guys!" Jessi turned back, smiling. "And do take your time and enjoy all your treasures, before bringing them down."

"We will," Alex laughed lightly, when recalling some of the times they'd had collecting most of the things that were laying there.

Once out back, in the brisk morning air, after meeting up with Marcose and Baker, the two women walked down a path Jessi had been down before.

"Jessi?" Beth spoke up, sadly.

"Yeah...?"

"Alex needs me back at the Inn!"

"What...? When...?"

"In an hour, maybe two!"

"What's going on...?"

"Ted needs some rest, and it wouldn't look right to have one of his other men standing in for him. Besides, he has to cover Alex's area, as well."

"Alex's area...? I had thought that that was what the extra help was for."

"It is, but you know how he feels about catching Tony?"

"Yes, all too well!"

"Yes, well, it worries me to see how driven he is over the whole thing."

"Beth," Jessi turned, as they reached a nice hilly area, near a running stream, where the two found a nice spot to sit and continue with their talk, "I have a feeling it's only going to get worse," she concluded, while taking a seat on the soft patch of grass.

"Yes, and when it's all finally over, do you think..." She stopped.

"Oh, Beth... don't do this."

"Jessi, I have to do this! After all, I had to accept our fate. But at the same time, I don't want him to be alone anymore, either!"

"What are you saying?"

"Jessi," she had to say it anyway, knowing how much it was going to hurt, "it's obvious that he cares for you."

"No... not you too! I would have thought that you of all people..."

"Me?"

"Yes, and don't tell me, you don't still love him...!"

"Yes, I do...! And, yet, enough to let him go...!"

"But why me...?"

"Jessi, haven't you noticed it too...?"

"It? What are you talking about?" She looked away to hide what she already knew.

"H...he loves..." She had to stop, as the tears began to burn the inside of her eyelids.

Looking back, to see them, Jessi replied, "No, Beth, I can't return it!"

"Maybe not now, I know! But after all this is over, and you have had time to heal, you will come to grips, and then..."

"No! I don't do things that way, Beth! Why can't you guys understand that?"

"Oh, but I do! More than anyone could possibly know!"

"Then why do it at all?"

"Because, once this case is over, I'll be moving on!"

"On? Where to?"

"Detective training."

"Detective training? Is that more important than love?"

"We have our careers now. I can't expect him to leave his, and he won't ask me to leave mine!"

"So, the two of you just give up."

Beth looked away again, and began crying. *It has to be this way!*

"No, little Sis, it doesn't," Craig's thoughts came through.

Smiling back at the house, Jessi picked up on him, as Beth turned back to look at her. "Did you hear him?" Jessi asked, smiling.

"I...I think so...! But..."

"Don't give up, Beth. Not yet. And yes, I do care for Alex. Lord, I find him to be so... irresistibly handsome, but..."

"Then, please... consider it? If anyone can make him happy, you can."

"Why, because we both can drive him up a wall?" she laughed, while reaching over to give her a sisterly hug. "Oh, Beth... don't you dare give up."

Chapter Thirty-One

A short while later, Alex and David came down, carrying the old crate with them, before going back up to get the other things. That which, being a couple of antique tables, one antique queen size bed frame, and a couple of chest of drawers to match.

"Hey," Alex spoke up, setting down the crate, "why don't you bring your truck around front, it'll make it easier to carry this, and the rest of the stuff out?"

"Alex," Beth spoke up, sounding concerned, when she and Jessi got up from the sofa to join them, "are you sure that's a good idea?"

"Yes, once I call the guys in to keep an eye on things. David?"

"Yeah?"

"Just give me a minute to round them up, before you head out."

"Sure!"

Taking out his radio, it wasn't long before Alex rounded up his men.

"All right, see ya soon!" he returned, when putting his radio back into its carrier.

"Alex?" Beth asked.

"All done!" he announced, turning to David. "They're just out back, and up the road a ways. So we should be all right to go."

Heading out to get his truck, David felt a shudder go through him, as he walked out the door. Passing it off he continued, as Jessi walked into the kitchen to see Craig standing there, she smiled, *"You are so mean, you know that?"*

"I didn't do it on purpose!" he smiled. *"He was there before I had a chance to turn around!"*

"Do you think he felt you?"

"He felt something, but right at this time he's hurting too much to think clearly."

"Guilt?"

"Possibly," he replied, shaking his head, as he turned back to watch David start his truck.

Meanwhile, waiting out front with Beth by his side, Alex was beginning to wonder what was taking him so long. "I should go and see if there's any trouble," he groaned, while pulling out his service revolver, when then they heard his truck pulling around.

"Looks like he's all right," she nodded toward his truck, when it appeared around the front of the house.

Shaking his head quietly, Alex went over to drop the tailgate, after David went to shut off the motor. "You had me worried!"

"Sorry, but..." he shook his head puzzledly.

"What?"

"Coming out the back door..." He stopped to look up at Jessi, when she came out onto the porch to stand next to Beth. The look on her face was one of surprise. But then seeing it, he knew then, something had to have happened.

"David? Hey, are you all right?" Alex asked, taking his arm. Then turning to see what he was looking at, with his own broad smile, he saw Jessi's face light up, as she nodded her head slightly to let him know that the two had a rather close encounter with each other. "Come on, we have work to do."

"Yeah, work," he repeated, shaking off the thought.

"Oh, David..." Jessi called out.

"Yeah?"

"How's my girl's doing over there?"

"Last I knew, they were cheating at cards with my dad!"

Laughing, she knew how good they were, when it had also come to playing cards. "Oh? And how would you know they're cheating?" she asked, smiling down at him.

"Because," Alex laughed, "no one beats Allen."

"Until now!" Beth joined in on the laughter.

Turning to look into Beth's baby blues, Alex had almost forgotten that lily-like laugh of hers, when he and David walked up to get the crate from inside. "That reminds me, did you two have a nice talk?" he asked, while taking a hold of the screen door handle.

"Yes we did!" Jessi continued to smile.

"Good! Shall we!" he offered, while fanning his hand in a friendly gesture to let them go in ahead of him.

"Oh, David," Jessi turned back, before heading into the kitchen to get dinner started, "why don't you stay and join us for dinner?"

"No thanks, mom probably has dinner on now!"

"In that case," Alex interrupted, "we had best hurry then, and get the rest of these things loaded, before she skins you alive for holding up dinner."

Agreeing, the two hurried and picked up the crate to carry out, while Jessi and Beth went into the kitchen to get started on their own dinner.

"What about the girls?" Beth was asking, while getting out the plates and silverware.

"Oh, gosh… I'm glad you said something."

Going back into the living room, Jessi grabbed up her phone to call them. While waiting, she turned to see Craig standing at the front door, his expression blank, as the guys came back in to bring down the bed frame next.

"Hey, handsome!" she called out telepathically.

Turning to see her warm smiling face, he grinned. *"It's just hard to see it go."*

"Yes, but it'll be taken good care of. And as for the other things, Jodi is great with antiques, and once she is through with them, they'll be brought over to the Inn!"

"Good, it'll be nice to see them get used."

Before they could say anything more, Jessi heard Rose's voice come over the other end. "Hi, Rose, it's me, Jessi."

"Hi, I was just fixin' on calling over there. Is David about through?"

"Yes, they're getting the last of Craig's old furniture out of the back room now!"

"Good, supper is about ready, and the girls were asking if they were to be eating here, or over there!"

"There, if you already have something fixed for them!"

"Not a problem, we have plenty. And if the three of you want to join us, come ahead!"

"I'll ask Alex. I know he has Beth going back to the Inn as soon as we're through eating."

"All right, if you decide to come, we'll see you shortly."

Getting off the phone, Jessi headed back to the kitchen, after seeing that Craig had gone.

"Well?" Beth turned back to see her going over to turn off the camp stove.

"She's asked if we would like to join them."

Biting down lightly on her lower lip, Beth thought for a moment, when they then heard Alex's voice filtering in through the front door.

"Well, I guess I'll see you later," he replied, when walking back up to the house, after giving him another brotherly hug that came with a pat on the back.

"Yeah, and I'll take real good care of these things, until you get over to get them."

"It shouldn't be too long, maybe a week or two at most."

"All right. See ya later."

Studying David's expression, as he climbed back into his truck, there was something there that had alarms going off in Alex's head, while watching him pull away. Standing there on the front porch, he continued to watch him, as he drove on slowly down to his parents' house. *Damn, what is it, David,* he wondered, while watching the red pick up getting closer to the McMasters driveway.

"Sounds like the two of you had a good visit!" Beth was saying, as she joined him on the porch. But then, seeing the look on his face, brought concern to her own, as he stood watching for Tony to show up at any given moment. "Alex, you don't think..." She stopped to look down the road, as well. Not seeing anything, she asked a little more softer, while carefully bringing a hand up to lay on his shoulder. "What is it, Alex?"

Not answering her, he stood poised, with his arms folded across his chest, his right hand tucked in beneath his lightweight jacket, while readying himself for trouble.

Seeing this, she too had her free hand tucked in behind her back, resting it on her service revolver. "Where's our guys now?" she asked, not taking her eyes off David's truck.

"The extras are across the road, as well as down the road. Not to mention, Marcose and Baker," he told her, while pulling out his radio. "Marcose?"

"Here!"

"Stand ready. David's on his way back. He should be there any minute now."

"We're ready," he announced, taking Brandon with him to go out front, alongside the garage, to wait until David had gotten there safely.

"When did you send them back over there?"

"Just before he left."

Then suddenly, everything changed in an instant, as every fiber in his body tightened at hearing an oncoming car. Turning toward the door, he yelled inside, "Jessi... stay where you are. Kevin...?" he called out over his radio.

"I've got her covered," he called back, rushing into the house, through the back door, nearly startling her, as she spun around to see him standing there. "Sorry, ma'am."

Without any further adieu, Alex took Beth along with him to take cover at the side of the house, while waiting for their mystery car to pass.

And then it did.

Racing up the road, was a dark blue car, but not the one they had expected. The driver was only a teenager, out having fun.

"Damn...!" Alex swore, taking out his radio. "Chase!" he called out.

"Yes?"

"Was that who I think it was?"

"Fred's boy?" he laughed.

"Yeah, damn him," he cursed, while turning back to see Beth's corny expression.

"Who was that?" she asked, grinning up at him, while relaxing her hand from around the grip of her weapon.

"That brat was just one of the kids who had been breaking out Craig's windows."

"Oh?" she simply said, sitting back on her heals, while fighting back a giggle.

"Don't you even."

"Oh, but of course not. I wouldn't want to…" She covered her mouth, as she was losing the battle to keep from laughing at him.

"Beth…!" he growled, while deep down he was beginning to laugh, just as well.

"I'm sorry, Alex, but it was pretty funny."

"Yeah, this time!" he admitted, shaking his head.

"What now?"

"We wait to see if anything else happens. If not, we go on back inside."

Doing just that, nothing happened.

"Well," Beth spoke up again, while Alex stood, offering her a hand, after his men gave the all clear, "once again, how was your visit with David?"

"He had a lot on his mind," he returned sadly, while going back in to check on Jessi.

Arriving in the kitchen, she turned to see the two of them standing in the doorway. "Alex…" she began, when seeing the troubled look on his face.

"Everything's all right," he nodded back at Kevin.

"Yes, sir." Bowing his head to Jessi, and then Beth, he returned to his post, leaving them to talk amongst themselves.

"Okay, Alex, out with it. What is it? What really happened out there?" she asked.

"It was just a teenager, hot roding down the road, is all," he returned. "As for David, he made it all right. Marcose and Baker are with him now."

"Good. And aside from making it back all right, how is he?"

"He…" he began, shaking his head slowly, "he really feels guilty about Craig's death. It almost scares me to think where this guilt is taking him now."

"I can see why!" Jessi returned, when remembering something Doreen had said. "Alex, do you remember what Doreen said? 'We mustn't change their destiny.' What do you think she meant by that?"

"I don't know," he replied, going over to the stove. "Hey, it's getting late. How about I get dinner started?"

"Rose has asked if we want to join them," she replied, hopping up on the counter to sit, while he took out his lighter.

"Sounds good, but Allen said we were going to be getting in some more rain tonight."

"Well then," Beth spoke up, while going into the living room to get her things together, "I should be getting out of here, before it starts!"

Following her in, Alex came up behind her. "Beth?"

"Yes?" She turned back to see the worried expression on his face again.

"Are you all right with going back? We can wait another night. It won't matter that much to Ted. He has everything covered just in case I needed you out here."

"No, Alex. Really, I'm fine!" she fibbed, turning away to hide her sadness.

"No, you aren't."

"Alex," She turned back to see his own hurt expression, "I'm going to be fine. Take care of her, won't you?"

"You know I will. But just to be on the safe side, I'm going to send a few guys out to follow you."

"Some things just never change, do they?" she smiled, while reaching up to lightly touch her lips to his. "See ya when you guys get back."

"Yeah." Helping her out the back door with her things, Alex called a few of his men to follow her back. "By the way, Ted says that Tony is in town having a few drinks. One of our guys is sitting in the same bar keeping an eye on him now."

"Good, then I shouldn't have any trouble, will I?" Beth smiled.

"No, but just the same, keep your eyes open in case he were to leave, before you do make it back to the Inn."

"All right. I'll call and let you know that I'm there."

"You better, or I'll bust you down in rank so hard you'll never forget to call me."

"Yes, sir," she teased, while getting into her car to leave.

Seeing her off, he turned back to see Jessi standing there, when dropping his head to avoid looking into her eyes. "Listen, it may get cold tonight, down into the low sixties.

So we're going to be needing more firewood to keep warm. I'll just go and get it now."

"How about I fix us something to drink, while you're doing that?" she suggested, while watching him walk off toward the woodshed.

"Sounds good! How about some more of that iced tea of yours, and I'll just about bet that Max, here, could sure use something too! Don't you, boy?" he asked, while turning to wrestle with him.

"Okay you two, but you're going to owe me big," she teased, while going back inside to get their drinks. "Oh, but what about Rose and Allen?"

"Huh?" He turned back with an absent look on his face.

"Dinner?"

"Yeah, sorry, my mind has been on other things right now."

"Yes, I see that. So what do you want to do about dinner?"

Looking around him, he thought, *wait on the wood, or get it, and then go to Rose's.*

"Alex?"

"Let me get the wood in first, and then we'll head on over."

"All right. In that case how about I put off getting that iced tea, but put out some water for Max?"

"Sounds good," he returned, forcing a grin on his face.

Once he was done with that, arriving at the McMasters, dinner was good as usual. Afterwards, David and Alex teamed up against Lora and Cassi with the video games, and getting their butts handed to them.

"Yes!" Cassi laughed, while she and Lora got up to do their victory dance.

"Alex, what happened to you?" Allen laughed. "You would have never let a girl kick your butt so easily."

"What do you mean, girl? There were two beating up on me," he roared, echoing the room.

Everyone laughed, and for the rest of the evening they sat back talking, while the girls went on watching a movie Rose had gotten for them earlier.

After saying their goodbyes and leaving the girls to spending another night there, Alex and Jessi went back to the farmhouse, where he went right in to get a fire going for them. While doing that, Max went over to lie on the floor near Jessi, who plopped herself down on the sofa to watch Alex's handiwork.

"It's funny," she began.

"What's that?" he asked, going on with what he was doing.

"The girls. When I had asked if they were ready to come back with us, they looked as though I had stolen their favorite toy!" she laughed.

"Sue said they had a good time over there, as well," he stated with a warm grin to himself.

"What…?" she asked, seeing that look on his face, when getting up to go over and hand him a piece of wood.

"They saw Craig's picture on the mantle, over their fireplace, and asked why they had David's picture there," he laughed.

"Oh no…!"

"Lora was totally blown away, seeing his unique smile, when Bob brought out David's picture to compare the two."

"Now she knows who I was crying out to, when we got back from my parents' place."

"Why were you crying?"

"The dreams, it was when Craig reminded me not to forget him!"

"Hey?"

"Yes?"

"I was just thinking about going out for some fresh air. Would you like to join me?" he asked, getting up.

"Sure! Just let me put on something warmer. Oh, and Alex, why don't you take Max with you?"

"You heard her, boy! Let's go!" he laughed, looking back at Jessi. "Are you all right?" he asked, before heading for the back door.

"Yes, just a little tired. But go on out, I'll be right out just as soon as I get changed."

"Okay," he replied with a small grin, while leaving her to get changed.

"Jess?" Craig spoke up, just then, while walking into the room with a warm smile on his face.

"Hi…!" she greeted softly, with a warm smile of her own, "I thought you might be popping in soon!"

"I just wanted to see how you were doing," he commented, while going over to the fireplace to sit down across from her, after she went back over to the sofa to take her seat again.

"Tired, but a little better!" she answered. "Craig…"

"Yeah?"

"You know, Alex was really glad to see you. Your death has really taken a toll on him the past two years. I just hope those two men, especially Tony, don't see through his disguise."

"Me too. Not to mention, he is taking an awfully big chance, especially with Tony."

"Is it possible for him to see you again? He really needs to clear his conscience about the day he found you here."

"It isn't his fault," he replied. The look in his eyes deepened even more, as he started to reach out to take her hand.

Jessi, following his gaze, stopped just then.

"Sometimes I forget I can't just reach out and touch you."

"I know," she replied sadly, while wishing she too, could go over and wrap her arms around him. "Craig, this can't be any easier for you being like this."

"Yes, well, what about you?"

"Oh, Craig…" She dropped her head down, before looking back up at him.

"Well," he tried smiling, "we at least have this time together!"

"Yes, we do! As for Alex," she added, "Craig, we both know it wasn't his fault, but he loves you so much, and you know how your death is really hurting him right now," she explained, while getting up to go over and sit with him.

"Now that he has seen me, it will make it easier."

"Does this mean you will talk to him again?"

"Yes. He needs to know everything that happened that day. But not tonight," he replied. "You should go out and sit with him for awhile. I have a feeling he could use your company about now."

Getting up, she turned, looking down into his eyes, as a smile tenderly touched her lips. "All right, but just as soon as I get changed," she told him, when turning to go into the bathroom.

It wasn't long before she joined Alex on the back porch, when he looked up to see her standing there, wearing burgundy sweats, and a pair of thick white socks. "I thought maybe you had changed your mind!" he stated, when she went to sit next to him.

"No, I had something I had to do first. Sorry it took me a little longer to come out."

"Did it by any chance have to do with Craig?" he teased, while leaning his shoulder into hers to bump it playfully.

"Yes, it did!" she laughed.

Changing the subject, Alex commented on the weather, "It sure feels nice out here. You can even hear the rain coming off in a distance."

"Yes, I can!"

"Jess?"

"Hmmm…?"

"Just how afraid are you of storms?" he asked, thinking that he may have seen some lightning, before she came out.

"Not nearly as much as my cousin is!"

"Hmmm…" he replied, sitting there for a while longer, before either of them said anything.

"Alex?" she spoke up, breaking the silence.

"Yes?"

"Why haven't you settled down yet?"

Not answering her, he got up and turned, taking her hand, when they heard thunder off in the distance. "We should be getting back inside, don't you think, before we get caught in the rain?"

"You're right," she agreed, as he helped her up. "But first, answer my question."

Turning away to look at Max, he thought back to when he and Beth were once getting close. *But then…* He stopped.

"Alex…"

"You already know the answer to that. We just couldn't get involved."

Seeing how the subject was bothering him too much, she dropped it for now, as he went to whistle for her dog.

"Come on, boy, let's go!" he whistled again.

Once inside, they noticed their fire had died down.

"Looks like I had best be getting it going again, huh?"

"Yes," she agreed, while he took the poker to kick up what little flames were left.

While he went on attending the fire, Jessi went over to wrap up in one of Craig's old blankets that she had brought down earlier, when noticing how the temperature had dropped some, while they were outside. "Mmmm… you weren't kidding about how cold it was going to get. I'm freezing!"

"It is that!" He turned to see what she was wrapped up in. "Looks like you found one of

Craig's old blankets up in his closet! At least it'll help keep you warm, until I get the fire going again!"

"Yes. When I was here the last time, he had me go up and get a couple of them, since I had only brought a few of my own!" Smiling down on it, she took in his scent even more. "Mmmm… no doubt it must have been him that I had smelled. He even said this was his favorite!" she cooed, while pulling it up around her more.

"It was," he smiled, while going on to fix up his bedroll. "And now, what do you say we get some sleep?"

"I'm all for that!" she laughed, while getting up to fix up the sofa-sleeper.

Soon she had his blanket spread out over the others, before getting in under them. When she did, she rolled over onto her side, facing away from the fireplace. "Alex?"

"Yeah?"

There was silence, when she then rolled over to face him. "What was it that you used to call her?"

Staring off into the flames, as his nephew had done when he was upset, he answered, "Rookie," he smiled. "She was my rookie." Turning to look up at her, he saw how the flames reflected off her gentle green eyes, before adding softly, "She was my little rookie. And yes, I was falling in love with her."

"Oh? I see!" she said, letting it go.

"Goodnight, Jessi," he murmured, rolling over onto his side, while shifting his shoulder holster aside to get more comfortable.

"Goodnight, Alex," she repeated, doing the same, while going on to take in more of the scent of Craig's old blanket, while allowing the thought of it to take her mind off Alex and his situation. Just as she did, a warm smile came to her lips at the thought of what it would've been like to have lain under it next to Craig. *Mmmm…* she thought, burrowing her head down onto her pillow, before sleep swept her away into a dream state, while feeling Craig's presence, as he went to join her under it.

"Why think about it?" he smiled down at her, warmly, while placing his arm around her waist, to insure a beautiful dream. As he did, he went to run light kisses down the side of her neck, causing light tingling sensation to her body. "I love you, Jessi," he whispered.

"Mmmm…" she whispered softly, "I love you too, Craig…!"

Hearing that, Alex grinned to himself, at the thought of sharing the living room with his nephew, nearby.

Chapter Thirty-Two

The next morning, Alex was up packing the Blazer for the trip back to the Inn. "Are we ready to head out?" he asked, standing in the kitchen doorway, smiling.

"Yes," Jessi replied, turning then to see Craig standing behind him.

With a big smile on his face, they both nodded their heads, while Alex was preoccupied, looking down at his watch to check on the time.

"Alex?" she cleared her throat.

"Yeah?" Looking back up to see her warm smiling face, she went to point at something, or in this case, someone standing behind him.

Turning, he saw his nephew standing there, grinning at him. "Craig!" he laughed, shaking his head. "I should have known."

"I didn't want you to go, without talking to you first."

Seeing the two hitting it off, Jessi excused herself, while taking Max with her.

"Where're you going?" the two asked simultaneously.

"I'll just be out back with Max!" she laughed.

"Good. Just don't go too far," Alex returned, grinning at his nephew.

"Great," she went on shaking her head, laughing, while turning to leave them to their talk, "you can sure tell the two of you are related."

And talk, they did. When an hour passed by, Alex walked out, looking at Jessi with a feeling of sadness, and yet a sense of peace.

"Alex?" Jessi spoke up concernedly, seeing the look on his face.

"Craig wants to see you, before we leave."

"Oh. Okay!" she returned, walking up to the back door. Stopping alongside him, she placed a tender hand on his shoulder "Hey. Are you going to be all right?"

"Yeah," he replied quietly, while taking the ball from Max to give it a good, hard throw, before going on. "Jess…" he breathed in raggedly, "I know now just how you must feel about having to say goodbye. It's pretty tough! Though, now, I feel a lot better after we had our talk, thanks to you and this gift of yours," he added, while turning to give her a warm, heartfelt hug. "Thank you, Jess, for being here when you were. He's pretty lucky to have you in his corner."

Giving him a gentle kiss on the cheek, she smiled and went back inside to see Craig. Finding him waiting in the kitchen, she smiled even more. "Hey, Alex says we have to be going soon!"

"Yes, I know. Be careful out there, Jess," he said, sounding worried for the two of them.

"I will. I'll see you in a few days or so?" she questioned, while looking up at those wonderful eyes of his.

"I'll be waiting!" he tipped two fingers to his lips, as she did the same. But then they both smiled sadly, when he sent out a troubled thought to her, *"Damn it, Jess… why?"*

Picking up on it, she began to regret having to leave him at all, when seeing the heartache he was trying so hard to hide from her.

"Craig" she broke off crying.

"Jess, you have to go."

"No! Not like this! I can't stand seeing you this way! Oh, Craig… I love you so… much. Why does it have to be so hard leaving you behind?"

"I wish it did have to be this way, but it has to…!" he cried, reaching out to her, as he slowly began to vanish, *"J e s s iI wish it were different. Believe me, I d o"*

"No! No!" she cried over and over again, while sinking to the floor. "Oh, God, no!"

Just then, Alex came rushing back in, once he heard her cries, after Craig had vanished. "Jessi…!" he called out, going to her.

Reaching her side, he knelt down to hold her, while the two let loose their tears of sadness.

"Oh, God, I don't want him to go, Alex! N…not now!" she sobbed.

"Me, neither. But he has to do what he has to, to get the peace he deserves."

"But I...I love him!" she continued into his shoulder, while reaching up to wrap her arms around him.

"Yes, and he sure loves you, too!" he cried even more, while wiping away the tears from his eyes. At that moment, looking heavenward, he uttered out a prayer for the two of them, while they continued to sit together on the floor, crying. *"Please, Lord, don't let this end to where they both get hurt by what Tony had done to him."* Once said, he looked back down into her tear-dampened face. "Jess, we have to go now. I know you don't want to, but it's for the best," he concluded, while going to wipe her tears away.

"No, I...I'll be okay," she stammered, while getting up with his help to go into the living room to grab Craig's old blanket, before leaving. "If it's all right with you, I had taken this home with me once before, and I'd like to take it with me again, to somehow feel him close to me."

"That's fine! Shall we?" he asked, pointing to the back door.

Looking once more around the old house for any signs of Craig, she turned back to Alex, "I'm ready," she replied sadly, while walking on out to the Blazer.

After getting in to start it up, just as he reached for the gear shifter, something out of the corner of her eye caught her attention. Looking up at the upstairs, back window, she saw him looking so sad, as Alex was about to back out from behind the house.

"No!" she cried telepathically at first, and then out suddenly, while throwing open her door, "I can't go! Not yet. He needs me! I have to go to him!"

"Jessi!" Alex yelled, shoving the gear shifter back into park. "Jessi..." he continued, while getting out to run after her, "wait!"

Taking the steps two at a time, she was up in the back bedroom well before Alex could reach her. "Craig!" she cried, finding him still standing at the back window, as he turned slowly to look into her pain-filled eyes. "I can't go! Not yet!"

"B u t y o u h a v e t o!" he whispered ghost-like at first.

"No! I won't!"

Turning back to hear Alex running up behind her, she looked to him pleadingly.

"Jessi…" He stopped, as if he could read her thoughts. Shaking his head, he looked to his nephew, and saw the same unspoken request to be with her once again.

"Alex…?" he pleaded painfully.

At that moment, the emotion in the room was almost more than Alex could handle. "All right, if it'll make the parting any easier."

Still feeling choked up over the situation, going back down to the living room, where he could get more comfortable, Alex sat on the sofa, and close his eyes, while the other two came down to join him.

Once the transformation took place, Craig stood up in his uncle's body to pull Jessi back into his arms, where, once again, they could hold each other, while letting their love grow to such unimaginable heights. "Oh… Jess," he groaned, while pulling off her top to slip both hands in through her bra straps, to slide them down off her shoulders, to where he could have her luscious breasts again.

"Oh, God…!" she cried, while bringing her fingers up to course through his hair, when his usual tingling sensation began on her senses, until it had finally reached down to her very toes.

Scooping her up into his arms, he laid her down on the sofa, before going on to remove her jeans. First, unfastening the snap, then the zipper. As he slid them down, he traced his lips down over the smooth, flat, surface of her tummy, and then down to where the zipper ended. "Mmmm… Jessi," he murmured, while discarding her jeans, before going on to pulling off his uncle's things. As he did, she laid back with heated desire, watching as each article of clothing went off to the wayside, until there was none.

"*Oh…Craig…*" she thought out, using telepathy to reach him, "*how I want you…!*"

"*And me, you shall have,*" he thought back, while bringing her legs up around his waist.

"Oh, yes…" she cried, feeling the ecstasy he was bringing to her, as she brought herself into his passion.

Before she knew it, he was there, bringing himself up to join her in one hot passion of fire, as the union brought new meaning to their love. And with each thrust of his power, more tears of desire were brought, and with it, bliss.

After the time seemed to have flown by, so did the fountain of their desire, as it runith over.

"Oh, girl…!" he groaned, when coming back down to cradle her in his arms, while fighting to slow their breathing down, before adjourning to the shower.

"Craig?"

"Hmmm…" he responded, when running his fingers through her tangled hair, while wanting to lock this time, as well as all the others, in his memory forever.

"I…" She stopped, not wanting to sound so repetitious.

"I love you, too," he smiled, while wrapping his arms around her, tightly, before getting up to go into the bathroom.

Once the time had come, she was able to say her goodbyes without too much regret.

"See you soon!" he smiled down at her, in his spirited form, as she and Alex turned to head out to the Blazer.

"Yeah, see ya!" she smiled back, warmly.

"Alex!" Craig smiled broadly. "Thanks!"

"Yeah, you're welcome!" he nodded quietly.

On the way home, after picking up her girls, Alex filled her in on what he had planned for the next few days. "If you want to go out, take Max with you. However, don't go without telling one of us first."

"Yes, sir," she teased lightly.

"You had damn well better! I have enough to worry about without thinking Tony has gotten to you, too!"

"I will, Alex. I promise."

"Good! So, now, did the two of you get your needs taken care of?" he teased.

"Uh, huh!" she smiled, seeing the gleam in his eye at what they had done to him.

"Great! I'm so glad to be of help!" he laughed, running his hand over his dampened hair.

Nearly an hour had passed, when pulling into the driveway to see that Tony's car was gone. Getting out of the Blazer, Alex called out for Ted. "Where is he?" he asked, going up to meet him on the front porch.

"It's all right. He's being tailed now."

"Good!" he sounded relieved. But then seeing the look on his friend's face was one of strong indication that he was trying to hide something from Jessi, when she walked up carrying Craig's old blanket and suitcase.

Turning then, as well, Alex smiled, hiding any reason for concern, so as not to alarm her.

With a small gesture of her own, she walked on by, to go inside with her girls. "I'll be in seeing Ashley and Renee, before going downstairs."

"All right, I'll bring in the rest shortly," he offered, while watching after her. Once she was inside and out of sight, he turned back to Ted. "All right, out with it. What's really going on?" he asked, leading him over to the Blazer, to get the rest of their things.

Reaching into his vest pocket, Ted pulled out a folded piece of paper and gave it to him.

The looks the two exchanged, just then, were almost frightening, as Alex began to unfold it.

Meanwhile inside, Jessi's friends greeted her warmly.

"Hey... is that you?" Renee teased.

"I know, it's been awhile," she laughed.

"Are you doing all right?" Ashley asked, handing her her usual, before noticing she had something hanging off her arm. "What's this?" she asked, seeing the old multicolored blanket.

"Oh, it's just a keepsake!" she smiled, while taking her coffee over to sit down, to tell them everything that had been going on. But then stopped, when recalling she wasn't supposed to be drinking any more coffee for a while.

Meanwhile, coming back inside to discuss the newest turn of events concerning Tony, Ted and Alex went into Jessi's office to close the door behind them.

"Damn him..." Alex growled, walking over to slam his fist down on her desk, "he isn't going to get anywhere near her."

"And just how are you going to stop him?"

"Kill him myself!" he continued to growl, but stopped when seeing Ted's expression. "No, I won't be doing that, but..."

"Alex..."

"Get all the guys together. And then fill them in on what's going on. I want this place secured so tight Tony won't dare make a move on her."

"All right. And you? What are you going to do?"

"I have to tell her, Ted! She has to know!"

"Alex, she won't be too happy if you don't give her the freedom to move around. And you know if we increase activities too much around here, Tony might get suspicious and run."

"And God help us, if he does."

"Yes, and if we're not careful, we won't know where, or even when the hit will go down."

"You're right, we'll have to play it careful, but damn it anyway, why her?" he muttered, heading for the door.

"Where you off to now?" Ted asked, following after him.

"To sign my death warrant, once I've told someone the bad news!" he groaned, just outside the office, when they stopped off at the front desk.

"Alex, just maybe..."

"No, she will," he laughed regretfully. "Anyway, take care of the men. At most, put them all on alert," he ordered, while looking off toward the Boutique, where he could hear her voice coming out softly.

"Good luck," Ted laughed, going off to take care of his end of things, while Alex headed off in another direction.

Meanwhile, sitting back, Jessi went on with the latest events for the Fourth of July.

"What are your plans?" they asked in unison.

"Something really big. I have already contacted the newspapers and television stations. Now to get the rest of the plan going."

"Jess," Ashley spoke up, laughing, "what is it?"

"Oh... just some good, old fashioned, down home cookin'!" she laughed along with her.

Just then, their laughter was cut short, when Beth walked in, looking solemn.

"Jessi," she spoke up timidly, "Annie needs to see you in the kitchen."

"Oh? All right!" she returned, while getting to her feet. "I'll see you girls later."

"Hey!" Renee called out. "How about dinner out on the front porch later?"

"Sure! Just let me tell Annie to fix us something special," she agreed, taking her things with her. Once out in the foyer, she turned to Beth, "I'll be right in, I just want to drop these off down in my quarters first."

"All right."

Knowing what was going on in the kitchen, Beth turned to go on up to her quarters, while

Jessi went down to drop off her things. Once done, arriving outside the kitchen, she walked in. "Annie, Beth said you needed to see me?" she asked, having no more than closed the door, when she saw the look on her cook's face.

Turning, Annie nodded her head toward a corner stool, where Jessi spotted Alex sitting.

The expression on his face was hard, and yet, it had a look about it that frightened her. "Alex, what's going on?" she asked, detecting something was very wrong.

"Jess, you'll want to see this," he announced, getting up to hand her the note. "Ted found it on the front desk, waiting for me. He said he didn't know where it came from, or how it got there, but then…"

Hesitating at first, she took it from him and slowly began to unfold it with shaky hands, when the writing on it became visible to her.

Storm; The note began.

If you care anything at all about the lovely owner of this Inn, you will stay out of my business. Drop this case now, or you won't only find another dead body on your hands, you will find hers, as well as her dogs.

T.

"Alex," She looked up from the handwritten note, "we knew this was going to happen, eventually."

"Yes, but I wasn't expecting it quite so soon," he explained, taking the note from her. "I've got to keep you safe, Jess. At least for a few more days."

"A few more days? Just exactly what is that supposed to mean?"

"I can't say for sure. It's just a gut feeling. But God help me for what I'm about to tell you next."

"Alex...?" she asked slowly, while taking a step back to brace herself for what he was about to tell her.

"Jess, please believe me, it's for your own good!"

"Alex... if you are about to tell me that I have to stay inside, you can just forget it."

"Jessi, you have too...!"

"What...? But no! I'm supposed to be meeting the girls out on the front porch for dinner in a little while. How am I supposed to explain that to them?"

"Damn it, Jessi, I'm trying to keep you alive, for God's sakes. You're not going to make this any easier for me, are you?"

"No, Alex, I'm not!" she started to complain, while pacing the floor. "I'll...I'll stop going out at night to meditate. Yes." She raised a finger in the air, just as she stopped in front of him. "But don't expect me to stay inside all the time. I won't do that," she screamed, then turned on her heels to go over to Annie. "Could you please fix me up something to snack on until dinner? I have some work to do in my office. But, like I was saying, the girls are wanting to have dinner out on the front porch this afternoon. If," She turned to Alex. "And I'm only saying *if* it's not too late in the evening to eat out there."

"Y...yes, dear," she replied, looking over to Alex questioningly.

Giving her a nod of approval, she turned to get started on Jessi's request right away, as Jessi started for the door.

Grabbing her arm to stop her, his voice thundered, as he turned her around to face him, "We're not done yet."

"Oh, yes we are!" she glared back, when the look in his eyes scared her.

"Jessi, damn it..." he growled. And for the first time since meeting her, just the mere thought made him cringe at the idea of finding her lifeless body laying somewhere, knowing just how much she had come to mean to him. "Jessi, please...! It would kill me if I were to find you like I did my nephew." He swallowed hard. "As I told you before, if it had of been anyone other than Craig, I would have taken you from him in a heartbeat."

"Oh, God, Alex..." she cried, knowing what he was about to say, as she tried futilely to break free of his hold.

"No, damn it, you're going to hear me out," he growled, pinning her back against the doorframe, while glaring down into her eyes.

"Alex, no! Don't say it. Please!"

"Yes, Jessi, yes, I am in love with you, too. God help me."

"Oh, Alex, no! Please, we have been through this. You promised not to push me about this. So please, drop it..." she cried, as she continued to try and break away.

"Jess, I know, and I'm sorry, but it's true."

"Alex, this is insane! You have a wonderful girl who loves you, and yet you are so willing to give that up all because of departmental rules. Well that is crap! Don't be stupid, Alex! Find a way around it!"

"I wish I could, but we both have our career in front of us. I can't just ask her to give it up. No more than she would mine!"

Having a feeling that Beth would for him, Jessi didn't say, but just wanted the whole subject to go away, and now. "Alex," She closed her eyes, and sighed, shaking her head.

"Jess, I'm sorry," he groaned, sick at the thought of possibly losing her to that sick bastard that threatened to take her away from him, like he did his nephew. Leaning in closer, without so much as a warning, while letting her guard down, he pulled her up into his arms and began to kiss her.

Chapter Thirty-Three

Just as she began to feel the warmth of his kiss start to flow through her, she placed her hands up along his handsome face, before bringing them down to break up the moment. "Alex..." she cried, not wanting it to go any further than that. "I am so sorry. I don't want to cause you any more pain than you already have, and I do care for you. Really I do. More than I should, but..."

"I know," he said, putting up a hand to stop her, "you're in love with Craig."

"Yes," she returned, while able to pull away now, "I am."

"Damn it, Jessi, I know you don't want to hear this, but he isn't always going to be there for you."

"Alex, don't you think I know that?" she cried. "Just why do you think I go out there? Lord, I don't want this to end! Not ever."

Bringing her back into his arms, he apologized, "God, Jessi, I'm sorry. I know this has to be killing you."

"Killing me? It is killing me. I can't bear to say goodbye to him. It's just too h...h...hard!" She went on crying into his shoulder, while forgetting they weren't alone.

Holding her for another moment, he gently pulled back to look down at her. "Hey, stay here for a moment."

"W...what...? W...where are you going?"

"To check out your office. We can talk more in there."

"Oh... Alex, no...! Please," she shook her head, "I don't want to talk about this anymore. I just want to drop it, because, like it or not, what I'm feeling is never going to change! So please get that through your head!"

Shaking his own head with a frown, he walked out to do what he said he was going to do.

"Oh, Annie..." she whined on her way over to slump down on a stool, "what am I doing? This is all so ludicrous."

"Yes, and it sure sounds like he has it pretty bad for you."

"But I'm in love with his nephew!"

"Yes that does present a problem for them. Have you tried avoiding him?"

"I haven't been able to do much of anything lately. Just trying to keep the Inn up and running smoothly has taken a lot out of me!"

"Why not just stay to your office, the Boutique, and your quarters? I can bring your meals to you until all this is over!"

"Sure," she agreed, getting up to start pacing the floor again. "Oh, Lord," she stopped, "I'll have to call Jodi and see if she will come and get the girls. At least they'll be safer with her."

"Yes, but I was under the impression the girls each had an officer watching over them."

"Oh, yes, of course they do," she groaned, while laying her head back against the wall. "Oh, darn him anyway, Annie, I'm to the point where I am about to say to heck with all this and just go back out to the farmhouse alone."

"You're not going anywhere alone," he thundered, when walking back into the kitchen. "Damn it, Jessi, when are you going to start taking me more seriously?"

"I am, darn you! For crying out loud, Alex, my work is falling behind, my life is being threatened, and I'm running out of time with him!" she shouted back. "Alex, I want to spend some time alone with him."

"When?"

"In a few days!" she returned, while going over to get the snack Annie made up for her.

"Come on then," he ordered, taking her free hand.

"What...?" she sounded confused.

"Your office!" he reminded, when looking back to see the confused look on her face. "Remember?"

"Alex...!" she cried, hopelessly, before deciding to give arguing with him a break, as she allowed him to pull her out of the kitchen and on down the hall to her office.

Once there, closing the door behind them, he turned back to glare down at her, "Listen, I know you're upset. We all are. Just try to hang in there!"

"Hang in there?" she glared back. *'Great, so much for that break!* she fumed. "How dare you ask me to do that, when my whole life is up in the air, because of all this. Not saying that meeting Craig, and falling head over heels in love with him was a mistake. It's that man out there who has the audacity to be here in my Inn that I'm mad at. God, I am so angry that if he doesn't leave me alone, I'm going to have it out with him, myself. And I won't be alone when I do."

Giving up to her hot temper, he threw up his hands. "I give up!"

"What?" she asked, thinking she would never hear those words come out of his mouth.

"You heard me. You don't need a blasted bodyguard! Just give you a baseball bat and you can kill him yourself! But I should warn you," he roared, "Craig wouldn't be too happy knowing that, because you would have taken his job away from him."

"Alex, it isn't funny!" she yelled, while sitting down at her desk to attempt to do some work.

"No, it isn't," he was saying, when there came a knock at the door. "Who is it?" he yelled back, not thinking to disguise is voice, while looking hard at her

"I...it's Lisa. Room three wants to talk to Jessi!"

"Just a minute!" Jessi called back, looking to Alex. "Well, what now?" she asked, sounding unsure of herself.

"Find out which one," he suggested, while coming around to give her the house phone to call the front desk.

Calling the front desk, Jessi didn't have long to wait before it was answered.

"Front desk! Lisa..."

"Lisa, it's me," she interrupted. "Is it Tony or Harry who wants to talk to me, and why?"

"It's..." She looked up at Tony, hesitantly, "the first one. And I don't know why," she said hastily, when he reached out to take the phone from her.

"Is that her?" he asked, grabbing the phone. "Let me talk to her."

"No!" she cried, pulling her hand back to rub it.

"Listen, lady," he growled over the phone, "I have something to say to you."

"Oh, you do, do you?" she returned, signaling Alex. "It's Tony," she whispered, covering the mouthpiece so that he could listen in on the call.

"Damn! Find out what he wants," he suggested, while pulling out his radio to call the others in.

"Well, I have something to say to you, too," she went on, while giving Alex time to call his people.

"Ted! Beth! We have a problem." He said, in a hushed, yet hasty tone.

"What's going on?" Ted came back, while sitting up in his room to listen in closely..

"Tony's at the front desk. He's on the house phone with Jessi, and I think he's about to cause trouble."

"We're on it," Beth cut in, heading down from her quarters, as Ted left his room at the same time.

Though, before Alex could stop her, Jessi had lost her cool for the last time, and went out to the front desk to confront Tony on her own.

"Darn you, Jessi...!" Alex swore under his breath, while heading for the side window to climb out onto the porch, where he was sure not to be detected.

Making it around to the lobby in no time, he found her and the others standing around in one of the most intense moments ever.

Catching the middle of their conversation, Tony was bearing down on her, while pointing back at Ted, "Your night clerk there thought he was being cute, when he had those balcony doors fixed the other night. Well, I've got news for you lady, he picked the wrong man to mess with. And as for your Captain Storm, his days are numbered, as well. If he doesn't back off, he will be sorry."

"You think so?" she glared back, just as heatedly. "Well, for your information, Mr. Belaro," she nearly hissed, while bobbing her head from side to side, "my desk clerk was only doing his job. You were told not to open those doors. And until I get around to repairing the balcony, those doors are to remain locked. So if its fresh air you want, use the front door like everyone else here."

"Well, just maybe I didn't want to use the front door."

"Well, that's just too damn bad! And for your information, I also know that you didn't just go out onto the balcony for some fresh air. You climbed down off it, as well, didn't you? So give me one good reason why I don't just have you thrown out of here on your ass, since you lack a great deal of respect for my Inn and its employees. And as for my so-called Captain Storm...?" she screeched, seeing Alex, now, standing behind him. "Don't you even go there with me. I saw the note you left him. And for your information, we are not a mailing service. If you wish to leave that jerk a note, take it to the police station. As for me, I don't know where you get off connecting me with him, anyway."

"Because, I..." He stopped suddenly, not wanting her to know his business.

"Because, you saw us? Was that what you were going to say? Well, was it?"

"And what if..."

"And what if, nothing. I was looking into an old farmhouse he has control of, as if that's any of your concern," she implied, having overheard Alex telling Beth earlier.

"No, it isn't."

"Well, then..." she started, when Ted stepped forward to peel her off this guy, before someone got hurt.

"Sir," Ted spoke up, "whatever this rift is that you have with Officer Storm..."

"Detective," he corrected.

"Who cares?" she flared, pulling away from Ted, as her eyes lit up in dangerous sparks of heated amber. "He is nothing but an egotistical hot head, who thinks he's above us all. So leave me and the rest of us here out of it...!" she yelled, while shoving him out onto the porch, and right into Alex's hard body, as he stood firm with his arms across his chest. Although, ignoring his warning looks, she went on to attack the overbearing Italian, who now stood between her and the man who would rather see him dead, "And Mr. Belaro," she continued, while glaring up into his bitter, yet surprised face, "for future references, don't you ever threaten me again. I am not now, nor will I ever be a part of that cop's life. Do I make myself clear...?"

"Loud and clear, Ms. Rae. Loud and clear," he continued to glare down at her, before putting his hands up, as if to say *'I give up'*.

At that point, she just shook her head. "I don't know why I don't just call the police and have you arrested. Except for the fact I don't want the hassle or the bad publicity on my Inn. So," she started, before she could lose her nerve, "unless you want to be thrown out of here by my hired hands, I strongly suggest you back the hell off and leave me and everyone else here alone. To make it plainer for you to see, people come here to relax and enjoy themselves. So from this point on, leave your business elsewhere and not here at my Inn."

"I'm sorry, Ms. Rae," Harry spoke timidly, as he stepped out cautiously onto the porch, "but Tony and Captain Storm have a history."

"Well, again, don't bring it here, we want no part of it. You got that?" she told him heatedly, before turning to go back inside. "Oh, and Mr. Belaro, I am not your enemy, here, but you'll soon find out who is, if you continue to threaten me. And just a little warning, the people here who work for me, don't much like hearing that someone is threatening to hurt me."

"She's right about that," one of the groundskeepers spoke up, when he and a few others came around from the side of the Inn, along with Alex's men, who were dressed like hired help.

"Are you all right, Ms. Jessi?" Hank asked. "We got a distress call saying that you were in trouble. So we all came runnin' to offer our services."

"Ma'am," one of Alex's men spoke up then, "is this man here, hurtin' you?"

"I don't know!" She turned back to Tony. "Are you planning on carrying out your threat, or are you going to drop it? And remember, I'm not your enemy. I don't even want to know what your beef is with this cop. So please, leave all of us here out of it. I don't want to have to ask you two to leave. But if I continue to feel the tension in the air, I will get my hired hands here to have you both removed. Got it?"

"Fine! It won't happen again," he returned, while eyeing at the others, until it came to Alex. When he did, the look on Alex's face was so full of hate that it brought on suspicion from Tony when he saw it. "You can all relax," he went on. "It's quite apparent that she feels the way I do about cops. And with the kind of help you have here," he turned back to Jessi, "who needs cops?" he grinned unnervingly, when turning back to study that one particular hired hand.

Seeing this, Travis gathered up his courage to come forward and pull attention off Alex, knowing most of what was going on, since Alex's arrival. "Hey, most of us here owe her!" he spoke up, taking a step closer. "If it weren't for her helping me when no one else would, I'd still be out there panning for money on a street corner. I had nothing. No job. No money. And nowhere to go. Until one day this lady, here, came out of the grocery store and gave me a bag of food with fifty bucks in it."

"You see, Tony," Jessi started back in, "they're not only my employees, they are also my friends and family."

"I can see that," he continued, while looking back at Jake, who remained glaring down at him angrily.

"Mr. Belaro," she cleared her throat to draw his attention from Alex, as well, "during the next few days we are going to be hosting an Old Fashion Down Home Cookin' Shin-Dig. It's sure to be full of fun and food. So, if you can behave yourself, you are both invited to join us. That's if you can handle that sort of stuff," she explained, when feeling her body about to give way. But fighting it, she knew she had to keep her wits about her for a little while longer, before he could see her weakness, "So, Mr. Belaro," she pushed forward to finish what she had to say, "feel free to relax and have some good, honest fun."

"We'll just see about that," he came back, looking down into her eyes.

"Good, Lord, is that a threat I still hear in your voice?" she muttered exhaustedly.

"No. But, for now, Harry and I are just going to run in to town and shoot some pool."

"Fine," she returned, just as he went to take Harry's arm to leave.

Standing by in silence, she and the others watched as the two got into their car to go.

"Damn!" Ted exhaled sharply. "That was really intense!"

"You're right about that," Beth replied, while relaxing her hand from around her service revolver, when Hank walked up after Jessi's friends turned to go back into the Boutique.

Alex didn't say a word he just stood glaring down at her with jaws clenched tightly, and eyes looking even colder and harder into hers than usual.

Out of nowhere, she threw him a kiss, and a wink. "And now,

Captain Storm," she smiled, "you know just how I've had to feel." With that she turned to Hank, who stood waiting to see if she were really all right.

"Ms. Jessi," he began, seeing how Alex wasn't going to be just brushed off to the side so easily, "are you sure you're all right?" the man asked, worriedly.

"Aside from feeling like I want to throw up! Yes Hank, thanks to you and the rest of the guys," she added, while calling out to the others, before heading for the kitchen. "Oh, and Hank...?"

"Yes, little lady?" he smiled.

"Will you get the guys together out on the back lawn? We need to go over the finalities of this shin-dig we were discussing earlier."

"Yes, ma'am," he then turned his smile into a proud grin, as she turned to walk back inside.

"Oh, no you don't," Alex said, with a warning tone in his voice, while reaching out an arm to stop her.

"Mr. Green..." she cried out, pretending to protest. "We have a lot of work ahead of us. I have to fix up a large menu, rent two hay wagons, find two Clydesdales to pull them with, and get a smoker for a beef roast. Plus more horses for two trail rides. Not to mention, a band!" she groaned, while stopping long enough to take a breath.

Meanwhile, Beth and Ted stood back watching the two of them with amusement.

"Yeah, well, just hold on there one darn minute," he growled. "Just when were you going to tell me about all of this?" he asked, looking totally confused, when she started to laugh at the look on his face, while at the same time, bringing a smile to it, as well.

"In about..." she replied slowly, looking down at her watch, "fifteen minutes! So," looking back up at him, she casually asked, "would you get your men together out on the back lawn, as well? I need to discuss how to pull off a big party in just one afternoon."

"Jessi..." he groaned, looking up at the ceiling, while letting out a laugh that nearly shook the house.

"Well..." she too laughed, "come on! Let's get moving! We don't have all day!" she announced, while turning back to take Beth with her to the kitchen.

"Jessi..." Alex called out again, stopping her. But then, turning to

Beth, he nodded his head toward the kitchen for her to go on ahead. "Would you mind?"

"No." Leaving them, she hastily walked off toward the kitchen.

"Alex…" Jessi turned back to see his apologetic expression.

"Ted?" he turned.

"Yeah, I'll take care of getting the guys together out back," he smiled, knowing what his friend wanted, without having to ask. But then, stopped to express his approval of how Jessi handled Tony so well.

"Thank you," she smiled proudly.

Smiling back, he headed out to the crowd still hanging around out front, while Alex took Jessi by the hand to go back into her office.

After closing the door behind them, he didn't know whether to shake her, or to kiss her. However, after what had happened in the kitchen, he just walked over to take a seat on one of her overstuffed chairs. "Jessi," he began quietly.

"Alex…"

"No, please let me finish."

"All right!" she agreed, going over to the sofa to take a seat and hear him out.

"I had said some pretty harsh things earlier…" He stopped to shake off the building of emotions. "However, I was angry about seeing that letter, and didn't want to see the same thing happen to you that happened to my nephew." And then, with a heavy sigh, he looked into his hands. "Jess, I had no idea that meeting you was going to be like this. All I had on my mind was to get the man responsible for Craig's death. I wasn't planning to fall in love again. Beth, I had thought, was a 'one-of-a-kind' woman."

"She isn't?"

"No," he laughed. "And I hadn't thought it could happen again. Yet what you have with my nephew, I had no idea the two of you had gotten so close. I mean, yes, I know the two of you love each other, but what he has with you is really beautiful."

"Yes, it sure is!" she smiled warmly at the thought of their heated passion, but then the sadness of the love they feel for each other coming to an end, she knew would be the death of her. "Well, Alex," she shook off the last thought, as it scorched the corners of her heart, "we have a lot of work ahead of us. Shall we go and see if the guys are together?"

"Sure!" Getting to his feet, he headed for the door.

"Alex?"

"Yes?"

"I do care for you. Really I do."

"I know!" he smiled broadly, while opening the door for her.

Once in the kitchen, Jessi turned to Annie, "Thanks for calling the others up to lend their support. It was really good of them to come running when they did," she commented, while going over to snatch up one of Annie's famous home-baked cookies.

"Yes, well, I thought you could use the extra help," she smiled sweetly.

"And I did!" she agreed, going over to lean against the counter, while shaking her head. "Although, I didn't know at the time what was going to happen. I just decided that it was time that I took back control of my Inn. Oh, and that sob story, Annie," she grinned. "That was a real nice touch!"

"I kind of thought so too! But I have a feeling he wasn't lying about the whole story."

"You're right," she said, thinking back to a conversation she had had with Hank concerning Travis.

"Now," Annie went to change the subject, "what is this shindig thing all about?"

"It's a plan to put some life back into this Inn, and we sure have a lot of planning to do," she commented, while rolling her eyes at the thought of all the work she had ahead of her in order to pull it all off. "First thing is to make out a list of food we will be needing, and then get a menu put together. That'll be your job, with Beth's help of course. Beth, is that okay with you?"

"Sure!"

"And the theme of this," she smiled, "will be 'An Old Fashion Down Home Cookin'. It will include having a beef roast. That'll be on Wednesday and Thursday, and open to the public with a cover charge. Hank will be in charge of that, while Alex and Ted are in charge of the trail rides."

"Oh, my, it sure sounds like you have it all covered!" Annie cried, breathlessly.

"Well, the plan is there. I just need to put it all together on paper, and make some more phone calls."

Just as Jessi went to get another cookie, Alex and Ted walked in.

"Jessi," Alex interrupted, "we have everyone together out on the back lawn, like you asked. Now, what exactly is going on?"

"We're going to liven' it up around here, and at the same time keep those two up there busy," she pointed overhead.

"Them," Ted pointed in the right direction, "busy? Doing what?"

"Wait and find out!" she smiled, while heading for her office to get a pen and paper. "Oh, and Beth...?"

"Yes?" she asked, from the open doorway.

"I want you and Annie out there, as well."

"All right!"

Stopping by the Boutique, Jessi went in to get her friends, and then stopped by the front desk, "Lisa, will you stay and watch over things here? I'll be out on the back lawn if you need me. Oh, and let Alex or Ted know when Tony gets back," she commented, before going into her office to get her pen and notebook.

"All right!" she returned, not seeing Alex coming up to take Jessi by the arm again.

"Wow, just hold up there a minute!" he grinned.

"Alex...!"

"Jessi, do you have any idea just what you are doing here?"

"No!" She stopped to look back at him, when the look in her eyes told him she was tired of what was going on there, "I'm just praying that it will work," she finished, before looking around her lovely old Inn.

"Yes, well, I'm not one for saying this, but what you did here by facing Tony the way you did, really took courage. Just don't do it again without some kind of warning first."

"All right," she smiled, before going off into her office.

Chapter Thirty-Four

Heading out back to fill everyone in, Travis called out, "What's this all about, Ms. Jessi?"

"This, my friends, is about the Fourth of July," she announced, while going over to stand at a table that was set up for her, inside the gazebo, where Beth, Alex, Annie, and Hank were sitting. As for Ted and the others, they remained standing around to hear what she had to say.

"Is this what I think it is?" Lora asked.

"Yes," she returned, seeing her girls standing off to the side with their bodyguards. Smiling, Jessi continued. "We are going to have what is known as a 'Good Old Fashioned Down Home Cookin'. Hank here, gave me the idea last week when the subject of the Fourth came up. Both days we will be offering two trail rides, one at an hour, the other a half-hour. Jake," she pointed, smilingly, "will be in charge of the trails, along with Ted. And Jake," she turned to gaze down at him, "if you don't mind, I will need you on the half hour trail with another guide. You'll handle the walkie-talkie, while he handles the first aid kit. You will each have a canteen with you on account of the heat. And Ted…"

"The hour trail?" he asked, grinning.

"Yes, along with the same equipment as Jake. However, you'll need an extra guide. As for who two of them will be, I'll let you both know later. The third one is up to the two of you…"

"Jessi," Alex interrupted.

Holding up a hand, she gave him a reassuring look, "Annie and Beth are in charge of the menu for Wednesday and Thursday's 'Home Cookin'. We'll be looking at a wide variety of pancakes. Along with eggs, bacon, ham, but no steaks," she explained. "And Annie, make sure we have plenty of coffee, tea, iced tea and lemonade. Oh, and Hank, we'll be needing a couple of smokers."

"What about bathroom facilities?" Travis asked.

"Glad you asked!" she grinned mischievously. "That will be your job," she announced, just as everyone began to laugh. Then holding up both hands, she lightly laughed shaking her head at the expression on her groundskeeper's face, "All right, you guys, that will be enough. Travis, we'll be needing four johns, two men's, and two women's. And while you're at it, get Andy here, to help you with that."

"What...?" a tall, lanky, blond haired, teenager groaned.

"You heard me! And Hank," she turned, "when Jake isn't tied up on the trails, have him give to you a hand with the smokers."

"And just where are we getting them?" Alex asked, when she went to sit next to him and Annie to jot down a few notes.

"I have one out behind the barn!" Hank offered.

"Is it still usable?" she asked, before looking up from her pad of paper.

"Yes, ma'am, it sure is!"

Turning quietly to Alex, a thought came to her. "Isn't there one out at the farmhouse?" she asked quietly.

"Come to think of it," he smiled, "yes!"

"Great! Can we use it? Or," she leaned in to ask, with a grin, "should we ask Craig?"

He broke down laughing at the thought of asking his nephew. "No, I'm sure he won't mind."

"Won't you be needing some help getting it?" Andy asked, in a surprisingly low voice, when he went to lean down between them.

Looking up at him, Alex couldn't help but grin, "Yeah, I will," he replied in a normal voice. "Hank," he turned, getting to his feet, "what do you say the three of us go and get the other smoker?"

"All right!" Andy cried, thinking this would get him out of work.

"Oh no you don't, Andy..." Jessi spoke up, laughing.

"Ma'am?" He stopped, short of the gazebo entrance, to turn back.

"That won't get you out of your assignment quite so easy. You will just have to do it when you get back."

"Oh, well, sure I will!" he promised, crossing his heart.

With the look he gave them, she and Alex both laughed.

"Hey, we shouldn't be gone too long, but in any case, can I use your truck to get it?"

"Sure," she smiled, when he turned and started for the steps of the gazebo. "Beth, you know what you're to do, while I'm out."

"Alex..." they both spoke up quietly, "please... be careful!"

"I will," he replied, when turning to Ted. "Stick to her like glue."

"I will," he assured him.

"Come on, guys...!" Alex called out, heading for the garage to get Jessi's, pick-up, "We have a mission to run."

"See ya later, boss lady!" Andy yelled back.

"Yeah, see ya!" she returned, waving a hand. "And don't take too long," she added, before turning to send Craig a quiet message to remind his uncle that he's there watching him. *"You there?"* she thought warmly.

"Yes, and it sounds like fun!" he laughed. *"How are you holding up?"*

"Oh, I'm fine!" she smiled, while looking over at the others, before telling him what had taken place earlier.

"Jessi, I know."

"About Tony's letter, too?"

"Yes, and I have to say, like my uncle, I'm really scared for you. So again, please don't take any unnecessary chances!"

"Don't worry, Alex would rather hang Tony out to dry first."

"And with good reason! As you of course know," he was saying, when Ted was about to interrupt their conversation.

"Craig, I have to go, I need to talk to Ted."

"All right, but behave yourself."

"Uh huh!" she smiled to herself, before turning her attention to Alex's friend.

Seeing her enlightened expression, not knowing it wasn't about Alex, Ted smiled. But then, when it changed, he knew what she was about to ask. "Jessi, the answer is yes. We carry our service revolvers on us at all times. Besides, I made sure of it, before we came out here."

"Good!" she sighed, before turning back to fill her friends in on what their part was.

Watching her from the sidelines, while acting as though he were reading over some notes handed to him, Ted grinned at how she had taken control of things, when then hearing Renee's chipper voice speaking up.

"Boy, all this sure sounds like a lot fun!" she commented, smiling.

"It will be, but I have a feeling the Boutique will be pretty busy, as well."

"You aren't a kidding!" Ashley added, while smiling particularly at her friend. "Oh, and by the way, we had just gotten our new fall catalogs in yesterday!"

"Uh, oh... I know that look!" Jessi laughed.

"Well, it's in there!" she announced, referring to a beautiful, long, black, satiny nightgown Jessi had been eyeing for some time.

"Oh, my," she cried happily, with a gleam in her eye, "I've been anxiously waiting for that particular gown to come in."

"Oh, yeah...?" Renee asked, with a sheepish grin. "Is there someone special you have in mind for it?"

"No...!" she fibbed, thinking briefly of Craig. "But now I have a lot of work to do. So if you will excuse me," she said, getting up to return to her office with Beth, Ted and Annie following behind.

Meanwhile, having just arrived at Craig's place, Alex had just pulled in to get the smoker from behind the garage, when out of nowhere, a clap of thunder sounded around them.

"What was that?" Andy cried, jumping out of the back of the truck. "There isn't a cloud in the sky!"

With a huge grin on his face, Alex turned to look up at the house. "Oh, that?" he laughed, shaking his head. "That was nothing. Just one of those strange things that happens, once in awhile, around here." he grinned. *"I hear you, nephew. I hear you,"* he laughed to himself.

"Then am I to presume that was thunder we had just heard?" Hank asked, while coming around to join them.

"Yeah, we've been having a lot of those strange storms popping up from time to time, that's all," he offered, turning back to lead the way to where he and Craig left the old smoker, before his death.

"Great!" Andy grumbled, as he continued to watch the sky, while giving them a hand.

Reaching the back of the garage, Hank spoke up quietly, "I guess this is where it had all happened! In the house, that is?"

"Yes," he explained, while stopping to clear away some over-growth, before getting to the smoker.

"Sorry to hear it, but I can see why Jessi likes coming out here so much."

"Hank," Alex turned, "have you known Jessi long?"

"Just since she and the girls bought the old Inn!"

"The old Inn? Just how old is it?"

"The house itself is about a hundred and ten years old. But the Inn is at least forty to fifty years old."

"And the original owners?"

"Oh, well…" he grinned sadly, shaking his head, knowing the story behind their deaths, "they really loved the old place. In fact," He had to stop to force back the tears, "it was their whole life's dream to open it up to the public."

"Man," Andy shook his head at how the subject got to Hank, "that was some dream!"

"And the attic?" Alex asked, thinking about the strange occurrence that took place a few weeks ago.

"Attic?" Hank looked shocked at the mere mention of it.

"Never mind, it's nothing," he replied, looking puzzled.

But was it nothing? He wondered. For the look he had just seen on the stable hand's face had him curious, as to what had happened up there.

Once the smoker was loaded up, Alex called Ted to see how things were going there.

"It's pretty quiet as far as our friends go. They're still in town. But for how much longer, I couldn't say."

"Just call me when you hear anything."

"Sure. I gather then you aren't coming back right away?"

"No. It's hot yet, and I want to treat the guys to a nice swim, before coming back, as long as things are quiet there."

"Yeah, well, we have it covered here, and there's still a few guys keeping an eye on you, yet," he grinned, having Chase, and now Marcose, knowing he would be the better man to act in Alex's defense, if something were to happen.

"Yes, so I've noticed," he laughed, seeing Marcose's grin, when nodding his head at him, from off in the woods, between Craig's and the McMasters place.

Looking around even more to see if he could spot Chase, Ted radioed the man to make himself known.

And then he did.

"Good!" Alex nodded back at the man standing off near the line of trees, along the roadside. "And just where did they park their trucks?"

"Same place we always do, where Allen goes to plow his field!"

"Good thinking, since we're about to head that way anyhow!"

"In that case, have fun, and I'll let the others know, so they won't be worried."

"Thanks, buddy, we will." Getting off the phone, the three headed over to Rose's for a quick swim, before returning to the Inn.

Meanwhile, back at the Inn, Jessi was in her office, waiting to go over the price list with Ted, when he walked in.

"Are we ready?" she asked, still pondering over her list. But then looking up to see his smile, she asked, "What is it?"

"I just heard from Alex. They'll be back after going over to the McMasters to take in a quick swim."

She smiled, knowing how hot it had gotten that day. "Good, they will certainly enjoy it."

"Yes, well, back to this, now. How much are you going to charge for everything?" he asked, going over to sit on the sofa, while going over a few notes of his own for the added security.

"Well, here's what I've come up with so far," she started, while getting up from her desk with a few copies of her list to hand out to Alex and Hank, while keeping one for herself. "Oh, but keep one for yourself, of course."

"Jessi," he got up to take the list from her, "just who are these two guides you were referring to?"

"Aside from the fact that I haven't asked them yet, you really don't know?"

Seeing her all knowing gleam, he shook his head in disbelief, "Oh, no...! You're kidding, right?"

"Think about it! It's sure to keep them busy, and all awhile, under your thumbs!"

"Yes, but which one are you planning to go with Alex?"

"Harry, of course! That's why you will be needing an extra man with you."

"Uh… I'm beginning to see now, to keep Tony away from Alex."

"And from me. So, instead of me doing the asking, will you do me the honors of asking them, for me, when they get back? It's getting late, and I am really beat."

"Going down to your quarters now, to relax a little?"

"Yes, before going on to bed, that is."

"All right. Shall we?" he smiled, while walking her to the door.

"Don't tell me."

"Sorry, boss's orders. Alex should be back soon after they get through swimming. So you won't have to be alone long."

"Good."

On their way to her quarters, they said very little in case Tony got back sooner than they had expected. Though, upon their arrival, she spoke up first, when seeing a couple of other sleepyheads. "You don't think they may have gotten into any kind of trouble, do you?"

"No. He would have called if they did. That and I sent Chase and Marcose to keep an eye on them while they were out."

"Oh? That would explain Kevin being here," she smiled, when recalling the young man having scared her, when rushing in to watch over her at Craig's, during that time the teenager raced by in a similar car as Tony's.

"Yes."

"All right," she smiled tiredly, before leaving him to go off into her room to get out one of Craig's old work shirts that she had found, when she went back up to get another one of his old blankets from his room.

Meanwhile, back out in her living room, Ted called Beth to come down and stay with her, until Alex got back.

"I'll be right down," she returned, while untying her apron.

"Thanks. I would just assume be up there in case Tony was to get back, before Alex did."

"No problem. I have a few notes to write down, while I'm waiting anyway. It'll give me something to do."

"Good. See ya soon."

Later that evening, seeing the others return with the smoker, Ted went out to greet them. "Hey there, did you have any trouble getting it?"

"No…" Andy hollered out, before Alex could say a word, "but you should have heard the strange thunder we heard!"

"Thunder?" he asked, turning to Alex.

"Yeah, well," he grinned, getting out on the driver's side to reach around back and grab a large package, before Hank could jump in behind the wheel and drive the truck down to the stable to unload the smoker near the other one. Waiting until they were alone, he asked, "Where is she?"

"In her quarters."

"Is she all right?" he went on, while turning to head in.

"Yeah, she's fine. Beth is with her now."

"Good, but just for the heck of it, I think I'll just go on down and check on her myself."

"I rather thought you might," he smiled. "Oh," he called out quietly, "you had better be checking on you know what." He pointed to his own hair. "It needs a little touching up."

"Yes, I know," he grinned, holding up a bag. "I'm hoping she would fix it up for me."

Shaking his head as they reached the front porch, Ted watched Alex head down to see Jessi.

Upon reaching her quarters, he walked into the living room, spotting Beth sitting on the couch, while flipping through one of the Boutique's catalogs.

"Hi, boss!" she whispered, when seeing his questioning look. "She's in the bathroom."

"Oh. All right. How are you doing with your assignment?"

"Just fine! Annie is out shopping now for the food, and one of our guys to keep an eye on her, as well. That, and Jessi has been on the phone all day. She sure is a miracle worker."

"Yes, she sure is!" he agreed, smiling. "Hey, you know, if you have something else to do, I can stay with her, now that I'm back. Besides, I'm sure the others could use an extra hand in getting ready if you want to go up and help out."

"Okay!" Getting up to head for the stairs, she stopped and turned back. "Alex?"

"Yes?" he asked, looking up from the couch, where he sat down to pull off his boots.

"Thank you"

"For what?"

"This assignment!"

"What's so great about it?"

"I get to do what I love most!"

"Oh, and what would that be?"

"Creating delicious foods!" she returned, before pausing for another moment. "You really do love her, don't you?"

"You mean, since you and I..." He stopped to think back to when he had first met her.

"Alex," she interrupted his thoughts, when seeing his unhappy expression, "you know what had happened, couldn't have been helped. We both know that."

"Yeah, right." He got up to set his boots aside. "As for Jessi," his expression deepened, "her heart belongs to someone else."

"Yes, so I've noticed! And what a shame, too! You sure would have made someone a great catch, you know that?"

"Yeah, sure!"

After she had gone upstairs, leaving him to think about things, he headed down the hall, to check on Jessi.

Stopping outside the bathroom, he knocked at the door, "Jessi, you coming out soon?"

Not getting a response, he called out again, while slowly opening the door. "Jessi?"

Meanwhile, lying in a tub of hot bubbles, she was nearly asleep, listening to her soft music. Seeing that, he couldn't help but admire her, for she, like Beth, was everything he had ever wanted in a woman, strong, independent, and all so darn beautiful. *Damn you, Craig, you just had to beat me to her, didn't you,* he thought to himself, with a generous smile, before calling out to her again, "Jessi...! Wake up sleepyhead!"

"A...Alex...?" she called back, as she slowly came around.

"Yes," he responded, while watching her reach out to catch her towel, before it could fall off a nearby chair.

Though, what he saw got his attention and held it, she stood to wrap the towel around her. In doing so, more of her voluptuous breasts appeared, before the towel could cover them.

Seeing this, he began to ache to feel them once again. *Oh, God, why does she have to be so beautiful,* he groaned, while turning away to clear his throat. "Jessi," he began, while looking back over his shoulder, "I'll be out here waiting on you, after you get dressed."

"Okay."

After getting dressed in Craig's old, gray plaid work shirt, she walked out to the living room to see the hair dye sitting on her table. Not to mention, her girls had already gone to bed.

Going over to pick it up, she asked, "I guess you need me to do your hair, huh?"

"Would you mind?" he asked, seeing how the shirt she had on barely covered her hips, while making the rest of her even more appealing.

"All right, let's go do it," she said, turning to head into the kitchen.

"Great," he laughed, following her in, "I just love the way you talk dirty to me."

"Alex…" she turned back, catching him in the doorway.

"Well?" he continued to laugh, as he went on to tell her about their trip out to get the smoker, before going on over to Rose's for a swim. "Oh, and she gave me something to give you."

"Oh?" she asked, looking passed him to see a large package leaning up against her couch. "What is it?" she asked, going back into the living room to check it out.

"She wouldn't say!"

Not able to wait, she put off doing his hair to unwrap the package.

"Alex…" she cried softly, finding a picture of him, Craig, and David sitting together by the McMasters pool, "is this what I think it is?" she asked, sitting back on the floor to run her fingertips over Craig's bright smile, while fighting back the tears.

"Are you all right?" he asked, coming over to kneel down next to her.

"All right?" she cried. "Oh, Alex… he looks so handsome here! So alive!" she continued sadly, while looking into Craig's deep blue eyes, as she continued to trace his smile.

"Yes, he does."

Seeing how it had affected her, he took her by the hand to help her up. "Come over here," he suggested, sitting her on the couch next to him to hold her, until she cried herself to sleep.

After sitting there for a short while longer, before getting up to carry her into her room, he thought back to the picture, *I know just how you feel,* he went on sadly, when remembering the day they all got together. It was also his birthday, two years ago. *Damn you, Belaro, why did you have to go and kill him? Why Craig...* he cried, while slowly getting to his feet to lift her into his arms, not once waking her, as he carried her into her room.

After coming back out, he went into the kitchen to take care of his own hair, before going back in to look at the portrait a little while longer.

"Damn it, Craig, why?" he cried, while tiredly shaking his head, when fatigue had soon caught up with him.

Stretching his long, lean body out onto the couch, he groaned out Jessi's name just before nodding off.

Chapter Thirty-Five

The next day, everyone was running around shouting out orders to each other.

"Travis, just how deep does she want these holes?" Andy asked, wiping the sweat from his brow.

"Four feet!" he called back, heaving a shovel full of dirt out of one, as the sweat rolled off his back.

"Jessi..." Beth called out, smiling from the back door, "I got the tickets, and are they sure pretty," she cried, waving them in the air. "What do you think?"

"Looks good!" she laughed, seeing their different colors, from the gazebo. "Why don't you run them over there to Jake," she pointed. "He's with Hank, working on the smokers?"

"Alright."

Heading back up to the Inn, Jessi walked into the kitchen to see how her cook was doing on her assignment. "Hey, there, how are things going in here?" she asked, tossing her pad of paper on the counter, before going over to get a pitcher of lemonade from the refrigerator.

"Pretty good!" she returned with her usual bubbly personality.

"Good. I sent Beth out to give the tickets to Alex and Hank. She shouldn't be too long."

"That's fine. I see that he has gotten his hair done!"

"Yes, well I was supposed to have done it for him last night, but..."

"I know. I heard him talking with Mr. Jones earlier this morning."

"Yes, well, seeing that picture was quite a shock."

"I can only imagine. But just the same, I'm not one for believing in ghosts."

"What...? What do you know about..."

"His nephew?" she smiled thoughtfully. "From what I've heard, enough."

"Does anyone else know?"

"Only Hank."

"Good."

"Ms. Jessi," Annie took her by the hand, "is it true, then? Have you truly fallen in love with his nephew...?"

"Yes, I have," she replied, seeing the look that came over her face. "Lord, Annie. I know how this all must sound, but I can't go into it right now with you. I have so much I have to get done, in order for this shin-dig to go off without a hitch."

"Yes. And obviously from what all that has been going on around here, those two men up there are dangerous."

"They are. Well, at least Tony."

"Well, just the same, I'm glad that Captain Storm is here to protect you and the girls. So whatever you're doing for this nephew of his, just be careful."

"I will. And now, for this shin-dig."

"Well, I thought if I prepare the pancakes ahead of time. All I would have to do is heat them up."

"Good thinking!" she smiled, while heading for the back door with her lemonade in hand. "My mom does the same thing."

"Where do you think I got the idea?"

Jessi smiled.

"Are you going back out, now, to check on the others?"

"Yes, and I'll let Beth know you need her."

"Thanks."

Meanwhile, out in the backyard, the tables were being erected right along with plenty of chairs. As luck would have it, the weatherman called for sunshine both days.

"Hey, boss, lady!" Andy called out, cheerfully, while waist deep in the last hole. "They're nearly done...!"

"Good!" she laughed, walking on out to see that everything was almost ready for the next day. "Beth?"

"On my way!" she called back, seeing where Jessi was gesturing with a nod of her head.

"Good. She really needs your help."

"Gotcha," she smiled, while running off to the Inn.

Turning back, Jessi called out to Hank.

"Yes, ma'am," he smiled, seeing her lively expression.

"How are the smokers looking?" she asked, walking up.

"Stick around and see," Alex spoke up, leaving Ted to join them. "We're just about to fire them up, now!"

"Alex?" she turned, quietly, with a smile on her lips, at hearing his deep voice.

"Yep!" he spoke up, putting an arm around her shoulder. "How are things going inside?"

"Pretty good, but I'm worried that Annie may need more help!"

"What about the girls helping out?" Hank suggested, while lighting one of the pieces of charcoal.

"Oh, but they are!"

"Good," Alex grinned, before going over to start up the second grill. "Oh, but don't worry too much, I'm working on getting you some extra help."

"Good," she smiled with a sigh of relief, while watching the first smoker sputter a few times, before it had finally kicked in, and then the second.

That evening, everyone, but Tony and Harry, met down in Jessi's quarters for one last meeting for the following day's activities.

"Jessi," Alex spoke up from across the living room, "I just got a call from Sue and Rose. They'll be here in plenty of time to lend a hand with whatever you need, and so will my other sister, Donna."

"Great! I had also called my cousin. But Karen, her friend, says she's out on a buying spree and won't make either day!"

"What about our cousin's?" Lora asked.

"They went with her. But Karen said she'll be here."

"Well, as for the smokers," Hank announced, while leaning back against the kitchen doorway, "they're both up and running, now, after having been given an extra cleaning. They should be fine for the feast."

"Well then, Ted," Jessi turned, smiling, "were you able to talk to our two guides?"

"Yes, though one was slightly reluctant to do so, he soon changed his mind, when the other gave him a little push."

"And I can only imagine which one that was," she laughed.

"Yep!" he smiled, when both turned to see Alex's growing curiosity.

"Are the two of you ever going to tell me just who these two are?" he asked, looking questionably at Jessi.

"Nope!" she continued to smile. "But Ted will after we're done here."

Looking over at his friend, Ted just smiled, shaking his head. "Sorry, pal."

"Jessi… why do I feel like I'm not going to like this?" Alex grumbled.

"Oh, but you will!" she teased, while reaching up to give him a quick peck on the cheek, before going on with the rest of the meeting.

Later that night, all but a few of Alex's men got to bed early to be rested for the next day. Before turning in herself, Jessi went up to check on the front desk, to make sure everything was running all right.

Arriving there, she picked up on the scent of a cigarette burning out on the front porch. Going out to see who it was, she saw one of Alex's men sitting there, drinking coffee and reading the evening paper. "Frank!" she spoke up, joining him.

"Yes, Ms. Jessi," he stood, putting out his cigarette.

"Just checking on things."

"Yes, ma'am, everything's just fine. I have the cordless with me if anyone was to call."

"You know that the doors are to be closed and locked by eleven, don't you?"

"Yes."

"Are you out here alone?"

"Not for long. Ted is with Marcose now."

"I see!"

Jessi knew exactly what that meant. The other officers were all out walking the ground, along with Ted, Alex, and even Hank, just to make it look like another night of security rounds.

"Well, goodnight then!" she said, turning to go back inside.

"Goodnight, ma'am."

Arriving back down in her quarters, Alex was just walking in from the patio.

"Is everything all right?" she asked.

"Yep!"

"Good. It's late. I'll see you in the morning," she called back tiredly, heading into her room, after checking on her girls.

Plopping himself tiredly on the couch, to pull off his boots, before going on to take a shower, setting them aside, he got up and headed down the hallway. "Jessi?" he called out, stopping outside her room.

"Yes?" she answered, opening it.

Seeing a mixture of concern, and a hint of humor, he asked, "Have you ever thought about being a cop?"

"No. Why?"

"Your plan for Tony and Harry. I was mad as hell at first, but then Ted made me see reason. You're damn good at this. I'm proud of you."

"Gee, thanks, Alex! I'm proud of me too!" she laughed, as he shook his head and turned to go on into the bathroom, while closing the door behind him.

The next morning, a crowd of people were already forming out front to pay their cover charge to get in and enjoy the festivities. Seeing this, while standing in the foyer, Beth tugged on Jessi's arm, while she was engulfed in a conversation with Ashley, at the time, "Uh, Jessi..." she cried, "I think you should see this...!"

Before Jessi could respond, Travis came running in, short of breath, "Ms. Jessi..." he cried. "You have to come out here. The parking area, we set up in the field, across the road is beginning to fill up!"

"Oh, Lord, you're right," she agreed, seeing all the vehicles and the crowed gathering as well. "Travis," she turned back to pull out her walkie, to call Jake, "get over there and give them a hand. And for goodness sakes, let's hope the parking lot doesn't turn into a fiasco."

"Yes, ma'am." He turned then to head out across the front lawn.

"Jake!" she called out over her hand radio.

"Yeah, boss."

"Get the boys together. We need to have a quick meeting, before all heck breaks loose. Oh, and I had to send Travis across the road to help get people parked. Do you have an extra man to help out over there?"

Turning to see one of his men, Travis's age, he came back, "Sure, I'll send Rick right over. As for the meeting, the usual place?"

"Yes."

"We're on our way," he announced, standing over by the smokers with Hank and Ted.

Putting her walkie back into her dress pocket, Jessi brought Beth and Annie out with her. Just as they rounded the corner, Beth looked back to see Harry and Tony heading out back.

"Heads up!" she leaned in to whisper.

"Uh, huh!" Jessi muffled her response, while approaching the gazebo.

Getting closer, she couldn't help but see Alex's heated expression, when seeing Tony walking up.

"Alex, smile for crying out loud. Or he will start to wonder about you again," she whispered, while she had a chance to say something to him.

Doing just that, as hard as it was, he thought of something that would keep the smile on his face.

Seeing it, she nodded, while looking around to see that everyone was there. "Ladies and gentlemen…" She stopped to wait for everyone to get quiet.

"People!" Hank called out, "Let's hear what the boss has to say, here!"

"Thanks, Hank," she smiled. "Okay. Good! Now to get this meeting over with so we can let the people in. Does everyone here know what their job is?" Hearing a lot of yes's and a few no's, she turned to Tony first. "Tony, you do know that you're riding with Ted, and one other guide, don't you?" she asked, studying his hard expression, while he glared at Jake suspiciously. *"Great, so much for the smile he has on his face."*

"Yes, but if you only knew what it was about," Craig returned, laughing.

"Do I even want to know?"

"Oh… I think you have an idea!"

"Let me guess, Tony's tombstone?"

"Pretty much!"

She turned, laughing to herself, when even Alex saw the humor in her smile, which followed.

Clearing her throat, she started to ask again, when he pulled his attention away from her groundskeeper to answer.

"Yes."

"Thank you. I think. Oh, and Mr. Belaro."

He looked back to her, when starting to look back at Alex.

"Yes, we need to clear this up right here and now."

"Clear what up?" he asked coyishly.

"Mr. Belaro, don't act like I haven't noticed. If you have a problem with my groundskeeper, here, forget it. Yesterdays' fiasco had only put a lot of my people on edge, because of your actions. And to help smooth things out, I had Ted, here, ask you to offer your help to show that there was no more trouble between us. Are we clear on that?"

"Yes, of course!" He bowed his apologies, and avoided Alex's glares altogether.

"Mr. Green, are we square, as well? And people," she turned, "that goes for all of you who were here the other day, to see what went down. I have extended my invitation out to both these men to be a part of the festivities. And I want them treated as such. Is that clear?"

"Yes, ma'am," Harry spoke up, liking her. Not to mention, some of the others.

"Good. And now let's hurry this up some," she commented, while turning back to hand Harry the tickets for the trail rides. "Harry, I want you and Andy to handle the ticket sales. Is that all right with you?" she asked, when seeing how Tony glared at him.

"Are you sure you want me to do that, Ms. Jessi? What if I mess up?" he asked, timidly.

"I have faith in you!" she smiled thoughtfully at him, while ignoring Tony's subtle glare. "That, and you won't be alone. Besides, Andy is giving you a hand, and Hank will be there to take the money for the cover charge."

Feeling Tony's disapproval, Harry chose to ignore him, as well, because he liked being asked to help out. "Yes, I'll do it," he smiled sheepishly.

Having seen Tony's behavior over her favoring Harry, she, as well as Alex and Ted, watched him closely out of the corner of their eyes.

"And now," she asked, as a strand of hair blew free of its tie, "are we clear now on what we are doing?"

"Yes," everyone called back.

"Well, then, let's go!" she smiled. "Hank…?"

"Gotcha, Ms. Jessi!" he waved, while going over with Andy and Harry to do what they were assigned, when she turned along with the others to finish getting ready.

"Ms. Jessi?" Alex called out, catching up to her.

"Yes, Jake?" she asked, when stopping to hear a couple of trucks pulling in with extra tables and chairs for the meals. "Hank…" she called out, interrupting Alex, "forget the booth and let Andy cover that. I need you and the other boys to help unload the trucks! Jake…" she turned back only to see his big, handsome grin, as he stood shaking his head in admiration.

"Yes, ma'am," he smiled, while running off and getting a few of his own boys to help.

"Wow, I can't believe how much you have gotten done!" Lisa remarked, when Jessi walked back in to take a breather.

"It wasn't just me! The guys all jumped in and worked through the night on everything. Which reminds me," she turned to go into her office, "we need to hurry and change!"

"We…?"

Bringing out two old fashioned dresses, Jessi held them up for Lisa to see.

"Is this for me?" she asked, taking the long, blue, plaid, dress Jessi was handing her.

"Yes, and what do you think of mine?" she asked, showing off her long, maroon, floral print.

"Nice!"

After getting changed, she went back out to join the others, when she heard a familiar voice call out from the crowd.

"Hey, Cuz'!"

"Jodi…?" she cried, seeing her cousin, and her cousin's two girls, walking up with Karen, not only Jodi's best friend, but business partner, too, of Jodi's Antiques & Collectables.

Giving each other a big sisterly hug, Jessi pulled back to look her over. "I can't believe you're here!"

"I can't stay long, but when I heard about what you were doing, I had to check it out."

"Great!" she smiled, while turning to the girls who weren't much different in age from her own two. As for her cousin, the two looked a lot alike. "Hey you two, Lora and Cassi are over at the tables, getting them setup. Why don't you go over and give them a hand?"

"Sure!" they agreed, running off.

After seeing them off, Jessi, Jodi and Karen went for a walk to check things out.

"So, how are things?" Jodi asked, seeing that Jessi was preoccupied. "Jessi?" she spoke up again, breaking into her thoughts

"W…what?"

"Okay, what's up, Cuz'? You haven't heard a word I've said."

"There has been a lot going on, that's all," she replied, while looking around for Alex. Seeing how he, Ted, and their guides were all out on the trails, she turned back to her cousin. "Are you hungry?"

"Starving! Why else would we have come," she laughed, walking over to see Annie come out with a platter of food. "To eat Annie's cooking, of course…!"

"Jodi…?" Annie cried, seeing the tall, brunette, walking up to lend a hand.

"Hey, there! How's my favorite cook?"

"Waiting to serve," she laughed, setting the platter down, before greeting her with a big hug, as well as her friend.

"Did you see the girls?" she asked, while taking a seat, when Annie sat them each a plate of food down in front of them.

"Yep, and I got them busy helping out!"

"Great! And perhaps after we get done here," she turned to Jessi, "we can go for a ride!"

"Sure!" Jessi agreed, while the three of them went on to talk and enjoy their food.

After they had finished, taking their girls with them, they headed over to the stables to see a group coming back in. However, Jessi didn't see Alex leading it, but Harry, however, was still at the tail end, when he had finished at the ticket table.

"Hank?" she spoke up, going over to talk to him, after he had left the smoker to one of his boys to watch, while he went to check on the other horses.

"Yes…?" He turned then to see a familiar face behind her. "Jodi…?" he grinned.

"Hi, Hank!" she smiled at the graying haired stable hand, in his upper fifties.

"Hank…" Jessi spoke back up, worriedly, "where is he?"

Seeing her concern, he grinned, "Don't worry none, he's out tailing Ted's group. And he's not alone."

"Good!" she breathed a sigh of relief.

"Now," he went on, "what is a couple of beautiful gals like you two doing here?"

"Having fun!" Jodi laughed.

"Well, if you haven't already tried out my cookin', you best be doing that," he teased, while looking especially at Jessi.

"Okay, okay…" she smiled, before running off to grab her own personal horse that he had saddled up for her.

Afterwhich, her group joined in with Baker's, who was now leading up the half hour trail.

By the end of the day, with everyone exhausted, Jodi left with her gang, before Alex returned. As for the money collected, it was more than anyone could have imagined.

Meanwhile, after everyone else called it a night, Alex and Jessi stayed up in her office to wrap up on what they had brought in for the day.

"Well, that's all finished," he announced, while closing the accounting book. "We pulled in quite a bit for one day."

"We sure did. I'll go over the bills tomorrow night to figure out what will be left over after everything is paid. Maybe then I could get started on those plans to have some cabins built next spring," she explained, while sitting back tiredly in her chair.

"Sounds good!" he agreed, getting up to stretch his legs. "And now what do you say, we close up here and get some sleep? Tomorrow is going to be another busy day."

"You won't get an argument out of me!" she yawned, as he went to pull her up from her chair, "I am so… ex…hausted…!"

"Yeah, me too!"

Heading for her quarters, he commented, tiredly, out in the foyer, "The girls sure had a lot of fun today, didn't they?"

"Yes, they did. In fact, they were so tired, they went right to bed after dinner!"

"No, doubt," he laughed, when stopping to see Marcose talking to Kevin on the porch.

With a nod of their heads, they continued watching over the area, while keeping a close eye on the inside, as well.

Reaching her quarters, Alex grabbed his gear, before heading for the bathroom. "If you don't mind, I'm just going to grab a quick shower, before calling it a night."

"All right," she called back over her shoulder, while going in to check on her girls. Just before reaching their room, she felt a tingling sensation running up her neck. *"Craig… what are you doing?"* she smiled, while standing outside her daughter's bedroom door.

"I just thought I'd say hello!"

"And a very nice way of doing it, I might add," she laughed, while going on to peek in on them.

Seeing how they were all right, she went back into her room, and closed the door behind her, before going on to change.

Once again, slipping into bed, wearing his old work shirt, she continued their talk, until she had fallen off to sleep, leaving her with a pleasant thought, as he sat back visualizing the two of them dancing in front of his fireplace, while wearing what she had on at that moment.

"Mmmm…" she murmured quietly, feeling his arms around her, as the music played on softly in her head. And with a coy little smile, she began to hum in her sleep.

Chapter Thirty-Six

When the next day got there, the band was playing a festive tune, while Ted and Alex, having decided to give the horses a rest, got a baseball game started up instead. And to Jessi's surprise, Alex's other nephew, Jarred Stanton joined them.

"Jessi?" Alex called out.

"Yes?" she turned back to see a tall, dark brown haired man, with his freshly shaven face, smiling over at her. And yet, seeing him, there was something in his eyes that looked so familiar to her.

Walking up, Alex introduced the two, "This is my nephew, Jarred," he whispered, seeing Jessi's expression. "He's…"

"Craig's cousin," she returned, smiling up at him. "And your…" she stopped.

"Yes, exactly!" Alex grinned, knowing she had remembered their conversation about Jarred being his new partner.

"You look so much like him!" she returned.

"You knew him?" Jarred asked, looking to Alex puzzledly.

"I'll fill you in on that later," he laughed, leaving Jessi along the sideline to join in on the game at hand. "Hey," he called back, "are you going to watch us?"

With a bright smile, she nodded her head, but before the two could get too far away she called out to his nephew, "Oh, by the way… it's a shame you weren't here yesterday."

"Oh. Why's that?"

"My cousin was here. You would have liked her."

"Oh? Does she look anything like you?"

"A spitting image!"

Great, he thought back to the beautiful girl he had lost out on years ago, if it hadn't been for her grandmother stopping him from going out with her. Jodi Tate wasn't just any ordinary girl though, she was beautiful and sexy, but not in a disrespectful sort of way. She was from a decent family, and unknown to him and Alex; she was also Jessi's cousin.

Catching up with his uncle, their team was in the outfield, while Harry and Tony's were up to bat.

"Come on, Harry, hit the ball!" Lisa yelled, as Ted was about to pitch.

Meanwhile, out in centerfield, Alex was getting ready to catch what might turn out to be a line drive.

As for the beef roast, Hank was back to cooking up a storm.

"Hey, Hank, how are you doing over here?" Jessi asked, while walking over with more ears of corn to put on the smoker.

"Just fine! How are you holding up?"

"As well as to be expected! It sure looks like everyone is having a ball!"

"Yep! Not to mention, how well everything turned out," he indicated with his meat fork, while pointing out over the crowd.

"Yes, it sure has!" She had no sooner said, when amongst the crowd, she spotted a couple of familiar faces walking up with their husbands. Joining them was a man she had not seen before. But then, she broke out into a grin, when realizing who he was. "David…?" she whispered, covering her mouth to keep the others from hearing her.

Grinning back, he nodded his graying head, which was only a disguise, while Bob spoke up, interrupting them.

"How's my favorite patient doing?" he asked, walking up to take a quick look into her eyes, as the sun came beating down over her.

"Better, thank you!"

"Good! You look happy. And Alex?" he asked quietly, while looking around. "Where are he and the others?"

"Out playing ball!" she was just saying, when Lisa came running up to grab her arm.

"Jessi…" she cried, "why aren't you watching the game? Jake is going up to bat next!"

"Already?" she cried, turning back to the others, "I guess I had better be getting back over there! Why don't you guys join me? You'll love to see this! Oh," she stopped, "Jarred is here, too!" she announced, knowing that he had been close to David at one time.

"We'll be right there!" they laughed, as Lisa tugged a little harder on her arm to hurry.

"Come on, girl, we've got to hurry!"

Just like Lisa said, Alex was up next, and when Jessi walked up to the fence, he turned to wink at her. "Go get'em tiger!" she whispered, while watching Harry about to pitch a foul ball.

After that, he took a moment to walk over to the fence to talk with her. "Is everything going all right?" he asked, having seen her smiling face, while over talking with Hank.

"Better than I could have ever imagined. Rose and Sue are here with their husbands, as they had said they'd be."

"And David? Is he…"

"Only until the game is over," she whispered, while pointing to where Hank was.

"Where?" he asked, trying to pick him out of the crowd.

"He has the graying hair, just like yours!" she laughed, turning back to Alex.

"And just what are you trying to say, lady?" he laughed. "Are you calling me old?"

"Well…! It is your birthday coming up."

"Hey, Jake! Are ya going to bat, or flirt with the boss?" Travis called out from first base.

"Well, I guess I had better be getting back up there. Tell David, he is not to leave without first seeing me," he ordered, before turning to head back up to bat.

"All right. Hey!" she called out, stopping him.

"Yeah?"

"Jarred?"

"What about him?"

"Does Tony know him?"

"No, and besides Jarred becoming my partner here recently, Tony had been gone all that time. That, and I asked him before he got here, to be sure it was safe for him."

"But there had been no other cases connecting him to Tony or his people. And let's face it, a guy like that has to have people out there somewhere."

Thinking of only one, the case they were wrapping up on, when he came out there, she may have been on to something. "Damn, you may be right! I'll say something to Ted, and have him talk to Jarred so it won't cause any suspicion."

"Good, besides, that's all you would need."

"Yeah. Now I have to get back to the game," he grinned.

Shaking his head, he readied himself for the next pitch.

Just as she took her seat, the most exciting thing happened, while watching as Harry went to throw the ball, Alex swung the bat as hard as he could, sending the ball so far out into centerfield, it had gotten Tony's attention.

"All right, Jake!" the crowd called out, while doing the grandstand wave.

"Is that Alex?" Bob asked quietly.

"Sure is!" she smiled, while calling out to him again, as well as David.

"Yeah, go Jake...!" he laughed. And for a brief moment, he didn't look nervous. But then suddenly, he stopped, when Tony turned back, hearing a familiar voice. "God... no... I've got to go," he whispered, nervously to the others, just as he was about to get up and leave.

"No!" Jessi whispered back, grabbing the sleeve of his denim jacket. "You can't!"

"Jessi, please!" he pleaded, while trying to pull away.

"David, listen to me!" she exclaimed, while looking up at him sympathetically. "Unless you want Tony to see right through your disguise, you can't just run out of here like that."

"But..." he started, when Alex, Jarred and Ted ran up to join them after winning the game thirteen to seven.

"Hey! You're not leaving yet, are you?" Alex asked, while putting a brotherly arm around his shoulder, when sensing his fear.

"I uh, I..." he stammered nervously.

Then Ted joined up to put an arm around his other shoulder to calm him down some. And in a low voice, he introduced himself, "David, take it easy. I'm Ted, Alex's old partner. Do you remember me?"

"Ye...yes!"

"Good! Now, try to look relaxed, Tony won't even notice you, unless you bolt out of here, whenever he looks at you. Besides, I didn't even know it was you, until Alex said something!"

"Yes, besides…" Jarred laughed, while looking his disguise over, "what do we call you?"

"Dusty!" he replied, smiling once again.

"What…?" Alex laughed, shaking his head. "That's what I used to call you, because you were always getting dirty from sliding into bases!"

Seeing her son's changed expression, Rose and the others walked up, asking, "Are you all right?"

"Yeah, I'm fine now!" he smiled, while heading over to the Beef Roast with everyone.

"Man, I'm starving after that play!" Alex laughed.

"Yeah, but did you see…" Jarred stopped to have a look around, before going on.

"What?" Alex stopped to do the same.

"No. It's nothing. I just wanted to make sure it was safe to talk openly."

"What were you about to say?"

"The look on Tony's face. That *was* who was out in centerfield, wasn't it?"

"Wait a minute," Jessi jumped in. "You don't know him?"

"Who?"

"The guy out in centerfield?" she groaned.

"No! All but what I was told that happened to my cousin! Why?"

"She was concerned that he may have known you," Alex explained, quietly, "through the arrest of Delgado. Is there any chance at all that those two may have had a run-in with you in the past on any other raids you may have been on?"

"No, I was always in some sort of disguise, like you, so if we had to do another undercover job, I wouldn't ever be known!"

"Good," Ted returned. "And no about Tony. He was just mad because he had to go after the ball," he laughed quietly.

"Yes," she laughed too, while turning the conversation back to David. "Alex, I'm worried," she stated, pulling him aside, when they reached the table to get their food dished up. "You don't think he recognized David's voice, do you?"

"No."

"But it did look like he heard something familiar from out of the crowd," she added worriedly, while Hank handed them a serving of buttered corn.

Looking over at David, who was laughing it up, now, with Jarred, Alex nudged Ted in the side.

"What is it?" he asked, seeing his hardened expression.

"Tell Jarred to stand ready. We may have a problem."

"What?"

"Jessi noticed the look on Tony's face, when David had called out to me, using my alias. We think Tony may have recognized his voice after all."

"All right, I'll get right on it."

He had no sooner started to turn away with his plate of food, when Alex stopped him again. "Hey, I don't want David alarmed. So try and handle it as quiet as possible."

With a nod of his head, Ted was off to join the others, just as Beth walked up, seeing the three of them looking pretty serious.

"Boss?" she whispered, seeing Tony watching David closely, now.

"We may have a problem. Just be ready on my word."

"Sure thing!" She, too, turned to go off in the guys' general area to keep watch, while Alex took out his hand radio to call Marcose and Baker.

"Jessi, where are your girls?" Alex asked.

"There!" she pointed with a nod of her head, while at the same time trying to put a smile on her face. "Alex?"

"Yeah?"

"Something just hit me. Wouldn't Tony know your connection to Beth or any of the others that are here?"

"No. What came down between Tony and I, the others were never around. I made sure of that, because of his family connection to the mob."

"Thank God, or all of this would have been for nothing."

"Yes. Now listen to me, I want you to stay with Hank," he ordered, getting the stable hand's attention.

"Sure!" she agreed, without argument, while he called out to Hank.

"Yeah," he returned, handing his meat fork over to one of the other groundskeepers, before coming around to take Jessi's arm, having sensed what Alex had on his mind.

"Take her over to her girls, while I call the others to put them on notice."

"Sure thing. Shall we?" he smiled calmly.

"Alex…!" she cried quietly, while trying not to look too frightened.

"Just go!" he ordered, before putting the radio up to his mouth to call out to his best man.

Doing so, she and Hank joined her girls, who were talking to Bob, Sue and Rose. As for

Allen, he stood over by David and Jarred, when Ted walked up to nudge Jarred off to the side.

"What is it?" he asked, getting the impression there was trouble.

Filling him in, Beth was busy keeping an eye on Tony, while acting as though she was carrying on a conversation with Annie. Turning then, she saw where Jessi and her girls were. *This isn't good,* she thought. But then, turning back to see what Tony was doing, at that moment, he was pulling Harry off toward the front of the Inn. "Alex…" she called out over her radio.

"What's going on?"

"Our bird is taking his side kick, and heading up front. Do we follow?"

"Yeah. Ted…"

"I'm with you."

"Let's go then! Oh, and Ted, take Jarred with you. Beth…"

"I'm with you," she spoke up, when coming up behind him.

"Good. You ready?" he asked, while passing their plates off to the closest person to them.

"Let's do it," she smiled.

With a nod of his head, giving the word, the foursome ran off in the same direction to see where they were going.

"But Tony… I don't want to go…!" Harry was saying, when Tony went over to open Harry's car door to shove him in.

"You're going, and that's all there is to it," he growled. "And the next time someone asks you to do something you say *no*!"

"But I like her, Tony…!" he groaned, while falling onto his seat.

"Yeah, and she knows Storm. So how would I know you won't go and say something to her," he sneered, while slamming the door shut.

"Alex," Beth whispered at the side of the Inn, while shielded behind some bushes, "he…"

"I heard," he growled.

"What are we going to do?" Jarred asked, while kneeling down next to his uncle.

Reaching for his radio, he looked on at their car, "Call Kevin and have him follow."

"He shouldn't go alone," Ted warned, while peering out around the same set of bushes. "How about we send Shane with him, since Tony hasn't seen either one of them?"

Making the call, the two undercover officers ran for Kevin's blue Jeep Wrangler, and were soon tailing after Tony's car, when he pulled out.

After sitting back on their knees for a couple more minutes to collect their thoughts, Alex stood back up, while putting his service revolver away. "We need to be getting back to the others and see how they're doing."

"Yeah, they're probably wondering the same thing!" Ted put in, while the rest of them stood, doing the same.

Checking first to make sure the coast was clear they went back, while hearing the band playing on.

A short time later, and a great deal of tension still in the air, it was then, Jessi heard her name being called out over the microphone that had been setup earlier in the gazebo, "Ms. Rae! Ms. Jessi Rae!" the announcer called out. "Will you please come up here? We have something for you," a tall man in his late fifties announced.

Having been rejoined by Alex and the others, Jessi asked, wondering who he was, while Alex and Hank walked her up to the gazebo.

"That's the Mayor, and my boss!" Alex whispered.

"Ms. Jessi," the Mayor, spoke up, "the people of Crawfordsfield County have all expressed their deepest admiration of your reopening of the Inn, and especially the choice of name in which you have given it," he stated, as she, Alex and Hank arrived at the gazebo. "Because of your ongoing services in our county and state," the mayor went on, "we the people would like to present you and your staff with this plaque of Continued Excellence."

"Thank you, Mayor Donaldson, Commissioner Garrett. I couldn't have done it without my friends, to name a few;" she pointed, "Annie, Hank, Travis, Ted, and even you, Jake, my real pain," she smiled, while turning to the others. "And I don't want to forget Beth, who Annie could not have done without. These are the people to whom we should thank. They helped to make it all happen."

Leading the applause, she turned back to continue smiling up at Alex, who had just given her a big brotherly hug, before sweeping her out onto the lawn to dance, while handing Hank the plaque.

"Just you wait, Ms. Jessi," he teased, while running his hand over her smooth back.

"You're the one who's going to have to wait. I'm leaving soon!" she whispered, when looking up into his icy blue eyes, while watching for the expression on his face to change. Even the shade of his eyes deepened, when he backed away.

Looking at her in total surprise, he brought her back into his arms even closer now. "Not by yourself, you're not!" he whispered in her ear, while looking out over the crowd of people, when seeing Rose and Allen enjoying their dance, as well as both his sisters with each of their husbands.

"Yes, Alex, by myself," she whispered back firmly.

"Jessi, please don't!" he pleaded sadly.

Looking deep into her eyes, he hoped she would change her mind.

"Alex," she whispered, when then lowering her head so to avoid looking into those sad eyes of his.

"When?"

"Tonight!"

"I'm going to follow you then. Just to make sure you get there all right. And then I'll come back and work on the papers for you if you feel that you have to go."

"Thanks, Alex," she replied, while fighting back the tears in which his feelings for her had caused, while trying to smile.

"And the girls, where are they going, or are they?"

"Yes, they're going back over to Jodi's."

"Jessi…"

"Alex, we should stop," she cried softly, when seeing a few eyes fixed on them at that moment.

Seeing his nephew looking their way as well, the look on his face looked puzzled, knowing how Alex had felt about Beth. "Yeah, you're right!" He turned back to see her loving smile.

Chapter Thirty-Seven

Finishing their dance, Jessi went in to pack, while Alex went over to talk to Beth, Ted and Jarred. "Has any of you heard back from our men who are out tailing Tony?"

"No," the three shook their heads.

"Great." Calling them himself, Alex waited to hear Kevin's voice on his end.

"Yes, sir?"

"What's the word on our friends?"

"They're shooting pool and having a drink!"

"Good. Let me know right away when they leave!"

"Yes, sir."

"All right," He turned back to the trio, "when Tony and Harry get back, keep them busy."

"After what happened up front, what if Tony won't let Harry do anything?" Beth asked.

"Then I suggest one or more of you guys do what I would do if I were here."

"Divide and conquer!" they each laughed, looking to one another.

"Harry needs our help, that's obvious. So watch him and make sure Tony doesn't do anything to hurt him. Beth," he turned, knowing, like Jessi, she has a heart of gold, when it came to misfits like Harry, "When you can get him off by himself, talk to him and let him know we are his friends, and that we won't let Tony hurt him. But he mustn't let on to Tony that he has a friend in us, or it won't work."

"Alex, what are you going to be doing?" Ted asked.

"I'm taking Jessi back out to the farmhouse for a few days."

"The farmhouse? As in Craig's old place?" Jarred asked, looking surprised.

"Yes," he returned, still not ready to get into a long discussion about it. "Beth?"

"Yes?"

"I want you to stay in her quarters. Listen to her music so Tony thinks she's still here. And Jarred," he turned back, "stick around, but stay low, unless you're needed. I don't want any more dead bodies on my hands, let alone another nephew."

"Are you staying with her or coming back?" Ted inquired.

"I'll be back. I'm just going out to check on the house and grounds. Once I'm certain she'll be safe, I'll be back to take care of things here."

"And the girls?" Beth asked.

"They already left with her cousin's friend, since she couldn't come back to get them herself."

"Is that where you sent Marcose?" Jarred asked. "I couldn't help but notice that he left right after they did."

"Yes, just in case he's needed."

"Good, but what about Craig's place?" Ted asked.

"It's covered. I put a few other guys out there to keep an eye on it, as we speak."

"Okay!" Ted returned.

Following Alex, the four went into Jessi's quarters to check on her.

"Jessi," Alex asked, while getting his service revolver ready along with the others, "are you taking your truck?"

"I guess I could, why?" she asked, bringing out her things.

"They know your car too well," Ted explained, while putting his revolver back into its shoulder holster. "If they see it here, they'll just think you haven't left!"

"Good idea!" Alex agreed, while turning to the stairs this time to head out to her garage.

"Stay here while I go and get it for you."

"You're bringing it up front, aren't you?" Ted asked.

"Yeah, why?"

"Just asking!"

"In that case, let's get moving. I don't want to waste any more time than necessary," he groaned, while heading on up, taking the stairs two at a time.

Still puzzled over the turn of events, Jarred just stood by watching, while Jessi turned to Ted, looking worried.

"Don't worry about him, he'll be all right," he smiled, thoughtfully. "Is this all you're taking with you on this trip?" he asked, looking over her luggage.

"Yes."

"All right!" he replied, while picking up her things to carry upstairs for her, as the others followed.

Getting there, the wait was short, when Alex came back in winded. "Are we ready?"

"Yes, and I had already said goodbye to the girls, before they left with Karen," she returned, while fighting back the unexpected tears.

Seeing this, Alex felt bad, when he came up to offer her a warm shoulder, "Jess, I know this isn't easy having to see them leave, but it's for their own good."

"I know, it's just that I don't like for it to be like this!" she shuttered, when pulling away to head on out to her truck.

Same here, he thought.

"Jessi," Ted cut in thoughtfully, knowing they must hurry, before their friends return, "while you're out there, watch yourself, and call us no matter what."

"I will," she promised, while smiling up into Alex's concerned expression, before getting into her truck. "If I don't..."

"You'll have me to reckon with," he growled.

Turning away to open her truck door, she smiled back at the strong hint of warning his, now, steely blue eyes held. "Oh, Alex, as if I were to put you through the hell I already have."

"You would," he growled.

"Alex, the two of you ought to get going, while the going is good!" Ted called out.

"Yeah, you're right!" Seeing now that Beth was back inside, talking to Lisa, he turned to Jarred and Ted. "What about the two of you?"

"Jarred and I will keep an eye on things here until you get back."

"Good. And like I said..." he looked to his nephew warningly.

"Yeah, I know," Jarred grinned, "stay low."

"Real low," he growled.

Just then, Kevin's voice rang out over their radios to warn them that Tony and Harry were on the move again.

"All right," Alex acknowledge, while heading for his own vehicle. "Let's go! They're on the move again!"

"Be careful out there!" Ted called out, as he and Jarred remained out on the front porch, when Beth came out to join them.

Waving their goodbyes, the two headed on out.

"Think one of us should follow?" Jarred asked, while keeping a focus on Alex's Blazer.

"Someone is!" Beth smiled, while pointing off toward one of their men in his black pick-up truck.

"Frank?" Ted asked, suspiciously.

"No. Rick."

"Problem?" Jarred asked, concernly, looking to Ted.

"I can't say just yet, but there's something about him that doesn't ring out right."

"Great. That's all we need, is a wrinkle in the works," he grumbled, while they stood on the front porch, while listening to their radios for further news from their men, while the clean-up was going on in the backyard.

A short while later, having arrived at the farmhouse, Alex went around checking things out, while Jessi went into the living room, where Craig was waiting for her.

"Hello, beautiful!" he greeted her warmly from the fireplace.

"Hi, yourself!" she returned, while trying to hide the fatigue, and yet the question some were still wanting an answer to.

"It's useless to try and hide it, you know? I can see how tired you are."

"Oh? Does it show that much?" she asked, avoiding his eyes.

Before answering, Alex interrupted them, after making his rounds, to say his goodbyes.

"You're done already...?" she asked, spinning around to look at him.

"Yes. Are you all right?"

"Oh, yes, sure! I'm fine!"

"Uh huh! You're sure? Because I can stay, if you want me to."

"Oh, Alex, I'll be fine! Really! Besides, you have to be getting back to Ted and your other nephew."

"Yeah, well, just the same, I have a few men out walking the ground, and Marcose will be here later."

"That's great! How about I just walk you out to your Blazer, then?"

Finding her behavior odd, and still hesitant about leaving her, he had to get back to find out what went down with the case he and Jarred were wrapping up on. "Yeah, well," he turned back, once getting to the Blazer, "I'll be calling on you tomorrow to see how you're doing."

"No doubt, you will!" she tried to smile, when he went to open his door. *"Come on, Jessi, don't be such an idiot. You have to do something! He looks so unhappy leaving you here alone."* Just then, she spoke up, grabbing his arm, "Alex, wait!"

"What is it?" he asked, turning back.

"I... just wanted to thank you," she began, while feeling the pain wrenching away at her. However, just saying thank you didn't seem to be enough, when she wanted to say more. *"But what?"* Then out of gratitude, she reached up and gave him a hug for all he had done for her.

"Jessi," he returned her hug, when he saw her saddened expression, "don't thank me, yet. Wait until all this is over, before you do that."

"Will it be?" she cried into his shoulder.

"Sure it will!" he thought sadly of all she would be giving up, when his nephew's time there was over.

Getting into his Blazer to get ready to pull away, he looked back at her one last time.

"See ya!" she smiled, as it began to lightly rain.

"Yeah, I'll see ya," he offered her one of his rich smiles, just as he pulled out.

Going back inside, she saw the small grin on Craig's face. "You know, don't you?"

"About Alex? Yes, for some time now. And you? How do you feel about him?"

"Oh, Craig, I care a lot about him. Perhaps more than I should! But..." She turned away to go over and sit on the sofa.

"Jessi, give it a chance!"

Give it time! Give it time...! She wanted to scream, hearing those words again. *When it was him, she was in love with.*

"Jess, I feel the same way, but still, why...? Why haven't you answered his question?"

"His question?" she cringed, wishing she didn't have to answer it at all.

"Yes, Jess. I want to know, as well, what *are* you going to do when all this is over?"

Shaking her head, she pushed herself up off the sofa, to walk into the kitchen. "Craig, please...!" she cried. "I am so tired of people asking me that same question over and over again! I don't even *want* to think about it."

"Yes, and I can understand why," he continued, while following her into the kitchen, "but understand me, I just don't want you to be alone! Because, as I'm sure you have already heard this, if anyone out there could be there for you, it would be my uncle. So please, think about it. I really don't want you to be alone once I'm gone."

"Craig, noI won't! I...I can't! So just stop it! P...please!" she began sobbing. "Just... stop it!" she cried out, feeling that her heart just couldn't take it anymore. And though, he wasn't setting out to hurt her, she suddenly turned and ran blindly out the back door and into the rain, not caring at all where she was going, when she just went.

"Jessi, no!" he called out, instead of using telepathy, to reach her. In doing so, the sound of his voice brought on a sudden clap of thunder overhead, as she continued to run further and further down a path.

"No" she went on crying, while not feeling the drops of rain, slowly seep into her clothing, "it's just too soon!" she sobbed. "It's just... to... soon!" Stopping to catch her breath, she continued to sob. "P... pleaseI just want to think about what we have now! This moment!" she continued, while dropping to her knees. "If only..." She breathed, but then, turning back to see how far she had gone, while knowing Alex's men were out there somewhere, not seeing any lights on back at the house, she became frightened. *"Oh, God... C...Craig, w...where am I?"*

Using telepathy, he called back, *"Jess, it's going to be okay! Just follow my thoughts!"*

"But they're all around me! How will I know which way to go?"

*"The thoughts, they will only get stronger as you get closer. Trust me...
I'll get you back safely...!"*

At that moment, having heard the thunder, one of Alex's men
spotted Jessi looking lost out on the path. Calling it in, Alex's voice
came back over the radio.

"Where is she now?" he asked, bringing the Blazer to a stop,
alongside the highway, not far from where he had just turned off of
Craig's road.

"Several hundred yards out behind the house! And sir...?"

"What is it?"

"She looks to be frightened about something."

"Stay close and then call me once she gets back to the house."

"What...? You don't want me to intercede?"

"No, you might scare her even more by simply popping up out of
nowhere. Just watch her, and make sure she gets back to the house all
right."

"Yes, sir."

Damn... he thundered inwardly, *before leaving the house, I had a
feeling something was wrong. But what,* he asked, sensing he had walked
in on their conversation. But then, not wanting to have left at all, a big
part of him wanted to go back at that moment. Meanwhile, looking
out at the rainy night, he continued to sit there, while waiting on word
from his man to see if Jessi made it back all right. *Damn it, Craig...* he
growled, *what the hell is going on back there?* Then suddenly, it dawned
on him. *The look on her face when I walked into the living room! Oh,
God, that's it, he knows how I must be feeling about her!* Shaking his head
sadly, he decided not to wait on word from his man. But instead, put
his Blazer back into gear and drove back to the Inn, through the light
misting rain, while feeling bad about the whole ordeal, both, at Craig's,
and the Inn. "Damn it, anyway, I wasn't planning for something like
this to happen. Why?" his voice roared out angrily.

Meanwhile, as the rain increased, Jessi walked even quicker, when
soon the house came back into view.

Going inside, she went straight to the living room and sat at the
fireplace to get warm.

"Jess," Craig spoke up, coming over to join her, while she sat, staring off into the flames, contemplating on whether or not to go back to the Inn that night, or call on Rose or Sue for shelter.

Picking up on her thoughts, he looked away, shaking his head. "Jess, please...! I'm sorry...! It's just that I care so much about what happens to you. I know you don't want to talk about it. But still, I just want to know that you're going to be all right, when the time comes!"

"When the time comes," she gulped back on renewed tears. "If Alex still wants me after I have gotten over losing you, I might turn to him, but not right now. I...I can't think about that! So, please... just drop it for now...!"

"All right," he whispered, while putting a kind smile on his face.

"I wish things were different for us," she cried softly, as she went to get up and pace the floor, while taking her hands to rub over her cold arms.

"I do, too! Until you came along, I had never felt so much love and compassion for anyone, as I do you. I just wish I knew why David couldn't have told me that he was in so much trouble. Damn him, anyway..." he swore, turning to look back into the flames, "my whole life has been taken away, because of him. It's just not fair!"

"No, Craig, it isn't fair. But for now..." she whispered, while coming back over to join him, as he turned back to look at her, "can we please talk about something else? I just want to hold on to this time we have together, for as long as we can! I don't even want to imagine life without you in it."

"What would you like to talk about?" he asked, when one of her thoughts came to him.

"What do you think?" she smiled.

"Really...?"

"Yes, really," she blushed, thinking about the man-made shower. "It felt so real, as if you were really there! But how could that be?"

"What makes you think I wasn't?" he grinned, while looking down at her damp clothes as the imprint of her breasts pressed against her top.

Seeing where his attention had gone, she grinned.

Changing the subject, he looked back up to see the gleam in her eyes. "Why don't you go and get ready for bed. We'll talk when you get back."

"All right," she smiled, while going over to get out her favorite sweats to change into.

Once in the confines of the bathroom, she slipped out of her wet things and took a quick shower, before putting on some dry clothes.

"So, how is my cousin?" he asked, turning just in time to see her coming back into the living room.

"Fine, I guess!" she laughed lightly, while going over to get comfortable under one of his old blankets, when a yawn came.

Seeing how tired she was, he smiled, "Why don't we table this until tomorrow, so you can get some sleep tonight?"

"Mmmm… you're…uh, uh, uh, right!" she replied, yawning once again. "Craig…?"

"Yes?"

"Will you stay with me?" she asked, before closing her eyes.

"All right," he smiled, coming over to stretch out by her side. "Sleep now, and dream…" he whispered softly in her hair, as she turned over onto her side and closed her eyes.

"Mmmm…" she murmured. And soon a dream began to form, as he laid light kisses along the side of her neck, which brought a smile to her lips.

Meanwhile, getting back to the Inn, Alex went up to Ted's room to talk him and Jarred.

"How's our guests?" he asked, walking in.

"One of them left right after they got back," Ted replied. "I tried to call and warn you, but you couldn't be reached!"

"Damn it!" he growled, while going over to look out the window.

"It's all right," Jarred spoke up. "It was Harry!"

"Oh…?" He glanced back into the room.

"Yes, Lisa heard him, as he walked out passed her to go to their car," Ted explained. "He was grumbling something under his breath about wanting to be through with all this."

"Through with all this?" Alex questioned, as his eyes bored down on the two of them. "And just what exactly does that mean?"

"I can't say," he offered. "But she also said he looked pretty upset, and yet, troubled!"

"You don't think…" Jarred began.

"That he's having second thoughts?" Alex returned, while looking back out the window. "Possibly, but Harry isn't the one that concerns me. I am however, after Tony. So out with it," he turned back. "What's going on with him?"

"Well, to start," Ted went on to explain, with a hint of concern on his face, "he's been on the phone ever since he got back. And, God help me, I'm afraid to say there's more. It seems that he has been talking with his boss. As it turns out, one of their other flunkies had just been sent to prison."

"What...? But I thought Tony was the ringleader here," Alex grumbled.

"No. A man named Martin..."

"Santos?" both Alex and Jarred spoke up simultaneously.

"You know him?"

"Know him...?" Jarred groaned. "We had just put his second right hand man behind bars, is all...!"

"Who would that be?" Ted asked, not recalling everything that went down with that case.

"Vince Delgado, one very angry man right about now," Jarred laughed.

"Which reminds me," Alex spoke up, "how did that go, anyway?"

"Up until the end, pretty good!"

"Meaning...?"

"Only that he made some hairball threat, as they hauled him out of the courtroom. Really, no big deal."

"No big deal...?" Alex growled.

"What sort of threat?" Ted interceded, just then.

"To the tune he will get even with us, when he gets out."

"Damn, that's all we need on top of what we have going on now," Alex grumbled.

"Well, I hate to say it," Ted went on, "but there's still, yet, more to tell."

"What the hell now?" Alex asked furiously.

"The hit on David!" he groaned, regretfully.

At that moment, Alex and Jarred's faces turned grave.

"When?" Alex asked.

"You don't want to know."

Studying his old partner's expression, Alex felt his blood about to boil. "You know something, don't you?"

"Yeah." He shook his head sadly. "And it isn't good, either."

"Oh, God, what the hell now?"

"It's worse than you think, Alex!" Jarred put in, knowing.

Still studying his old partner, Alex was beginning to regret asking the next question, but knew it had to be asked. Though, somehow he knew the time was getting close, as Tony was having too much fun playing around. And now it was time to get down to just why he was back. "All right," he asked, heatedly. "What's going on?"

"Alex," Jarred began.

Putting up a hand to cut his nephew off, he thundered, quietly, "Everything. And now!"

"It's time, Alex," Ted returned. "The hit is going down, and soon."

"When?"

Hesitant to answer, Ted shook his head.

"It's..." Jarred spoke up again. "It's taking place the day after tomorrow."

"Alex," Ted regretted having to go on, "it's happening all over again. It's all going down on the Fourth of July. Just like it did then."

"What the..." He shook his head in disbelief, when not thinking it through at first. Then suddenly, having a sick feeling in the pit of his stomach, a thought came to him, "Oh... my... God" he cried, painfully, "it's Craig's anniversary, marking two years since his death! And why not, they screwed up the hit two years ago! Why not get it right this time? Only this time it isn't going to happen...!" he growled, hating the memory even more of what had happened to his other nephew.

"Alex..." Jarred started in, but only to be cut off once again.

"No..." he turned to nephew and thundered quietly, "I'll be damned if I'm going to just sit back and let another innocent man get killed, damn it! I wasn't there for Craig when he..." he broke off, "but I will be there for David."

"Yes. Well at least we don't have to worry about David going back to the farmhouse any time soon," Ted interjected. "He hasn't been there since Craig's death!"

"Wrong." Alex shook his head.

"What?" both men asked, sounding surprised.

"Yes, well, he was there Friday to get Craig's crate and a few other things out for me. And he'll be back again this Friday."

"No way!" They both shook their heads.

"Yes, way," he explained, seeing their expressions change right in front of him. With a shake of his head, he nearly laughed, knowing he was going to have to tell them eventually. "Oh, boy," he continued to shake his head with a huge grin on his face, "I can see now that it's time that I fill the two of you in on just what has been going on out there, both, while I've been there with Jessi, and even now, while she's out there alone. But first, you both just might want to sit down for this," he suggested, while pointing to a couple of chairs in the room.

"No, thanks," Ted politely declined. "I think I'll just stand, if you don't mind."

"Have it your way!" He continued to shake his head at his friend. "But once I'm through, you would've wished you had!"

Knowing the look on his uncle's face the way he did, Jarred laughed, while taking a seat, as he knew it could only mean one of two things, that whatever he had to say was going to be pretty deep, or just simply pretty weird.

Meanwhile, going over to the bed, Alex sat down for what was guaranteed to sound pretty weird. "Well, it all started when Jessi and her girls were caught up in a bad storm, awhile back."

"Yes, having to hold up out at Craig's old place. Yes, I know that part of the story," Ted interrupted, "but..."

"But what you don't know, is about these dreams of hers, which by some miraculous means had brought them to Craig's place on that particular night! While there..." he hesitated, "she met, and agreed to help his troubled spirit, by getting David to come out to the house, so that Craig could get some answers!"

"Answers of course that only David could give him?" Jarred asked, shaking his head.

"No... way, man!" Ted said, while refusing to swallow the story.

"Oh... yes," Alex grinned, while looking over at one very confused friend.

"Now wait one minute, here," he cried, shaking his head, "Craig is gone! He was killed two years ago, by those very same two men, who just happen to be back to finish the job that they screwed up on."

"I'm aware of that, damn it!"

"Come on, Alex, I know just how much losing Craig meant to you, and to you too, Jarred. But spirits...? Get a grip here! You're insane!"

"No, Ted," Alex shook his head, "I am very sane. And furthermore, I've seen him for myself, and so has Beth."

"What...?" Jarred stood at that moment, hearing Beth, too, had seen him.

"Yes, Jarred," he grinned. "And yes, we have even talked to him. Only with me, Craig and I talked again later, to tell me everything that he could about what had happened to him. Starting with when he had gone over to borrow David's truck, which put him in that bad predicament in the first place. And worse yet, I have a feeling his spirit is going to show itself Friday."

"Great," Ted groaned. "Now I know you've lost it. But just for the sake of asking. Why?"

"If I didn't know better," Jarred was now getting in on this supernatural stuff, "I would wager a bet that he is there to even the score!"

"Exactly!" Alex agreed, while getting up to face his nephew. "Then, at least you believe me, don't you?"

"Well, Uncle, you're not the type to believe in things like this, and since you seem so all sure fired up! Yes. Yes, I believe you."

"Thanks," he grinned, patting him on the arm, as Jarred went to get up.

"Well, in that case," Ted spoke up, running a hand over the back of his neck, "we had better be getting some sleep, tomorrow is going to be a long day."

"You're right, I'll see ya in the morning," Alex replied, while heading for the door.

"Are you going back down to stay in her quarters?" Jarred asked.

"Yeah, why?" he asked, looking back at his nephew.

"Just thought I'd ask!" he exclaimed, while saying his goodnights to Ted, before walking out with his uncle.

On their way down to the foyer, Frank was at the door, talking to one of the guests.

"Frank!" Alex nodded politely, before turning to Jarred. "Why don't you plan to stay here tonight. We can talk more down in her quarters?"

"Sure! Besides, there's something about this Jessi I would like to ask you."

Not wasting any more time, upon reaching her quarters, Beth was just closing her book, when she looked up to see them, just as they reached the landing.

"Any word from Craig's place, yet?" Alex asked, while getting a fire going in her coned shaped fireplace, near the kitchen door.

"No, not yet. It's been pretty quiet."

"Why, what's up?" Jarred asked, when sensing concern in his uncle's voice.

"Oh, it was probably nothing," he fibbed. "It seems that she was upset earlier after I left."

"Oh...?"

"Yeah, one of the guys saw her run out into the rain, and was worried."

"Then, am I to assume that the others don't know about..."

"Craig's spirit...?" he laughed.

"Nope, they don't," Beth got up, smiling, while walking over to Alex. "But we do!" she beamed, while placing a hand on his shoulder.

"So I hear!" he laughed, while still feeling the shock of having found out about it himself.

"Heck, our seeing him was purely by accident!" he laughed, setting the poker aside.

"Oh?"

Shaking his head, he went over to stand at the back door, to look out at the rain, as it continued to fall softly over the ground. "We were just getting ready to head on over to Sue's, when the two of us," He stopped to turn back and look at Beth.

"When we walked back in on their conversation," she finished, while continuing to look into Alex's eyes.

"Wow...!"

"Wow is an understatement," he laughed.

"Yes, that's for sure! He was like a brother to me. And seeing him there, well, it was a tossup between kind of scary, and well... kind of heavenly all at the same time!" she sadly smiled, with tears running down her cheeks, when wiping them away.

"Yes, well it was an experience neither one of us will ever forget," Alex put in, when offering to wipe them away for her.

"No doubt!" he agreed, changing the subject. "And now on to more earthly matters. How are you and Beth doing?"

Looking to each other, she turned to avoid the sadness in Alex's eyes, just then.

"We're all right!" he returned grimly, as she went to excuse herself.

Once hearing the door to Cassi's room close, Jarred turned back to his uncle, "Damn, I guess that was the wrong thing to ask."

"No, I'm afraid it hasn't been easy on either of us. Let's face it, she and I are cops. And once all this is over, she's on her way to Detective training."

"Oh...? And how do you feel about that?"

"Aside from Departmental Rules, you mean?" he groaned, while going over to pull off his boots. "It sucks! Damn it, Jarred, what do you think? I was pissed! And just when I was beginning to fall in love with her, too!"

"Hmmm, sounds like something I went through several years ago, when I was a Rookie, myself!"

"Jodi?"

"Yeah!" he groaned, going over to the fireplace, while running his hand over his hair. "Alex," he turned, not seeing the picture of a woman sitting right next to Jessi's, "this cousin of hers, have you met her?"

"No. All I know about her is that she deals with antiques, and is just as afraid of storms as Jessi is. Oh, yeah, and that they have a lot in common, starting with losing their first love in bad automobile accidents; where now, both are divorced and raising two daughters, why?"

"Oh, it's probably nothing," he fibbed, shaking off the thought of wondering if the two could have been somehow related. "Hmmm," he smiled, "some cousin! What's her name?"

Laughing, Alex shook his head, "I honestly don't remember! She told me, but it had slipped my mind!"

"Oh, but she said she was here the other day. How did you miss meeting her, then?"

"I was out tailing Tony. In fact, she wasn't supposed to have made it to this shindig at all! Something to do with a buying spree?" he questioned, while setting his boots aside.

"Oh, yeah? Well, not to change the subject, but does she have any coffee around here?" he asked, while turning back to warm himself up a little.

"Sure. I'll get some started."

Still, not giving notice to the picture sitting up on the mantle, the answer to his question was staring him right in the face. The woman for whom he had met years ago, and had come to fall head over heels in love with, only to be stopped by her over-protective grandmother. At that point, he had then turned to bury himself into his work, a lot like his uncle did.

Now, years later, having put Jodi Tate out of his mind, Jarred was faced with a picture, only to have been taken some years later.

"Hey," Alex asked from the kitchen, "do you still remember how the two of you met?"

"Yeah, I was out on a burglary call for Jodi's Antiques, back when her grandmother had the shop over in Ripley."

"That was some time ago! And you still think about her after all this time?"

"Yes. She, like Beth was to you, was a one of a kind. How do you forget that?"

"You don't," he agreed, standing at the sink, preparing the coffee, while now, thinking of Jessi. "How can you forget that?" he repeated more to himself, while grinning mischievously. "Hey, not to cause you any more grief, but have you seen her since then?" he asked, as he went on to measure out the coffee grounds, before turning on the coffee maker.

"No, not since you and I went to check on a case we were wrapping up on back then."

"Oh… you mean since after she had gotten married to that jerk you saw hanging out with some bimbo in a night club?"

"Yeah…!" he finished angrily.

"Didn't she ever know how you felt about her?"

"No, I never had the chance to tell her, damn it!"

"Oh, let me guess, her grandmother?"

"Yeah, she said Jodi had already lost one man in her life, and she wasn't going to go through that again."

"All because you're a cop? Damn!"

"Yeah, damn!" he groaned sadly, while thinking of those sad eyes of hers, both at the Antique Shop, when it had gotten vandalized, and again, sitting out on her front porch after she realized she had gotten married to the wrong guy.

"If she's anything like Jessi, or even Beth, I can see why you felt so strongly about her."

"Yes, well," he groaned, smelling the coffee, as it was about ready. But then going over to pull off his boots, he commented, when seeing the old brown faded ones sitting next to the couch. "Hey, I see you still have Craig's old boots!"

"Yeah, I sure do!" he replied sadly, when looking over at them. As he did, the thought came back to him, remembering when the Coroner gave them to him, along with the rest of his effects, before he was to be buried.

"Oh, by the way! Happy birthday, uncle!" Jarred laughed.

Chapter Thirty-Eight

The next morning, Jessi was once again awakened by the sound of her cell phone, which was lying next to the sofa on her suitcase. "Hel...lo...!" she grumbled into the receiver.

"Well, I see I woke you once again!" Alex laughed.

"Yes, so it seems you have this great sense of timing. You must really hate me, Alex, or why would you want to wake me out of a beautiful dream?" she asked, while rolling over in bed.

"Sorry, but something came up. I'll be out later to talk to you."

"Sure. Fine. Okay! See ya!"

With a soft roar of laughter, he continued to shake his head at how she sounded over the phone. "Okay, I'll see you later. And Jessi?"

"What?" she grumbled, tiredly.

"Call me if anything comes up, before I get there. You hear me?"

"All right...! I will...! Now goodbye, Alex."

"All right, goodbye."

"Emmm... Wait! There is something I have to tell you."

"What?" he asked, when hearing her laugh.

"Happy birthday, you old fart!"

"Gee, thanks!" he laughed, letting her go, while sitting there for a short while longer, before pulling on his boots.

"Is everything all right?" Craig asked, taking her by surprise.

"Craig!" she screamed, when they both started laughing.

"Sorry! I just wanted to tell you that you might not be seeing me for a while. But don't worry, I'll still be around. I just need some time to regain my strength."

"Okay... I'll just be out taking a walk with Max, then."

"All right, but be careful out there. If you see Tony's dark blue sedan, get back in here and let me know."

"You don't really think he would come back here today, do you?"

"You never know what he'll do. Just be careful," he added, so as not to scare her.

"All right!"

After working around the house, while listening to her music, she decided to take a break.

"Oh, what a day," she thought out to herself, tiredly, while grabbing up a towel and a bar of soap to get cleaned up.

Heading outside to clear her mind, she stopped on her way over to the shower. *"No,"* she thought quietly to herself, *"I think I'll wait on that, until after I go for a quiet walk."* Doing so, she looked around, noticing how late it was getting. "Boy, where has this day gone?" she asked, taking a path out behind the house to look for her dog. Just then she heard him coming up the path in front of her. Looking half wet from what looked like he had gone for a swim, she cried out to him, "Max... where have you been...?" she laughed, shaking her head in an amusement.

"Rrrr...!" he groaned, when turning to head back down the same path with her following after him.

"Max..." she called, running after him. But then, she saw it, as she caught up behind him.

"Oh, my, gosh...! So this is where you've been going all this time!" she cried, seeing what looked to be a rather large creek out in the middle of the woods. "This is great...!"

Going over to set her things down on a rock nearby the water, before slipping out of her clothes, she looked around to see if any of Alex's men were insight. "So far so good!" she murmured quietly, while slipping first out of her tennis shoes, to go up check out the water.

Seeing how it wasn't too bad, she then decided to get washed off there, while doing some wading around, before going back up to the house.

"Okay, boy," she commanded, while slipping off most of her clothes, "stay here while I go in and get cleaned up."

Doing so, he picked a nice spot near the creek and laid down, while she walked out further into the water, before wading out a little deeper, where she could feel its coolness do its magic on her tired and achy joints. The air by then was nice and warm, and carried a breeze, which made it that much nicer for taking a bath.

"Oh, yes, this is really great!" she cooed, stopping long enough to slip off her bra so that she could wade around a little while longer.

Unbeknownst to her, she wasn't going to be the only one out there for long. Having forgotten about Alex telling her that he was coming out, she continued to wade around even longer than she had planned.

Meanwhile, driving up to the house, it was dark and quiet. A little too quiet as far as he was concerned. "Marcose!" he called out.

"Sir?"

"Anything to report?" he asked, getting out of his Blazer.

"Nothing. It's been pretty quiet."

"Where are you now?"

"Out here in the tree line!"

"All right, stick around."

Approaching the house cautiously, he drew out his service revolver, and held it up next to his right shoulder, as he went on up to the front door. Upon entering the house, he started with the upstairs first, while checking out Craig's old room. Going in, he got a strange feeling he was not alone. "Is someone in here?" he called out, not thinking about Craig.

Not getting an answer, he turned to leave, but then suddenly stopped when a cool breeze passed him by in the doorway, and with it, was the scent of aftershave lotion, the same scent his nephew wore.

"Craig…?" he smiled, realizing then, that his nephew's presence was there in the house with him, as he went on downstairs to check out the rest of the house.

Arriving in the kitchen doorway, he saw the cleaning supplies out on the counter, and continued to smile, figuring she must have taken a break and gone out somewhere with her dog. "Good," he commented, as he turned to walk back into the living room to put some wood into the fireplace, "I'll just get a fire going to warm it up a little in here."

While about to do that, at that precise moment, something strange happened.

"Oh, God, what…" he cried out, when suddenly he fell to the floor, feeling as if the room was spinning out of control around him. "No…!" he continued to cry out, while fighting to keep control, but then stopped, when he felt there was no way to win over what was happening to him.

At that time, his large body fell hard to the silence around him.

Meanwhile, enjoying her relaxing time in the water, while not giving any more thought to

Alex's men out walking the woods, something or someone was about to invade her space.

Hearing the water off in the distance, her intruder headed down the path toward the sound, not knowing what he was going to find. Then coming to a sudden stop, he spotted her things on a rock nearby, and next to them was her dog, sleeping soundly. At that moment, turning to look slowly over the water, he saw her standing waist deep in the middle of the creek, running her fingers up through her long, wet hair, as she stood with her back slightly to him.

However, with her mind still focused on the glorious feeling the creek was giving her, she was totally unaware that someone was standing nearby, watching her from the trees.

"Hmmm… this is going to prove to be interesting," he groaned, quietly, so not to alarm her dog.

While he continued to watch, her wet hair clung to her bare shoulders. As if that wasn't bad enough, with the aid of the moonlight pouring down through the trees over her beautifully wet, glistening body, it had only served to make what he was watching that much more enticing, as she continued to run her fingers through her hair.

By then, with her head held back, her intruder took in every inch of her body. Trying hard not to notice when she had turned even more, the shape of her ample breasts became even more pronounced to him now, than ever before.

"Damn you, girl, you are driving me out of my mind!" he swore under his breath, while trying hard to keep her from hearing him. "And so you should. With a body like that, you could drive a vegetarian to eat meat," he thought out loud, groaning to himself, while also giving thought to what Alex would do, if only he knew what was going on, at that moment.

By now his desire for her had grown so deep that he needed her, wanted her, and had to have her. That's when he decided it was time to join her.

Walking up to the edge of the water, unnoticed by Max, he removed his things and went on in to come up behind her. *Oh, this is going to be great,* he thought to himself. And with her back still toward him, as he got up closer, he reached out, placing his arms carefully around her waist, causing her to scream.

Not thinking what that was going to do, Alex's men heard her; and both Marcose and another man came running with their service revolvers drawn.

"Freeze!" they both commanded, while standing ready.

Turning around slightly to face them, her intruder kept her covered so that the men wouldn't see her body in the moonlight, as he began to grin up at them.

"Alex...?" Marcose cried suddenly. "Hey! Sorry! I thought you were..."

"Don't mention it. And at the same time, don't, and I mean, don't say a word of this to anyone, unless either of you wish to be doing some crappy jobs for the next year or so."

"Yes, sir," the other man nodded, as they backed away to give them total privacy.

Hearing them leave, Jessi turned around ever so slightly to see Alex standing there with a broad grin on his face. "A...A...Alex... what are you doing out here?" she shrieked, while attempting to cover herself with her own arms.

Not once releasing his hold on her, he whispered something in her ear.

"What?" she cried, while turning even more in his arms to come face to face with him, while he still wore that sexy grin of his that she had come to love so dearly. "No...! Craig?" she gasped, as her eyes opened wider with even more surprise.

Still grinning, he pulled her up into his arms, nodding his head. "Yes, Jess, it's me," he replied, as she wrapped her arms up around his neck.

"Oh, Craig, I can't believe it! You're really here! Oh, God... I love you so... much...!"

As she continued to cry, the heat of their bodies rose between them, causing an instant combustion, when at that moment, Craig's lips claimed hers with so much heated passion, it swept them both away.

"Jess, I want you so… much!" he breathed heavily into her ear, as the wind picked up, making his presence there even more alluring and mystical, while being so far away from the house that held him, and yet, still holds him a prisoner of. "I've got to have you, now, Jess, right now…!" he groaned, knowing their time will soon be up, when it comes time to even the score.

"Oh, yes. Yes!" she cried, feeling the body of his uncle against her own, as his manhood, rugged as it is, pressing its way against her small, flat tummy.

Once again claiming her lips, her body sang out with desire. "Oh, girl…" he groaned, lifting her up into his arms to carry her out of the creek.

"Mmmm…" she too groaned, while aching to be one with him again.

Upon getting out of the water, while taking her over to lay her on a soft patch of grass, just beneath a weeping willow tree, he knew they would still have a certain amount of privacy to pursue their passion.

"Oh, Craig…" she cried out yet again, only this time in agony, and in joy, as she reached out to him as he came down to join her, "please, make love to me… now…! I want you so… much."

"You will always have me," he whispered, while claiming her lips again and again, just as their tide of passion drove them to much greater heights, and then some.

When the time finally came, he entered into her with so much searing heat that her nails found their way into Alex's very own shoulders, where they dug deep into his hot flesh, causing him to bleed unknowingly. And together, they reached the pinnacle of time and slowly drifted back down to an awareness, as time itself, drifted by.

Rolling over onto his side, he looked into the eyes of the woman for whom he had come to love so very deeply. "Jess?"

"Yes?" she returned breathlessly, as they continued to lie in each other's arms.

"I love you so… much," he went on, while choking back on his emotions. "You could have left and never came back to help me, but you did. Why?"

"I can't really explain it," she replied, while looking up into his deep blue eyes, as they sparkled in the moonlight. "For some reason we were brought together."

"I know, but for how long?" he asked. "You know I have to even the score with those men. That's the only way I'm ever going to be able to end this nightmare, once and for all."

"Oh, Craig… what's going to happen to us then? Will there even be an us after you have settled the score?"

"Only God knows the answer to that," he replied, while getting up to help her to her feet, as he then went over to retrieve her towel, before putting his uncle's clothes back on.

Feeling her sorrow, he came up behind her. "Are you all right?" he asked, as he pulled her back into his arms.

"Yes," she replied, still feeling the heat of their love coursing through her veins, as she turned to put her arms around him. Not caring if the towel fell or not, all she could think about was how good her body felt against his. And yet, for a forty-eight year old detective, his uncle was pretty tall, and built really well. For Craig though, he had many of his uncle's features, without the graying hair of course.

"Jess," he broke into her silent thoughts, "you feel so warm standing here in my…" He stopped for a moment and laughed softly into her ear, when thinking what he was just about to say. "Well," he smiled, "in my uncle's arms."

"Mmmm… I wish we could just hold each other like this all night," she smiled tearfully up at his own, now, tear-filled eyes. "It's been so long since I've ever felt like this."

"Me, too," he groaned, while making himself pull away, "but we need to be getting back up to the house, it's getting late, and…" he hesitated, "I don't know how much longer I can stay in his body like this."

"You mean, because you're so far out from the house?"

"Yes."

With that, she went quietly over to pick up her things, before calling her dog.

"He sure has been a great companion, while you've been here!"

"Yes, he has! I wouldn't want to be anywhere without him."

Taking the path back, they walked together hand in hand in silence, with Max walking up ahead of them.

Pat Gillespie

Once inside, Craig went to take care of the fire Alex had started on, when he turned to see where Jessi had allowed her towel to drop to her feet. And without any exchange of words, he turned back to write a quick note for her, and then another that she hadn't seen for his uncle.

Fastening them both up on the mantle, he removed his shirt and went over to join her on the sofa.

"Jess," he whispered, looking into her tear-filled eyes, while running his fingers lightly through her long, wet hair, thinking then of their recent passion, and how it was still yet, lingering on his mind. *"Oh, God, Jess, I wish this could be real for us, and not just some stolen moment in my uncle's body!"* he cried, when then, at that moment, turning to look upon her soft creamy-like skin, he went to run his hand over it. As he did, their passion ignited once again.

"Oh, Craig! Craig! Craig!" she cried out over and over again, until she couldn't take it any longer.

Not long after their passion had exploded, he put forth every ounce of energy he had left to give her.

Sometime afterwards, she cried out in short spurts, while trying to catch her breath, "S...stop!" she cried.

"It's all right... let it happen..." he whispered gently, as he began easing up.

"I wish I could, but..."

"I'm not hurting you, am I?" he asked, looking down into her eyes with a sense of concern in his own.

"No... no..." she replied, while still fighting hard to catch her breath.

Seeing her struggle, he began laughing so hard, he nearly fell over on her.

"W...what's so funny?" she asked, when unable to keep from laughing herself.

Rolling over onto his back, while pulling her along with him, he told her how he was able to get out to her.

"You what?" she laughed.

"Yes, Uncle Alex owed me a favor, and in the morning he'll understand why I had to do this to him."

"And just how do you think he will take it?"

| 356 |

"Oh… he'll probably be a little ticked," he laughed, while looking into her sleepy eyes.

That night, after grabbing a quick shower, the two went back in to lie down, whereas, they were both too tired to dress after all they had just shared together. Meanwhile, snuggling up next to each other, while taking in his fresh manly scent, he wrapped his arms securely around her, while feeling her heart beating against his chest.

"Craig…?"

"Yeah…?" he returned, while feeling her inviting breasts pressed up against him, as the two laid beneath his old blanket.

"I love you…!" she whispered softly against his chest, just before drifting off to sleep.

"I love you too, Jess," he returned, while running his hand over her hair, "I love you, too…" he repeated, painfully.

As the hours passed, his spirit had to leave his uncle's body, before his strength had gone away completely.

Looking down on them from where he was standing, Craig felt, with regret, that having to leave them this way would be for the best. *"I'm sorry, but waking in each other's arms this way, without your clothes to cover you, just might give you the kick-start you both need. If only you, Jessi, would let it,"* he whispered, while finding his strength quickly diminishing, now. *"I'm so sorry, but unless God were to grant me this second chance, you would be better off with Alex a n d n o t a l o n e…"* he cried, feeling his voice, now ghost-like, as he began to fade away, leaving the two most important people behind, as he went off to restore his strength for what was to come.

When morning came, waking first to find Jessi sleeping soundly in his arms, her hair felt so soft against his chest, as he ran his fingers through it for a moment, before feeling her shift ever so slightly beneath the blanket. And yet, there was something different about the situation. "What…?" he asked, half under his breath, as he lifted the blanket slightly to see what he had suspected. Having a feeling of what he felt lying so warmly against him, he discovered, was not his imagination, as he swore even more under his breath, at what he saw, *Damn it, Craig… why didn't you leave me on my bedroll… damn you…?* he asked, while finding the two of them without their clothes. But yet, he couldn't help but notice her warm, soft breasts lying so perfectly against his bare chest. *Oh, God,* he continued. But then, just when he thought matters couldn't get worse, at that moment, his own body took on a mind of its own. "Not now, junior!" he growled quietly, while feeling his groin begin to throb.

Though, smiling at her beautiful features, while lying there across him, he couldn't blame his body for wanting her, when things started to heat up. However, taking that moment, he attempted to slide out from beneath her, so as not to wake her. Though, all attempts had all but failed, when she rolled over onto her back, while stretching out her beautiful body, forgetting that she hadn't anything on.

Unable to pull his eyes away, he gazed over those luscious mounds of hers, aching to run his hands over them. "Damn it...!" he growled once again, under his breath, as his eyes burnt with desire, while feeling the ache in the back of his throat, as well.

Just then, reaching over to run her hand across his chest, she dropped it down to begin to lightly stroke it over his sensitive shaft, when nearly causing it to explode upon contact.

"Oh... girl..." he groaned, closing his eyes to the sensation she had brought him, "not now. God, girl... not... now...!" he breathed, taking her hand away to give it a slight squeeze.

"Mmmm..." she began to moan, as she slowly started to stir even more.

Going back over onto her back, he modestly covered her voluptuous breasts, so as not to embarrass her, when she woke to the realization of being in bed with him, and not his nephew.

Thinking then, as she was starting to wake, he greeted her with a half-baked smile, "Good morning! Did you sleep well last night?" he murmured softly, as she reached up to rub the sleep from her eyes. However, in doing so, the blanket slipped down once again, baring her breasts to the room.

"Mmmm...?" she mumbled sleepily.

"I was wondering if you slept well?" he repeated, while trying hard not to glance back down at them, as he attempted, yet again, to cover her.

"Uh, huh...!" she replied, with her eyes still closed to the morning sunlight, as it streamed in through one of the side windows. "And you?" she asked, yawning.

"Well... yeah, I did!" he smiled, while giving in, just then, when he found it difficult to cover her up, as she had laid her arm across that part of the blanket, making it hard to move it without her awareness. Yet, having been gazing upon her luscious swells awhile longer, he looked back up to see that she had fallen off to sleep again. "Great..." he continued to smile, while propping himself up on one elbow, "you just have to go and start something, didn't you, nephew?" he groaned again, while aching to have her for himself. And have her, he soon did. As all attempts to fight off the urge failed, he slowly caved into his desire.

As she lay there looking all so inviting, he leaned down and ever so lightly began tracing his lips over one of her perky little nipples, as the cool air reached them. "Oh, hell," he groaned, finding the taste to be heavenly.

Meanwhile, while continuing to take in its nectar, she arched her breasts up even more, as he went on to suckle them with a little more power behind it. "Mmmm... Jessi..." He stopped long enough to bring himself around to lay in between her long shapely, legs, as they gave way to his weight when placing himself there, "I've wanted you for so long, and now..." he groaned, bringing his passion up to meet hers. "Oh... God..." he continued, while feeling it as he slid inside her, the glory of its ecstasy over how she felt surrounding him. And yet, he somehow knew it wasn't him that she was thinking of, though it didn't seem to matter much at the time, as he had to have her.

Meanwhile, taking the strokes slowly, he watched as her expression intensified with every passing moment, when their passion grew to such fiery depths.

Before long, the moment came, as she reared up, digging her nails into the bed linen, as he gritted his teeth, when feeling the pressure exploding from within.

"Ah... yes!" she cried softly, when dropping back down to the bed, as the perspiration ran off her.

As it did, he went to kiss away some of its moisture from between her breasts, as she heaved to catch her breath.

Soon though, he looked back up, as her eyes were about to slowly open. At which point, he knew he was in for trouble if he didn't do something, and soon.

God... now what am I to do... he asked, knowing what it was his nephew was asking of him. However, it was too late to get up and leave the room, before she saw him lying next to her.

Before he could go back over to his side of the bed, the look on her face, when she saw him then, was one of puzzlement, at not seeing the familiarity of Craig's handsome smile looking back down on her. Instead, it was Alex's icy blue eyes she was looking up at, as a sheepish grin came to his face.

"A...Alex?" she cried softly.

"Yes," he replied, bringing the blanket back up now to cover most of her breasts. "I...I don't know what to say," he started, while glancing down over her beautiful form.

As he did, she began to realize then that she was naked, as she too glanced down to see half her breasts still visible to them both. "What..." she started, while feeling the heat of their bodies so close together, as she found it increasingly harder to fight him off.

"I'm sorry," he offered, "but it seems that Crai..."

Cutting him off, she knew that Craig must have had something to do with this. "I think I know," she smiled, as she took the hand that she too was holding the blanket with, to trace over his ruggedly handsome face. As she did, she allowed the blanket to slip ever so slightly off her breasts, but just enough to catch his attention, as one of his hands went up to catch the blanket. However though, he had caught one of her breasts instead.

Feeling its soft delicate skin beneath his touch, he ran a thumb over its inviting nipple, as she went to close her eyes to its erotic sensation. When she did, she had also brought herself up into it, as he fought not to go any further.

"Mmmm..." she felt the moan escape her lips. But just then, she opened her eyes again to feel the tears seeping out.

"I'm sorry, Jess, I'm not trying to..."

"No," she cut him off again, when placing her fingers to his lips, before rising up to kiss them. "I know."

"What...?" he asked, forgetting about her conversation with his nephew.

"Craig! He told me how he wanted this for us, but…" She stopped to look away, while feeling the pain of her love for his nephew came flying back at her.

Seeing how it was hurting her, he offered to change the subject. "Hey, how about some coffee?" he asked, while getting up to slip on his jeans, as she rolled over onto her stomach to give him some privacy.

"Sounds good! Are you making it?" she teased, when he headed for the kitchen.

"Sure I am!" he returned, while putting on some water.

After he had, she turned back over onto her back and laid there for a moment to look up at the ceiling, while listening to him rattle around in the cabinets.

Before too long, he returned with two piping hot cups of coffee in hand, as he went over to the fireplace to set them down, before starting a fire to throw off the chill in the house. That was when he spotted the two notes tacked up on the fireplace mantel.

"What's this?" he asked, taking them down.

"What's what?" she asked, sitting up just as he turned back to hand her a note that was addressed to her.

"I don't know!" he exclaimed, but then, slowly recognizing the handwriting to be his nephew's, as he smiled.

"Alex…?"

"It's from Craig!" he announced, while watching, as she began to open hers.

Tracing her fingers lightly over the writing, it read;

Jessi,
If God were to grant me just one last prayer, it would be to give me
a second chance, so that I could come back and ask you to be my
wife. I love you, Jessi Rae, with all my heart. Hold on to that.
Hold on to it forever, and don't forget me.
Yours For Eternity,
Craig Alexander Mathews

When she finished, she wrapped Craig's old blanket up around her more, before going on to get up and get her coffee. "Alex…" she spoke up, handing him his cup, as he went on reading his letter, "what does he have to say?" she asked, while going back over to have a seat.

"He says he has to even the score alone, and to protect the only woman for who has truly gone the length to be here for him."

"What else?" she asked, seeing the regretful expression on his face, just then.

"He says he could never love any other woman the way he loves you." At that, he felt bad for what he had just done to her, when he crumpled the letter up in his hand, just as he turned back to the fireplace.

Feeling the same, she turned to look away.

"What?" he laughed, realizing then that there was more to the letter than he had thought, as he went to uncrumple it.

"What?" she asked, turning back.

"This sounds kind of crazy! He says here, to go into the bathroom and look into the mirror...?" he questioned.

"What...?" she asked, when he looked up at her.

"I'm to give you this folded note first, before I go!"

Giving her the note, he went into the bathroom. Once there, he turned to look into the mirror. At first, there was nothing to see, but then feeling a stinging sensation, just between his shoulder blades, he turned a little more to see a set of long gashes right where the stinging was.

"Jessi!" he growled, coming back out into the living room, when she went to stand up with the blanket still wrapped around her.

Still glaring at her, she held the note out to him. "A...Alex...?" she asked, looking puzzled. "What is it? What were you supposed to see?"

Not answering her, he ripped the folded note right out from her hand.

Chapter Thirty-Nine

Reading it out loud, it read:

"SURPRISE"

"Well, well, well..." he raked his fingers through his graying hair, and laughed, shaking his head, "was it all that good for you, Jess?" he asked, showing her his back.

"Oh my, gosh...!" she gasped, looking at the deep scratches she had placed there the night before.

"Well... was it?"

"Well" she began timidly, "it was wonderful!"

"Wonderful?"

"Yes! You see, Alex, I was out at the creek cooling off, when you... I mean, Craig snuck up behind me! I thought at first it was you! But then, he whispered my name in my ear!"

Nodding his head, "Must be nice!" he grinned, while looking at her with a playful sort of contempt in his eyes. "However, with that gorgeous body of yours, I certainly can't blame him for wanting you so badly."

"Alex...!" she blushed.

"Okay, I'll try to stay away from that subject, but on another a more safer one."

"Last night?"

"Yes. With my men out there, what if one of them had seen him? I mean me?"

Laughing, while getting out a change of clothes to put on, she told him what all had happened while out at the creek.

"He said what?" he roared.

"If they said anything about what they saw, you would assign them crappy jobs for a long time. Or something along that line."

Shaking his head, he walked over to the front door to give her some privacy in getting dressed.

"Alex..." she stopped for a moment, as she felt the room start to sway slightly around her, "you asked me what I was going to do when all of this is over."

"And..." he turned back to face her, just as she went to pull her long hair out of her sweatshirt, "have you decided?"

"Oh, Alex, it isn't as easy as all that," she began, while coming up to stand in between him and the door. "I can't just turn to you, like my feelings for Craig didn't mean anything!"

"Jess, I know that. And I admit, it was wrong of me to push as I did. Believe me, I'm sorry, but we both just want the same for you."

Turning to look out at the bright, sunny morning sky, he stood in behind her, while placing his arms around her waist. In doing so, she hadn't meant to lay her head back against his chest, but when she did, she could feel his heart pounding intensely against it.

"Jessi..." He voice was soft and undoubtedly warm against her cheek, when he went to hold her more snuggly, "I know that it isn't as easy, as all that. I've gone through losing someone myself."

"No. And as you know," She turned back to look up at him, "I'm going to need some time to get passed all that has happened, before I can just simply pick up the pieces and move on with my life. Oh, God, Alex, I don't ever want to say goodbye to him! Not after having already done that, years ago with my first love!"

Just on the verge of tears, she reached up to throw her arms around him. As she did, he tightened his hold on her. "Damn it, Jessi, I know it isn't going to be easy, but you have to know that I'll always be there for you, when you're ready to start your life over again."

Hearing that, she swallowed back the tears, before going on, "A... Alex?"

"Yes?"

"C...Craig told me that if anyone could be there for me, that person would be you."

"Oh..." he asked, pulling back slightly to look down into her eyes, "what else did he say?"

Smiling, she looked up into his sparkling eyes. "Not to brush the idea off too fast. And to at least think about it."

"And have you?" he asked, taking a hand to run it through her hair.

"Have I…"

"Thought about it?"

"Oh… Alex…" she cried softly, while placing her fingertips gently to his lips, when he instinctively went to kiss them, causing her to shutter at the tingling sensation it had just caused her. "That's not fair," she cried, while letting out a soft giggle at his expression.

Toying with her, he asked, cocking his head to one side, while grinning sheepishly down at her, "What's not fair?"

"You and Craig! You two are so much alike," she stated, just as they broke out laughing.

But then, looking over his shoulder, at that moment, she saw Craig standing inside the living room doorway, laughing as well.

"Why you…" she broke off, as Alex turned to see what she was looking at.

"Hey, there!" he called out to his nephew, smiling.

Seeing how amused the two had become, she shook her head, acting as though she were put out over their behavior. "Okay, you guys," she spoke up, placing her hands up on her hips, "what are you up to now?"

"Why… us?" Craig asked innocently. "What makes you think that?"

Looking at his uncle with a questioning look, Alex just shook his head, as he dropped his hands down to where he was now holding her loosely.

Not asking what that was about, she just pulled away, while shaking her head. "All right, be that way! If you're not going to fess up, I'll just go on out back with Max and let the two of you talk for awhile."

Laughing, the two watched, as she went through the kitchen to go out the back door, before calling her dog.

"You didn't say anything to her, did you?" Craig asked, while going to stand at the back door to watch her with her dog.

"No. I want to wait until she has had some time to get passed all this," he explained, while joining him. "I have to admit though, I wish things were different for the two of you, when it's you she loves."

"I know, but I can't give her what she deserves. Though, you can!" he replied, while turning to look back at his uncle.

Seeing the look on his face, Alex stepped back away from the door so that she wouldn't pick up on their conversation. "No, Craig!" He shook his head. "Not this way. Not on the rebound. Surely you know that she had already lost her first love some time ago. And now *this*? This is really tearing her up inside."

"I know. God, I wish things were different for us. Believe me, I do. Damn it, Alex, ever since she came along, I have been praying like crazy to get a second chance...!" he cried. "Damn it... it wasn't even me they were after! Why the hell didn't David say something to one of us? God..." he growled, while turning to walk over to the counter.

"I don't know, Craig. But I'm going to get to the bottom of it. I promise you that," he swore, looking over at his nephew, while leaning back against the counter, with that hurt expression on his face.

"Alex, what Jessi said about your leaving to be a cop, do you think it may have any real bearing on his attitude change?"

"Well, if you think about it, it wasn't long after that, that he started hanging around the wrong crowd!"

"I can't believe I never noticed it," he growled, shaking his head, disgustedly.

"Yeah, well, if I remember, you were seeing Abigail, at that time."

"Yeah, don't remind me," he replied, thinking how his marriage turned out.

"You know, Craig, Abby couldn't hold a candle to Jessi."

With a small chuckle, "You're right about that!" he grinned, while going back over to look out the back door at the most beautiful woman who had come into his existence, when Alex walked over to join him.

"You know, or maybe you don't," he laughed, thinking about something Jessi had told him, 'when it comes to spirits, they don't have any concept of time'.

"What?" Craig asked, when turning back to see the amused look on his face. "Oh, really!" he laughed, picking up on what his uncle had realized, just then. "It's okay. Around here, what is there that I need to keep time on?"

"Yeah, well."

"It's getting late, huh?"

"Yes, and I had better be getting some breakfast on. But just the same," he grinned, while looking down at his watch, "it's already going on ten, and I haven't told Jessi yet, that Sue and Bob are coming by later with the others for a cookout."

"Mom and Dad? Really?"

Knowing his time was vastly coming to an end, Alex felt bad. Though, he tried to hide it behind his smile. "Yeah, they are!"

"Oh, but, no…!"

"What…?" he asked, feeling as though he had just made the biggest mistake ever.

"Alex, only the two of you can see me, aside from Beth, that is!"

"Are you sure?"

"Yes! I tried to get mom to see me, but it's just not possible!"

"Man, don't let it tear you up. Besides, you have to reserve yourself for what's about to happen."

"I know," he replied, turning away to look back out at Jessi, "it's coming real soon."

"Yes. I know. Tomorrow some time," he sounded sadly. "And I can't seem to bring myself to tell her yet, either."

"Yes, and it doesn't give us much time, does it?" he replied, looking back at his uncle.

"No, I'm afraid not."

"Hey you two," she interrupted, when walking back in, just then, "what's with the sad faces?"

"It's nothing! Are you hungry?" Alex asked, changing the subject.

"Starving! And so is Max!"

"So we've noticed!" Craig laughed, while going back over to lean against the counter.

"Ah huh!" she grinned, suspiciously, at the two of them, before excusing herself to get a shower. "And while I'm at it, I'll just give the girls a call, too."

"I'll see you later then," Craig returned with a warm, crooked smile, while giving her a wink, as he faded away.

"Oh, by the way," Alex went on before she could get too far, "Sue is coming by in a little while with the others,"

"Oh? What's going on?"

"I thought we would have a small cookout in the backyard. So if our not so friendly friends come around, they won't see us."

"Alex," she started, while leaning her shoulder into the kitchen doorframe, "you're really doing this for Craig, aren't you?"

"Yes."

"Thanks," she smiled up at him, before leaving the room to go and get her shower over.

After a short time in the bathroom, and then on the phone with her girls, she returned, wearing a pair of blue jeans and a black V-neck sweater. "Mmmm…" she commented on her way through to the kitchen to join him out on the back steps, "something sure smells good!"

"Glad you still think so!" he returned, looking up at her, just after she closed the screen door. "I thought it would be nice to eat out here for a change," he added, while tossing Max a piece of bacon.

"Yes, it is. And before I forget," she exclaimed, pulling Craig's medallion from her pocket, "I have something here of Craig's to give you!"

"Oh, what is it?" he asked, when she placed it in his hand.

"Don't you recognize it?"

"Oh, my God, yes, I do!" he replied, putting his plate down to examine it more.

"Good! I found it while cleaning, and I've been meaning to give it to you, but, you know, with what all that has been going on, I have kept forgetting to do it, until now."

"Oh, but this belongs to you now!" he said, handing it back to her.

"Oh, but no…! Alex, I can't take this! You had given it to him to have!"

"Yes, and now you should have it," he explained, placing his hand over hers, while the other rested on her shoulder. "Please. Keep it for good luck."

"Oh, all right," she agreed, while rubbing the medallion between her fingers.

Meanwhile, while enjoying their meal, Alex told her all about the different things he and his nephews got into as kids growing up.

"David though, must have really felt proud having you three as acting big brother's, without one of his own."

"Yes, it was fun having him around," he agreed, when looking down at his plate.

"I bet!" she smiled, seeing how quiet he was getting. "Hey, take a look at those!" she called out, while pointing up at some cottony-looking clouds overhead. "Don't they look beautiful?"

"They sure do!" he sighed heavily. "Well, we had better be getting things cleaned up.

They'll be here pretty soon."

"All right!" she agreed, while getting up to take her own in, when he interceded.

"No, I'll get that for you!"

Knowing better than to argue with him, she followed him inside, while he went over to the sink to get their plates both washed up. "Have the guys out there eaten?"

"Yes, I sent out some food, while you were on the phone with your girls."

"Good. And as for the cookout, what are we planning on fixing?" she asked, while taking a plate he had finished rinsing off, to dry.

"I thought we'd have some steaks and potatoes. I had picked some up on my way back from the station earlier."

"That sounds awfully good! I just hope nothing goes wrong, while they're here."

"That makes two of us!" he agreed, after she had dried the last plate, while he headed out to the Blazer. "But just the same, I think I'll give Ted a call to see what they're up to!"

Doing so, Jessi set the dishtowel aside, and went on into the living room to make up the sofa. As she did, the memory of what they had done played lightly on her mind.

"Thinking about this morning?" he asked, walking back in unexpectedly.

"Yes, how could you tell?"

"It was in the way you were holding that blanket, just now."

"Alex, what did we do?" she asked, turning back to look up at him.

"We..." He stopped a moment to think. "We made love, and under some rather strange circumstances I might add," he smiled warmly down on her.

"Yes, but..."

"Jessi, it's okay!"

"How can you say that? Craig must really think of me as being a rather..."

"No." He stopped her. "That isn't true!"

"Oh? Did he say something to you?"

"No, just pretty much what he has to you! Which was, he wants me to be there for you."

"So he..."

"Jess, I think Craig left us in that predicament for a reason."

"So we would find ourselves..."

"Vulnerable? Yes. And if it means anything, I found you to be incredibly exciting."

"Alex!" She blushed, while turning away.

Just then, catching sight of his nephew standing off by the front door, looking at her in a regretful sort of way, Alex knew what his nephew had done, took a lot of guts, as it must be tearing him up, not to be able to come back so that they could be together.

Somehow, able to get Craig's attention without her knowing it, he motioned for him to be with her.

Looking puzzled at first, he then saw what Alex had meant, when she had turned away to think to herself. And with a slight nod of his head, he came up to join with his uncle, once again, but only for a very brief time.

Finding her thoughts miles away, she had no idea what was about to take place, when she was easily caught off guard, as she felt the blanket being taken out of her hands.

"Alex..." she began, when he gave the blanket a toss, before turning her around to face him. As he did, she felt his hands, as they began to tremble.

"A...Alex... what..." She stopped then to look up into his eyes. At that time, she lost herself in them, as he went to claim her lips, while her arms went up around his shoulders.

Returning his kiss, it wasn't long after, his hands found their way up under her sweater, to unfasten the back catch on her bra.

"Mmmm…" she moaned, while feeling herself falling back slowly onto the unmade sofa, as he continued his pursuit of her taunting breasts, wanting them right where he could taste them.

Rising up to meet his passion, she gave way, as her sweater went up to bare them.

Running his tongue first over the peak of their blossoms, he took them in even more, while suckling on them until the heat had reached her toes.

"No…! Alex…" she groaned, feeling his hand reaching for the zipper on her jeans, "we have got to stop this!"

"No, Jess, it's not…" He stopped, unable to finish, as he went on to devour her lips again.

"Mmmm…" she moaned, while intertwining her legs with his, as she felt herself falling deeper and deeper into their passion. When suddenly, his hand found her most vulnerable spot, and took it.

Feeling his strokes, she went with it until she began ripping at his shirt, to get it off, before they plunged even further, while going on to take everything else off to have each other. But then, was it Alex, she began to think, realizing whenever Craig was around, making love to her, there would be such a tingling sensation radiating through him. "Oh… God…!" she cried out, feeling the intensity of his passion tearing at her very soul.

Lifting herself into it, her head went back as far as it could, when he brought a hands up to run through her long, thick mane, before his lips found her neck and began suckling at it, while leaving her his signature once again.

"Craig…!" she cried, dropping herself back down onto the mattress to pull his head back up so that she could look into his eyes. "You are so mean to me…" she commented, when seeing his glistening smile, just then.

"I can't fool you can I?" he laughed, when rolling over onto his side.

"No," she laughed. "I felt you in the room, but it wasn't until you had touched me that I knew."

"What was it about my touch?"

"You know the answer to that! You have always made me tingle.

That, and this time you were shaking, like you had the other night, when you had nearly collapsed!"

"And now...?"

"Yes, even now. But, Craig..." she cried, "you have already used up so much of your strength, and your parents are going to be here soon!"

He smiled. "I'll still have time to store it back up, before they get here. I'll be all right."

"But..."

"I know," he grinned sadly, knowing that they wouldn't be able to see him, "but at least I'll get to see them!"

"I wish you could do more than that."

"Perhaps, but now we need to get dressed."

"Mmmm... you're right!" she moaned, when he went to get up.

But then, he stopped and stole, yet, another kiss, just to hear her laugh.

"Oh... you... are so... bad...!" she cried, laughing up at him.

"Yeah, I am!"

"But I don't want to get up yet!"

"Oh, but you have to!"

"Why...?"

"Because..." he laughed, "just how would you explain away about you and Alex, when they get here?"

"I'll just say that I lost myself in those blue eyes of his!" she continued to laugh, knowing that it was partially true, as he went to kiss her yet again, while seeing that beautiful smile of hers.

Later that day, the others all arrived, as Alex instructed them to park in the back so that their cars wouldn't be seen from the road.

"Boy, doesn't this all smell good?" Sue commented to her brother, while walking up with a big bowl of chips in her hands.

"It sure does!" Jessi agreed, while coming out, carrying a pitcher of iced tea in one hand and a pitcher of lemonade in the other.

"Here," Alex called out, seeing how heavy the pitchers must been, "let me help you with those."

"Hey there, I'll help too," Allen offered, joining him.

"Thanks!" she smiled, looking around.

"What is it?" Alex asked, carrying the pitcher of tea over to a makeshift table he sat up.

"David! He's not here!"

"Allen, where's David? I thought he would have been here, too!"

"He said he had some stuff to take care of first, at his place, but if it wasn't too late he would be here later! Alex, is he in some sort of trouble again?"

"No," he said, looking over at Jessi, while not wanting to alarm anyone, "but just for the heck of it, I think I'll just give him a brotherly call to make sure everything is all right!"

"Alex," Bob spoke up first, from where they were sitting, off under a nice shade tree.

"It's probably nothing," Jessi offered, when seeing the look on Rose's face, when Alex headed to his Blazer. Patting her on the hand, she smiled, "He's just being careful, with Tony around, is all. He doesn't want to see anything happen to him."

"We know that," Allen replied, while turning to his wife. The expression on his face was along the lines of worry, and yet, there was something else about it that Jessi couldn't quite pick up on.

Sensing her thoughts, Craig cut in just then, *"What is it, Jess?"* he asked, with a strong hint of concern.

"I'm not sure! Can you pick up on what they're thinking?"

"I wish I could, but all I can feel is sadness!"

"Jessi," Sue broke into her thoughts, "what is it, dear? What's wrong?"

"W...what?" she asked, looking up to see everyone staring at her.

"You looked as though you were a million miles away!"

"Oh, I'm sorry!"

Catching Bob's attention, as well, he got up to check on her, while asking if she were all right.

"I...I'm fine...!" she exclaimed, while gently pulling away. "I was just thinking, is all."

"Does it have something to do with our son?" Sue asked, when recognizing the look on her face, whenever she and Craig would have their talk.

"Yes. Well, sort of!" she grinned, shyly.

Getting up, she excused herself and went into the house to seek him out. While there, Bob and Sue followed her in, while leaving Alex with the others.

Once in the living room, Bob spoke up, "Jessi, were you really just talking to Craig out there?"

"Bob…" she started.

"No, wait, let me explain. In the seminar they told me that there is a certain look, which comes over a person's face, when they are conversing telepathically with someone. Was it Craig?" he asked.

Hesitating at first until seeing Craig in the kitchen doorway, nodding his head, she turned back, "Yes it was. I was bothered by something, when he picked up on it, but wasn't able to clear it up for me!"

"Does it have something to do with Allen and Rose?" Sue asked, sadly, having picked up on the same feeling earlier.

"Yes, I'm afraid so!"

"We kind of figured it did, but whenever we would ask, they would refuse to talk about it!" she exclaimed, while looking up at her husband. But then suddenly she stopped, when seeing Jessi look off at the same doorway, as she cried nervously, taking her husband's arm. "Oh, my, Lord! Jessii…is our son here right now?"

"They can't hear me or see me. Only you and Alex, aside from Beth, can."

"What do you want me to do?"

"Tell them I'm here, but explain why they can't see me."

"All right!"

"Jessi?" Bob spoke up this time.

"Yes," she turned back to say. "Yes he is, but unfortunately only a few of us have been able to see him."

"We understand that! But he can hear us, right?" he asked, hopefully.

"Oh, yes," she replied smiling, while watching Craig go over to the fireplace to sit down.

"Where is he now?" he started to ask, when seeing her attention go from the doorway, over to the fireplace.

"I bet I know!" Sue replied, smiling. "His favorite spot in the house! He's sitting down, isn't he?" she laughed.

"Yes," Jessi smiled.

"The fireplace?" Bob asked, with a warm smile, while shaking his head.

Jessi continued smiling, when Craig spoken up again. "Tell them, I said hello."

"All right."

"What?" Bob asked eagerly.

"He says, hello!" she smiled, while turning to see sad, yet excited faces.

But then suddenly, Sue's knees began to go weak on her. "Oh, my! I think I had better sit down," she cried, when Bob helped her over to the sofa. Going on, she wept, as he continued to hold her. "I've wanted so much to tell him how I have missed him!"

"You just did. Remember, he can hear you. You just won't be able to hear him!"

"But you can tell us what he's saying, right?" Bob asked, hopefully.

"Bob?" Sue looked up, just when they heard the back door open, and Alex walk in.

"What's going on in here?" he asked, coming into the living room.

Seeing his sister and brother-in-law on the sofa, he turned to see Jessi's expression, as he too saw Craig sitting on the hearth. "Can they..."

"No."

"Damn, I wish he could do more for them, they need closure so that they can go on."

"Oh, but perhaps there is something you can do!" his nephew grinned.

"Oh... no. Why do I have a feeling I just got myself into trouble here," he laughed.

"What do you mean?" Sue asked, when she and Bob looked at each other puzzledly, before turning back.

"Alex?" Jessi asked, as Craig got up to move aside.

Turning to indicate for his uncle to have a seat, Alex did so. As he closed his eyes, Jessi went over to take his hand, while he smiled.

It wasn't long, before opening them again, that he looked into

Jessi's warm and smiling ones, as that all too familiar smile of his came through.

"Well," she smiled, "I think I'll just go on out and visit with the others, while you talk to your folks!" she whispered, while kissing him tenderly on the lips, before getting up to leave. "I love you!"

"I love you, too," he whispered back.

"Jessi..." Sue called out, as she started for the back door, "wait! Where are you going?"

"It's okay!" she turned back. "He'll explain it all to you!"

Once she was gone, he smiled and went over to stand in front of them.

Getting up, they looked into his eyes.

"Son...?" Bob spoke up, seeing a glimmer of their son standing there, as he continued to smile on them. At that moment, they realized it was their son, and not Alex.

"Mom! Dad!" he spoke softly at first, not sure if he should reach over to hug them.

Smiling at the fond reunion, when Sue and Bob had finally accepted the idea of what was taking place in front of them, Jessi, having watched just inside the kitchen doorway, turned then to head on out the back door.

Chapter Forty

Reaching the backyard, she found David talking to his parents. "Hey, there!" she greeted, while going over to take a seat.

"Is everything all right?" Rose asked, while Allen took over the grill for Alex.

"Sure! Everything's just fine!" she replied, while hoping to ease the moment, until the others returned.

It wasn't long, though, before Sue, Bob and Alex walked back out to join the others. The expression on their faces was sad, yet when Sue and Bob walked over to Jessi, they gave her a warm and loving hug for all she and Alex had done for them.

"You're welcome!" she replied, while smiling over at Alex.

"Well, now," Bob spoke up, rubbing his hands together, "when is this wonderful food going to be ready?"

"Just as soon as David, here, gives me a hand on getting things set up!" Alex laughed whole heartedly.

It wasn't long, after the food was served, that everyone took their seats around the table.

While eating, the conversation was kept to a minimal, while covering things, such as the weather, the crop, and Bob's practice, while not once bringing up the case, until Marcose walked up, a short while later, to talk with Alex.

"Do we have a problem?" Alex asked, while walking over to throw away his trash.

"No. We just got a call from Ted."

"And...?"

"He says everything's quiet. I just came in to see how things were doing here. Oh, and to let you know that the boys had all smelled the steaks cookin'..." he grinned, humorously.

"They're hungry?" he laughed. "Well I guess, since our two friends aren't an immediate threat! Tell them to come on in and get something to eat. I brought enough for them, as well."

"Sure will."

Just as he was about to call his men in, Alex stopped him, "Leave one at each point, and have the others take them out something."

"Okay."

"And Marcose?"

"Yes?"

"Make certain that they clean-up after themselves. I don't want any signs of anyone being out there."

"You got it." Calling in a few of the guys from out back, he then called the others to let them know that food was on the way.

"Thanks!" Baker returned, while keeping an eye on the road from where he and another man sat, perched up in a tree.

"You want me to get us something?" Kevin asked, while feeling his stomach start to grumble.

"Sure," Baker returned, while feeling if anything were to go down, he would be the best to spot trouble if it came.

As for Kevin, young and agile, he was faster on his feet and quick to duck out of sight if necessary. "Be right back!" he smiled, on his way down the tree, before Baker could say anything.

Shaking his head, with a smile, he turned back to keep an eye on the road ahead of him.

Meanwhile, after the others had gotten through eating, Bob and Sue got up to leave. "If you'll excuse us, we're going to head on out now," Bob spoke up, taking Sue's hand.

"Oh?" Jessi asked, while looking up from a conversation she was having with Rose.

"Yes." Sue returned, looking to Jessi one last time, before going over to give her brother a hug. "However, we will be seeing the two of you tomorrow, won't we?"

"Sure will!" they both agreed.

"Good!" Bob called out, waving goodbye. "Rose! Allen! David! See you tomorrow!"

Nodding their response, Bob and Sue were off, when Alex turned to Jessi, while nodding his head off toward the house.

Knowing what he was trying to say, she headed for the back door, when Rose called out interrupting her, "Jessi, we're going to be heading out too."

"Oh, but…" She turned back to see their saddened expressions, and then looked to Alex. Seeing his own expression grow dark, she too felt a sense of what was going on. But not knowing the full extent of it, she turned back and offered them one of her sweet smiles. "All right, see ya tomorrow!"

With the exception of David, who Alex had pulled off to the side so that they could talk, Rose and Allen both headed over to their car, while she went on inside.

"David?" Allen turned back.

"I'll be right over. I'm just going to give them a hand cleaning up."

"All right, son," he turned sadly to leave.

Meanwhile, just inside, after everyone had gone their own way, Jessi found Craig where she had last seen him.

Stopping short of the fireplace, she saw the saddened expression on his face and knew she didn't have to ask. Instead, he just laid his head down on his clasped hands, while resting his elbows on his knees. "I can't stand seeing them like this," he groaned, shaking his head sadly.

"No, I guess not," she returned, coming over to sit next to him, while going on to look into his clouded eyes, when he turned to gaze upon her own.

"Where's David now?"

"Out back with Alex!"

Getting up, he went into the kitchen to look out the back door with her coming up behind.

"You know, he's not looking all that good either?" she commented, while looking sadly over his shoulder, before going over to sit on the counter.

"No, he doesn't," he replied, seeing the two standing at the picnic table, in what was sure to be a deep conversation, concerning what had happened, "but, God, Jessi," he turned back, "I know he's hurting, yet it still floors me how he had just let this happen to me."

"I know, but Alex is, now, trying to find out why!"

"Yes. And…" He turned back to look out at the two, before making his announcement.

"Craig…? What?"

"Tomorrow…" he began slowly, "tomorrow it'll be my turn to ask the questions."

"Tomorrow?" she asked, while hopping down off the counter. "Why tomorrow?"

Turning back to look at her, the look in his eyes frightened her.

"Craig…?"

Coming over to the counter, he stood, looking deep within her tear-filled eyes. "It's all right, Jess," he fibbed, knowing this wasn't the time to tell her. "As for David," he turned back one last time to look out at him, "I'm not ready to talk to him yet."

"But…"

Placing a finger up to her lips, he smiled reassuringly, "I need to get some more rest."

"Oh. All right!" she smiled warmly, as he too did the same, by touching a finger to her nose, before fading away. By then, Alex came walking back in.

"Alex," she asked, seeing David getting back into his truck to leave, "where's he going?"

"Back over to his folks' place for the night," he explained, while going over to pour the two of them a couple of glasses of iced tea, before going on.

"Thanks," she smiled, taking her glass, as he turned back to hand it to her.

"I told him that I wanted him to stay close by, in case Tony was to show up."

"Good!" she replied, noticing the questioning look, on his face. "Craig?"

"Yeah. Where…"

"He said he needed to get some rest."

"Good. How about we go out for a little walk then?" he suggested, while helping her down off the counter.

"Sounds good! Besides, the air feels really nice out at this time of the evening," she said, heading for the front door, with him in the lead.

"Yes, it sure does!" he grinned, taking her hand to lead the way, once they were on the porch, while closing the door behind them.

"Where are we going?"

"Just out back, here! I want to check on something I haven't seen in awhile."

As the two walked around the side of the house, they headed for the old, block garage that they had gotten the smoker from out behind, which was hidden amongst some trees.

"Alex?"

"Yeah?" he asked, pulling out a set of keys.

"What's in here?"

"I don't really remember! I just thought it might be interesting to have a look, while things are quiet back at the Inn!"

Opening the door, he saw it, sitting there, right in front of them. At which time he growled, feeling sick to his stomach. "Damn…!"

"What?"

Though, going over, he opened the larger set of doors to allow in what light was left of that day. When he did, she saw it too.

"Oh, God, Alex, is this what I think it is?" she shuttered, covering her mouth, as the hot tears began to stream down her face.

"Jessi…" He turned to see the look on her face, as he came back over to offer his support.

"This is it!" she cried, while reaching out a shaky hand to run over the tailgate of Craig's nineteen eighty-four, red, Chevy pick-up, while feeling all its dents and dings from the bumps it took over the years of construction work he had done. "This is the truck he had been having troubles with the day he was killed?"

"Yes, I'm afraid so," he returned, while the expression in his own eyes was full of pain, from seeing his nephew's old truck again.

Turning then to look up at the house, where in the upstairs window, Craig was standing, looking out at them, sadly. At that moment, she never felt more horrible, as she did then. But then, suddenly, picking up on a much more frightening feeling of danger coming their way, she turned back to look out through the large double doors, while hearing a car approaching the house. "Alex…" she cried out, frightfully, while taking a shaky step back, "the doors! We have to close these doors, now!"

"What..." he started, when suddenly he too heard what she did. "You're right!"

Going over quickly to close the large double doors, he then turned back to take her arm to head out the side door, in an attempt to get her back to the house. But just as they started for the door, she stopped him in his tracks.

"Jessi?" He too stopped short, seeing the expression on her face had changed to an alarming one. "Jess, what is it?" he asked again, still having a hold of her arm, when she pulled back to muffle a cry. "Jessi, answer me!"

"Oh, my, God! He...he...! Tony! He's here!" she cried out, pointing, in a hushed-like whisper.

"Are you sure?" he asked, pulling out his service revolver, while at the same time, shoving her behind him.

"Yes! Down the road! Craig says he's still in his car, and..."

"And...?"

"Alone!" she finished.

"All right, let's try and make it back to the house. We'll go in through the back door."

Luckily for them, the old garage had been built back off in the trees, where under the growing evening sky, couldn't be seen from the road.

"Alex..." she pulled back fearfully, as he went to pull out his radio to call one of his men, "what if he never goes away?"

"Just try to hang in there. If anything were to go down, Marcose and the others will be right on it."

Having no sooner said that, he turned to give Marcose a call.

"Alex?" the man's deep voice came back in a hushed-like manner.

"Yeah, where are you?"

"About twenty feet or more from our uninvited guest."

"Great. Stay there," he growled, while reaching the side door, but then stopped, when she suddenly pulled him back again. "Marcose?"

"Yeah?"

"Hold on there a minute," he ordered, just as he looked back to see the growing look of fear come across her face. "Jess, what now?"

Picking up more of Craig's warning, she covered her mouth out of fear that it was all going to happen that night. And just as she had, they heard something approaching the side door. Shoving her ever more in behind him in hopes to shield her from what was about to come, Alex turned back to aim his gun at their impending intruder. But then, at that precise moment, Max came running in through the open doorway, scaring the two of them.

"Damn you, Max..." he roared under his breath, while lowering his gun, "I could have shot you, just now!"

"Damn! Alex..." Marcose called out quite suddenly to warn them.

Before he could respond, she too cried, pointing out the front window. "Alex, h...he's right there...!"

"So I see," he returned, glaring out at Tony's dark blue sedan, as it drove slowly by.

"What are we going to do?"

"For now, hang in there, and see what he's going to do," he explained, while trying to sound calm, but then Max began to growl. "That goes for you too, boy," he added, while concentrating on watching Tony, when Marcose came in quietly through the side door, while making himself known.

"He must have gone by the McMasters' place to see if David was there," he commented, while joining Alex at the front window.

"Yeah, but why is he here?"

"Haven't a clue. Unless..."

Turning to see the look on his face, Alex's eyes grew dark and stormy. "He was out to get me too?"

Shaking his head, the two continued to watch, as the car slowly drove on by.

After a brief, but unnerving moment, Jessi spoke up in a low, but hushed voice, "Alex, it isn't going down tonight, is it?"

"No," he returned, feeling the pain of regret, as it tore him up inside for not telling her that it was going down a lot sooner than she had expected.

Meanwhile, Craig called out to her, to hurry back inside, in case Tony was to decide to come back. Turning, she told the others, "It's time!" she whispered. "Craig says to hurry back inside, in case Tony was to decide to come back!"

Hearing this, while looking at the two of them puzzledly, Marcose just stood back waiting on Alex's next orders.

"Okay, let's go," he commanded, while getting everyone out of the garage. "Oh, and Marcose, stay nearby," he ordered, while locking the door, before stuffing the keys back down into his pocket.

"Just in case our friend was to come back on foot?"

"Yes."

"Not a problem! I'll tell the others to keep their eyes open, as well."

"Good." Taking Jessi's hand, Alex called out to Max, while running back up to the house, "Come on, Max, you too, boy!"

Once inside, he closed the door, while calling out to his nephew.

"Right here!" he answered from the living room doorway.

"What is he doing now?"

"Nothing! He's gone! It's safe!" he explained, as Jessi quickly pulled away to go into the living room.

Passing Craig in the doorway, he could sense her emotions building up to a boiling point, as she quietly went about taking out her sweats for the night. *"Jessi…"*

"No…! I won't take it easy," she returned, knowing what he was about to say. *"I can feel the time getting closer,"* she cried, while turning to look into his troubled blue eyes.

At that moment, Alex too, saw the tears building up in hers, before she turned quickly to head for the bathroom. "Jess…" he called, reaching out to grab her arm.

Feeling herself being pulled back, she cried even harder, while pulling away to run off some place where she could close the door behind her, as the tears began to pour. "Oh, God, no" she continued, while slowly sliding down to the floor. "Please, not yet! Not now! P…p… please, I can't do this again!" she sobbed, shaking her head. "I can't say goodbye! NoI…I can't!"

"Alex," Craig spoke up, looking worried, "I need to go to her, but I can't without you to make it happen."

"Yes, but won't this cause problems for you later? You have to be strong enough for tomorrow!"

"Alex, I'll be ready, but tonight…" He stopped to look back at the bathroom door, when the two walked into the foyer.

"I know. Tonight she needs you," he finished, seeing his nephew's pleading eyes, when he turned back to his uncle. "All right. Go to her. She does need you!"

A short while later, walking back out into the living room, she didn't see Craig standing where she had last seen him. And for the first time she really felt all alone without him there to comfort her. "Oh, God... why does it have to be this way...?" she quietly cried, while trying to decide what to do next.

Looking around, she discovered that Alex, too, wasn't around.

"Alex...!" she called out, somewhat more to herself, than him.

Not getting anywhere with that, she went out onto the front porch, in hopes that Tony wouldn't return. Doing so, she found Alex sitting on the steps.

"Alex..." she cried again, having not expected to see him sitting there, "I didn't know you were out here."

Not answering her, she walked over to sit next to him. "Do you think Tony will come back tonight?"

With a slight shake of his head, he still didn't answer.

"Alex?" The silence was beginning to bother her. "What is it? What are you thinking?" she asked, trying to get him to say something, anything, but dead silence. It was too quiet. By then she turned slowly to look into his eyes. Seeing something familiar, she placed a hand along the side his face. "A...Alex?"

Still he chose to remain mysterious, as he took her hand to give it a slight squeeze, before turning it over to kiss the palm ever so gently. In doing so, it caused the heat to quickly rise in her veins, as he turned to look deeply into her eyes. "Hello beautiful," he whispered seductively, while pulling her over onto his lap with one hand, while placing the other alongside her face to bring her lips down to meet up with his.

"Oh, you...!" she whispered, while pulling at the snaps on Alex's shirt to reveal his firm, tan, masculine chest, before running her fingers lightly over it.

"Jessi?" Craig whispered deeply.

"Mmmm..." she moaned in return, just as he went to pick her up.

"How about we go back inside and hold each other?" he groaned, not wanting this time to end for them either.

"Let's!" she returned, as he went to carry her back into the house.

Getting there, he gave the door a light kick to close it, before going over to lay her gently on the sofa, where he soon began pulling off his uncle's shirt, just as she had done her own. At that moment, in the firelight, gazing down upon her thinly laced covered breasts, with their raised blossoms peeking through, he slowly went to slip off the rest of her things, before going on to lightly run his lips over her tummy, and then up to those delectable nipples of hers, just as he moved to slip off her bra.

"Mmmm... so much for holding each other," she teased, when knowing their time was running out. But then, needing him, as she did, she arched up into his caressing lips.

"Oh, Lord, Jess..." he cried, hungering more and more for her. When that moment came, with it, the feeling of agony as it built up between them.

Wasting no more time, he hurried out of the rest of his thing, before either one of them could lose control.

Breathing heavily, as he looked down into her sultry eyes, he smiled. But then, without warning, the two reversed positions, where now, smiling down at him, her eyes sparkled in the flickering firelight, as he reached up to run his fingers in through her thick brown hair, while she sat upright, straddling his hips.

"Jessi..." he began.

"Hmmm...?"

"How is it that you remained divorced for so long?"

"Most men I've known were always jerks!" she replied, while coming down to nuzzle on his neck.

"Alex isn't a jerk!" he stated, while taking a hand full of her hair to bring her back up to claim her lips.

"Ha!" she laughed, when suddenly she felt the pressure of his passion pressing up to get into her. Bringing herself back up to make it possible, she gasped while trying to get the words out. As she did, a sudden urge to laugh again came out instead, while thinking of the first time she and Alex had met.

Seeing her face light up, he asked, "What...?"

"Alex," she laughed even more, "he was a jerk when we first met!"

"Oh...?" he began, when the room felt as though it were about to spin out of control, just as the feeling of his raw power was brought forth and thrusted once again inside her.

"Ahhh…!" she cried out, lifting her long hair back out of her face, as it felt as though the earth was beginning to tremor beneath her.

Soon after, when the heat exploded within them, the feeling of his hands coming up to the small of her back caused her to quiver all over. As at the same time, she felt the pressure of their release hit.

"Damn you, girl…" he cried, feeling the pain being drawn out of his uncle's body, as the final release hit. When it did, it tore away at his senses. "Why?" he cried, while pulling her back down to claim her hungering lips, before rolling her over onto her back to look down on her beautiful smile.

"Craig…? What…"

Stopping her words, while looking sadly, he slowly pulled her up off the sofa. "Let's go on out to the shower where I can hold onto this moment for as long as I can."

"Sure! All right! But you should know that one of Alex's men is out there."

"Oh well, he should know by now to turn his back, shouldn't he?"

"Oh, Craig!"

Grabbing a few towels on their way, she wrapped one around her, while he did the same.

Once outside, Craig looked around and spotted the same man from out at the creek, now standing up front, near the road.

Turning slightly around, Marcose saw Alex, as he turned to go into the shower. And with an understanding grin, he turned back to keep his eyes open for Tony, in case he had stayed in the area.

Meanwhile, in the privacy of the shower, while feeling the water cascading over them, he continued to woo her. And like before, when she had first used the shower, he pressed her body up against the wall, while bringing her hands up over her head. As he did, in one quick fluid motion, he had her up, wrapping her legs around his hips, while taking their love even further than before.

"Oh, Craig…!" she cried, bringing their lips back together hungeringly, while feeling even more of his raw power when he deepened his desire into hers.

"*Oh... yes... Jessi...*" he groaned deeply, while allowing his voice to drift off in the night air. "*Remember... this... always.*"

As time went on, the two slowed themselves down to catch their breath, before getting out to go back in and dressed. Once done, he carried her over to the sofa sleeper to lay her down so that they could cuddle, before having to leave his uncle's body. Sadly, he lay listening to her call out his name after she had fallen off to sleep. "It's going to be all right," he whispered. "I'm right here. I won't leave you. And somehow, if only..." He stopped to look up toward the heavens, knowing their time was running out, he closed his eyes to pray even harder. "Oh, Lord, please...!" he cried out, feeling the pain of what he was about to lose, rip at his heart like no pain had ever done before. "Please grant me this one prayer. Please... give my life a second chance...! Don't take me away from this wonderful woman for who has come to meaning so very much to me! I love her, Lord!" he continued to cry. "I love her as I have never loved a woman before."

As he continued to cry, while turning to look upon the love he was about to have to say goodbye to, suddenly she woke long enough to look up into his tear-filled eyes. And even as she had slept, she too prayed that somehow God would grant them eternal love. However, for her, she wasn't able to hold back her tears any longer.

"Oh, Craig, I will always love you. Always...!" she cried painfully, while choking back on her own emotions, as she turned to hold him, hoping that somehow, the pieces of her seemingly exploding heart, could keep them together.

"And I, you...!" he returned sadly. "*And I you*" he repeated, while kissing her passionately one last time, until his spirit left Alex's body.

Chapter Forty-One
'The Day of Reckoning…'

Waking the next morning, before Jessi, Alex found himself once again lying on the sofa next to her. Smiling, he tried sliding out of bed so as not to wake her, when at that time he heard a truck pulling in. Unfortunately, the slightest movement woke her anyway.

Looking up at him, he smiled, "Good morning, lady. We have company!"

"Mmmm…" she moaned, while stretching out, "you should go and see who it is, then!"

Laughing more to himself at her corny comment, while getting up to see who it was, he stopped to watch as she got up smiling to get a change of clothes out, before going off into the bathroom to get dressed.

Hearing the door close behind her, he went on to open the front door to greet David, as he walked up onto the front porch, not looking all too sure about being there, especially on that particular day. "Hey, there, nice to see you back again!"

"Yeah, well, Jessi asked me to stop by this morning. Is she up?"

"Yes, she's in getting dressed. Why don't you come on in and wait on her? I was just about to put on some coffee!"

"No…" he replied nervously, "I think I'll just wait out here."

Meanwhile, in the bathroom, she was talking with Craig. "You know David's here?" she asked, while slipping on her sweater.

"Yes," he replied regretfully, while leaning against the sink, watching her.

"Oh…?" she smiled, while turning back to see the troubled look in his eyes. Then it hit. "Oh, God, no…! Craig…?"

"Jess…"

"No…! Please, tell me it isn't today."

Not answering, she shook her head.

"Oh, Lord…!" she shook her head, looking up at the ceiling, and then back at him, "I was right about the time running out for us, wasn't I?"

"Yes."

"No… Craig…! Not yet….! Not today…!"

"I'm afraid so, beautiful!"

"No!"

At that, they both cried together, as he tried forcing his famous smile, just for her.

"Craig…"

Putting a finger up to her trembling lips, she wanted to look away, but didn't, knowing he needed answers.

"It's time, Jess. I have to know why he didn't tell me about all the trouble he was in."

"I know, but…" she sniffled, while wiping the tears away.

"God, Jess, I wish it were different for us! Really I do!"

"Yes, well, you don't know how many times I've prayed for that," she told him, while going over to the door, shaking her head frustratedly.

"You're not the only one!"

Looking back up at him one last time, before going out, with their eyes filled with so much pain, he just wanted to hold her but couldn't.

"I love you so much, Jess!" he cried, raising a hand out to touch her cheek. And when he did, feeling its tingling sensation along the side her face, a tear found its way down to where his fingers were nearly touching her. As it did, he felt the dampness running over them. *"What…"* he started, when blocking the thought from reaching her. Looking down at the moisture running over his fingers, the look, which came over him, was one full of disbelief, at what had just taken place. *"But I felt that…!"*

"Yes…" came the sweetest sounding voice he had ever heard.

"But, I…I don't understand…!"

"Go..." the voice whispered out only to him. *"Go now and talk to your friend...!"*

Looking back into Jessi's eyes, he wanted to say something, but couldn't. Instead, he just told her to bring David inside so that he could talk to him. "When you get him in here, come up and get me."

"Your room?" she asked, opening the door.

"Yes," he smiled, heading for the stairs.

Going into the living room, she found Alex and David still out on the front porch talking. "Hi, David, I'm glad to see you decided to come!" she greeted warmly, while walking out to join them.

Looking puzzled at first, he asked, "Why did you want to see me?"

"I'll explain it all when you come inside. It isn't all that safe out here."

Coming up shy of the front door, he stopped.

"David!" Alex spoke up, from behind.

"No, I...I can't!" he cried, backing away. As he did, he ran into Alex, while shaking his head. "I just can't go in there. Not today!"

"David," Alex spoke up again, while placing his hands firmly on David's shoulders, "I know how close you and Craig were, but those two men who killed him are still after you. If we stay out here, we're sitting ducks," he explained, while pulling out his cell phone to call Ted.

"He's right, David," she murmured worriedly, while still standing in the open doorway. Though, looking at him now, she still couldn't get over how he looked so much like Craig, tall, dark, and handsome, except there was something missing in this thirty-nine-year old, *"Something, but what?"* she asked herself. "Please David," she began, sounding a little more worried, when Alex was about to get off his phone, "it isn't safe out here in the open. Especially if they followed you here!"

"Jess..." Alex interrupted, as his voice held an alarming sound to it, "I just called Ted."

"And...?" she asked, seeing the look of alarm on his face.

"I'm afraid it's not good."

"What is it?"

"He didn't come back to the Inn last night, and Harry, well Harry wasn't found in his room either."

"Who? Tony?" David asked, looking back at Alex, nervously.

"Yes, your buddy, Tony!" he announced, while nudging David toward the open door.

"Now, shall we take this inside?" he ordered.

Taking a moment after David went inside Alex looked into, what were once, her tear-filled eyes. "Are you all right?" he asked, placing a hand around her waist.

"Not really!"

"I'm sorry, Jess, I really wish this didn't have to happen."

"Yes, but why to such a great guy...?" she asked, looking out across the yard, while trying hard not to cry.

"I don't exactly know, but just remember what Doreen told you. It's going to work out somehow. We have to believe that."

"Yeah, sure, I'll try...!" she said, tremblingly. "But please don't expect me to say goodbye to him... I can't do that! No... not now...!"

"I know. Just the thought of saying it, kills me!" he exclaimed, while looking off toward the woods that were in the opposite direction of where his men were. *"Damn it, Craig, something tells me that even you knew this was going to be happening today,"* he thought, when just then, another bad feeling hit, as he turned back to look for his men. But they were nowhere to be seen.

Taking Jessi's arm, he turned her back to go inside.

Before going, she reached up to give him a warm hug, not knowing what was just going through his mind. "Thanks, Alex," she whispered.

"For what?"

"For being here!"

"I wouldn't be anywhere else, at this very moment," he returned, while looking back at the woods. "I just wish it wasn't going down so soon!"

At that, the two went back inside, while closing the door behind them.

"I'll be right back," Jessi announced, heading for the stairs to go up to Craig's room. "I just have to do something first."

"We'll be here," Alex nodded quietly, while taking out his radio to call his men.

Meanwhile, reaching his room, when walking in, the door closed behind her.

"Craig…?" she cried, turning to see him standing near it, while looking so sad.

Knowing the time was running out for the two of them even sooner than he had expected, he tried real hard to smile, but it was useless. "I know," his eyes said what he hadn't, while walking over to the window to look out over the same woods Alex had, "the time is almost here, and those men are already nearby."

"What…? Where…?" she cried, going over to peek out from one side of the window, while standing next to him.

"Just past those trees!" he explained, while turning back to her. "As for the three of you, there isn't enough time to get you out of here, but you will be safe up here, when the time does come. As for Ted, he won't make it in time."

"But there are Alex's men!"

"No. They've already been spotted sometime during the night."

"Are they…"

"Dead? No." He couldn't help but grin. "They're just tied up out in the woods, but very pissed that they hadn't seen it coming."

"That's a relief, but then why won't you let Alex help you then?"

"Because, as I told you before, I have to do this alone, since I was alone when I died."

"I know, but…"

"I know, I feel it, too!"

For what had seemed like a long moment, neither one said a word, just looked sadly into each other's eyes, until he spoke up, breaking the silence, "We have to be getting downstairs now, I have to find out what had happened, and why they wanted him dead."

"All right."

Together, going downstairs, they heard David try to explain what had happened.

"But then why didn't you just get out of it?" Alex was yelling at him.

"I tried to! But they wouldn't let me!"

"Who wouldn't let you? Tony?"

"No! Santos! Tony is, supposedly, just one of his right hand henchmen! So he says."

"That's what we heard. Then what happened?"

"When I did get away, Harry and I called the department to talk to you."

"To me…?" Alex was stunned not to know that.

"Yes!"

"But I never got the message!"

"The guy who took the call…"

"What about him?"

"His name…"

"Come on, David, don't stop now! What about his name?"

"It was on the list of crooked cops!"

"What?" he yelled. "And where is this list now_____?"

"I don't know! Harry had it last."

"The cop that took the call. Who was it?"

"Frank something!"

"Peters…?"

"Yeah, yeah that's him!"

"Damn it!" he thundered, while grabbing his cell phone.

After a short wait, Ted's voice came over the other end, "Yeah!" he called out.

"We've got big trouble!" Alex barked over his end. "Where's Frank Peters?"

"He's right behind me in his Suburban, why?"

"Damn it!"

"Alex, what's going on?"

"I'll tell ya, but first, where was Frank last night?"

"Out walking the grounds, or so he had said!"

"Damn it, Ted, he's a crooked cop!"

"What…? Damn, I had my suspicions, but…" he yelled, while looking up in his rear view mirror at Frank's car.

"What's going on?" Beth asked, worriedly.

Hearing her voice, Alex asked, "Was that Beth, just now?"

"Yes, I brought her along with me. Why?"

"Good. Ted?"

"Yeah?"

"Keep her away from Frank. And Ted…" There was silence, as Alex looked back at David, "call for back up, and tell the commander the situation. And for God sake's, get Frank out of the way, before you get here. He's bound to cause trouble for us."

"Got it."

Before hanging up, Alex turned back to David and asked, "Who else, David? Who else was on that list?"

Stopping to think, he looked back to Alex, "Terri?"

"Shaw?"

"What?" Ted hollered out on his end.

"God…" Alex stopped, while raking his free hand over his hair, "you heard that too?"

"Yes, loud and clear," Ted returned heatedly, while doubling up his fist, just as Alex had done the same.

"Get her, Ted. Get her before I do. So help me, God, if you don't, I'll kill her."

"I'll take care of it personally. But first, let me take care of our crooked friend here."

"That reminds me, have you heard from any of our guys?"

"No. Why?"

"Damn it! That's what I was afraid of. Looks like, if not one of our uninvited friends, Frank, himself, may have gotten to them."

"That's not good."

"No. And to make matters worse, I'd go out and look for them but…"

"You wouldn't know where to start. Not to mention…"

"There's no time!"

Getting off his phone, Ted filled Beth in on what was going down.

"Terri was involved in this, all along?" she asked.

"Yes, and if I don't get to her first…"

"I heard." She cringed at the thought of Alex's vengeful expression. "What do we do now?"

Dialing headquarters, he put up a finger to hold her thoughts. "Commander!" he called out once the man answered his private line.

"What's going down?" the commander asked, knowing the only time the private line was ever used, was when something bad was about to take place. That, and the fact that Ted, Alex, Jarred and Marcose were the only cops he trusted with this number, along with his growing like for Officer Lamb, when hating to have to put an end to hers and Alex's relationship.

"We now know who two of our bad cops are."

"Who?"

"Peters and…"

"Shaw?" the commander guessed.

"Yes. How did you know?"

"I had my suspicions when she peeled out of here in a souped up sports car, not more than a few days ago. Seeing that, I had her bank records seized upon investigations, once Delgado had gone down for drug smuggling."

"And Frank? What about Frank?"

"That, I had no clue."

"We've got to get him off the road, and now, Commander."

"Hang in there, I'm sending out a few good men I had to call in, in case something like this were to happen. You know, with Santos, we can never have too many men out there."

"Which reminds me, you can forget about Baker and Marcose."

"Them too?"

"No! No!" he came back right away. "I can't reach them on their radios. And from what Alex had told me, I think Frank made an unscheduled trip out to the farmhouse late last night, and put them both out of commission."

"He didn't…"

"Kill them? I don't think so. Frank doesn't come across as killing his own. No, I think he's got them tied up somewhere."

"What about Kevin?"

"He's been sent to watch her girls."

"All right, then, anytime now you should be seeing a couple of SUVs coming at you.

Signal them when you see them. And Ted…?"

"Yeah?"

"Get the hell out of the way."

"Why?" he looked to Beth puzzledly.

"Just do it. Oh, and Ted?"

"Yeah?"

"Get to Alex, as quick as you can."

"I'm on my way," he groaned, hanging up.

Within minutes, just like the commander said, two unmarked, Special Forces vehicles showed up. Knowing them once they appeared, just like Alex's, made with specially treated glass, upon signaling them, both Ted and Beth watched as they sped by.

Suddenly, hearing them squalling on their breaks, both vehicles, and one other, while coming up from behind, surrounded Frank's Suburban and quickly made their arrest.

"Wow!" Beth cried excitedly.

Smiling, Ted continued on.

"Is there something you want to tell me?" she asked questioningly.

"Oh…" he grinned, "you recall an assignment the commander pulled Alex and I on about a year ago, after Alex started to calm down some from Craig's death?"

"Yes…!"

"What you had just witnessed, was a part of it."

"The Special…"

"Yes," he cut her off.

Meanwhile, back at the farmhouse, the others had just enough time to talk, before Tony and one very unwilling sidekick, 'Harry', were about to show themselves.

"Alex…" David was just saying, when both Jessi and Craig walked in.

"David," Jessi spoke up, "there's someone here who wants to talk to you."

"Who?" he asked, turning to look at her nervously.

Seeing the look on her face, Alex looked over at the staircase, where Craig was standing. "Jessi does this mean…"

"Yes. It's time."

"Will someone please… tell me what is going on here, and just who wants to talk to me?"

Without warning, his answer came. "Me, David," Craig said, standing behind him, as David jolted around so fast, he stumbled into Alex. And with a look of surprise on his face, he looked as though he were going to pass out at any moment.

"What's wrong, David?" he asked, breaking out into a grin. "You don't look so well."

"C...Craig?" he stammered, when finally able to find his voice, while breaking down crying. "Oh, my, God... it really is you! Then it's true! You have been here all along."

"Yes, David," he groaned, "I have."

"Oh... God, I didn't want you to get killed. It wasn't supposed to have been you. They were after me!"

"Why, David?" he asked angrily. "Why were they after you?"

"I...I was suppose to turn my back on something that was about to go down! I...I couldn't do it. It was wrong! They were dealing in drugs!"

"Then why didn't you just get the hell out of there? I lost my life, because of you."

"I tried! But..."

"Tell him, David," Alex ordered. "Tell him what you told me."

"What?" Craig asked.

"I...I..." David turned away.

"David," Alex growled, while turning him back to face Craig, "tell him!"

"All right!" he yelled. "I turned him in, or at least I tried to. Are you happy now?"

Looking to Alex, Craig wondered what could have happened. "Alex...?"

"He spoke to a dirty cop," he groaned, "who I assumed was on Santos's payroll."

"Yeah, and now he wants me dead!"

"You could have told me!" Craig yelled.

"I didn't want to get you involved! You had Abby, and the two of you were happy! And I...I..."

"Didn't have anyone?" he finished. "God, Alex was gone, and I was too busy with my own life to see that you were feeling left out!"

Going over to the window, David looked out, when at that time, Jessi nudged Alex in the arm, "Let's leave the two of them to talk," she whispered, while pointing to the door.

Turning to look back at Craig, she smiled sadly.

"Where are you going?" he asked, looking into her eyes.

"Just out on the porch!"

"Please be careful. They're not very far, now."

"Where are they?" she asked, when the expression on her face looked more frightened now, as she learned of their new hiding spot.

"Not in their car, but near it."

"All right."

After going out onto the porch, Alex asked, while closing the door behind him, "What was that all about?"

Scared, she told him, "They're getting closer, Alex. You've got to call Ted back, and now!"

"But he's already on his way!" he explained, taking her by the arm to calm her down.

"But he's going to be too late!"

"How do you know that? Did..."

Not waiting, she blurted it out, "Alex... Tony is already here!"

"Where?" he asked, just as he turned to look down the road, when suddenly it came to him, as he caught a glimpse of morning sunlight reflecting off the car's windshield. "Damn...!" he swore, when at that moment, every muscle in his body tightened, as he quickly looked around for her dog. "Where's Max?" he asked, looking back off toward the trees, waiting to see if either of them comes out into the open.

"I'm not sure!" she replied, while watching off in the distance for any movement, as well. "He was in the kitchen eating earlier!"

"Damn it..." he growled, pulling out his cell phone again, "they must have been watching David ever since last night. That explains why they never went back to the Inn."

"Oh, God, I had almost forgotten to tell you..."

"Tell me what?" he turned back to look at her.

"Marcose and Baker! Craig says they're tied up somewhere out in the woods, but they're all right, just, well... uh..."

"Pissed?" he finished for her, while unable to help but grin, while shaking his head. "I think I can see why. Ted said Frank was supposedly out late last night checking the grounds."

"But he was out here?"

"Yeah, and no doubt Marcose had no clue, when they were over taken."

"Alex, do you think he may have told Tony who you were?"

"No," he paused, before punching in the last of Ted's numbers, "but if that's the case, it could have set Tony off."

Having said that, Ted's voice came across the line.

"Ted?"

"Y...ah!" The reception was breaking up on Alex's end.

"Where the hell are you?" he asked hurriedly, while at the same time, trying to strain his ear to hear his friend.

"A...out t...enty min...tes away! W...at's going on n...w?"

"Our friends are already here! They're down the road, heading this way on foot!"

"Ar... you th... at the h...se?"

"Yes!"

"Who's all th...re w...th you?"

"Jessi, David, an..." he caught himself just in time, when turning to look to Jessi. "Max," he finished.

"Damn! Y...u s...id D...vid was go...ng to be th...re, but I h...d my d...bts!"

"Ted..." Alex cut in, as the reception was getting too hard to make out, "I'm afraid you are going to be too late, getting here."

"H...ll, I'm floor bo...rding i... as it i...!"

"I know. Just get here as soon as you can. Something has obviously gone wrong. And Ted..."

"Ye...h?"

"Just to be on the safe side," he stopped briefly, when seeing the expression come over

Jessi's face, "get an ambulance here, as well, we may need it."

"I already put in the call for one." His voice came through clearly then.

"Good thinking. Hey," seeing some movement down the line, he quickly added, "I've got to let you go. We've got company coming up through the woods now! If anything goes wrong, take care of my nephew and... Beth for me, will you?" he groaned, thinking he may never get the chance to see her again. "Take care, buddy!"

"I will," he returned, looking to Beth, who had heard his last statement.

"Ted...?" she nearly wanted to cry.

"He's going to be fine. We just have to get there, is all," he said, while putting in a call to Jarred.

Without warning, Craig sent Jessi a message, *"Get back in here. Both of you! They're coming up through the woods, now!"*

"Oh, Alex... Craig says..."

"I know," he pointed out. "Let's go!"

Taking her by the arm, they rushed back inside. Though, once there, she grabbed up her phone to call her girls.

"Your girls?" he asked thoughtfully, when knowing the pain she must be feeling, while leaving them behind.

"Yes." Her expression saddened.

After closing the door, Alex took out his service revolver to quickly check it over, while she spoke hurriedly with her girls.

"But, Mom" Lora cried, "why can't you just get away, while you still can?"

"It isn't safe anymore, besides, Alex is here, so I'll be just fine...!"

Meanwhile, standing off to one side of the entryway, while talking with both her girls, coming from the window that faced the woods, Craig ordered everyone upstairs, before looking to his uncle, "Protect them for me, Alex," he said, when turning back to Jessi, who had just gotten off the phone with Cassi, while no longer able to hold back her tears any longer. *"Lord... I'm sorry Jess..."* he thought out telepathically, *"if we only had more time. God knows I wish I were able to love you. I mean really love you the way you deserve, but..."*

"Oh, God, Craig... no!" she cried out uncontrollably, while reaching out a hand to him.

"Yes, Jess." He reached back. "Now, you have to go. Alex, it's time. You guys have to get upstairs, and now!" With his last glance to everyone, he nodded his head. But then, turning to Jessi, he smiled his crooked smile. "I love you, Jess!" he softly whispered, just as he slowly faded away. *"R e m e m b e r I w i l l a l w a y s l o v e y o u"*

With that, she ran over to the sofa to grab up his old shirt and blanket to take with her for safekeeping. As for the rest of her things, she had already taken them out to her truck earlier, when somehow sensing something was going to happen. But then suddenly, thinking about her girls again, she prayed she hadn't made a mistake by leaving them behind.

But then, Alex spoke up, cutting into her thoughts, "Damn, I don't feel right about this. I should be down here with him!" he commented, on their way up to Craig's room. Stopping, as they were about to enter, he turned to look at Jessi, and shook his head, "That had to have sounded pretty strange."

"No. He knows what he's doing," she offered, hoping to sound reassuringly, while walking into the room, and over to stand at the side of the window, to continue praying.

Looking confused, while Alex closed the door behind them, David asked, while walking up beside her, "Did I miss something, here? Why does he feel he has to do it alone?"

"Because..." she started, sadly, when looking over at him.

"He was alone when he died!" Alex finished, while standing at the door, listening, before going over to join them.

As silence filled the room, each of them carefully watched and waited, wondering when it all was going to happen.

Just then, seeing the two coming out of the woods, David cried out, "They're here...!"

"Take it easy, David. Everything is going to work out, just fine," Alex told him, while looking to Jessi for some sort of sign.

"Sorry. Nothing," she said, turning to go over and have a seat in a corner, where she closed her eyes to pray even more for Craig and the others, while still holding tightly to his things in her arms.

At that time, Alex too, went over to join her, when taking her free hand to hold, while paying close attention to their surroundings. "If we are to be doing anything, this sure is what we need to be doing right about now."

"Yeah, you're right," David agreed, while going over to join them.

Meanwhile, outside, the two men were making their way around the house, while looking in every window, and trying every door, until coming to one that was unlocked, due to Craig making sure of it.

Finding it, Harry knew if he didn't cooperate, Tony wouldn't hesitate killing him, too. So putting his own feelings aside, regretfully for the others, he called out, "Hey, Tony, over here!"

"What did you find?" he asked, when Harry went to step aside.

Entering quietly, neither one said anything, while glancing around the area.

"Where are they, Tony?" he asked, standing just inside the doorway.

"They're probably hiding somewhere," he commented, smugly, while proceeding into the living room. Seeing how the sofa was pulled out, and unmade, he knew someone had been staying there. "Well, well, well," he said, cynically, "what do we have here?"

"What did you find?" Harry asked, while coming up from behind.

"From the looks of it, someone has been staying here."

"The owner of the truck out back?"

"You could say that, along with that Blazer that looks awfully familiar."

"You think it's the one from the Inn?"

"Oh, yeah, it's the same one all right, belonging to that nosy groundskeeper. But he ain't no groundskeeper," he sneered. "It's that cop I hate. Alex Storm!"

"What now? We were only supposed to get McMasters, not the others...!"

"So!" he laughed. "The cop has been a pain in my neck ever since we killed his nephew by mistake. And as for the other person, well let's just say, they should have stayed home today."

"Yeah, well, you sure made the boss mad. I thought he was going to kill you for what you did."

"How the hell should I have known that McMasters was going to loan out his truck to his friend? Besides, what's done is done. Now let's start looking for McMasters and do what we were sent out to do in the first place."

"Yeah, well, I felt like hell after what we did," he groaned, while following Tony around.

"Harry," Tony growled short of the kitchen doorway, "you're going to have to get over that. The guy is dead and buried. Now shut the hell up, and start looking."

It wasn't long, when the two split up to look for David and Craig's uncle.

While taking the first floor, Harry went upstairs to have a look around. "Where are you, McMasters?" he called, out quietly, once he got up there. "You know I'm not like Tony, I don't want to hurt any of you. But Storm has made him real mad, and now he wants him dead, too!"

At that moment, a chill came up around him, when Craig appeared, standing behind him. "*H a r r y...*" he called out in a whisper.

"Tony?" he called back, turning around to find no one there.

"*N o... H a r r y...*" Craig whispered again, while moving around to the other side of him.

"M...McMasters, is that you?" he asked, turning to look the other way. Still, there was no one in the hall, but him. At that time, he was beginning to get really nervous. "I must be hearing things, or this house really is haunted," he coward down, while looking overhead for some sort of apparition to come floating by. As he continued to look, he thought once again, "W...what if... No..., that c...can't be...! He's d...d...dead. It must be all in my head."

"*N o H a r r y! D o n' t y o u r e m e m b e r? Y o u a n d T o n y, H a r r y. Y o u k i l l e d m e. M e, H a r r y. R e m e m b e r? Y o u a n d T o n y!*" he repeated slowly, again and again. "*Y o u a n d T o n y!*"

"Ma... Ma... Matthews? I...it can't be. Y...you're dead! Tony killed you!" he cried, while turning around and around.

"*B u t y o u w e r e t h e r e t o o, H a r r y! Y o u w e r e t h e r e t o o!*"

"Yes I know it was wrong. But Tony, he...he doesn't care!"

"He, who?" Tony asked, angrily, when coming up behind him. "Did you find them?"

"N...n...no, not yet!" he replied, with growing fright in his already shaky voice.

"Then who were you just talking to?"

"No one, Tony, just thinking out loud," he replied, when walking up to the door that the others were behind. And just as he did, Craig's spirit appeared between them and the door.

"Tony!" Harry screamed, backing away. "I knew it! I knew it! He is here to get even with us for killing him! Come on, we have to get out of here, before it's too late!"

"What are you squalling about? Who's here?"

"M...Matthews!"

"Harry," Tony growled, not picking up on what he was seeing, "you're talking nonsense. Now shut the hell up. We've got a job to do. So get back to work and find them!"

"NoTony! No more killing!" he pleaded, as he started to back away even more. "I want out, Tony. I want out, now!"

"You're not getting out of anything," he growled, while going for his gun. "You got it?"

"No!" he yelled, when Tony aimed his gun at him.

Chapter Forty-Two

Hearing this, David and Alex looked to each other. "Alex, we can't let Tony kill him!"

"I know," he growled, wanting to go out and aid Harry from what was about to happen.

Before making a move toward the door, while confronted with what Tony was about to do to him, Harry suddenly got up the courage to throw him down the stairs. "No" he cried out, "you're not going to scare me no more!"

Seeing Tony go head over heels down the stairs, Harry turned to look back up at Craig, "I...I'm s...sorry, M...Matthews," he replied sadly. "Like your friend, we both got caught up in something neither one of us wanted no part of!"

"Then go, Harry," he said in a ghost-like tone. *"Tell Alex. Tell him everything you told me, and clear yourself."*

"Where?"

Pointing to the door where Alex and the others were, he repeated, *"Go, now, Harry,"* he ordered, just as he started to disappear, knowing his nightmare wasn't quite, yet, over with.

Slowly opening the door to Craig's room, Harry went in with his hands held out in front of him. "I'm not here to hurt any of you!" he announced, walking in, though, not stopping until he reached the window. "I just don't want to do this anymore. It was wrong when we killed your nephew, Storm. I know that! But you have to know that I wanted no part of this, either!"

"Give me one good reason why I should trust you," Alex asked, while going for his gun.

"Tony has you right where he wants you. Who's to say, if he were to tell you to shoot us, you would do it out of fear for your own life?"

"But I..." he began, when turning around to face them. When he did, seeing the gun trained on him, out of poor judgment, he reached out, grabbing Jessi's arm to pull her over in front of him.

"No!" she screamed, as he placed his own gun up to her head.

"Harry, no...!" David, too, cried. "You don't want to hurt her. You said it yourself you don't want to do this anymore. So please, put the gun down, and we'll talk."

"H...Harry! P...please!" she cried, feeling the hard, cold barrel pressing against her temple.

Hearing her cries, Craig came back into the room, as the hand inwhich Harry was holding the gun in began to shake.

"Come on, Harry," David went on, while Alex continued to train his gun on the man holding her hostage, "you don't want to hurt her. Not Jessi, she hasn't done anything to you."

"No, she hasn't. But I will if he doesn't drop his gun. You hear me?" he shouted out at Alex, as his hand began to shake even more. "I mean it! I don't want to hurt her, but I will if you don't drop your gun first."

"A...Alex" Jessi cried, while unaware of Craig's presence, due to the amount of fear that was pulsing through her, "p...please!"

Going over to stand next to Harry, Craig began to whisper chillingly so that even Jessi could hear him, and know that she was going to be all right, "*H a r r y...*"he started ominously, "*d r o p t h e g u n... H a r r y...! Y o u a r e n o t h i n g l i k e T o n y. S o d r o p t h e g u n b e f o r e I c h a n g e m y m i n d!*"

Suddenly, just as his expression changed, he did as Craig told him. "A...all right! I'll drop it!"

"A...Alex!" Jessi cried, frightfully. "P...please..., put yours away too...!"

"All right! All right! Just don't hurt her," he growled, while slowly putting his gun back into its holster. "Okay, now let her go," he ordered, while holding his hands out in front of him.

Doing so, while feeling Harry loosening his grip on her, she turned slowly to face him, while unbeknownst to everyone in the room, Tony had slipped out. Suddenly, at that precise moment, a shot rang out, sending a bullet, piercing through the window, sensing glass shrapnel flying.

"No!" she screamed, while reaching out to grab onto Harry, just as he slowly slumped to the floor.

While the expression in his eyes was so full of pain, he turned to look up at Craig one more time, "F...forgive me, M...Matthews, p... please... for...forgive me for not st...stopping him!" he cried.

Feeling the pain of what he had just heard, Craig's eyes darkened over what had just happened, when Alex and David hurried over to see if Jessi was all right.

"Jessi...?" Alex called out. "Are you hurt?"

"No! I'm all right! It's Harry..." she cried out tearfully, while they all went to see what they could do to help him.

"It looks like he has taken a bullet through the back," Alex announced, while rolling him over to see if there was an exit wound. Seeing one, he stopped to have a look around the room.

"What is it?" David asked, while he too looked around for something out of the ordinary.

"The bullet," he exclaimed. "From the looks of Harry's wound, it had just barely missed his heart! But..."

"What?" Jessi asked, emotionally.

"It went right through him." Looking once again at Jessi, he pulled away from Harry to look her over thoroughly. "Are you sure you're all right? You didn't get hit too, did you?"

"No. It must have missed me."

"David, you were standing right behind her. Are you all right?"

"Yes." Turning then to follow the path of where the bullet could have gone, he saw it. "Alex...! Look...!" He pointed to the wall nearest to the door.

Getting a closer look at it, Alex turned back to the others.

"St...Storm..." Harry uttered out painfully.

"Take it easy, Harry." He rushed back over to offer his help. "Help is on its way."

Meanwhile, as Jessi attempted to stop the bleeding, Alex and David rushed over to the window just in time to see Tony heading off away from the house.

"No!" David cried, thinking Tony was about to get away. Grabbing for Harry's gun, he headed for the door. "I've got to stop him. He can't get away this time."

"David, no!" Jessi cried out, turning to Alex, "You have to stop him, Alex, he mustn't get killed...! And Tony..." She stopped to look to Craig, now that she could see him. "He can't get away this time either, o...or Craig..." she choked back on her emotions, while seeing his expression go grim.

Not having to say another word, Alex knew what she was about to say, when he took off after David. Catching up to him at the front door, he made a rash dive from one-third the way up the staircase to tackle him to the floor, when knocking the gun out of his hand.

"Alex...!" he yelled. "He's getting away! We have to stop him!"

"Not this way, David. And not without me!" he yelled back, when unaware that Tony had doubled back, and was now walking in through the front door, while glaring down at them.

"Well, well, well, what do we have here?" he snarled at the two of them, lying on the floor. "One soon to be dead duck, and one gonna be dead cop," he laughed out loud, while kicking Harry's gun off to the side. "I've been waiting for this day, Storm. Now I have the both of you right where I want you."

"Tony Belaro," Alex growled, while glaring up at him. "You're not going to get away with it this time. You're going to pay dearly for killing my nephew."

"Yeah, yeah, yeah. And just how do you plan to carry out that threat? From where I'm standing, you don't seem to have a rat's chance of getting yourself out of this mess," he laughed. "Your gun. Toss it out here, now!"

Begrudgingly, Alex did just that. Pulling it out slowly from its holster, he slid it off to one side, opposite of where Harry's gun had landed.

"Good. Now, where is the driver of that other truck out there? Get him down here, now!"

"Leave her out of it, Belaro," David yelled. "She doesn't deserve to get hurt."

"So it's a girl we have here, do we," he sneered, while looking up the stairs, grinning.

At that moment, Alex and David wondered where Craig was, while upstairs helping Jessi with Harry's wound; the two were trying to make him as comfortable as possible. "You're going to be all right, Harry," Craig was saying, while looking over Jessi's shoulder.

"I can see him!" he whispered to her with a softened expression on his face. "I can really see him!"

"Yes, I know," she returned, looking back at Craig, while smiling, when he went to give her a kiss.

"Matthews, it was Tony who did this to you. I didn't really want no part of it. I swear!"

"I know, Harry. And Tony won't get away this time. He'll pay for what he did to me."

"Harry," Jessi started in puzzledly, "if you and David were so close..."

"Why didn't I know this wasn't David?"

"Yes."

"At first, seeing the truck pull away, we both thought it was David."

"When did you first realize it wasn't?"

"Here, when we came face to face with..."

"Me?" Craig asked cynically.

"Yes," he said, seeing the look on Craig's face go a little more grimmer. "I'm sorry, Matthews, but it all happened so quickly from then on out."

"Go on," he instructed, while folding his arms across his chest.

"Well, Tony had his gun out already and...and I...I was scared...! So please, you gotta believe me. I didn't want to do this."

"Craig..." Jessi started, only to see him look off in the direction of the stairway, when the expression on his face grew even darker, while thinking back to when his nightmare had first began.

Just then, his thoughts were interrupted, when Alex called out, sounding a little strange, as if to warn them that he and David had been caught by Tony. "Jessi...!" he called up to her.

"Well, well, well, if it isn't Ms. Jessi Rae," Tony sneered once again, hearing her name, when looking back down at the two of them.

'Come on, Jess,' he groaned inwardly, while looking back up at Tony.

Hoping that she was smart enough to pick up on his warning, she would tell Craig. And it worked, though, it was Craig who picked up on the warning, when he turned to Jessi, "Tony," he warned. "He's got them!"

"Alex, no, he can't!" she cried softly, when Craig held up a reassuring hand.

"It's going to be all right. I won't let anything happen to him, but we do have to get them back up here. I have to deal with Tony alone."

"I know," she replied, thinking of a way to do just that. Just then a thought came to her.

"Jessi... no...!" he shook his head, while picking up on what she was thinking.

"It will work, Craig, trust me!" she exclaimed, while looking down at her blood-covered hands.

Studying her for a moment, he gave in, seeing the determination she had on her face. "All right, just be careful."

"I will. Besides, what could go wrong?" she asked, nervously. "I have all three of you hear to protect me."

"We'll do our best," he grinned, not liking what was about to take place.

"All right, now, Harry, you're going to have to go along with this if you want to get out of here alive."

"Sure. What is it?" he asked, eagerly, as Craig listened too, to what she had to say.

After all was said and done, she took the bloodied rag and held it up to her own shoulder, to make it look as though she had been shot.

"Jess..." Craig looked at her with deep concern, "are you sure you really want to do this?

It's pretty dangerous, and Tony is not one to mess with."

"Well, I'm sure of one thing, I'm sure I don't want to lose you, or Alex. But knowing how much you want for this nightmare to end, for your sake, I'll do it," she cried, as a tear found its way down her cheek, while not wanting to see Craig go at all.

"Jessi," he smiled sadly, while wiping the tear away, "it's time to call them up, then."

Nodding her head, she looked to Harry, "Are you ready?"

"Let's do it," he replied, closing his eyes.

"Okay..." she returned, while taking in a deep, cleansing breath, as she went to look for another rag to apply to his shoulder, though the bleeding seemed to have stopped.

Meanwhile, positioning herself for what she was about to do, Alex called out again, while watching Tony out of the corner of his eye, and yet, still wondered where his nephew could be, and why he hadn't shown himself, yet. *Come on, girl, what is going on up there?* he continued, heatedly, while knowing his gun wasn't too far away. *No, this isn't the time to go for it. Not while Tony's gun is still trained on us.*

Just then, they heard Jessi's voice, yet there was something strangely odd about it.

"A…Alex" she cried out, staging her voice to sound as though she were in great pain, "I…I c…can't…! I…it h…hurts too much…! A… Alex, help me…! I…it really h…hurts too much…!"

'What the hell…?' He looked to David, as his own expression turned from being full of anger, to concern, while silently shaking his head. *'Damn it, Jessi, you weren't hurt when I left you. Just what are you up to now…?'*

Hearing her, Tony turned back to the others, "How do I know she isn't lying?"

"Because, she doesn't like to lie…" David fibbed, looking to Alex out of the corner of his eye, when he knew for a fact she was all right when he ran out of the room earlier.

Together, they nodded their heads quietly, and decided to play along.

"Hmmm," Tony grunted, "we'll just have to see now, won't we? Let's go," he ordered, waving his gun at them.

"Where?" Alex asked, while trying to stall for time, as he and David got up slowly from the floor.

"Upstairs," he pointed, while going over to pick up Harry's gun.

Seeing his chance to retrieve his own gun, while Tony's back was turned toward them, David saw what he was about to do and gave a nod of his head, before going over to stand in between them. Meanwhile, quickly and quietly Alex retrieved his weapon and returned it to his shoulder holster, before closing his vest around it. And none too soon, when Tony turned back to face them.

Not realizing what he had just done, Tony gave the two a hard shove toward the steps, "Let's go," he ordered.

With a knowing grin, the two tripped up the stairs ahead of him.

Arriving at Craig's old room, Tony shoved them both over to where Jessi was slumped over, while holding the bloodied rag to her shoulder.

"Jessi…?" they both called out, stumbling over to sit next to her.

"Are you all right?" Alex asked first, pulling her over into his arms, as she went to look up at him.

With a warm smile on her face, Tony was unable to see her expression, when Alex let out a silent grumble.

Meanwhile, David moved around to check on her for himself. "How are you holding up here, girl?" he asked, checking out her supposed wound, when she turned to look over at him.

Understanding the message he saw in her eyes, he tried hard not to smile.

"Mmmm… I feel like… I'm going to faint…!" she replied weakly, when then letting her body go limp. In doing so, she dropped her head back onto Alex's arm, as if she had.

"Come on, girl," he shook her gently, "just hang in there, you'll be all right," he spoke up, while keeping watch on Tony from out of the corner his eye.

"Mmmm… A…Alex…" she acted as though she were starting to come around, "H…Harry, he…he didn't m…make it! He's… d…dead! H…Harry's d…dead…!"

"Oh…?" Reading the expression on her face, he knew Harry was still alive, "I'm sorry to hear that," he returned, going along with her scheme, while giving her a knowing wink. "He should have never gotten killed."

"No, h…he sh…shouldn't have. Oh…." she moaned. But then, as she turned to look up at Tony, with a smudge of blood on her cheek, seeing Craig standing in the doorway behind him, she tried to sit up on her own, when Alex ended up helping her. "Mr. Belaro," she began, "by any chance have you seen your prosecutor lately?"

"What…? What are you talking about?" he asked smugly, when turning around to see the ghost of Craig Matthews standing, there, behind him.

"Why, Tony Belaro," Alex grinned, "I do believe you are about to be prosecuted."

Just then, the look on Tony's face was turned to one of utter horror. "No" he cried out, "this ain't real!"

"Oh, but I am real! And now it's your turn!" he thundered, while throwing Tony one powerful backhand, which sent him flying across the room. On the other side, he landed up against the wall, leaving several cracks splintering in the old plaster, as he slowly slid down to the floor.

When he finally straightened up, he stood, looking over at Craig, and then Alex. Taking out his gun, he aimed it directly at Alex, and yelled, "Not before I kill you, Storm! This is for all the years that you have been a pain in my neck!"

As if in slow motion, they all cried out, before Alex could get to his own weapon. By then it was too late, Tony had pulled the trigger, spewing an immensely hot piece of lead out of its short black barrel. Hitting its intended target through the right shoulder, Alex was made to propel back away from Jessi, and onto the floor, while sending blood pouring out through the whole the bullet had made.

"Oh, God, no!" Jessi sobbed, reaching over to pull Alex into her arms, just as Tony took off out of the room. Looking down into his pain stricken eyes, she sobbed even more, remembering how she had last seen Craig in her nightmares. "No... Alex! Pleasedon't you die on me, too!" she continued, while placing her hand over the area in which the warm, thick liquid was oozing out of.

"Jess..." He reached up, touching her tear-dampened cheek. "I...I'll be all right. Really!" he said, while groaning at the pain the bullet was causing him.

"Alex" Craig too hurried over to see about his uncle, as did David. "Are you sure you're all right?"

Looking to his nephew reassuringly, he nodded his head. "Now stop him, Craig. Do whatever you have to, to get him for what he had done to you. Just stop him."

Hearing this, Craig looked to Jessi.

"Do it, Craig. Whatever it takes," she said, choking back the tears.

"I love you, lady," he groaned, looking deeply into her eyes, before reaching over to kiss her one last time, while sending a small amount of electricity through it, as before.

"Mmmm... same here...!" she returned, lovingly.

Backing away, Craig smiled his crooked smile, and looked to the heavens, just as the sky turned dark and stormy, and the thunder roared out all around them. Soon, as the lightning lit across the sky, his spirit had vanished, leaving David and Jessi to tend to the two wounded men.

Meanwhile, downstairs, Tony was making a run for it. "This is crazy...!" he yelled, just as Craig reappeared at the front door, before he could get away.

"*C r a z yy o u t h i n k?*" he yelled back, eerily. "*Y o u t o o k m y l i f e a w a y f r o m m e, a n d n o w I w a n t i t b a c k! B a c k! B a c k!*" he thundered, when throwing another powerful backhand, sending Tony back into the living room, before going on to do it again. Only this time, up against the fireplace, where blood began to trickle from his nose and mouth.

Wiping it away with the back of his hand, Tony asked sarcastically, "Yeah, well, just what are you going to do about it now, you're dead?"

Walking up, Craig glared down at him, "You've heard a life for a life? Well now, meet your maker...!" he growled, shortly, before disappearing.

"Is he out of his mind...?" Tony yelled, looking around the room, wondering what was next.

Upstairs, David looked as though he wanted to go after him.

Sensing this, Alex attempted to get up, when Jessi began to protest against it, "Alex, no...! You shouldn't try to move...! You will just start to bleed again...!"

"I can't just sit here. You're going to need help with Harry," he explained, when turning to David, "As for Craig, I know you feel you owe it to him to do something. But it's his battle now. Tony isn't going far this time. Craig will stop him. He has to in order to finish this war."

"I know," he replied sadly, when Harry began to move.

"Is Tony gone?" he asked.

"Yes," she replied. "He's downstairs."

Pulling himself up to lean against the wall, near the window, Harry told Alex everything. "Captain Storm, David didn't do anything to break the law," he explained, while looking up at David's empty expression. "He really wanted out, and so did I, but..."

"Thanks, Harry," David put in, sadly, while walking over to the window, "but because of what I had done, it doesn't matter much to me anymore," he replied, looking out.

"David, what are you saying?" Alex asked, while David stood there, looking so lost.

"Just that," he said, looking back at him. Then, with a heavy sigh, he turned back to the window to continue looking out.

Meanwhile, downstairs Tony was making a run for the front door once again, when Craig reappeared, cutting off his path.

"No...! This is crazy. You're dead. I killed you...!" he continued yelling, while shaking his head. But then turning, he thought he saw his way out, as he turned to head for the back door. "I'm out of here...!"

"Like hell you are!"

Before he could reach it, Craig summoned up all the power he could gather to bring down the ceiling in the kitchen, not realizing it would weaken the structure for the rest of the house, just to finally stop Tony dead in his tracks.

Looking up at the same time the ceiling, with all its plaster and beams, came crashing down on him, Tony cried out in horror, while covering his head, as the rubble began to pelt him. Then soon, that one beam struck the final blow, silencing him forever.

Soon after the rest of the house began to shake.

"Alex!" Jessi cried out, just as a beam came crashing down toward her.

Seeing this, as he turned away from the window, David threw himself in the path of the beam to knock her out of its way. "Uh!" he groaned, when stricken across the back of the head and shoulder by the heavy two-by-eight, sending him to the floor, rendering him unconscious.

"Oh, my, God! David!" she cried out, as she and Alex rushed over to move the beam off his back.

"David!" Alex called out, while carefully rolling him over. "David! Come on, David, talk to me!"

Not getting anywhere with that, Jessi suddenly saw just how much blood he was losing, when she pulled her hand back from beneath his head. "A…Alex!"

"I know. It looks pretty bad."

"Oh, Craigwhere are you?" she cried, sending out a message to him, while Alex did all he could under the circumstances, while trying to keep his own shoulder from bleeding profusely.

When Craig appeared in the doorway, before she could resume what she had been doing, the room lit up brightly overhead.

Looking up, to see what was going on, everyone saw an angel appear, hovering over them.

Raising her hands, she temporarily slowed time to a near stop, and looked to Craig with her sweet angelic smile, "Craig," she softly spoke, "God has chosen to grant you, David, and even your prayers, Jessi!"

"Me…?" she asked, not thinking clearly. "But I…I don't understand…!"

"It's simple! Craig, you have been praying for a second chance, so that you can be with the one you love. And you, Jessi, you have already lost one love in your life. You too, have been praying for the same thing, to be with Craig."

"But what about David?" Craig asked.

"David has been praying that God would take his life so that you could go on living, as you should have. Craig, to Him, you weren't supposed to have died! And because of the guilt he has had to carry these past two years, his spirit, now, has no will to live! Therefore, Craig, God wants you to continue with your life in David's place. You must hurry, however. Time is running out. This house will be collapsing very soon."

Standing near his best friends' unconscious body, stunned by what he had just learned, he didn't know what to do.

"Craig" Jessi cried. "Please come back to me! I need you. Please!"

"Do it, Craig," Alex spoke up, looking to his nephew. "Come back to us. To Jessi."

"Oh, yes, and Alex," the angel added, "God has plans for you, as well!"

"Me? Why? What have I done?" he asked humbly.

"Because of your willingness to give up your love for Jessi so that your nephew could be with her, God feels that you have sacrificed a lot for the love of your nephew. Not to mention, the love you recently had to forfeit. You too, shall be rewarded," she finished, when turning back to Craig. "It's time, Craig. You must decide, and now. For I can't hold back time much longer."

Looking into Jessi's tear-filled eyes, and then his uncle's, he shook his head. "But, the two of you, you could've had…"

"No, Craig," Alex cut in. "Do it for Jessi. It's you she loves, not me."

"Craig…! P…please…!" she cried, holding out her hand to him. "Don't leave me now…! I…I love you…!"

"All right. What do I have to do?" he asked, while kneeling down next to David.

"The same as before!" she smiled, sweetly, when looking up toward the heavens, as she raised her hands to open the gates for David's spirit to be received. As she did, her wings expanded to their fullest width.

Before long, David's spirit had arisen, and while looking to Craig, he sadly smiled, "I'm sorry for not telling you the truth. And when the time is right, tell mom and dad I just couldn't go on like this anymore. Tell em'…" He stopped to look at the others. "Tell em' that I love them."

"I…I will," he replied sadly.

And with a smile, the two exchanged their last farewells, with Craig entering David's body, as David's spirit left with the Angel, but not without tears from the others, as they watched him go.

Not long after, Craig started to come to, as the house again, began to shake.

"Craig…?" Alex called out his name. "Can you hear me?" he asked, bending down to help him up.

"Y…yes," he replied lightly at first, until he was able to think more clearly. And with their help, he was soon able to stand on his own, as well. "Jess!" he groaned painfully, while turning to look once again into her tear-filled eyes. Doing so, he tried to smile.

"Craig…? Oh, God, Craig, is it really you…?" she asked, touching her hand to his face.

"Yes, beautiful, it's really me," he flinched, while carefully pulling her up into his arms. "Damn…!"

"Are you sure you are all right?" Alex and Jessi both asked.

"Yeah…!" he laughed. "But boy, I sure know I'm alive now…!"

"How's that?" Alex laughed along with him.

"Because… it hurts…!" he continued laughing, while carefully rubbing his head.

"Well, good, I'm glad to see you're okay then," he grinned, while going over to get Harry. "Now, what do you say we get out of here? This place is about to go at any time now."

"Let's do it, then," he agreed.

With Jessi's help, the four of them rushed out of the bedroom, missing all the falling debris and crackling floorboards, as they reached the steps.

"Lord, you guys…!" Alex groaned, seeing the staircase sway, before they attempted to hurry down them.

"We don't have much choice in the matter," Craig returned, while holding Jessi close to him. "How about you?" he asked, feeling her shake, "Can you handle it?"

"Like you said, we don't have a choice in the matter! So let's just hurry," she shivered nervously, while still holding onto his things.

Going down the stairs with bated breath, they reaching the front door, when hearing the sweetest sound ever, coming from outside, the sound of sirens, from the approaching ambulances, as they pulled in.

"Good, they're here," Alex announced, while yanking open the front door. But then, turning back to take one last look at the place, all three of them felt the pain of seeing it go.

Though, just as each one stood there, they saw their own memories flashing back in their minds of all the time they had spent there. Jessi's, were of that stormy day, which had brought her and her girls there to take refuge out of the weather, then seeing Craig for the first time. Adding to that, tossing the cleaning rag at him, when that wonderful smile of his came through to warm her heart. Then all the passion the two had shared. Not to mention, Alex and all they had shared.

As for Alex, the times he and his nephew had spent working on getting the place ready to move into. The times he brought Beth out, and not wanting to think about that horrible day of finding his nephew's body, he thought of more pleasurable things. Like the times Craig stepped into his body, and after, when waking to find Jessi lying so warmly against him. And then their passion and the wrestling match out in the backyard that led to the deep-bedded desire to have her for himself.

And Craig, the memories were so many, but only one seemed to have mattered, and that was Jessi. Finding her on the floor of his room, dazed after having hit her head, and yes, the searing passion the two shared through the willingness of his uncle. *My uncle,* he thought, looking over at him, and sensing all that he must be feeling right about now.

And Harry, well Harry was just a victim in Tony's vengeance like they were.

But then, as if in unison, they all looked back on where the kitchen used to be, only to find the doorway filled with rubble.

"Come on...!" Alex ordered, breaking into everyone's thoughts, as he held Harry up with his good arm. "Let's get out of here...!"

Just as they cleared the front porch, they heard Ted's voice in the crowd, as he, Beth, and now, Jarred, ran up with a few ambulance attendants to take Alex and the others to safekeeping.

However, just as they reached Ted and Jarred's vehicles, they all heard the most horrifying noise ever. For coming from the house was the sound of wood groaning, and glass crackling, as it echoed throughout the air.

Looking back in time to see the roof come crashing down, Ted yelled, shoving everyone out of the way, "Clear the way! It's coming down!"

And so it did. Just as everyone jumped in behind the vehicles, parked out front, suddenly the house, itself, came crashing down all around them, while scattering debris all over the place.

Meanwhile, over at the McMasters, where the others were waiting on Alex, David and Jessi to show up for the Fourth of July cookout, they began worrying, when hearing sirens racing up the road toward Craig's place.

"What on earth...?" Rose cried, as they all got up to head out toward the front of the house, to see what all the commotion was.

Shortly after the ambulance raced by, no sooner had they all gotten out to the road, they heard the most horrifying sound ever coming from the direction of where the ambulances were heading.

"Oh, my, God" both Sue and Rose cried, while looking over at Craig's old place.

"Was that coming from where I think it was?" Bob asked, just as Allen's face went white with horror.

"Dear, God," he cried, hearing the sirens pull up into Craig's front yard, "David!"

"You're right!" Bob shouted, while grabbing Sue's hand, as the others followed. "And if something has gone wrong over there, they're going to be needing us!" he yelled back over his shoulder, while running to their cars.

Heading out first, Bob took the lead.

Meanwhile, back at Craig's place, Ted, still crouched down behind his truck, turned back to others, once all the dust had settled, "Is everyone all right?" he asked, looking over at Jessi first, then Alex. Seeing what had happened to his right shoulder, he called out for a medic, while going over to him, "Alex! Your shoulder! You've been shot!" he began, while scooting around to have a better look at it.

"No. I'm fine, but we need to get Harry and Cra..." He stopped, when realizing what he was about to say, as he saw the look on Ted and Jarred's faces. "I mean David," he corrected, "to the hospital."

"And what about you?" Beth asked, while coming around to look at his shoulder, as well.

"I'll be fine," he smiled up at her. "I just want to get them taken care of first."

"Oh, I think we can fit you into the ambulance, as well," Ted ordered, while flagging down a medic once again. "Get these people over to be checked out," he ordered the young man.

"Yes, sir," the attendant replied, while coming around to take Jessi first, followed by Alex, and then Craig.

As for Harry, he was led to a separate ambulance to be taken in to the hospital under guard, until they could sort out all the details of the shooting.

"Jarred," Alex called out, "how is it that you happened to show up?"

"The Commander called and told me to drop everything, after Ted had already called me. Besides, hearing what was going down, I just had to be here."

"And I'm glad you are," he grinned, while looking to Craig.

"Yeah... I sort of thought you would be," he returned puzzledly, when looking to Beth, who looked more preoccupied with what was going on around her.

Wanting to tell them the news, Alex had more important concerns on his mind, and that was to see to his nephew's injuries. And now, with Jessi and Craig standing at the back of the ambulance, while he was being looked over, Alex looked sadly into her eyes, just as Craig exchanged thoughts with her.

"Go to him. He needs you," he prompted, while nudging her toward his uncle, once they were through with him.

Doing so, she went up to give Alex a hug, before going on to thank him once again for everything he had done.

"You're welcome. However, I should be thanking you!" he grinned, while looking down into her smiling, yet blood smudged, dust covered, and tear-dampened face.

"Oh, Alex..."

"No." He put up a protesting finger to her lips, before looking around them. "Jess," he spoke softly, not wanting to draw any more attention to what had taken place in the house, "it's because of your belief in him that brought him back to us. You're the one who deserves the thanks."

"Captain Storm," the EMT spoke up, "we're ready to see Mr. McMasters now."

"All right," he returned, while getting down out of the back of the ambulance so that they could get Craig checked out.

Just as he got up inside to take a seat, they all heard two other cars pulling in, followed by the sound of doors being closed.

Looking up at his nephew, it was then they both heard familiar voices calling out from the other side of the ambulance. "Alex! Jessi!" both Sue and Bob called out.

Hearing his parents' voices, Craig's expression changed drastically.

"Take it easy," Alex warned, just as Bob and the others rushed around to the back of the ambulance to see who was inside it.

"Are you guys all right?" Bob asked, while looking over Jessi first, and then Alex. When he got to Craig, he suddenly stopped, when looking up into his eyes. Seeing a flicker of pain that wasn't connected

to his son's injuries, Bob swallowed hard at what he had seen. "D...
David...?" he began, "h...how... about you?" he asked, feeling a little
uneasy at first. "A...are you okay?"

"It hurts a lot," he replied, while fighting back the sudden surge of
tears, as Bob went to check out the nasty bump on his head.

"Well," he spoke up, seeing how bad it looked, as he went on to
get into the back of the ambulance with him, "let's get you all over to
the hospital and get these injuries taken care of. Sue..." he called out,
"take the car and follow us. And Rose..." He turned to look at David's
mother, "we can possibly make room in here for you, if you want to
go."

"Allen...?" she looked to her husband questioningly.

"Go ahead," he replied, knowing something was different about
their son, when he reached down into his pocket to bring out a letter
David had written that morning. Shaking his head sadly, he put it back.
"I'll be right behind you."

"Okay."

"Jarred...?" Alex called out, seeing him talking with Beth and a
few other officers.

"Yeah?"

"Get a few guys out to search for Marcose and Baker."

"They're fine," Ted called out, when pointing over toward the fallen
debris.

Seeing the two sifting through the rubble, Alex felt a sense of relief
come over him.

"Yeah," Ted was saying to one of the attendants. "Alex?" he called
out, walking up.

"Yeah?"

"If you're ready, they're wanting to get going."

"All right, let's hit it," he said, as the doors were being closed.

Watching, as the two ambulances pull out, Allen turned to look
back at the house that had once stood there. "What happened here?"
he asked, now seeing what was left of it.

"I don't know," Sue exclaimed, puzzledly. "But we should get going,
they're going to be needing us."

"Yeah. Yeah, you're right," he agreed, turning to head for his car,
while fighting back the tears, until he was alone.

Chapter Forty-Three

Arriving at the hospital, Bob got ready to go into surgery to remove the bullet from Alex's shoulder, while Craig was taken down to X-ray. "How are we doing?" he asked, walking in, in his surgical clothes, while they were getting him prepped.

"Just about ready," the female nurse replied, while taking a pan mixed with blood and dirty water away.

"Good. Alex, as you already know, they'll be in shortly to get an IV hooked up to your arm, and administer the usual stuff, before taking you down to surgery. How are you feeling?"

"Fine, I should be used to this by now."

"Well, yes, but it's always better to try to avoid these things," he explained, while trying to laugh it off. But then seeing Alex's growing concern, he asked, "What's on your mind? Is it the others?"

"Yes. Any word on..." He stopped to keep from saying Craig's name.

"David?"

"Yeah, David."

"He's in, now, getting an X-Ray. We should know something by the time I'm through here with you."

"Good."

Just about that time, the nurse walked back in to administer the IV, while Bob stood by and smiled, knowing how much Alex hated needles.

"Shall we?" he asked, once she was finished, when two male attendants arrived to wheel him down.

"Let's get this over with," he sighed, while feeling the drugs kick in.

With a nod of his head, the attendants released the brakes on the gurney and started for the door. As they went through, the lights in the corridor began to blur, and soon Alex was at the mercy of his brother-in-law. While down in the waiting room, knowing that it was going to be awhile, before anyone was to hear anything, Jessi filled the others in on what she could, while holding the letter Craig had written her.

"And Tony?" Sue began.

"He's dead."

"Thank, God," Rose cried, while looking to her husband, who hadn't said a word, since he had gotten there.

"What about you?" Sue went on, knowing the connection she had with their son, had ended so sadly. "How are you holding up?"

"Me?" She looked off in the direction they had taken Craig in. Turning back she thought sadly of his friend, and what he had given up so that Craig could come back. "How am I holding up?" she questioned. *Like I've just lost...*"

"Jessi, what is it?" both, Sue and Rose asked, seeing a tear running down her cheek, just when an attendant came out with a couple of washcloths and towel so that she could clean off a little, before the others came back.

"Oh, just thinking, is all!" she fibbed somewhat to keep from saying too much, knowing how it would only serve to devastate David's parents, if they only knew what their son had done so Craig could return to them. *Come back,* she thought tearfully, when turning away again, while using the washcloth to cover her face, as the tears came flooding out. *"Oh, Lord... why did someone have to go at all...? Why couldn't they have both made it through this together? Why...?* she cried inwardly, before calling her girls, to let them know she was all right.

Coming over to offer her a shoulder to cry on, Sue and Rose joined her to cry over their loss, as well. Whereas, Allen hid his tears from them, he turned to head for the Hospital Chapel, to cry out his sadness over what David's letter had to say.

Getting there, he pulled it out to read it once again.

Dear Mom and Dad, it began, as the tears fell freely, now.

This comes really hard for me, but you must know that Craig's death was because of my own selfish stupidity. If it hadn't been for me, he would have still been here with us. How can I face myself in the mirror each day, knowing that I had caused it? It hurts too much. It has for far too long now. I'm sorry, Mom, Dad, but what I have to do, I know is going to wind up hurting yet more people. People that I love. And now, even seeing Jessi's love for him, I can't take it any longer. Bob says that there is a way for him to come back, but a very slim one. It sounds kind of crazy, but I have to try it. It's the only way I could ever live with myself. If it works, Craig will be back with those he had left behind because of me. I love you both. Remember that. And remember, how sorry I am for doing this.

All my love
Your son, David

"Oh, David, what have you gone and done now..." he cried into the letter, while sitting there the remaining time in silence.

Meanwhile, back in the waiting room, the others continued mourning over their loss, though different from what only Jessi had known.

"Honey, we're all going to miss him," Rose was saying, while offering to wipe her tears away. "Yet, I know it's going to be harder on you, since the two of you had gotten so close."

"Yes." Jessi had to bite back on her lip to keep from telling her the rest of what she was thinking, at that moment.

"Oh, honey," Sue pulled her back into her arms, as the tears kept coming, "we all have to give it time. It's all going to work out somehow. Just remember, he can rest now. His nightmare is finally over," she sobbed quietly.

"Yes, it is. But not for Rose and Allen," she cried silently. "Listen, I need to call my girls and let them know I'm all right."

"Oh, but I've already done that," Sue replied, when showing her the business card from the Inn, with its number written in bold ink.

"When?"

"On the way here, while you were in the ambulance. Your cousin was so upset over hearing it from them, right after you call the girls, I guess just before it all went down? She's bringing them here to see you, now."

Looking around, Rose asked who she was looking for?

"Beth and the others?" she asked, just when she heard familiar voices coming down the hall, toward the waiting room.

"Ms. Jessi…" Annie called out first, followed by Hank, and then the girls, and her cousin.

"Are you all right?" he asked, seeing the old damp blood on her sweater.

"Oh, that's not mine."

"Alex…?" they asked, worriedly.

"No, but he is in surgery to have a bullet removed from his shoulder. It was Harry's, when Tony shot him. I had to pretend that he was dead, and that I was hit to fool Tony so…" She stopped at what had happened, when shaking her head. "Well, we can talk about it later, if you don't mind."

"Mom," Lora came around to hug her, as did Cassi.

"I'm fine! Really!"

"Are you coming home right after you get done here?" Cassi asked.

"Not just yet, sweetie. I have something I need to do first. And I have to find Max."

"Max…! Where is he?" Lora asked.

"At the farmhouse, or what's left of it."

"And Tony?" they asked.

"Dead." She left it at that until another time.

"Hey, cousin," Jodi came over to sit next to her, when Sue got up to check on the others. "Are you going to be all right?" she asked, knowing about the story.

"Yeah." Turning, she looked to Jodi and gave her one of those 'I'll tell you later' looks.

"Okay. For now, how about I just take the girls back with me, and you can call when you get back to the Inn."

"That sounds great. Girls," she turned.

"We heard," they replied disappointedly.

"Do you mind?"

"No. She has us helping out in the shop," Cassi smiled quietly.

Laughing, just as they heard Beth and Jarred coming back, Jodi said her goodbyes, and took the girls over to wait on the elevator. After getting on, and the doors were closing, Jarred walked by, glancing in, when he thought he had seen someone he knew.

Seeing this from the doorway of the waiting room, Jessi asked what that was about, when he came walking in with a look of puzzlement on his face.

"It's probably nothing. I just though I saw someone I knew."

"Did you ever see my girls while you were at the shin dig?"

"Yes. Was that them getting on the elevator?"

"Yes, with my cousin. They will be staying with her until I get back to the Inn,"

"Speaking of the Inn," Hank spoke up. "We should be getting back there to keep an eye on it. Is there anything you want us to tell the others?"

"Just that I'll be back soon. And that I'm fine."

"Okay."

Giving her a hug, Annie and Hank were out of there. And not all too soon, when what seemed like hours, a nurse came walking out to let them know that everything was all right with Captain Storm.

"He's in recovery now, waiting on the anesthesia to wear off."

"And the bullet?" Beth asked fretfully.

"Doc. Matthews got it out," she smiled, while turning to Sue. "Your brother was lucky, as usual," she continued, having known Doctor Matthews, Sue, and especially Alex, for all the times he had been in and out of surgery for gunshot wounds.

"Yes, and one of these days," she laughed, shaking her head, "he's going to get the better of me."

"Oh, and David," Rose asked, worriedly. "How is my son?"

"He'll be all right. Doc. Matthews is in with him now. He just has to finish sewing him up a little."

"How bad is he?" Jessi asked, holding back even more tears for her man.

"Not too bad," she exclaimed, just before walking away.

"Thank, God," she cried quietly, while turning away, once again to hide her concern.

Shortly after getting started on Craig, getting a call from a nurse in Recovery, Bob left one of the nurses to finish up for him so that he could go back and check on Alex.

"Hey, there," he called out, while walking in through the swinging doors, "just what do you think you're doing there?"

"I can't stay here like this," he groaned groggily, while reaching out for his blood-covered shirt, "I've got to see about..." He stopped to look back at his brother-in-law, "D...David! Is he..."

"All right?" Bob questioned, puzzledly. "Yes. He'll have to take it easy for a few days, but he should bounce back all right. However, you're my main concern. You shouldn't be rushing around like this. That shoulder of yours still has a ways to go to heal. Not to mention, you have lost a lot of blood, to boot."

"I'll be fine. What about..." he started to say, when he suddenly dropped down against the bedside table, at the pain that just wrenched through his shoulder, as he went to put his arm in through the sleeve.

"Yeah, sure you are. Now, how about I give you a hand here. Or better yet, we get you a different top to wear out of here," he offered, while picking up a blue and white sling to keep Alex's arm mobile.

"No, this will do until I get back to my Blazer, where I have some clothes still in it."

"Fine." After putting on the sling, he asked, while making a few last minute adjustments, "How does it feel?"

"Fine," he groaned, when the nurse walked back in, carrying his service revolver and shoulder holster.

"Captain Storm!" she smiled, handing it over to him.

"Thanks," he grinned, taking it.

"Why don't I just hold onto that for you," Bob offered, while taking it out of his hand. "You won't be able to wear it for awhile, yet."

Nodding his head, the two walked out to join the others, when Rose had just returned with Allen.

"Alex..." Sue cried, as she went up to give her brother a tear-filled hug.

"I'm going to be fine. No serious damages," he smiled.

"Good...!" she nearly yelled, as he pulled back to see the look of worry on Jessi's face.

"Hey..." He went over to hold her against his good shoulder. "He's going to be fine."

"He has to be," she whispered, while fighting back yet, more tears. "He just has to be."

"He will be," he smiled, while holding her warmly, until seeing Beth standing off by his other nephew.

"Alex…" she cried, when coming to give him a hug too.

"Hey there, save one for me!" Jarred grinned, coming up to shake his good hand.

"Well, if you will excuse me," Bob spoke, while clearing his throat. "I had a nurse finish up on David, as I had gotten a call, telling me that our tough Detective here was starting to come to a lot sooner than expected."

"Oh…?" Sue laughed.

"Well, I had things to do!" he laughed, while looking over into Jessi's glistening eyes.

"Oh, Alex." With her own warm smile, she reached around to give him another hug. "I'm just glad that you're all right."

"Me, too," he returned happily. "Me, too."

Smiling, Bob walked away to check on David, while the others went to take a seat.

"Alex," Jessi spoke up, asking, "do you really think he's going to be all right?"

Picked up on her concern for their son, Rose asked, "Jessi, what is it, dear?"

"I was just worried about David, is all," she exclaimed, when looking up to see everyone looking at her so intently.

"Oh?" Allen asked, suspiciously.

"Yes," she returned, looking then to Alex, who was wondering himself, what was on Allen's mind.

"Allen, it's only natural to be concerned," he put in. "After all, he took a pretty bad hit on the back of the head. We're both just worried that he may have gotten a concussion out of it."

"Yes, I know," he went to say, when then hearing the door to the waiting room open.

Turning, everyone stood, seeing Bob and Craig come walking in to join them.

"Bob?" Rose spoke up, seeing her son, as Jessi pulled away from Alex, when wanting to go to him, but knew better not to, at least not at that time.

"Well, aside from some bumps and bruises along with that one nasty cut, he'll be all right," he explained.

"Good," she and Allen sighed.

Turning to see Jessi's growing concern, he smiled, while looking deep into her troubled eyes, when he went on to surprise himself, by still being able to reach out telepathically to tell her that he was all right.

"I'm glad, I was really frightened," she returned, while still clinging tightly to the letter he had written her.

"And you?" he turned to his uncle.

"I'm fine," he replied, while quietly welcoming his nephew back with a brotherly hug.

"Thanks, Alex," he returned quietly.

"Well, we're glad you guys are okay," Sue smiled, while giving them each a hug. However, when it came to hugging Craig, something suddenly occurred to her, when he returned her hug. There was something undoubtedly different about it. *'That's odd!'* she cried to herself. *'That isn't like David to hug me quite like that! It's like... like...'* she thought. *'No... I'm just imagining things,'* she continued, while looking up at him, and yet, wondering if it could be. *'But no, how could it be?'* she asked, when seeing his pain-filled expression, when he looked down at her.

"Oh, Mom..." he cried to himself, while wanting so desperately to tell her that he was back and to say he had missed them.

"Well," Bob spoke up, interrupting the moment, while taking his stethoscope off from around his neck to place down into his jacket pocket, "what do you say we get out of here and get these three cleaned up?"

"Sure," they all agreed, while heading out of the waiting room.

On the way out, Rose asked if anyone was hungry.

"Starving!" both Alex and Craig laughed, while unaware of Bob's reaction to hearing his own son's familiar laughter.

"Well then, let's go on back to the house. The food is already cooked. All we have to do is warm it up."

And so headed out, but not Bob, as he hung back a little to study David. And like Sue suspected, there was something different about him. *Very,* he thought puzzledly.

"Bob... are you coming?" Sue asked.

"Yeah. Yeah, I'm coming."

Reaching their car, the three were invited to ride back with the McMasters, while Sue and Bob followed in silence. As for Jarred and Beth, they followed in separate vehicles, while having been invited to join them.

On their way back, though, Alex asked to be dropped off at the farmhouse. "They should be done going over it by now," he explained.

"What on earth do you need there, other than your vehicles?" Allen asked, while looking back in his rearview mirror at them.

"Jessi's dog," he explained, while looking beside him, where she sat, while quietly being held by Craig.

"I hope I can still find him," she wondered, sounding worried.

"We will," Craig replied, as he uncomfortably turned to look out the window, when they pulled up to his old place.

Looking over at him, while noting his expression, Alex leaned in to ask quietly, "Are you okay with stopping by here so soon?"

"Yeah, I'll be fine. Besides, it isn't like I won't be able to leave here, again!"

"Craig…!" Jessi nearly yelled beneath her breath.

"I'm sorry, that had to have sounded pretty bad," he laughed, while giving her a silent hug, before getting out to check on their vehicles.

About that time, Sue and Bob pulled up behind them, as did the others. "Alex…" Sue called out, "what are you doing here?"

"We're here to get my Blazer, and to try and find her dog," he called back.

"Oh. All right. We'll see you guys over at the house then?" she asked.

"Sure."

"Hey, Alex," Jarred called out, tiredly, "Beth called to let us know that she's going on back to the Inn to get some sleep."

"What about you? Are you going on over?"

"Yeah. I'll see you guys when you get there," he waved, while pulling away.

"Well, where do we start?" Alex asked, looking over the area, when at that very moment they heard the familiar sound of Jessi's dog running up, when hearing their voices.

"Max" Jessi cried out, happily, while dropping to her knees to give him a hug, "you're okay!"

"He should be!" Craig smiled, while kneeling down next to her. "Oh...?"

"Yeah, I sent him out, before things started to get a little too hot."

"Thank you," she cried, while reaching her hand over to give him a light kiss.

"Mmmm... you had better be careful," he teased, as his eyes twinkled with joy at the thought of being able to really hold her whenever he wanted.

"Oh, yeah...!" she grinned, threateningly.

"Mmmm..." he groaned, seeing how he was going to enjoy his life again.

At that time, the two stood back up to see Alex at his Blazer.

"How is it?" Craig asked,

"It's still drivable," he announced, while the two of them walked over to her truck that sat in next to his Blazer, while having to climb over a heap of boards and siding to get to it. "Oh, and Craig...!" he spoke up, seeing how it was safe to call him by his real name.

"Yeah?"

"I should warn you," he laughed. "She likes to claw."

"Hmmm, I'll have to keep that in mind," he laughed, when turning back to Jessi with his warm crooked smile on his face. "What do you say, we come back here later after we're done?"

"Yeah... I'd like that," she replied, while looking back over at where the house used to stand, only to see yellow police tape and a pile of rubble. "Besides, I'm going to really miss this place, and the times you and I had spent getting to know each other here. And yes, even..." She stopped to feel the heat of their love coming back, as it wanted to be renewed.

"I know," he smiled, while picking up her thoughts, when feeling his own desire for her building back up inside him. "Someday we'll get all this cleaned up, and maybe even rebuild it," he suggested, while holding her up against him in the growing darkness of the evening sky.

"We sure will," Alex added, when coming around to join them, while they looked on at what remained of Craig's old place. Which at that time, was one part of his old room at one side of the house, and the fireplace at the other side. "Oh, and that reminds me," Alex spoke back up, "What about David's truck?" he asked, looking over at it.

Doing the same, though with a sickening feeling, when remembering what all had happened when he drove it last, putting his hand down into David's pants pocket, he pulled out a set of keys, realizing then they were the same set he had used before.

"Are you all right?" Jessi asked, when seeing his face go grim.

"Yeah," he laughed sadly, while Alex went back over to get into his Blazer. "I'll just come back and get the truck later."

"Craig," Alex called out, having heard his nephew, "there's no real rush on getting it. Just when you are ready, it'll still be here."

"Yeah, just like it was then."

Alex and Jessi both shook their heads at what he was going through, but knew he had to put it all behind him, himself, though, with their help. Meanwhile, starting up his vehicle, Alex turned to the two of them, "Hey, see you two over at Rose's, okay…?"

"We'll be there shortly," Jessi called back, as he put the Blazer into gear, and began the chore of pulling away, while having to drive over a few boards to leave the two alone to take in all that had happened on their own.

But then, remembering she was still covered in blood, dust and filth, Jessi reached in to pull out her suitcase.

"What?" he asked, seeing what she was doing.

With a laugh, she said, "I can't go anywhere like this! I've got to get a shower first. That's if it still works."

"It should!" he exclaimed, when going over to check it out, while she went to dig out everything she would need.

Seeing how it was still working, she set off to take her shower, while he hung back to look over the area, knowing how much he was going to miss the house. "Well, Max," he groaned, while pulling the tailgate of her truck down to take a seat on it, when Max jumped up to check this new body of his out. Laughing, he patted him on the shoulder, "Yes, boy, it's still me," he continued, while seeing the dog's confused expression, when he finally gave in to the new Craig.

Meanwhile, it wasn't long before she reached over to turn off the water, before stepping out into the moonlight to get dressed and towel-dry her hair. At that point, she turned back to look over at him, and then smiled at seeing he had on his old work shirt, which she had worn so often.

"What?" he spoke up, interrupting her thoughts.

"Hmmm…?" she asked, while coming over to join him.

"You're holding out on me."

"Oh, and what makes you so sure about that?" she asked, smiling up at him

"The look on that pretty face of yours. What were you just thinking?"

"Just how nice that shirt looks on you!" she smiled even more. But then a thought did come to her that he would surely hear. *"Our thoughts! We can still hear each other's thoughts? I thought at the hospital, it was just some kind of fluke. But it can't be, when we can still hear each other. What does that mean?"*

Surprised, too, he smiled, *"Yes, well it seems that we certainly do still have that ability!"*

"Yes, but for me, knowing right after meeting you that I have a gift, those things just don't go away!"

"Yes, but I didn't have this gift, as you call it, before I died. And now…"

"Maybe there's a reason why we have it still! Meanwhile, that shirt on you looks…" she smiled down at it.

"Oh, yeah, a little big?" he laughed, speaking more normally, while looking at the shirt, too. "Yeah, but it'll work!"

Taking the time, the two looked again back over at where the house had stood, before getting into the truck to leave.

"Mmmm…" she cringed at the thought of Tony's body being buried beneath the rubble.

"Thinking about Tony?"

"Yes…!" she shivered, when turning away.

"They'll find him."

"I know. It's…"

"Just what shape he'll be in when they do?"

"Uh huh!"

"I don't know. But I'm sure Alex will get it all taken care, before we ever start rebuilding this place."

"Craig?" She looked up at him.

"Yes?"

"Can we have it the way it was?"

"Sure! Just the way it was," he smiled warmly, while holding her for a little while longer.

With a sigh, they knew they had to be going, when letting go of each other to close the tailgate, while Max remained in the back of the truck.

Meanwhile, going around to open the driver side door for her, he stopped her, before she had gotten in, "Jess?"

"Yes?" She stopped to look up at him again.

"I wish we didn't have to go, just yet."

"I know, but we have to!" she exclaimed, sympathetically, while seeing how all of this was still bothering him.

"Yeah, it's just facing them, is what's bothering me." And with a heavy sigh, he shook his head, while the two climbed on into the truck, with him sitting in behind the wheel.

Starting it up, he carefully maneuvered it out around the broken glass and debris. And once he got it over to where the old driveway that led up to the garage was, heading out onto the road, the two rode the brief distance in silence, until pulling into the driveway of the McMasters place, where they could hear the sound of laughter coming from the patio out back.

Meanwhile, pulling up alongside Alex's Blazer, Craig saw Jarred's motorcycle, instead of his truck.

"Whose bike is that?" Jessi asked, looking it over.

"Jarred's? But I thought he came right over in his truck!"

"He must have run home and got it."

"Yeah."

"Nervous?" she asked.

"Very. I just wish we could sit here for a few more minutes, before joining them."

"That would be nice, but..."

He laughed. "I guess not, huh?"

"Nope!"

Turning to look into her caring eyes, he asked, "How am I going to pull this off? When all I want to do is go up to my own parents and tell them I'm back!"

"I know this isn't going to be easy, but you're going to have to try!"

"But how? And suppose they ask me something that only David knows?"

"Either change the subject or just say you forgot!" she shrugged.

"Sure, that'll work for awhile, but then what?" he asked, while turning to shake his head, and staring out at the house, before reaching for the door handle.

"Well… you can always smile and say you haven't been yourself lately!" she said, when suddenly laughing at the reaction her last comment had gotten from him.

Shaking his head even more, he cracked up laughing too.

Chapter Forty-Four
'Two for the price of one'

Meanwhile, sitting out in the backyard, while enjoying the smell of the steaks cooking on the grill, Jarred was laughing along with the others at some of the stories told about the last two cookouts Alex and Jessi had been to. "You must have really enjoyed that?" he laughed at Alex's expense, when hearing how Jessi gave him the heave-ho, not once, but several times into the pool.

"Yes, well, she has that knack of getting under ones skin." he grinned.

Having just heard a truck pull in a few minutes prior, Bob asked, while setting his iced tea down to get up, "Did I just hear someone pull in?"

"Sure sounded like it," Alex replied.

"Well, let's go and see if that was them," he suggested, heading off to go around the side of the house.

"We'll be right there," Alex returned, while he and Jarred got up. But then stopping his nephew, he turned back to motion toward the others.

"What?" he asked, seeing the look on his uncle's face. "Alex," he lowered his voice, "does this have something to do with what happened back at Craig's place earlier?"

"What do you know about that?"

"Not much. But let's face it, you've been acting pretty strange, since you guys came running out of the house, just before…"

Cutting him off, he took Jarred off to the side to tell him what he could, without raising too much suspicion.

In the meantime, not feeling anymore calmer about seeing the others, Craig started once again for his door handle. "Well, I guess we should be getting out, huh?"

"Yes, I guess we should."

No sooner had they gotten the words out, they heard footsteps coming up from around the side of the garage. When then she saw his father coming toward them, while wearing a warm, yet, nervous smile on his face.

But why, she wondered, while keeping her thoughts to herself.

"Hey, I see the two of you have finally made it. Are you going to come and join us, or just sit there all night?"

Laughing nervously, Craig and Jessi got out to greet him, while walking around to the front of her truck. "Yes, well I guess we should be getting on back there then, shouldn't we?" he laughed, while putting an arm around Jessi, when not thinking that she and David's relationship wasn't all that close.

In doing so, Bob stopped short, while looking at him even more suspiciously. "Just a minute," he called out, before going on any further. "Before we go back, there is something that's been bugging me here recently."

"Oh? What's that?" he asked, while looking to Jessi for help.

"There's something here that is definitely different about you, and I can't quite put my finger on it. But ever since this morning, and after the accident over at the farmhouse, you even seem different, somehow. Now," he pulled back a little to place a hand on Craig's good shoulder, "I know the difference between David and Craig's walk. And at the hospital I noticed something else, too!" He stopped, to see the expression on Craig's face change, realizing he must have hit on something. *'Especially when Craig turns to Jessi. As though communicating amongst themselves, as they had in the past!'* he speculated to himself for a moment.

Looking into her loving eyes, he cried out, *"Oh, God, he knows...!"*

"Yes, Craig, he knows," she smiled inwardly. *"You can't hide who you are."*

"And son," he went on, knowing he had something, "when you and Alex were laughing at the hospital, it wasn't David's laughter I was hearing. It was Craig's. Plus, all this time you had never called Rose or

Allen, mom or dad. Nor have you referred to Sue and I, as Uncle Bob or Aunt Sue. And judging now by the expression on your face, I'm right, aren't I? Correct me if I'm wrong, son, but..." he cried, hearing those words coming out of his own mouth, not once, but twice, "you aren't David, are you?" he asked, demanding now to know the truth, as the tears of pain brimmed to the surface. "Please... tell me the truth!"

"No, Dad. It's true. I...it is me... Craig," he replied sadly, as he too started to cry.

"Dear, sweet, Jesus!" Bob cried out, while pulling his son into his embrace, when they both began to cry.

"I've missed you, Dad...! God, how I've missed you...!" he sobbed.

"I've missed you too, son. I've missed you too!" he repeated, just as Alex came walking up, with Jarred coming along anyway.

Seeing the reunion, he asked, when placing an arm around Jessi, "He knows, doesn't he?"

"Can you believe it!" she smiled in return.

"Wow, Bob has his son back," Jarred smiled too, while getting in on the excitement, once he had grasped onto what Alex was telling him, while the others were busy getting things ready.

"Yep," Alex grinned. "And he needs his son, as well as my sister does. Although I feel bad for Rose and Allen, but Bob and Sue have gone through a lot in the past two years, too."

"I know," Jarred replied, while looking on at the two of them.

Turning just then to interrupt the others, Bob spoke up, "Let's go eat."

Dropping his arm from around Jessi, Alex went to join the others, as they headed on back to the backyard, with the exception of Jessi, who suddenly felt out of place, as she chose to stay behind with her dog.

"Oh, Max, I wish I knew what to do!" she cried, while going around to the side of the truck to fondle his fur, when he came over to sit near her. But then, she stopped when hearing Alex calling out to her.

"Hey, aren't you coming?" he asked, when seeing that she wasn't following along.

"Sure, I'll be there soon! I just want to see to Max first," she fibbed, while feeling as though she ought to leave and give Craig some time with his family.

"All right."

"Yeah, right…" She turned back to continue to cry quietly, while not realizing she wasn't going to be alone for long. "Max, what do think? Should we just get out of here and go on back to the Inn? I don't want to get in the way of their reunion!" she cried, when suddenly feeling like that part of her life was over, and now it was time to move on.

"Would you really do that?" came a voice from behind her. "Would you really just leave here without saying anything to me?"

Turning, she looked back to see Craig standing there, looking so bewildered. "No…" she returned, as her tears began to fall freely now, "I could never really just leave without saying goodbye to you. I just didn't want to be in the way of your happy reunion!"

"You're not in the way, Jess," he replied, while holding out his hand to her. "Come with me," he smiled, when pulling her into his arms, to look deeply into her tear-filled eyes. "I promise, we won't stay too long. It's just that I want to be alone with you, as soon as we can leave, that is."

"All right!" She smiled at a thought she was having, when they started to head back to the cookout, with Max jumping out of the back of the truck to tag along.

"Oh, yeah…?" he laughed, while stopping long enough to bring her back up into his arms to place a light kiss on her nose. "Sounds good to me!"

"That's not fair!" she laughed, while smacking his arm playfully. "You weren't supposed to hear that."

"Well then, stop thinking about it so hard," he continued laugh as he bent down to kiss her desirable lips.

"Oh, Craig…" she moaned, when feeling herself wanting him. "Mmmm…"

"I know, but we have to be getting back there so that the others don't start thinking you and David are an item. But darn… I don't know just how much longer I'm going to be able to behave myself."

"You won't if I have anything to do with it," she returned telepathically, while heading on back to join the others.

"Oh… Lady…" he warned, while feeling the blood pounding in his veins for her again, *"you had better behave yourself if you know what's good for you."*

"Wooo... I'm shaking in my shoes...!"

"You will when I get a hold of you."

And misbehave she did, while deliberately sending him seductive messages all through the meal, when finally Rose spoke up, "David, are you feeling all right?"

"Huh? Na, I'm just a little tired, is all. I think I'll call it a night," he replied. "If you all will excuse me." Turning back to Jessi, he asked for a ride back over to the farmhouse to get his truck, while with every intention of being alone with her. "Would you mind?" he asked, while controlling his own thoughts from going out to her.

"I suppose I could," she smiled, while getting up to leave, as well.

"You know you're going to get it, when we're alone!"

"Oh, yeah...?" she thought smiling.

"David, make sure you call us tomorrow," Allen called out, interrupting their thoughts.

"All right," he returned, while heading out after saying their goodbyes.

Turning to his wife, Bob whispered, "Sue, you have to watch this. Watch the way he walks, and listen to his laugh without looking at him."

"Bob!" she protested quietly, while thinking of her own earlier encounter at the hospital.

"Please...! Just listen," he pleaded, before turning to their son, "Hey, David!"

"Yeah?"

"Where are you staying tonight?"

Without thinking, he answered, "I'll be at the Inn visiting with Jessi and Alex," he teased, as that grin of his became obvious to some of them.

Right then, Sue's face paled, when seeing her son's crooked grin. "Bob..." she cried quietly, "what are you trying to say?"

"Come with me and see for yourself!" he told her in a hushed-like manner, while getting up to take her hand. "We'll be right back, folks, we're just going to see them off," he explained, while looking to Alex.

With a nod of his head, along with Jarred, they knew it was meant to keep Allen and Rose occupied for a few minutes longer.

"Rose!" Jessi called out. "I'll call you."

"All right!"

Heading around to the side of the garage, Sue continued to protest, as the two caught up to the others, "Bob, this is crazy," she continued, in a lower voice, so as not to arouse suspicion, once they reached the driveway.

"Then ask him," he said, when stopping Craig and Jessi near her truck.

Turning slightly to face his mother, she looked at him, tearfully, "I...is it true? Are you..." she began, but couldn't. Turning back to her husband, she cried, "I can't do this. I just can't!"

"But..." he began, when looking back to his son. "It's up to you, then," he pleaded. "You have got to tell her the truth."

Craig too could feel the pain, she was feeling, at that moment, when she turned to start for the backyard, while hoping to put some distance between them, when her own tears began to fall.

At that moment, he looked to Jessi.

With a nod, she smiled. "Tell her, Craig."

Nodding as well, he agreed, while turning back, before his mother could get too far.

"Mom..." he called out, tearfully. "I..." he stopped when she did.

"Tell her," Jessi coaxed.

Watching as her back tensed up, he went up quietly to tell her what he had been wanting to, since seeing her at the hospital. "Mom...!" he said it again, once he had gotten closer to her, "I love you...!" he whispered.

Slowly turning back to look up at him, the tears ran down her cheeks. "No...!" she cried, looking into her son's eyes. Yet, seeing that familiar glimmer of his spirit shining through, she cried out again, while slowly shaking her head, "I...it can't be!"

"Yes, Mom, it's me."

"But..."

"It's our son all right," Bob spoke up. "You heard his laugh, and saw his crooked smile. Heck, you even saw the way he walks! Good, Lord, woman, I saw the look on your face. Jessi and Alex had even seen it all happen!"

"I don't understand...!" she continued to cry, while holding a hand up to Craig's face to study it.

"David came to me," Bob went on to explain, "one day, not too long ago, to ask if it were possible for Craig to come back. I didn't pay much attention at first, until I overheard him praying."

"Mom..." Craig broke down, taking her hand in his, "I didn't know David was in so much trouble. These past two years, I've been praying to end this nightmare. Then I met Jessi the night it stormed out here. At that moment, I knew I had to pray to get my life back. I had no idea, it was going to be in David's shoes, though!"

"Oh, my, Craig...?" she cried out, taking her son into her arms, while sobbing the whole time through. "When you hugged me at the hospital, I somehow knew then, but I didn't dare hope. And if it weren't for your unique smile, I would have not known it now!"

At that, they all started to laugh.

"Wait. What about Aunt Rose and Uncle Allen?" he asked.

"What about us?" Allen spoke up, when coming up to hand Sue, David's letter. "We've known for some time that David has been eaten up with guilt over Craig's death. Craig was like a son to us, too!" he stated, angrily. "David... I mean, Craig, when I saw you in the back of that ambulance, you seemed different somehow. Something in your eyes said it all. And yes, even your smile. That is one thing no one could ever copy. And we all are very happy to have you back with us. It's just seeing you as David that's going to take some getting used to."

"Rose. Allen," Jessi spoke up, "for two years, you have both suffered right along with Craig's parents. Now look at him, you both have your son's here," she smiled ever so brightly.

"Mama Rose," he spoke up with a light laugh in his voice, at how he had always referred to her as Mama Rose, "David's spirit is finally at peace with himself. He had even asked that I tell you both how happy he is now, and that he loves you very much."

"Thanks, dear. It means a great deal knowing he's happy," she cried, as Jessi walked up to lend a loving shoulder.

Looking for a way to cheer up the subject, he laughed at just how David had neglected his body. "Yeah, well, now it's time, to put some weight back on this body of his. He has really let it go," he announced, as everyone started laughing along with him. "One more thing, though," the tone in his voice went serious.

"What is it?" Sue asked worriedly.

"It's okay, Mom," he said, seeing her concern, as he gave her a reassuring hug. "I would just like to hold a quiet memorial service at my old place for David, as soon as we can get it cleaned up."

"Thank you," Rose and Allen both said, while going over to give him a hug for his thoughts.

"I still plan on calling you mom and dad, though, if you don't mind."

"We would really love that," Allen replied tearfully.

"I guess now this means I have two birthdays, huh?" he smiled childishly.

"Listen to you," Sue and Rose both laughed.

"Yes, well," Allen added, "I could still use some help out in the field."

"No problem," he announced, turning to Jessi with a warm smile. "I'll be glad to, right along with my future wife, here."

"We pretty much figured that out," Bob laughed. "The two of you couldn't keep your eyes off each other throughout dinner tonight."

"And I knew that she was in love with you," Rose went on to explain. "Because, I tried to fix her up with Alex."

"But then he told us her heart belonged to someone else," Sue added, while going over to take Jessi's hand.

Looking fondly into her eyes, Craig interjected his own thoughts, "Well, she is a very special and gifted lady. She found me and stuck by me all the way. It wasn't easy, and her own life was in danger, as well, but she never gave up."

"That's for sure," Alex laughed, while putting in his own two cents at seeing her blush.

"Alex…!"

"Well, it's true! You're the most stubbornness, bull headed woman around. She had even told Tony off at the Inn. Heck, I even thought she was going to beat him to a pulp right where he stood!"

"Oh, and I wanted to," she announced, while looking up at Craig.

"Well now," Alex offered, seeing their longing expression, "I have a feeling these two have some catching up to do," he teased, while patting Craig carefully on the shoulder, so as not to hurt it anymore than it already was. "Take it easy you two. I'll see you when you're ready to start working on the farmhouse. And as for our unfortunate friend, we'll get that all taken care of first thing in the morning."

"Thanks, Alex," he replied, thinking of where Tony's body was last seen, before the house had come crashing down on him. Looking down on Jessi, he blocked out that thought, not wanting to upset her.

"That reminds me," Bob spoke up. "What are you going to do now with that place?"

"We're going to rebuild it," Craig said proudly.

"What...? What on earth for?" Sue asked.

"So that we can have a place to come to from time to time. You know, to take a break from work," Jessi exclaimed, while smiling at the memories the two, correction, three had created there.

"It also looks like we'll be building some cabins soon, too," Craig announced. "That's if I can get Uncle Alex and Jarred's help on it," he smiled over at the two.

"Hey, I wouldn't miss it," Jarred grinned broadly. "And for the record, welcome back, cuz'," he teased, while going up to give him a big, but gentle, brotherly hug.

Interrupting, Rose added, "Well, enough is enough, we could go on all night, but I can see we have some sleepy eyed people here who need to get home."

"Make sure you call us in the morning, though," Allen added.

"Allen, let them rest! They've had a rough day!" his wife chided.

"Thanks, Rose," Jessi replied, as she and Craig turned to put Max back into the back of the truck, before getting in.

Meanwhile, going up to give them one last hug, Alex stopped them, before they could get in. "I'll see you both later. And thanks for everything, Jess," he added quietly, while putting an arm around her, especially. "I won't ever forget what you have put yourself through for my nephew."

"And I won't ever forget everything that you have done, either," she replied, while fighting back the tears, when knowing just how much she was going to miss the times they had spent together, as well.

After saying their goodbyes, Jarred came up to lay a kind hand on Alex's good shoulder, "Well, Uncle, he's one lucky guy," he smiled.

"Yeah. That he is," he grinned, knowing right where the two were going, once they had left there. "Yep, that... he is."

And that they did. Once they were on their way, Craig turned to Jessi, while taking a hold of her hand, "Are you up for a walk?" he asked, nearing his old driveway.

"Sure."

Bringing her truck to a stop once they pulled in, he switched off the ignition and carefully got out to go around to open her door. "I know a spot that we can sleep out under the stars if you want to," he suggested, while grabbing his old blankets out of the back, along with her dog.

"That sounds wonderful," she replied, happily, as the two headed down a different trail with Max in the lead.

Thinking after everything they had gone through, she just wanted to cuddle up with him, and never, ever, have to say goodbye again. But then, suddenly, after walking a little further down the trail, she came to a sudden stop, while looking around her.

Turning to look up into his smiling eyes, when he grinned down at her, she couldn't believe what she saw. "Craig...!"

"I know," he replied, unable to help but smile that much more, when knowing what she was thinking. "In a dream?"

"Oh, Craig!" she laughed, while throwing her arms around his shoulders.

"Do you like it here?" he asked softly, while pulling back to lift her chin up to look into her eyes.

"Like it? Why, yes!" she returned, just as he went to claim her lips tenderly, before pulling away to lay out one of the blankets for them to lay on, and the other to cover them if it were to get chilly out, near an old oak tree, while listening to a babbling brook all night long.

Afterwhich, taking her hands, he led her over onto the blanket, where they kicked off their shoes, never once taking their eyes off each other.

"Jessi," he whispered tenderly, "now that I really have you in my life, will you marry me?"

"Oh, Craig, you will always have me in your life," she replied, warmly, with tears of happiness just waiting to come out. However, pulling out his note from her pocket, she placed it in his hand.

Looking down at it, he smiled, seeing that she still had it with her.

"And the answer..." she went on playfully.

"Yes?" he asked, already knowing her answer.

"Craig...!" she scolded, when picking up on his thoughts.

"Sorry. Old habits, you know?"

"Mmmm... don't I ever," she smiled warmly.

"And the answer?" he asked again.

"Is... yes. Yes, Craig, I'll marry you," she replied, while running her fingers lightly up his taut stomach to his slightly masculine chest, causing a small rise from him.

"Remember what I had warned you about, lady. You had better be careful," he laughed, as that warm, crooked smile of his lit up her heart once again.

"Oh? Remind me again, won't you?" she teased.

"All right. Let's just say that if you keep this up, it might get something started. You know what that was like up at the shower."

"Oh... yes, I do, and as for now..." she smiled coyly, when looking up into his deep blue eyes, while slowly unfastening each button of his blue flannel shirt, "I sure... hope so, Matthews. I sure... hope so..."

With that, he pulled her up into his arms to claim her lip hungeringly.

Epilogue

One month later, following Craig and Jessi's wedding, Alex was wrapping up on the last of Tony Belaro's case in his office, down at Headquarters.

"Well, that takes care of that!" he announced, closing his briefcase, before getting up.

"Yep!" Ted agreed, while kicking back on the sofa to stretch out his arms. "Tony's body has been found, and removed from the rubble, and Harry has been released, pending a trial. Do you think he'll go straight?"

"I hope so."

"Well, at least for now, we can relax."

"Yeah, relax," he grumbled, looking at the wedding picture of Craig and Jessi, sitting out on his desk. *You're one lucky guy, Craig,* he groaned inwardly, when thinking of the times he himself had held such a beautiful woman in his arms, and yes, even made love to her. And then again, not to mention, all those times his nephew had loved her through his body. *Man...!*

"She sure is beautiful, isn't she?" Ted asked, while breaking into Alex's thoughts, when coming up to stand beside him. "When you told me what all took place in Craig's room...! Man...!"

"Now you know."

"Yes, and what a love those two shared, and still to this day."

Just then, their peaceful moment was interrupted, when a call came in for Alex. Not taking it himself, Ted picked it up to see what it was about.

Suddenly, stumbling back to the sofa, his expression went totally grave, as he hung up.

"What is it?" Alex asked, when looking back over at his friend.

"God, not again…!" he cried, shaking his head.

Getting to his feet, Ted grabbed Alex's arm to head for the door.

"What the hell is going on?" he demanded, while pulling back.

"It's happened again."

"What…?"

"Delgado. He's gotten out."

"Damn…! I've got to get to Jarred…!" he groaned, while reaching for the phone.

"Alex," Ted stopped him. "H…he isn't there!"

"What…?" Suddenly seeing the look of anguish written all over his friends' face, Alex began to see red. "No! No! H…he didn't? Jarred?"

"No, not yet, but it's serious. He's taken a bullet to the chest, and they're rushing him to surgery, as we speak."

*　　*　　*

Watch for the ongoing series of this story in 'A Dream Worth Waiting For'. And see how Jarred Stanton and Jessi's cousin, Jodi Tate, are reunited. Moreover, how Alex is rewarded for what he gave up for the love of his nephew.

The reunion of hearts goes out to both, Jarred and Jodi, and Alex and Beth, but not without first dealing with Vince Delgado and his vengeance on still yet, Captain Alex Storm, while thinking Lieutenant Jarred Stanton was dead.

Plus, the Honeymoon couple 'Craig and Jessi' returns and all are joined together back at the Inn, where Alex and his team are back to protecting the innocent from Delgado's wrath.